I KILLED
Hemingway

WILLIAM McCRANOR HENDERSON

I KILLED
Hemingway

ST. MARTIN'S PRESS NEW YORK

DESIGN BY JUDITH A. STAGNITTO

Library of Congress Cataloging-in-Publication Data

Henderson, William McCranor.
     I killed Hemingway / William McCranor Henderson.
          p. cm.
     "A Thomas Dunne book."
     ISBN 0-312-08816-7
     1. Hemingway, Ernest, 1899-1961—Fiction. 2. Key West (Fla.)—Fiction. 3. Authors—Fiction. I. Title.
PS3558.E4946I18   1993
813'.54—dc20   92-42213
                              CIP

10 9 8 7 6 5 4 3 2

"What is glory? It is to have a lot of nonsense talked about you."

—GUSTAVE FLAUBERT

Part One

I STOOD ON *the train tracks and looked up into the darkness where the house was. After a while first light broke and turned the sky gray and purple and pink and I could see the mountain and the river and the house. He would be awake now. It would be a good day. I left the train tracks below and walked up the hill toward the house.*

Around the side you could see where someone had left a door unlatched. I pushed on it and slipped inside and walked through the kitchen and down a few steps into the living room. He was alone in his bathrobe, his back to me, looking straight ahead at the far mountains through a picture window. A double-barreled shotgun lay on the table by his side.

Yes, with his own gun . . .

I holstered my automatic and reached for the shotgun.

"Don't worry," he said toward the mountains. He spoke as a man would speak to his wife. Then came the sound of my boot scraping the floor and he knew it was not his wife and he spun to meet me. His face was twisted with surprise and rage. He stood in a slight crouch.

Let him come for me, I thought. Let him try me if he has his *cojones left, let him try the one man he could never fight fair and beat but only snipe at from the shadows, rob and slander and betray. I took the safety off and waited.*

"You," he said.

"Open your mouth, Papa."

He slumped a bit and obeyed me without protest, as a solitary prisoner obeys the commander of his firing squad. I jammed both barrels into his gash of a mouth and squeezed the triggers, blowing him back onto the cover of Life where he belonged. . . .

"Yuck!"

"Oh, come on, Elliot—"

"No. I sincerely mean it. Yuck!"

I'm holding the manuscript high between two fingers, like a rotten fish, as I pass it back into Craig Vandermeer's fluttering editorial hands. We are lunching at One Fifth Avenue and the lunch is on Craig, who is in a complete ecstatic dither over this obviously bogus fragment that some nut is trying to palm off as legitimate memoir.

"Is that all you have to say?" Craig sniffs into his Campari and waits, eyes endearingly agog, a characteristic little trick I've watched him pull since our college days nearly twenty years ago. "Tell me, what does *yuck* mean?"

"*Yuck* means I'm offended by this, this—"

Craig is already wagging his head. "Offended doesn't count, Elliot. Sure, it makes you sick, it's raw and upsetting, but we're not here to discuss sick or raw, et cetera." His face assumes a quick shrewdness and he arches over his bowl of chili, moving in on the point. "The issue, old boy, is authenticity, period. Could it have happened? The question of taste is neither here nor there."

"It's not authentic."

"How do you know?"

"I know."

We stare at each other with grim half smiles. I am already somewhat irritated since I thought I was coming to lunch to beat the drum for my own project, *LifeForms*, and instead all Craig wants to talk about is this other insignificant grotesquerie.

"Tell me how you know."

"It's painfully obvious—to most of us, anyway. The facts are well established."

"Oh, really?" He slurps a spoonful of chili. "No one saw it happen. Mary Hemingway was upstairs asleep. They simply found him with his head blown off. This Eric Markham guy could have done it."

Under the table my foot is peevishly whapping the floor. "Don't be an idiot. Of course it was suicide. He came from a whole family of suicides. He thought about it all his life. He'd already tried it four or five times—they had to wrestle the gun out of his hand. He tried to jump out of a plane, for God's sake. The man was a time bomb."

Craig raises his forefinger. "But the fact remains, *no one saw it happen*. Possibly someone else could have gotten in and—"

"Possibly who? Alice B. Toklas? Hey, don't count her out, she hated him, you know! Or the butler. Did Hemingway have a butler?"

Craig waves his hands in tactical surrender. "All right, very cute. But there's more—the whole Paris angle. Apparently this guy and Hemingway were pals back in the twenties, Hemingway plagiarized him—"

"Craig."

"Well, that's what he claims. And what if it's true? I mean, think about it."

"Craig, you're talking to the guy who wrote *Hemingway on the Terraces*. I've got stories on Hemingway that never even made it into print. In all that Left Bank gossip I never once came across the name Eric Markham."

"What if, that's all. *What if?*"

Craig sits back with an unyielding grin across his tiny mouth. Something is making him look unusually stylish today, very *GQ*, maybe his baggy tweeds or his creamy brown tortoiseshells. Craig has been an editor at Warren & Dudge his entire adult life. I watched him pay his dues as a grind. Now he is into Big Acquisitions and he likes it—the sense of discovery, the adventure, the risk. He's proud of his rise to the top and has devised personal insignia to go with it—his teal elbow patches, his silver Mont Blanc pen, his cultivated Angloid manner. Warren & Dudge has just been acquired by the British press magnate Sir Harry Taymore, who wants to mark his entry with something splashy and explosive. Craig, who recently edited *My Ten Days with Bigfoot*, is definitely playing in the right ballpark.

"Look, Elliot, you don't think I asked you to lunch just to sniff at a few pages of manuscript—"

Ah, maybe we're coming to *LifeForms* after all.

"Here's the situation. The editorial board, with a smattering of ritual dissent, has taken the bait—"

Yes!

"—at least so far as to look into this alleged assassin a bit further."

The assassin. "Oh."

"Elliot, think about it. If this claim has the slightest validity to it—any at all—I mean, just imagine: *I Killed Hemingway*, the life and times of Ernest Hemingway's real-life assassin! Is that a guaranteed best-seller or am I way off base?"

He's canoeing on a tide of sewage, but why stop the flow? *LifeForms* will come up in due time. Meanwhile, it's dawning on me that there must be some kind of a money role for me in all this, so I ought to shut up and listen. Who am I to be so high and mighty anyway, with my rent due, my fall clothes stuck in the cleaners, my cleaning woman dunning me for three weeks' pay?

"I suppose it might sell."

"You bet your sweet ass it will." He leans forward, ostentatiously serious. "Then here it is, Elliot. Sir Harry himself is a great Hemingway fan. He called personally to say that he wants somebody to go down to Key West and see what this guy is all about. He wanted to use a private eye but, thinking on my feet, I said, 'Wait a minute—Elliot McGuire's your man!' I mean, a Hemingway scholar, for heaven's sake—"

"That was a long time ago, Craig."

"I know, I know, but who cares? It's legitimate. Hemingway scholar—"

"Needy case."

"I didn't say that."

"Never mind. I assume there is money involved."

"Three hundred a day plus expenses."

"I accept." I signal the waiter for another Scotch.

"That was quick."

"Once I isolate the essential argument—in this case, the money—my reluctance melts away. So, tell me more."

Craig is bubbling over with conspiratorial glee. "Oh, Elliot, you're going to love this."

"Go on."

"You fly to Miami and take a connector to Key West, rent a car and drive to the Blue Conch Motel—don't you just love it, Blue Conch Motel? Eat, drink, whatever. Wait for somebody to contact you."

"Mm-hm."

"Remember, you're down there representing us, you're one of our editors, okay? Talk to him, feel him out. He wants a deal on what he's shown us. Five pages! Ridiculous, of course, but Sir Harry's hot for this. He doesn't want to get scooped so he's very reluctant to play hardball with the guy. Try to get a look at the rest of the memoir. Get a sense of whether or not it has an authentic *feel* to it. That's the operative word, *feel*."

"We're not interested in truth?"

"I wouldn't go that far. But watch my lips carefully as I reiterate: *feel*, Elliot, *feel*, okay? It may not be the Liberty Bell but does it go 'bong' when you ring it?"

"That's all?"

"I told you you'd love it."

The waiter sets my Scotch down and leaves. I stir the cubes with a forefinger. Something about this makes me feel a hundred and fifty years old. Not just lack of enthusiasm, but a deep dread, a gloom of anticipation that I can't fully explain.

"And if I find he's full of shit?"

Craig raises a hand to stop me. "Keep your mind open, that's all. Make your judgment on the totality. Even if you're convinced he never pulled the trigger, what else do you see? Is there a book there? That's what Sir Harry wants to know. *Is there a book?*"

Why am I so down on this gig? The Hemingway connection, I imagine, but I'm supposed to have made a lot of progress with my Hemingway problem. Really, I ought to look at it as a paid Florida vacation, even the possible beginning of a new side career: Elliot McGuire, literary gumshoe. So why so sour? Because, damn it all, if Craig had come through with an advance for *LifeForms*, I wouldn't have to accept errand-boy jobs like this to keep body and soul together.

"What about *LifeForms*, by the way?"

Craig dusts his lap with his napkin. "Patience, old boy. Sir Harry's only been on board for six weeks. He's got a huge stack of projects on his plate and he's going through them one at a time. *LifeForms* is in there."

"That's all you can tell me?"

"Relax, Elliot, it's a terrific idea, we all think it's going to be an absolute monster, but Sir Harry—"

"Sir Harry needs time."

"Exactly." Craig's little grin grows like a man-eating flower consuming itself.

TWO

HERE'S WHAT I came to lunch ready to say:

Listen to me, Craig: I am changing my life. How? By reshaping my LifeForm. It's almost done. You could do it too, in your spare time. LifeForms provides lots of ways. You can start with something as simple and nonthreatening as an obituary.

Elliot McGuire (1948–2037). Author, scholar, poet . . . (something like that, just to get started). *Writer and thinker Elliot McGuire died today at his East Hampton estate, age 89.* (Always give yourself what I call Maximum LifeExtent.) *Biographer and creator of LifeForms, a self-help system based on biographical analysis, McGuire's productive years spanned 1989 to the present. . . .*

This is an example of BackLoading, a LifeForms technique where you load the future with specific promises of achievement, thereby toning up your LifeSpring, which is a kind of conceptual trampoline, your launching pad to a firmer, more structural future. Let's go on:

Following LifeForms, McGuire published definitive biographies of Caesar, Mozart, Einstein, Jesus, Shakespeare, and Charlie Chaplin. His Pulitzer Prize–winning biography of Ernest Hemingway, Nada Man, is considered the standard work on that author. McGuire is also the author of twelve novels, two Broadway plays, and three volumes of poetry. In 2017, he received the Nobel Prize for Literature. . . .

And so on. This is a LifeForms exercise.

(Or it would have been if Craig had given me the opening.)

Funny how things grow. Out of a momentary exchange with Sven, my therapist, here I've gone and evolved this whole damned thought system. It's simple, it's profound, it's biography-based—it's all the things I am.

It's also a meal ticket if I play my cards right. Think what a corporate training program it would make! LifeForms seminars at Xerox, IBM, General Motors! A whole generation of middle managers changing their lives by changing their Life-Forms! All from a chance wisecrack. Sven was helping me come to terms with what he saw as a fundamental paradox in my nature—my compulsion to intellectualize—when in fact (as he politely put it) my intelligence was "unassuming." Dear Sven. What was he up to? Ever so gently he was inviting me to consider that, when it came to the sheer rigors of abstract thinking, I might not be playing with a full deck. But I forgave him.

As the prime culprit, he fingered my mother (isn't it always Mom?), a soft-spoken beauty whom my scholarly bulldog of a father married as a change of pace. Dad's original wife had possessed considerable status as a Mary McCarthy–type professional intellectual, but my mother was a different kettle of fish altogether—dark, sensual, prophetic. Her brand of intelligence was distinctly nonverbal. She had innate taste. She didn't have to *prove*: she *knew*. In looks and temperament, I'm a combination of the two of them: big and blustery, always ready to debate a point like my dad; dark and intuitive like Mom, and, yes—why not admit it?—maybe a bit shy on raw steel-trap mental virtuosity.

But add it all up and what do you get? A peculiarly potent form of brilliance: anyone can think fast, but I can think *new*. I'm unusually suited to spawn ideas. I'd take that even farther: without intending to brag, I'd say my personal balance of mind and magic verges on the unique. This is what lay behind my flippant remark to Sven:

"I may not be able to prove God as fast as you can, but I'll come in here next time with an idea you've never thought of in your life."

And I did. He had to admit it.

Not the entire thought system, just the beginning, lots of work remaining to be done. But the radiant kernel of brilliance was there.

Of course my stepmother, Kristin, who holds chairs in both English and philosophy at Columbia (though she's younger than I am), pooh-poohs it on intellectual grounds. No surprise there: it's still rather ad hoc. But with an ample advance from Warren & Dudge, I'll have breathing space to flesh out the theoretical details. Then, as my dad used to say, Katy bar the door! *Gangway for this man, the walking embodiment of his own master premise—Elliot McGuire, who started strong, stumbled, lived underwater for twelve long years, and is now poised to resurface, resplendent in his powerful new LifeForm!*

Okay, so Craig's not quite ready. Let this Hemingway triviality play itself out. This week, next week, in the long run it won't matter. I can wait.

THREE

CRAIG WALKS ME down Fifth Avenue puffing on a Players, ogling the women in their sweaters and their snappy fall skirts.

"Mm, look at that—divine. To schtupp her would be to die."

Craig is a creature of shallow obsessions, like Madonna, whom he just saw in concert from the front row. (He paid a scalper five hundred dollars for the ticket.) He waves his cigarette around in figure eights as he describes the rush, the orgasm of the heart, the happy death of it all. Yes, I suppose I condescend a bit to him—he is not what I would call *serious.* His milieu is the surface. He's a floater.

"I wouldn't say this about just any lady, Elliot—and I'm not really into degradation—but if Madonna volunteered to check my prostate . . ."

He finishes the joke graphically, a Hollywood kind of joke: I can tell he's just been to L.A.

He breaks off suddenly. "You okay, Elliot?"

"Sure, why not?"

"Well, your head is bouncing around."

"I'm, uh—it's an exercise."

Actually I was keeping time in my head to "Express Yourself," but Craig doesn't have to know that.

"What kind of exercise?"

"Just one of those stress-reduction things. Yoga actually. Got another cigarette?"

"Certainly. Oh, here's a joint. Shall we?"

The first blast sends my eyes reeling back into my head and I stagger heavily. This was a mistake: I haven't smoked a joint in six months.

"Whoa, guy," says Craig. "I better call you a cab."

I let him. It's easier than saying no. I have to sit for a minute anyway, just to pull my head together.

"Sure you're okay?"

"Yeah, yeah."

"I'll phone you tonight," says Craig, stuffing me into the taxi. He slams the door and recedes, like a film running backwards.

FOUR

ONCE UPON A time, I was going to write the first great Hemingway biography of my generation. It was more than just my own opinion: other people thought so too. Even Hemingway might have had an inkling. He and I actually exchanged a few letters shortly before his death in 1961 (I was a callow but promising thirteen).

But a funny thing happened on the way to the definitive EH bio: I found that the more I haunted his life, the more it haunted me, oppressed me—the more I became what I can only describe as an acute Hemo-phobe.

I don't think much about the man now, don't read him anymore, no longer write angry follow-up letters to him in my head or any of the sad silly things that characterized my Hemo-phobic period. I'm clean. I fought my own private battle with toxic Hemingway syndrome. I made my separate peace and walked off the battlefield. My admiration, my awe at his energy and brutishness and power, my horror at his pain and confusion—all gone, drained away along with youth.

So is it any wonder that I'm not comfortable with this project? Down in Key West, a man claims to have known EH, loved him, killed him. And I'm off to confront this? Years of therapy later, the eight-hundred-pound gorilla off my chest— and now I'm inviting him back to jeer over my shoulder yet again?

Actually, my own LifeForm, at this time, is in pretty good shape. I have evolved from a rather chaotic Reverse Vortex into the stability of a Rooted Wineglass.

What that says is: I was once a sort of big splash that narrowed to a trickle or (to mix metaphors—which we normally avoid doing in LifeForms analysis) a BIG BANG reduced to little more than what Craig calls a sparrow fart.

Ever tried living as a sparrow fart? It is perhaps the ultimate in reduced circumstances. Total marginalia. Not that marginal life is necessarily all bad. It can produce ferment. Indeed, LifeForms itself was almost a direct outgrowth of my six or eight years of intensely low-profile existence.

After a flashy entry into (and ignominious exit from) Hemingway studies, I was down and out, living anonymously, a beaten man. I supported myself by ghost-writing vanity autobiographies and teaching courses (New School, NYU Extension) in How to Write Your Own Story. LifeForms grew out of the observation that when students who were depressed by their lives *rewrote* them in a positive manner, depression disappeared, a major discovery!

My mother and I used to do this: we would tell each other the stories of our respective lives, over and over again, changing them for the better. Mom always wrote Dad out of her story. Likewise in mine, I was usually homeless, a street child she found and took home with her. Some of our tellings sprawled into endless complicated spirals. Some were perfect circles. Shape was a big thing with my mother. She told me that history formed shapes, that form wasn't just an element of composition, it had real historical consequences—an idea that set my dad's teeth on edge. I was thrilled by the notion; and it was a simple step to the observation that, by retelling their life stories, my dead-end students were doing something very powerful: they were creating new shapes, new contours—new *Life-Forms*.

Right now I would describe my "Wineglass" as a promising conflux (the base), tapering sharply to a restrained continuation (the stem), flourishing majestically into an ever-widening bell of achievement (the top).

And you know what? As I would have said to Craig, had he given me the chance, you too can change your LifeForm. It's not too late. You've got the power. Using LifeForms, you can literally reconceive the future and set forth the terms of your own success, just as I have.

FIVE

"WHERE TO?" SAYS the cabbie.

"Don't rush me. I have to think."

Lunch with Craig is over. According to my appointment calendar, "M. Skolnik" is next. M. Skolnik? Who's that? The context has momentarily escaped me. This is happening a lot lately. It's just the joint, it'll come. Let's start at the end of the day and work back. Astrid. Astrid is later. A bite to eat at a trendy SoHo truck stop, I suppose, then some sex done Astrid's way, lots of rhetorical desperation and pretend kinkiness, a real workout leaving me with chafed knees and elbows. But that's later. Skolnik is now. Skolnik—but who *is* Skolnik? I flip to the addresses and run a search. . . .

Skolnik, Skolnik—

Oh yes, of course. Another old man with a life story to tell. Myron Skolnik of Myron Skolnik Associates. Seventy-eight years old, wants his autobiography done while he's still got all his marbles.

"Where to?"

"Forget it." I don't need a ride. I feel fine now. I can walk to Myron Skolnik's. I step clear of the cab just in time to avoid being flipped as the cabbie floors it, cursing me in killer Hittite.

Let's see: Myron Skolnik Associates, West Sixty-something—no, it's too far to walk. I cross the avenue and head for the subway entrance at Eighth Street. This is the way to go: descend into a hole in the ground, no tip, no conversation, a dark roar through the colon of the naked city to one more meeting of no possible consequence.

SIX

THESE LITTLE MEMORY lapses, if you can call them that, don't concern me much. I know they're not medically significant. A little dope, a little less profusion to the brain, low blood sugar. If my life were falling to pieces I'd worry, but it isn't. Money is a problem, as always, but I'm well enough positioned. Craig is right: *LifeForms* is a monster. By the time we've had the book, the TV series, the seminars and cassettes, the research institute, the retreat center, it's going to change forever the way human beings look at their lives—to say nothing of *my* life.

I'm almost forty-one. When I look back at the postbaccalaureate stripling I was the year I retraced Hemingway's steps in Paris, I cringe. That was 1972. I hung out at the Dome and the Closerie de Lilas, grew a mustache, started a bullfight novel (in little blue composition books), and "researched" Hemingway's backstairs Paris life by gathering drinking stories from barflies who claimed to have known and drunk with him. The result was a new look at EH's hangout style (I concluded that he did a lot more drinking and screwing around than was assumed—and this sparked the notice of Carlos Baker, then the supreme Hemingway biographer, who took me under his wing), a series of articles and a book, *Hemingway on the Terraces* (*terrace* being French for the rows of outdoor tables at a French bar).

Who was that kid? Where has he gone, that kid who threw up at his only bullfight, stalked a deer in Michigan and couldn't pull the trigger? Why did he so fitfully and almost mournfully try to memorialize Hemingway, expose Hemingway, *be* Hemingway, all at the same time? That Elliot McGuire has gone down in history forever, down for the count, down and out. We don't mention him anymore, we don't think about him. Nor do we think about Hemingway. We are living in the present now. The era of LifeForms. We are teaching ourselves to wake up to a new morning, put our life on the potter's wheel and lovingly reshape it.

So it doesn't even bother me to do another vanity biography or two while I'm waiting for the advance. Why should I be in a hurry? Surely I could never have come up with Life-Forms any earlier than now. Youth is one-dimensional. When you're only twenty-three you're like the bushman who counts "One, two . . . *many*." Life is mostly whatever tiny mound of a past you have accumulated. There's today, next weekend, then . . . infinity. At forty, however, you begin to know what it means that there are things you'll *never ever* do. You get the drift: in a quick fifteen or twenty years you'll be elbowing the edge of the universe, slipping off into that great big blank vale of nothingness beyond. I bet this is what Myron Skolnik, Hollywood producer, is brooding on as he waits for me high in his office near the top of the Gulf + Western Building in Columbus Circle. I picture him in deep contemplation, behind a power desk of endless black marble, a skull in his hand, a raven perched on his hairless pate. He is thinking, *Jesus, didn't it all fly by fast!*

Myron Skolnik is a producer of what used to be called "B pictures." Most recently, he's had an unbroken string of successful "slasher" features. Posters from some of the big ones decorate his reception area. Also, according to my agent, Jerry Bronstein, he has done quite well in "quality porno"—glossy hard-core films for couples—although he may choose not to talk about this.

Skolnik's grandmotherish chief of staff escorts me into the Great Man's presence.

"The writer," she mutters to Skolnik as if to say "the poisoner." She's no fool: she knows this act of vanity will cost her boss plenty of silly money, and as far as she's concerned, I and anybody like me ought to be dropped like a bag of trash down the nearest elevator shaft.

Skolnik is posed at his window, to be discovered, book in hand (a copy of Cellini's *Autobiography*). "Ah!" He turns theatrically and emits a shaft of pipe smoke. "Mr. McGuire— Elliot, if you will. Sit, sit. I have a story to tell you."

The line has a crafted ring to it. He must have hired the guy who used to write "The Millionaire." The move, which ends with a hand thrust at me across his desk, has been overrehearsed, resulting in a jerky, robotic quality. I shake his hand and slump into a chair.

"Let's see—where to begin, where to begin . . . ?"

He opens with a roundup of his early years in the business: how he made a quick fortune as a purveyor of film cans, then backed a series of beach-blanket and monster movies, all hits. He was golden, he recalls, he could do no wrong. These were also the years of family, children—

I watch him warm to it, this ruddy-faced, goateed, seventy-ish, Brooklyn-bred little tough guy with a lifetime of experience in the dreck business. As he paces and talks, what emerges is the archetypal tale of a brainy youth who makes it out of the slum streets of the city, against all odds, to become—a what? How's that again? A *presidential advisor?* Here is where the project starts to shimmy and shake.

"You were a presidential advisor?"

"That's definitely one thing I want in the story. I have to have a scene with JFK, somewhere. Let's say, something where I advise him to stay out of Cuba, or not to go to Dallas or whatever."

"This happened?"

He chooses his words with care. "This is an element of the story I'm telling."

"I see."

The story goes on: Myron gets some interesting jobs—congressman, secretary of state—wins humanitarian awards. There's sex: he encounters an Oscar-winning actress in the prime of her classic beauty and screws her on his desk "wheelbarrow-style." Other "very chaste" young women, wives of congressmen, friends of his daughter, end up panting and whimpering as they do it with him "doggie-style."

I stop taking notes and instead concentrate on Myron's curiously shaped head: frontally, he is almost epic—a broad forehead, thick white hair—but in profile he loses it completely, with a mushed-in cranium, as though somebody stepped on his head at birth. As I listen to him tell about leaving a tryst with a certain famous leggy British royal ("pogo-style") to run some kind of secret mission for George

Bush, my heart suddenly goes out to the old guy, his red face blooming with a vision of how to make his life mean something more than film cans and slasher pictures. As I watch him operate, his rascal's soul is somehow washed clean; mortality surrounds him with the delicacy of an eggshell. I see his death and I'm touched.

Here's a question: Why do I continually find myself drawn into sympathy with these tiresome old mythomaniacs? God knows. Why is a suicide drawn to a bridge? I guess this is what has made me such a willing vanity biographer, this affliction, this inexplicable need to help aging also-rans like Myron Skolnik maintain their final dignity. And worse: to believe them.

"Now at this point, Myron makes a deal with the devil—"

"Symbolically."

"No, literally. A deal."

"Literally. We're into allegory, then?"

"No way, no allegory. This is a story for adults!"

"Mm. And what is the deal?"

"Well, the upside for Myron is success beyond measure, beyond possibility—even more than he's already achieved."

"As?"

"As a tennis star. He's fifty-five years old but he wins, he beats Lendl, Becker, he wins the Grand Slam. And of course there's the respect that goes with that, and the women—"

Stop there. "And the downside?"

"Well, we don't have to get into that too heavily."

"But what is it? Death? Is this a death pact?"

"Not exactly. The devil comes for him."

"Death."

His rosy face drains to white. "You could call it that, I suppose. Death. Whatever. You're the expert."

Whatever.

No, there will not be a meeting of the minds. I just can't make myself do this. I want to encourage people to rewrite their lives, but not this way. This is nickel-and-dime. I'm beyond projects like this.

Item: I've been invited to be a featured guest on WBAI's "Ecology of Belief," the alternative religion show.

Item: Sven sends patients to work with me as a legitimate adjunct to his therapy.

I don't have to get down in the muck with the likes of this

miserable ego tripper. I want to be out of here, out of his office. Out of his *life*. He doesn't want a biographer, he wants a screenwriter. In fact, as he talks, I realize that that's where this project is meant to go—to the Big Screen. The book will be bait for a deal; it has to contain big scenes, irresistible material. That's why we're bending the facts a little. "I want truth, not facts," he says. *The Myron Skolnik Story* will be true to the overall shape of his LifeForm (a volcanic mountain range, as he sketches it), true to the general theme of "the Myronic Quest" (his words) right down to finessing death itself, leaving the story open to a sequel if box office grosses are fat enough.

"I have to go, Myron."

"Huh? You just got here."

"No. I think I'm about to have a . . . well, it's a kind of seizure."

"A seizure? Oh my God!"

"Don't worry, I'm used to it—"

"Should I call an ambulance?"

"No, no, no. I just—I'll be fine. As soon as I get to the street . . ."

There is the voice in my head that says: *C'mon, be a man, stand up and tell the old roach the truth!* And then there is the other voice, the one I hear as I hit the street. It says: *What you need is some fresh air and a good stiff drink.* Well, a hike down to Spring Street to meet Astrid will be good for as much fresh air as any normal human being could stand. I buy a half-pint of Scotch and, nestling it in its brown bag, I drink my way down Ninth Avenue.

By the time I hit Chelsea I'm out of Scotch and out of money. I stand in front of an automatic teller machine trying to remember my code—oh hell, there's a line forming behind me, no one's saying anything but it's all whips, chains, and studs back there. This could get ugly, let's move on—Astrid will have money, she always does, thanks to the weak dollar, dear Astrid, my Brit, my own pearly drop of English savour here in the roiling stew of Gotham.

So it's on down Ninth Avenue, veering off at Bleecker, past my block, my neighborhood, haunt of my haunts. Around Perry Street someone's playing music loud. "Autumn in New York . . ." The young Sinatra's moist, lugubrious voice pours out a second-story window. It makes me want to cry. Something about lunch with Craig has left me in a state of dying fall. Hemingway. The shotgun blast to the head, the shabby inevitability of it, the *humiliation*. No, cram that back in its box, McGuire. Get it out of your head. Leave death behind, think about sex instead. Think about Astrid. Push on. There's Houston, Canal's coming, can Spring be far behind . . . ?

SEVEN

NO SEX TODAY, I can tell by the way she flips me the front door key from her loft window (the buzzer system is perpetually vandalized). Good, I'm not in the mood anyway. We'll talk instead. Astrid is rangy and aristocratic, with creamy English skin and reddish hair which she usually wears in a sensible French braid. She's younger than I am by a good ten years, an artist, makes elaborate sculptures with string. Her problem (one of them) is that knot-tying drives her into fits of anguish. By the end of a bad day she's pacing the cavernous space like a lioness. Or slumped in front of MTV. Or eating endless compulsive bowls of Cheerios that she metabolizes instantly. It's my job to calm her down, and sometimes, though not often, sex isn't the cure.

The elevator opens directly into her vast space. The loft is huge. A hundred years ago it probably housed a nationwide clothing concern. Now, one nervous sculptress. Astrid makes no attempt to keep house. Twice a year she hires a small army of professional cleaners to come in and swarm over the place while she spends the day visiting her ex-husband's new wife, whom she has a sort of crush on.

This is an MTV day. I can hear it going and see the play of light coming from a far corner about a thousand yards across the loft, where Astrid keeps a gigantic mattress and wide-screen TV. The blinds are drawn. In the darkness I have to pick my way through a forest of stringy objects, then I'm in the kitchen area (there are no rooms as such, only one vast rectangular space the size of a Saturn rocket hangar). There are sullen circles under her eyes as she watches the dark-haired young videojock waving her arms and laughing at something or someone off-camera.

"Do you think she's pretty?"

"Yes."

"So do I. She's the sort of pretty that appeals to a woman. She has spirit. I'd want her on my hockey team or something, d'you know?"

"Not exactly."

"No, men don't think that way, do they? A man thinks in terms of how she'd look with her breasts bare. Or on her back begging to have his baby—am I right?"

"Never mind."

"Well, what about it?"

"If you say so. Why get into it?"

"Come on, Elliot, let's get into it. Must I ball up my fists and physically pick a quarrel with you?"

"Must you?"

She's silent for a moment.

I sit on the edge of the mattress and take her hand. "I'll be out of town for a few days."

"Really? Where?"

"Key West." I tell her about my lunch with Craig. "I'm not a hundred percent certain I ought to do it."

"Why not?"

"Oh, you know. Anything connected with Hemingway . . ."

"But you're beyond all that now aren't you? Hasn't Sven gotten you beyond all that?"

"I don't know."

"This could be a sort of test, perhaps."

"Just what I need, a test of my Hemingway immunity. And anyway, I really ought not to leave town, the WBAI Life-Forms thing is just a few days off."

"Well then, don't do it."

"But the money's too good. It's perfect. How can I not do it?"

"Oh, for God's sake, just do it or don't and be damned. You're so precious with your delicate little psyche, Elliot, it drives me crazy. You lack boldness, darling, d'you know that?"

My delicate little psyche? Look who's talking. "I'm not sure I know what you mean."

"See there? You might have said something like Oh stuff it, but what did you actually say?"

"Never mind."

"Here you are, this big swarthy pirate-looking man, and you can't even tell me to stuff it."

"Is that really what you want, tough-guy moves? Want me to stand over you and be abusive? I could do that— *Stuff it!*"

"Oh, never mind. You just don't get it—"

"You're right. I don't."

Usually I'm not so touchy. I was never a hard guy to get along with. But she wears me thin during these wound-up afternoons. It's like fighting my way through a force field.

A sigh. Maybe we'll break this deadlock.

"Well then?"

"Astrid, sweetheart, what do you want? Do you want my opinion? I'll give it to you: get out of strings. Get into some other form of sculpture. Clay. Mash clay around, it would be so much better for you."

She's looking at me. I just don't get it.

"Don't you think I've thought of that? Why don't I just make messes with concrete like Sophie Luxembourg—I could have skinheads with muscles do it all, just like her. But that's not me. Sophie does absolutely marvelous things, but they're unique to her. I do my string work, that's me. The days it goes well, I'm happy. Most days I'm miserable. But how could I change it? Suppose I lost a leg, could I change that? My mother is a middle-class twit and my father is a faceless wraith of a nobody, can I change that?"

"You've been to Sven."

"Yes, but it's no good. I mean, he's marvelous. He does everything but slap me awake. I leave Sven's feeling like I've stepped out of a bracing shower. Then moment by moment I can feel the mold creeping back over my soul until it's only been a few hours and I'm my old horrible self again."

"What do you want to do now?"

"Mmm." She pulls me next to her. "Do my LifeForm."

"I've done your LifeForm. Believe me, it hasn't changed since last Friday."

"Tell me a story."
"Oh, come on, Astrid."
"Please. Please, Elliot. I feel so out-beyond. I'm so scared. Tell me a story, darling. The one about the meadow. Please, please."

She kills the TV so we hear nothing but muffled street noise—sirens, children playing hopscotch in the schoolyard down the block, distant backfires, screaming electric guitars.

"Once upon a time a little girl named Astrid toddled off into the meadow that stretched behind her house. It was Tuesday, and she knew that every Tuesday the water in the brook turned to pink lemonade and the rocks along the bank all turned to chocolate."

"Have it be a hot day and the chocolate is all soft and she smears it all over herself, okay?"

"Right."

"All over her body."

"Okay."

"And Elliot, pretend you're doing that, okay? Smearing it all over my body."

"Okay."

"Mm, that's wonderful. I feel better already. . . ."

EIGHT

AFTER THE LONG walk home, the long trudge upstairs, my message light is blinking.

Astrid, with second thoughts:

"*Elliot . . . (long exhalation) I'm such a witch. Don't pay any mind to whatever I said—I can't even remember what it was but I know it was beastly. Until you did that with the chocolate. It always does calm me, doesn't it? Chocolate, chocolate, chocolate—what is it about chocolate? (a yawn) You're a wonderful big goofy chap with a streak of the most unselfish goodness. Mmmmwah! There. Love you so. Good night, sweet.*"

Next, Craig:

"*Listen, big guy, this Hemingway proposition is getting hot. I can't go into the whole thing, but we're feeling some urgency here, so—assuming you'll go for it, I took the liberty of booking you a flight to Key West with car and motel. That's tomorrow, Elliot, okay? Get back to me tonight and I'll fill you in."*

Part Two

THE PLANE TO Key West is full of depressives, silent screamers, woebegone tourists, sullen business travelers who want to end it all and that's why they chose this flight, *my flight.*

God, dear God, don't take an ax to my LifeForm, I don't want to die!

The marvelous thing about fear of flying is how it snuggles like a ringworm into the contours and crevices of your uncertainty, hugs the curves of your guilt and horror. I've learned to keep a lid on it; by that I mean that I don't go screaming up and down the aisle begging the flight crew to turn the plane around. But normal life, normal thought, is impossible while in the air. I go primitive, seeing magic everywhere, curses and blessings in every face, hearing doom in every tiny whirr and titter of the engines, every innocent lurch of the giant silver coffin. Are there babies on board? God wouldn't kill a baby, would He? Yet you do read about it, babies dying in crashes. Grip the seat tighter. Pray. Drink.

It's worse this time because of Hemingway. While in the air I've started to cave in to the notion that vibes can kill. Is he wishing me dead? Could the dark force of his rage dash us all to earth? I know this is witchy thinking, but that's what I mean. I can no more hold it off than I could banish a sneeze.

Well, let's get a grip on ourselves, shall we? Let's order another Scotch, tip the seat back, loosen our tie. Let's listen to the sound of nylon stockings as the flight attendant bends over with our drink. Relax, wax expansive, get lost in the stunning prospect of the eternal sun warming the endless continent below.

Look. Creation!

No good—a brief attack of buffeting ruins it for me. All right, try something else: let's review my instructions. Eric Markham, the Hemingway-killer, has specified that I'm to check into the Blue Conch Motel and wait in the bar for an emissary who will escort me to him. Possible paranoia. Maybe he fears a plot to extradite him to Ketchum, Idaho. Could it be that he believes his own cock-and-bull story?

Oh, Jesus, we're upending, plummeting down, down, hooking around Key West and lining up for a desperation approach. I'm drained. To hell with the notes. If this project goes through I suppose some poor sap of a Hemingway scholar will have to rise up and swat the old spider. If I had stayed in the field, it might well have been me. Thank God I'm out of it. I had my brief moment as a junior Hemingway man, then contrived to get myself jerked off the stage through self-destructiveness and stupidity. No matter, the field was over-crowded anyway—so many careerists feeding off the bloated life of one man—and now this. Now comes some ancient psychotic to cheat Papa out of his final creation, his own lovingly self-crafted death—

Blam . . . blam. We're on the ground.

So be it: this was not my time. Let me now pick up my life and get on with it.

I step off the plane into ferocious tropical heat.

"It's not usually this bad in October," says the Hertz clerk, a smeary little blonde who is sweating hard in her polyester uniform.

I have rarely been south of D.C. I don't remember ever feeling heat like this, a plenum, through which I swim toward the Hertz lot like a slow-motion pearl diver. The car is so cooked I can hardly touch it. I start it up and wait outside for the air conditioner to cool down the interior. There are a couple of low-slung, shady-looking bars on the periphery of the airport, but I resist the urge to throw down a couple of beers. Let's get to the hotel first.

The Blue Conch resembles a set for *Casablanca*—lots of heavy stuccoed architectural masses, palm fronds, ceiling fans and such. They ought to give out fezzes at the desk. But there is a clean Windex-blue pool and I plunge gratefully into it as fast as I can strip off my sweaty New York gear. Unclenching from the ordeal of the trip, I float on my back a while, then rub myself dry with crisp white hotel towels. Inside, the air conditioner and ceiling fan have chilled my room, so I snuggle into one of the two king-size beds and flip on the remote TV. Let's see if I can find Yugo anywhere.

I go grazing: Henry Kissinger is being asked what to do in the Middle East . . . Elvis Presley is singing to a group of puppets . . . Big Bird is visiting a bagel factory . . .

And there he is: my old pal Hughie McDonough, a.k.a. Yugo, heartthrob and host of the raciest daytime talk show in syndication. Today's *Yugo* features a group of reformed spouse killers. A promo tells us to be sure not to miss tomorrow's show: "Dangerous Cuisine: Live Monkey Brains and other Forbidden Delicacies."

Yugo has gone to hell. This is a guy with a troubled childhood who pulled himself together, made Dean's List at Columbia, and went on to do some first-rate environmental reporting for the *Christian Science Monitor*. He drove an old Volkswagen. He canvassed for George McGovern. Now look at him—rich, divorced, coiffed. Watch him pacing, whirling like a rock 'n' roller, wheedling, praising, flirting, raising his hands in horror, chortling in various states of sleaze, pointing in accusation.

"*Yugo, I have to tell you, it's a whole new ball game. Killing my wife, God bless her, was the beginning of a new life for me.*"

"*But what about her life, Sam? The life you took?*"

Wife killer weeps. Seeing tears, Yugo springs forward and runs fifty feet to drape an arm around him.

"*Sure I'd like to have her back. But Yugo, what the Lord sees fit—*"

"*Hold that thought, Sam, we've gotta take a break.*"

Zzzap!

At some point I'll reveal how my dear old snake of a buddy screwed me out of a chance to boost *LifeForms* on his show. But later. The wound is still too fresh to think about, much less talk about, without bringing vile froth to the corners of my mouth. So we'll leave Yugo for now. I'm dimming out anyway. I'm drifting away . . .

. . . and he grins up at me, showing teeth at the side of his mouth, thick crow's-feet at the corners of his eyes. He is crouching in the dark in his bathrobe, like one of Francis Bacon's neurotic horrors. He pushes his thin white hair forward again and again into a Roman curl. On the table is a hat pin. Before I know what I'm doing, I've buried the hat pin in his fleshy butt. Instead of screaming with pain, he explodes, like a giant water balloon. That's it. He's gone. Aside from the blood and shards of bathrobe, there is no more Hemingway in my dream.

The nightmare again. It's back.

TEN

I WALK INTO the Blue Conch Lounge, as directed, dressed for business in editorish chinos and a rumpled seersucker jacket. A quick Scotch at the bar and I loosen my tie and move to a table to make myself more conspicuous.

I'm on my third Scotch when I become aware of some loud throat-clearing near the entrance. A tall, bony redneck, about my age, is standing by the doorway, squinting into the semi-darkness of the lounge. He's sunburnt, not like a tourist but raw, like a fisherman or a mate on a pleasure boat. Gangling tattooed arms stick out at crazy angles from the T-shirt, as if they were broken then badly reset. He holds a hand-lettered sign that reads: ELLIOT MCGUIRE.

My finger goes up. Spotting the gesture, he bobs his head with relief and limps broadly over to the table.

"Mr. McGuire?"

"Sure. Sit down. Would you like a drink?"

His eyes widen. "Tha's a pleasant thought." He settles into the chair like a sack of silverware. "Yo, Lil!"

He waves in the direction of the barmaid and makes a gesture that says "big." Lil nods solemnly and pours him a tumblerful of Seagram's.

"Guess Pappy ain't gonna mind if I smooth out for a minute or two here."

"Pappy?"

"Ah, Mr. Markham, that is." He cringes slightly. "Some folks calls him Pappy."

"And what's your name?"

"Aw hell, I'm sorry! Roland. Roland Munger!" He stands up halfway to shake hands, then falls back into his chair.

His drink arrives.

"Ah—mm. Tha's good. Ain't you gonna have a drink, too? Yo, Lil—"

"No thanks." It's tempting, but I wave off the barmaid. "I'd like to get on with it, if that's okay."

"Suit yourself."

Roland downs the rest of his whiskey and hangs a grin on his face. He doesn't seem to be in a terrible hurry to move on. As a broad hint, I stand and peer down at him. "We all through?"

Roland's grin wilts. "Well"—he clears his throat—"there's just one thing, a silly little thing."

"Let's have it."

"I'm gonna have to blindfold you."

"Hm?"

"Pappy's orders. Got to blindfold ya."

I should have known it—here come the kinks. "Uh-uh. I don't think so."

"Well, now wait a minute—put yourself in his position. A man that's confessing to cold-blooded murder. You could be the law, for all he knows."

"You know that's ridiculous."

"I don't know nothing. I'm just doin' what I'm told."

Reaching into his back pocket he pulls out a pair of satin black eyeshades and dangles them hopefully.

"Please?"

"No way."

"Oh hell, I told the old fool you wouldn't go for it. Wait now, try this: we'll forget it for now, but when we get there, just before we go in, slip 'em on and pretend you wore 'em the whole way. How about that?"

I consider the likely consequences of driving off with this possible maniac. But no, he's too clownish, too much the classic Hemingway "rummy" to be dangerous.

He holds the eyeshades out to me in supplication. "Pretty please . . . ?"

We pull to a halt in front of a weathered old wreck of a place, a shotgun shack, in a little back street called Gruntbone Alley. The front yard is choked with weeds and uncut grass. The paint has long since peeled away. Chickens peck at the ground. Derelict refrigerators rust away at the side of the house. There's an African wicker chair on the porch and I can see what looks like an old Cinzano umbrella set up in the yard behind the house.

"Remember now: you don't know where you are," Roland says, thrusting the eyeshades at me. I slide them on and let him help me out of the car. He guides me through the yard and onto the porch.

"Pappy?"

"Come on in."

Up a step—I'm inside the house, which smells like years of sloppy living. I sense his presence, just a few feet in front of me.

"Welcome," says his gravelly baritone of a voice. "You can take the peepers off."

I shove the shades up my forehead and open my eyes. Standing tall in the half twilight is a pale, decrepit old man, shaved bald Mr. Clean-style, white stubble blending with the map of deep anxious wrinkles that stretch across his face. Nervousness adds age to his already ancient bearing and causes him to writhe and twitch in place as he checks me out.

"Mr. Elliot McGuire from Warren and Dudge?"

"The same."

He squints hard and licks his lower chops. "Prove it."

"What would you like to see? My library card?"

"Something with a picture. How do I know you're not FBI?"

I hand him my driver's license. He takes a look, grunts and hands it back.

"All right. Sit down, McGuire. Make yourself comfortable. What can I get you to drink?"

"Scotch would be nice."

"Get him a beer," he orders without taking his eyes off me. I realize he is trembling all over, in waves, and it's not just the palsy of old age. There is a sheen of sweat across his forehead. He may be just a fly in my ointment, but from his side of the table this event is no less than the signing of the Magna Carta.

Roland slips a can of Budweiser into my hand.

The old man claps his hands once. "So, Mr. McGuire. What's next?"

"I'd like to look at the manuscript."

He grins faintly, a thin soup of politesse. "I'm afraid I have to say no to that, my friend. You'll have to go out on a limb with everybody else if you want to get into this auction."

"What auction?"

"I'm running an auction, don't kid yourself."

"But if we saw the manuscript first—"

He shrugs me off. "That's not the plan. Make a bid if you want in. You'll see the manuscript when you've bought and paid for it and not before."

Absurd. But this is a very old, very suspicious man, in the midst of what is surely the last big event of his life. Let's just assume he's going to sit on the manuscript, for whatever reason—it's not my job to push him around. That's Craig's problem. All I have to do is find out if it goes "bong."

I clear my throat and plunge ahead. "Okay, then maybe you could describe what's in the book. Besides the killing scene, that is—I've already seen that."

"Did you like it?"

"Well, sure. It's . . . gripping." (Is my nose growing?) "But what else? You say you were in Paris with Hemingway in the twenties. I assume you get into that."

"I'd turn that around to say he was in Paris with me—but yes, I do get into that, as you put it. In fact, it's largely about those days, the twenties in Paris, the expatriate stuff. Next question."

As he whacks the ball back at me, his eyes shine in his face like marbles embedded in an overcooked meringue.

"Did you know Jimmie Charters in Paris?"

"What's this, a little quiz? Sure, Jimmie, the bartender at

the Dingo and the Falstaff and just about every other American bar in town."

"How about Florence Martin?"

"Flossie Martin, the fat lady of Montparnasse. Try again."

"Raoul Mosely." A made-up name.

"Raoul Mosely? Never heard of any Raoul Mosely."

Okay, he knows his way around Lost Generation trivia. But he could have gotten all this from a number of easy sources so the exercise is probably pointless. Even he thinks so.

"Look, McGuire, anybody could know those names. They're even in *your* book. Yeah, I've read it. *Hemingway on the Terraces*, right? Not bad, except you missed the best of it, you guys always do. Why don't you try me on some folks who aren't in the books? What about Renée Mersault, the sculptress who did a cast of Hemingway's dick? Or the guy they called Le Chat who shot a drug dealer in the butt in Ezra Pound's flat, in front of Ezra, Dorothy, and a whole crew of people that Ezra swore to secrecy? You never heard of these things, did you?"

"Hot damn!" Roland laughs with delight, slapping his thigh.

Actually, Le Chat is a surprise, though I did hear about the plaster-caster, Renée Mersault, and lots of other gossip, too, when I was in Paris. I was a cautious young scholar in those days, meticulously ethical, burning to show how ruthless I could be with the ephemeral chitchat of history. The truth is I kept some of the best gossip out of *Hemingway on the Terraces* because I couldn't verify it. And there are good reasons for caution. Gossip is gossip; by definition it may never even have happened. I wonder about this Pound anecdote. Anything so deliciously scandalous would've gotten into the literature. Biography is tricky: you have to be careful.

"Go on," I say, but the sneaky grin on his face tells me he has just started his meter.

"You want more? It's in the manuscript."

"I see. And we pay to take a look."

"That's correct, son. As they say in Hollywood, it's pay or play."

There is a knock at the door. The old man widens his eyes theatrically. "Now who could that be?"

Roland jerks it open. Outside is a young woman in her

twenties, wearing a camisole and a longish skirt. She's prettier than she ought to be, standing on the threshold of this den of sleaze.

"Mr. Markham, I'm Lynn Bowen from *Vanity Fair.*"

Vanity Fair! It's possible, I suppose. . . . Markham looks back at me to make sure I'm taking all this in.

"Ah, Lynn! Didn't expect you till later. Come on in. Meet Elliot McGuire from Warren and Dudge."

Her hand is cool and soft.

"I can come back," she says.

"Sure, sure. Me and Mr. McGuire'll be finished in a half hour, max. Then I'm saving the rest of the day for you, my dear." He takes her arm and stage-whispers, "Mr. McGuire's trying to make up his mind whether I'm for real or not. What do you think of that, Lynn?"

She smiles, a pleasant, takes-all-kinds shrug of a smile. "I think he'd better get the word back before Warren and Dudge gets left in the dust." The voice is delicate and modulated, the accent mildly southern. She nods good-bye and withdraws.

"See what I mean? That's what's happening, McGuire. You better get it through your head: there's a line forming, and you guys better get in it."

"That's fine, but you should understand one thing: no one at Warren and Dudge is going to move this project an inch farther until you give me something I can walk away with."

"Here." He fishes around in his hip pocket and comes up with two snapshots, which he shoves in my direction. "Take a look at these."

The first one is a grisly Kodacolor, a man's dead body wrapped in a blood-soaked bathrobe and lying face down on the floor. Only there is no face. There is not even a head, only some fleshy stubble, above the neck line, and a puddle of blood. As I realize who it is (but, of course, it could be anyone at all, a model—a posed mannequin for that matter) a bolt of nausea makes me swallow hard. I flip to the next one: it's a black-and-white, from a different era, a genre of picture I've seen hundreds of—the young Hemingway on the loose, posing with literary pals or drinking buddies. In this one, he leans drunkenly against the shoulder of a man who could almost be his twin brother. The man is bigger than Hemingway, even better looking, and stands with a solid dignity that contrasts with EH's unsteadiness. In this picture there is no doubt: that man is the young Eric Markham.

"Yeah, that one's me and him. And you can guess who the other one is. Now hand 'em back, my friend, and as far as I'm concerned, that's it for this round of negotiations. If you don't have the authority to make a deal, you can just head on back to your bosses in New York and let 'em make any goddamned decision they want."

--- ELEVEN

BACK AT THE hotel I call home to beam up my messages.

First my agent, Jerry Bronstein: *"What the hell is going on, Elliot? Myron Skolnik says you had some kind of attack in his office? Are you okay? Call me, let's talk."*

Beep.

"Hi, babe, it's Yugo. What'm I gonna do with you, bubeleh? You never return my calls. C'mon, pull your head out of your navel long enough to meet me for a beer, okay? Call me at that number I gave you, it rings right on my desk. No, wait. Different number, hang on—" He reads the new number (he has to change it every few weeks to dodge persistent women fans and bothersome crazies). I don't bother to write it down.

Beep.

"Elliot, this is Coyote from WBAI. Um Shakti wanted me to check with you to confirm your guest spot for Wednesday night's program. If everything's cool we'll see you at the studio a half hour before airtime. By the way, we've been airing a LifeForms promo for the show—have you been listening? Looking forward to it—"

My radio debut. I really ought to make sure the right people at W&D will be listening. Perhaps distribute a tape. But later for all that. I'm tired. My mind is muttering like a bucket of deranged bees. I think I'll order something from room service and go to bed. I've done my job. Let's report to Craig, take the money, and run.

I call him at home.

"Elliot, great—hang on, I'm going to put you through the speakerphone."

Craig's voice has an adenoidal poignance that sounds like sensitivity until you get to know him and realize what a soullessly carnal creature he is—and proud of it. I like Craig. He lives from sensation to sensation, glitz to glitz. He is the fleshly little brother forever at my shoulder, his role to fatten up my spirit and guide it through this custard of a life.

"Okay, tell me everything."

"Want my better judgment? Thumbs down."

"Aww, now don't spoil it for me."

"Craig, there's going to be trouble with this guy, I just know it."

"But is it thumbs down because he doesn't have a story after all—or because you fear he's a bumpy ride? I can live with the latter, you know."

"He may have a story, but I've yet to see a manuscript."

Craig's voice lowers to bass register, full of confidential urgency. "Look, here's the problem: Sir Harry has fallen madly, insanely in love with the idea of this book. The *idea*, you know. I honestly believe that if such a book didn't exist he would want it written anyway. Get my drift?"

"I hear what you're saying."

"Off the record—what chance do we have that there's *something there*, even if it's a mess—something to work with?"

"As I said, he wouldn't show me the manuscript."

"Well, give me some images the man, the scene, what are we dealing with?"

"Okay: a big old wreck of a Hemingway look-alike, except his head is shaved, don't ask me why—probably so he *won't* look like Hemingway, whom he claims to despise—and yet he calls himself 'Pappy,' get it?"

"Mm. Go on."

"Most certainly paranoid—made me wear eyeshades on the way to his shack—but nervy: he obviously thinks he can sit on the manuscript and bluff his way to a contract. By the way, someone claiming to be from *Vanity Fair* was there—"

"*Vanity Fair?*" Panic enters his voice. "Oh, shit! If *Vanity Fair* was there it means he's all over the place with this thing. Next he'll have us in an auction."

"He claims to be doing just that."

"What's his phone number?"

"No phone."

"No phone? How am I supposed to talk to him?"

"He said go away and don't come back without a firm offer and a contract in hand."

"Jesus. Elliot, I'm going to put you on hold, okay? While I try to reach Sir Harry's plane."

Sir Harry's plane, a 747, is outfitted as an office and luxury living suite. This is a man whose feet haven't touched the ground since 1978. He holds the mogul's world record for consecutive deals done above thirty thousand feet.

And he's quick, too—Craig is back on the line in just under two minutes.

"Elliot, the man amazes me, absolutely amazes me." His voice warbles with new confidence. "The mind of the man—so fresh, so full of entrepreneurial recklessness. He's ready to throw a contract at Eric Markham's head. Get me the fax number at your hotel."

I open my mouth to protest, then close it. Why should I fight him?

"I want you to go back to him with the contract I'm going to fax you. It's a generous offer, almost too generous, if you ask me. But Sir Harry has three conditions, okay?"

"Mm-hm."

"Number one, Markham's got to take it or leave it. No negotiation. But it's so good he's bound to take it. Number two, he gets a minimal fraction of the advance on signing, with the big piece to come on approval of manuscript. Sir Harry is taking a chance as it is, he wants to protect himself if it should turn out unpublishable. And number three—and this is crucial—you *must* see a manuscript or no deal. It doesn't have to be *War and Peace*, mind you, only a memoir of some kind, starting somewhere, moving through something, and ending up with a bang in Ketchum, Idaho. We'll pay you to stay down there and edit. *Et voilà—I Killed Hemingway*. And you—more tan time in Key West, you fortunate dog!"

"I didn't bring any clothes."

"You're on expenses, old boy. Buy some."

TWELVE

OF COURSE, BUY some. Like any secret agent, merge with the territory. Look around—here we have sensuous open-air tossed salads of jungle greenery, salty breezes, sunlight, and hot sleepy endlessness. Blend in.

It's not hard: just outside the Blue Conch is the main drag, Duval Street, where every third storefront is a T-shirt emporium. I enter something called The Body Boutique, which seems particularly well stocked with fun-in-sun accessories. A dark-haired girl with a French accent waits on me.

"You will walk out of here looking so mmm *formidable*," she assures me. "We have everything but the shoes."

She reminds me of my mother. Mom was small and dark and had an accent too, but hers was southern: she spoke English and French and Hebrew the way she learned them down in Savannah, with a lilting soft southern warble.

The French girl sets me up with spiffy wraparound shades, two pairs of lemon-colored shorts, a sunshade that says HEMINGWAY DAYS, and several T-shirts silk-screened with exotic birds. Rather than walk out looking *formidable*, however, I have the clothes wrapped up so I can stay dressed for business, New York–style.

I think of my mom quite a lot these days, what with Life-Forms beginning to happen and all. I think mostly about what an honest kick she would have gotten out of it—unlike my dad, who would have found a way to trash it. Mom died at a bad time for both of us: I was out of touch, lost in college, and she was fighting a silent war against indignity (Dad had already taken up with Kristin) and, unknown to any of us, disease. Our good times had come much earlier, when I was a gawky little kid and Dad had only just begun his long siege of neglect. In those days we would spend whole afternoons together. We would eat marvelous things in the park, sausages and cheeses and candies we bought at Zabar's. We would *look* at things.

She would describe objects to me as if I were blind. To Mom, the world was exactly what you could see of it, no more no less. Thus you *literally* created the world by the act of perceiving it.

She left me a blessing and a curse: "Don't think you're like the other kids, Elliot," she used to say. "You came into the world with a *message*."

I used to think that meant I would be a mailman when I grew up. Maybe even something like a Pony Express rider. That seemed not bad at all. One day I came home from school complaining that I never won anything—footraces, spelling bees, that sort of thing—somebody else was always a little faster, a little smarter. "It's not that I'm a complete klutz or something," I said, reasoning it out, dealing with it rather well, I thought. "I don't come in last. I'm just in the middle somewhere. I'm mediocre."

Her eyes ignited suddenly. Her voice, hardly audible, crackled: "Don't you *ever* let me hear you say that word!"

I reeled back a step. "What word?"

She stamped her foot (I had never seen her stamp her foot before). "You are *not* mediocre. Nothing you will ever do will be mediocre, do you hear me?"

I heard her.

Yes, Mom would have enjoyed being around for Life-Forms.

THIRTEEN

"I HAVE A contract."

Pappy just looks at me.

"I have a contract," I repeat.

He stirs and scratches his cheek. He seems shy and unsure of himself. "We ought to have some coffee," he whispers.

"No thanks. Did you hear what I said?"

"I heard you," Pappy snaps. "Let me see it."

"First let me see the manuscript."

Roland is lounging around. He pops open a beer and

leans back against the old refrigerator, watching with intense interest.

Pappy's face breaks into a weak grin, then collapses under my gaze, settling into a mask of despair. "There isn't one."

A noisy gull flies over the shack raining down contempt on his shiny old head.

"I see." There goes my editing fee.

"Want a beer, Pap?" says Roland after a beat of silence.

"Yah."

Roland hands him a fresh can. Pappy rolls it back and forth across his forehead before taking a swig.

"No manuscript. Now let me get this straight. There's been a terrible accident—the manuscript was carried off by a marauding sea lion. Or it went down with the *Titanic*. Or there never was one to begin with." I turn my disdain up a notch. "But what intrigues me—not that I really care, I'm only a paid minion—what tweaks my interest is, what's this all about? What's the point here? Is it just a case of literary arson? A false alarm? A bomb threat? Are you one of these people who like to start forest fires—"

"All right, enough." Pappy rises to his feet and a strength I haven't noticed before flows into his face. His expression turns into a commanding scowl. "There's a manuscript. My whole life is a manuscript. There's a goddamn manuscript, I promise you that!"

"Where? Where is it?"

"Stolen."

"Stolen?"

"Stolen by Hemingway."

Incredible! "The manuscript was stolen by Hemingway? What are you talking about?"

"Sit down, will you?"

"I don't want to sit down."

"Get him a beer," Pappy says to Roland.

"I don't want a beer."

"Okay, okay. Just simmer down and listen, okay? Get him some coffee."

"I don't want any coffee. Say whatever you want to say and then I'm leaving."

"Well, don't jump on your goddamn horse just yet."

Pappy's emotional energy shrinks to depression level again and he retreats to his bed like a crab backing into a hole. "First off, I don't blame you for being confused, angry, whatever. I know what it looks like: like I'm an incompetent swindler that just got snagged in my own con game. Well I can answer the charges, point for point."

"Please do."

"Okay: Swindler." He clears his throat. "I'd be a swindler if I was lying, if there was no story here, no manuscript, as it were—"

"Please define 'as it were.' "

"All right, all right, there's nothing on paper, I'll tell you that up front, nothing beyond the pages you've already seen."

"Stolen by Hemingway."

"When I'm through it'll all make sense, pal, okay?"

The heat is overpowering. I don't know why I'm so irritated by all this. So he turns out to be a delusionary old nutcase. Should this be any great surprise? Relax. Just go back to New York and tell Craig to forget it. It's no skin off my nose. Meanwhile, let's hear how he tries to get out of this. . . .

"Go on."

Pappy stands up and begins to scuttle aimlessly around the shack as the words spin out of his mouth like abstract filigrees.

"I'm as old as the hills. Y'know how I got this old? I've always been able to get a good night's sleep. Not like our legendary friend—nighttime was like Halloween for Hemmy unless he was oiled up. You get as old as me, however, and time don't mean so much—ten years here, five years there, it goes by like a nap. The pages I sent up to Warren and Dudge, the assassination, to me that happened yesterday morning. Paris, 1925, that was last week. I've got a photographic mind and it's all there." He taps his head. "The story of me and Hemingway goes way beyond the assassination—which by the way is true, every detail of it—it goes all the way into the soul of the man and tells the one story he never wanted told."

"And what's that?"

"How he stole my life."

Little by little Pappy is straightening up, gaining stature, the scuttle turning into a stride. I realize again how large he is, a heavyweight.

Roland has curled up in a corner as if to watch his favorite TV show. He catches my eye and points confidently at Pappy: Listen to this, kiddo, he's saying.

"I can't tell you the whole story now. But I'll say this: there's plenty of it. Revelations! Things you never heard before about Ernest Hemingway. Things that'll sell books!" Pappy pauses significantly. "That's right, *sell books*. That's what we're going to do. There's a manuscript, all right, and I'm big with it, but for reasons yet to be revealed I need help. This book's got to be ripped out, I can't deliver it myself." He fixes me with a look that combines defiance and exhaustion. "I'm ninety-three years old, McGuire. I'm out of hormones. I can't get it up anymore. Figuratively speaking, that is."

A gap of silence widens between us. Ninety-three years old . . .

"You need a collaborator."

It's a simple enough statement, but coming out of my own mouth, it makes my head reel. I think of Myron Skolnik back among his film cans, pregnant with his own nutty vision of a life that would sell books and vault his myth to the silver screen. Is this my recurring fate? To encounter an infinite series of old men reaching out to tell their stories through Elliot McGuire, literary midwife?

Pappy's eyes are wide with anticipation. There is money on the table here. It is time to play poker.

"Okay," I open. "Correct me if I'm wrong. We are talking about I Killed Hemingway, a memoir by Eric Markham, as told to Elliot McGuire." Not that I want the credit—it's just a bargaining chip. We'll see if he falls for it.

"No. No way." He shakes his head and squints intently. "This is my story, you'll be using my words as they come out of my mouth. I want sole credit."

My gaze is rock steady. "Sorry."

"Sole credit or no deal."

I puff my cheeks out theatrically and head for the door. You have to be prepared to walk.

"Wait a minute, wait a minute," Pappy whines after me. "Just hear me out, damn it."

I wheel around and wait.

"You're offering a contract, what's the advance?"

"Ample."

"But how much? Gimme a figure?"

A casual shrug. "A hundred thousand."

Pappy breaks into an immense grin. "Well, aww right!"

"But don't let it swell your head. The cash is only a reflection of the demented office politics at Warren and Dudge. And you only get twenty-five up front; you don't see the rest until they have an approved manuscript."

"Do you want it? It's yours."

"What?"

"The seventy-five thousand part of it. It's yours. At my age, what do I care about the money, I won't have time to spend it. All I want is my place in history. I'll take the opening twenty-five grand, just to take care of my immediate needs. You get the rest. Just give me sole credit."

Now this is an engaging twist. I think it up and down.

"Look, McGuire, it's your lucky day. You come down here to edit a book—they'll pay you for that. But you go a little farther, you ghost the damned thing. When it's done I hand you seventy-five thousand dollars cash under the table. You make out like a bandit!"

There's a name for this: double-dipping. I'm just going to pretend this is a B movie, which it is. Corrupt but charming, I'm going to drive a hard bargain.

"All right, let's say I do it. Let's say I ghost for you. Publishers take forever to pay. By the time your second check is cut my work will be done and out of my hands. How can I be sure you'll give me the cash?"

"You can't," Pappy says. Silence fills the little room. "We're beyond the law now, this is sheer man to man. Once we shake hands we've got to trust each other, that's all."

His eyes are unblinking.

"Okay. Let me make sure I understand this," I say. "I produce a manuscript; in return I get three-quarters of your advance, plus whatever else I make from my separate deal with Warren and Dudge. You get sole credit."

"Plus royalties over and above the advance," Pappy hastens to add.

"Sure."

"You don't think there'll be any?"

I shrug. There might well be royalties. But sufficient to pay off a hundred-thousand-dollar advance? I doubt it.

"You wait, pal, you wait." Pappy holds out his hand. "Deal?"

I clasp the outstretched old paw. "Deal."

FOURTEEN

"THE CAFE DES *Amateurs was the cesspool of the rue Mouffetard, that wonderful narrow crowded market street which led into the Place Contrescarpe . . ."*

EH got it wrong, of course: it's *"de la* Contrescarpe." I ought to know. I did my time in the same festering Parisian swamp, although by the time I got there the whole square had grown gentrified and the café had changed its name to La Chope.

"Something to drink, sir?"

"Coffee, I guess."

I have *A Moveable Feast* open on the seatback tray table twenty-five thousand feet in the air, a slick new paper edition I picked up in Miami International on a whim. A stupid whim. I shouldn't read Hemingway anymore. It affects my bowels. I've even been known to break out in hives.

Hemo-phobia is a genuine psychosomatic condition that ought to be in the books. You can imagine how it played hell with my life as a Hemingway scholar. But there is a soothing by-product: it tends to cut into the intensity of my *other* problems. Today even my fear of flying has been damped down to an acceptable whine. Small bumps, pesky little pockets of funny air go by scarcely noticed—

Oof! A whopper! "Make it a Scotch, okay?"

"Yes, sir."

Read, damn it, keep reading:

"—and the hotel where Verlaine had died where I had a room on the top floor where I worked—"

Forget it, I can't concentrate. Why am I doing this to myself, this substituting one phobia for another? It's a prescription from hell. Well, should I curl into a ball and fibrillate? No, do something else. Occupational therapy. Make some phone calls.

Ah, my Scotch— "Miss, do you have an in-flight phone?"

"Yes, sir, would you like to make a call?"

"Please."

Phone contact should help. Something about cellular connections with the earth makes me feel a little safer. I dial Craig.

"Elliot! Where are you?"

"I don't know, somewhere over Delaware, I guess."

"Come again? This is a noisy connection."

"I'm on the plane. I'm on my way home."

"On your way home? Well, don't keep me in suspense. Is it a page turner?"

I release a breath into the phone. "It—it needs work."

"What are you telling me? Do we have a turkey here? C'mon, old boy, it's your Uncle Craig, you can tell me."

I'm not used to lying, but it isn't an altogether downbeat sensation. There's a tantalizing confusion in my sensorium— like being nauseated and aroused at the same time. Is this the thrill of degradation so irresistible to compulsive liars and self-soilers?

"It needs . . . *lots* of work." That isn't a lie. I wait, letting him twist for a few seconds. "But it could be hot. Really hot."

"Hot! That's what I need to hear! So where do we go from here, what do you need?"

"Time, mostly. Time to work with him."

"You've got it. Take as much as you need to do it right. Stay down there."

"But I'm not *down there* anymore, Craig."

"Huh?"

"I'm in a plane, remember?

"Ah, yes. Why the hurry to get home, by the way?"

"I told you. I'm going to be Um Shakti Lewellyn's guest tonight on WBAI."

"You didn't tell me that."

"I must have. She's interviewing me about LifeForms."

"Well, I hope you can get yourself back to Key West in due time."

"I don't see why not."

"You'll need a place to live down there, a condo or something."

"I'd rather stay on at the Blue Conch, if it's all the same."

"Whatever makes you happy, Elliot. How much time do you need? Will a month be long enough?"

"Should be. I'll need some cash—"

"Of course, of course."

"I mean now. In advance."

"All right, consider it done. And get the old geezer to sign his contract, okay?"

"He already has, I have it with me."

"I want it. I'll send a messenger over to meet your plane."

"Have him bring the cash, okay?"

"You drive a hard bargain, Elliot. I'll see if there's anything left in the kitty."

"And don't forget tonight."

"Tonight?"

"LifeForms, Craig. WBAI, eight o'clock. Assuming I land safely and all."

"Got it. I'm setting an alarm right now."

"Good-bye, Craig."

"So long, big guy. You're doing a fabulous job."

FIFTEEN

WBAI-FM IS LISTENER-SUPPORTED radio, which accounts for the unvarnished, disheveled look of the place. But the listenership is select: the artistic and intellectual vanguard of New York City keeps the dial parked here. This is exactly the audience I want to reach now at this critical seed stage. This is the soil I want to impregnate. Later for the Larry Kings, tonight I'm right where I want to be.

Astrid and I arrive and are met in the reception area by Um Shakti's producer, a tall bony hippy who calls himself Coyote, and looks like his last job was on a peyote farm. He takes an immediate shine to Astrid, hovering at her elbow as he leads us to Um Shakti.

I've never met "Um" (is that what I should call her?) but on the air she has a luscious radio voice that suggests sensuality, long golden limbs, nudism. It just goes to show. In person, Um Shakti is fortyish, short and plump, with a bad complexion and ratty brownish hair going to gray. However, as she holds out both her hands in greeting, there is a firmness of gaze, an air of gentle command that takes over once you get past her dowdy appearance. This woman could definitely lead a cult.

"Elliot," she breathes, viewing me intensely at arm's length.

"This is my friend Astrid Davies," I say, hoping to deflect some of the abundance of her gaze.

"Yes, of course!" Um Shakti breathes, shifting her entire attention momentarily to Astrid, who flutters and stiffens irritably under the scrutiny. I know how she regards people like this: "silly guruish harvest goddesses and such," is the kind of phrase she would come up with.

"D'you mind if I smoke?" says Astrid in her steeliest English manner. This gets the desired effect: Um Shakti blinks once, then leaves her alone.

"Smoke? Hey, sure sure," says Coyote eagerly. "Not right here, but I'll show you where, okay? Come with me."

Off they go, Astrid fishing for her butts, Coyote trying to keep his palms dry.

Um Shakti shows me into the interview studio and sits, radiating like a crystal chandelier as we wait for the show to begin. A thick pane of glass separates us from the control room, where I can see Coyote, behind the engineer, still working hard to connect with Astrid. He seems to be doing all the talking. She stands in various bony poses of nonchalance, watching us and blowing smoke in the air. The engineer points his finger and we're on—

"Hello, New York, this is Um Shakti, the program is 'The Ecology of Belief,' and I'm so pleased tonight to welcome as our guest Elliot McGuire, creator of LifeForms, a brilliant new system for human possibility. Elliot, welcome."

"Thanks, it's my pleasure."

"Elliot, what we're about here is more than just the analytical, wouldn't you say? Isn't LifeForms something you can live by?"

"Oh yes, sure you can. Most people think they're stuck in whatever form their lives have taken up till now, but Life-

Forms says no, you can change that form, and gives you therapeutic techniques to do it."

"Let's backtrack for a moment: how did you make this discovery?"

"Well, I'm a biographer, Um. I've written twelve or thirteen private biographies and naturally I'm sensitive to this issue of life-as-form. What happened was, in working with human stories, I began to realize that people—sometimes great and famous people—were literally trapped inside their lives. It simply never occurred to them to use LifeForm change as a tool to open up new realms of possibility for themselves."

"Give us an example."

"Okay, first you learn to perceive your primary form, the form you start with, your benchmark form, if you will. Then there are techniques for transforming the primary form in ways that make it more dynamic. Let's take author Ernest Hemingway, for instance. He began his life and career with such a flurry of creativity and achievement, then as the years went by he got stuck in a certain invariable pattern of life— frozen in a LifeForm that was no longer appropriate for him. So his gift, his vitality, his ability to write simply withered away. I would have encouraged him to redefine his form— which began as a sort of Christmas tree—lots of presents at the base, then mostly tinsel and cheap ornaments as he went along, till finally the whole thing petered out at the top—I'd have made that static phallic element over into something that could have powered him through the rest of a long and productive life, something more like a guided missile or a rocket, which picks up the basic Christmas tree form but reconceives it by adding power and motion to it."

There's a long silence, as Um Shakti simply looks at me, blinking once or twice.

"Okay," she says. "And then you began to put your theories to use?"

"Right. I began working with Sven Svensen, the Swedish analytical psychologist who practices here in New York—"

"Yes, and a frequent guest on our show, I might add."

"And with his help I developed a therapeutic approach with which I've been able to help a number of his patients."

"How does that work? Suppose I came to you for help?"

"First, as I say, we'd determine your base LifeForm, your PrimeForm, as I call it."

"How do you do that?"

"It takes a lot of training, but in the end it boils down to a largely intuitive process—I close my eyes, like so, and a form gradually appears in my mind."

"That's so simple. Can anybody do it?"

"Well, not exactly. The simplicity is deceptive. In Life-Forms training you learn to extract the key variables from a life. It's concentrating on those variables that makes it happen."

"So you wouldn't be able to do my LifeForm without knowing my life story?"

"Normally, that's the case. But I can come up with a pretty accurate spot reading just by being around a person for a while."

"Let's try it! Do my LifeForm!"

"Okay." In the dark, I see a pumpkin, a big fat sprawling pumpkin. I'm not surprised. Pumpkins are people who have no single direction, they just spread out at the edges. I don't want to tell her this.

"What do you see?"

"An ascending mountain range. This is very healthy. It means you're making an orderly progression up, from peak to peak."

"I like the sound of that."

How could I tell her she's a pumpkin, in front of all New York City? It's only a spot reading anyway—they can be way off the mark.

"Let's open our phone lines now and take some questions from our listeners. . . . Hello, you're on the air."

"Elliot, I really appreciate and respect what you're trying to do. Is there some kind of mantra you could suggest that would help us change our lives?"

Tap dancing time. "Well, you could try this: *I am changing my life. I am reconceiving my LifeForm. It's almost done. This is my Manhood*—or Womanhood or Personhood or whatever. Repeat this as you utilize some of the other techniques of LifeForm transformation and it'll support the process."

"Hello, you're on the air."

"Oh, hi. I'd like to know how we can find out more about LifeForms and where I could locate a LifeForms therapist."

"Well, I expect to have a book coming out within the year." (Are you listening, Craig?) "I'm in the process now of setting up a LifeForms Institute for training purposes. Actually at the moment I'm the only certified LifeForms therapist in New York, but we expect to change that before long."

"But how can I contact you directly for therapy?"

Um Shakti steps in.

"Caller, you can speak to Elliot about that later, off the air, okay? Hello, this is Um Shakti, you're on the air—"

And the calls roll in. They're out there. I always thought so but I never saw the proof until this moment: they're out there—a ready audience for this idea, a vast *market* for Life-Forms.

At one point, Um Shakti passes me a note: "This is unbelievable! We've never had so many calls."

Finally it's over. Um Shakti chants a little bit and says good-night over her theme music (by Ravi Shankar). But the switchboard is still jammed with calls. Coyote sets us up in a small room with a phone and as Astrid strokes my hair, I speak to about twenty or thirty more people desperate to change their lives, absolutely certain that the sound of my voice tonight was the first moment of the rest of their lives. They want LifeForms. They want it now. And more than that, *they want ME.*

Astrid takes me home with her. There's something almost respectful in her manner. She's not complaining about her life. She's soft-spoken and attentive. She makes love to me worshipfully.

"Elliot," she says, lying naked in the overheated loft, "do my LifeForm."

How can I say no?

I close my eyes. No form emerges at first. Then I start to see it: a dark blob, amoebalike, assuming a series of pseudoshapes until it settles finally into a vulvaish set of lips. This isn't good. This indicates she's consuming herself by some form of hypersexual cannibalism. I feel like the astrologer who keeps seeing bad luck, ill health, violent death in people's charts. What am I going to say? She is so vulnerable.

"It's a flower, a particular flower. It's a rose, a rose that's past the bud stage, mature, but still opening—it's at that point where every day a new flourish of petals appears. It's a very creative form. Unfurling beauty. You're okay, sweetheart, it looks good."

"Oh, Elliot, oh thank you." It's as though I just gave her a reprieve from death. She reaches for me in a fit of relief, which, like most of her emotions, sets off ripples of sexuality. I can feel myself slipping into the dark night of her true LifeForm.

At the airport, on a whim, I stop at one of those insurance machines. Of course, what does it matter if I go down—in insurance terms, that is. I have no wife, no children, not even a dog to howl at my death. But let's do it anyway.

I fill in the Hemingway Association as beneficiary. This is not because I want them to profit, God knows! What I'm up to is jacking up my numerical chances of safe passage by conniving an irony so extreme it could never come to pass: EX-HEMINGWAY SCHOLAR CRASHES ON SHAM PAPA MISSION, LEAVES THOUSANDS TO SCHOLARLY GROUP THAT DRUMMED HIM OUT OF HEMINGWAY STUDIES!

See what I mean? What's the law of averages that such a moral miscarriage could ever materialize? Practically nil, I would say. Irony too extreme.

I've heard arguments against this tactic, but sorry: I've had too much success with it—protecting myself by pushing statistical envelopes to the max. It works. The Hemingway Association, my beneficiary?—don't make me laugh. I feel better already.

SIXTEEN

THE MORNING OF Day One dawns, soft and tropical.

All right, let's read the rules.

Number one: proceed as if it's all true. What choice do I have? He's either lying through his teeth (not at all out of the question) or he's telling some form of half-truth (also plausible). As a professional, I accept the material at its face value. Otherwise this job will never get done.

Number two: This *is* a job like any job. He's just another old man with a story to tell. I've gone down this road so many times before, I know every twist and turn. I may be bothered by the creepy specifics of this one, but in the long run moral untidiness melts away under the heat of higher purpose: subsidy for LifeForms.

Would Nietzsche have hestitated? Not for a second.

So come on, shake off this malaise. Be a man. Stand up, start walking. The sooner we can get through the dictation stage, the sooner Craig and Sir Harry will have their manuscript, the sooner I can wash off the slime and forget the whole tawdry little episode.

He's waiting for me. I can see his gargoyle of a head craning around a gatepost.

"There you are, you're late."

Warren & Dudge's check for twenty-five thousand is burning my pocket. It is hot in more ways than one. I've never seen a publisher come up with so much money so quickly. It had to be drawn on the personal order of Sir Harry Taymore. This should impress the old guy.

He glares at the check for a moment, then folds it and stuffs it into his pocket. Nothing, not even money, is going to slow him down today. He's brewed coffee already and placed a pile of leathery Danishes on a paper plate in the middle of his kitchen table. This is a man who is ready for his appointment with destiny.

"Eat if you want," he says. "How do you like your coffee?"

"Black."

"You sit here." He points and beckons like a traffic cop. "Now how're we gonna do this? Where's your tape recorder?"

"Right here."

"That? That's a toy."

I plunk my Sony on the table. "It's big enough."

He folds his arms. "I want something else."

"Now wait just a minute." I rise and give him a hard stare. "There are going to be a few ground rules. One of them is this: I am the professional here. You are a job to me. It's going to be a good job because I have professional standards—I don't do anything halfway. But I don't want to be hassled over small details, okay?"

"All right, all right—"

"Here's how we're going to proceed: I'll ask you questions and you'll answer them. We're going to do this every day for as long as I think we have to. When the whole story is on tape, I'm out of here. I go back to New York, transcribe the tapes and weave the material into a finished memoir—and presto, you're an author."

He waves one hand like a hanky of surrender. "Whatever you say, boss."

I turn on the recorder.

"Now: relax your mind, forget about time sequence. I want something special for openers. Something emblematic. An image. Something you think of whenever you drift back to your days in Paris with Hemingway. An event. A party. A special day . . ."

His eyes flick back and forth.

"How about—hmmm—how about the day I first met him? It's so clear in my mind it could have been day before yesterday."

"Fine."

He pulls a deep breath. "Okay, I won't get into why I was in Paris. Let's just say I was there, poor as I am now. The Big War was over. I had a room east of what the Parisians called Boul' Mich, in the rue Descartes—That is, before I moved down to the rue Mouffetard, over the butcher shop there. Mornings I took my coffee in the little plaza up at the top of the Mouff. I had been in Paris ever since the Armistice, trying to pull myself together. I hadn't had what you'd call a good war. It was all I could handle just to follow my feet up to the café, find a piece of sun, drink a coffee or a brandy and let my mind drift.

"Well, the table where I sat was right around the corner from Hemmy's house. I couldn't write yet—my fingers would shake too hard when I tried—but I used to carry a notebook just to be ready. Hemmy spotted me right off. He noticed things about me: I wore old army clothes; I drank in the morning; I looked to be some kind of writer. And he also saw what I saw: that we were alike enough to be twin brothers. So one day he grabs a table next to me and just sits down with his paper, pretending not to look at me. The garçon had brought out another brandy and we were speaking French. After the garçon was gone, Hemmy leans over and says, 'Pardo, m'shoo'—oh, Jesus, what an accent! I says, 'Let's use the mother tongue, bub,' and he blushes and sputters a bit, then he's talking real broad, like a cornball from prairie dog country. Says he's a poet, he's seen me there and figured I'd be a poet too and was I a vet and so was he and where'd I see action and so on and so forth, buys me a drink, buys me another drink, and another drink, and before you know it we're shit-faced, up past the Pantheon, singing songs, pissing on the street, and all of a sudden Hemmy says, 'C'mon, let's climb this church!' Before you know it, we were halfway up the fool thing—hootin' and hollerin' and there were windows flying open and folks sticking their heads out, some of 'em cheering us on, some cursing at us and yelling for the police.

"Well, a couple of gendarmes come riding up on their bikes to make a disturbing-the-peace issue out of it. 'You come with us,' says one of 'em in French. I look around. Nobody near but a few drunk street people, so—I wink at Hemmy and let fly my Saturday night sucker punch. Down goes one *flic* like a sandbag. The other one jams his stick hard into Hemmy's diaphragm. Down goes Hemmy. The *flic* comes for me the same way, but I grab his stick, pull him toward me with it, and spit in his face, which gives me about a second's worth of shock time, long enough to put him down with two jabs, *bang-bang*, one to the nose and another to what's left of the nose. By now Hemmy's up, looking shaky but ready to run, and we take off for the Mouff.

" 'You can punch,' he says, after he gets his breath back. We're in the alley behind my place. 'But can you box?'

"I tell him I've been pounding assholes into the floor since before he was in short pants but he's not really listening; I see where he's going with it; he wants me to put on the gloves and step into a ring, wants to box me. He figures I'm a one-punch brawler but he can finesse me in the ring.

"He brings me over to the American Club, which is kind of like a YMCA, with guys in tank tops waving Indian clubs around, stabbing at their toes, grunting on the parallel bars and so forth. They all know him when he comes in. 'Hem!'

they say. 'Hem, old boy!' I figure they're mostly wire service guys and trust fund idlers keeping trim for the heiresses that hang around the cafés down along Montparnasse. But there's a boxing ring there, and a couple of candy-asses are circling each other with gloves on the size of pillows.

" 'One side, boys, here's the main event,' Hemmy tells them. He's smooth as pudding with these jokers, talking out of the side of his mouth like Boston Blackie. They love it, they go for the act—it's like 'Here, Hem, kick my butt!'—oh, they think he's marvelous.

"Now what happened next never got into the biographies and all I can think of is, Hemmy's buddies never understood what they were seeing. We put on the gloves and started circling. He threw some punches at my head and I kept countering, cutting him back whenever he led. Bam! Down he went. That was round one. Round two, the same again. I could tell the boy thought he was a boxer but he was up against real expertise. I could've knocked him out anytime and he started to realize that. He saw me pulling punches and it drove him crazy.

"Well, it goes on and on like this and Hemmy's face is looking pretty puffy, when all of a sudden he slams his knee right into my crotch. Take note—this was pure Hemmy: when it's slipping away, go for the nuts. I doubled up and rolled to the floor. Hemmy strutted around and waved at his buddies— 'Good boy, Hem!'—they thought he had knocked me down. Then he comes over, big grin, and holds a hand out for me. I stood up on my own and looked at him. The grin, the dimples, the little-boy squint, just like I had showed up for his birthday party. He was too good to be true. 'Pal,' I says, low, 'just between us, you ever do that to me again, ever, and I'm going to kill you.' That's all. Just a simple statement, but from the heart. The big grin faded. He looked back at me, all huffy, and nodded. He got it.

"Then I reached over and roughed up his hair and he grinned all over again and threw one of his big arms around me. 'Come on, fercrissakes, let's go get drunk!' he says. And we stepped down from the ring like that, pals, and I heard one voice say, 'Look at 'em, Jesus Christ, twin gods, what a pair of *men!*' "

* * *

Well.

What do we have here? He's a liar, of course. It's complete bullshit, it's got to be. And yet. And yet . . . this is well-crafted bullshit. Rooted in verisimilitude, *creative*. Against my will, he's got me wanting more.

Let's run a spot check of his LifeForm:

As he savors the end of his story, I drop my eyelids and concentrate. Out of the blankness, here it comes—a circular form, a self-referential mandala of some kind, but more, something living about it, something *frighteningly* alive. His is a particular variety of LifeForm that you almost never see, and when you do—it's trouble. A thick, sinewy slab of a snake with a mouth the size of a crocodile's is in the horrifying act of consuming itself. Its tail has disappeared into its own toothy maw and the entire body writhes and quakes in the grip of this hideous perversion of nature.

Pappy's LifeForm is a classic, all right. A rare, terrifying classic. It even has a name: *uroboros*—

My eyes pop open and he is staring at me. He winks.

SEVENTEEN

SOMEONE IS TAP-TAP-TAPPING at the door.

"Yo, Pappy. Is this a good time?"

"Come on in, sweetie-pie," he says, winking at me.

In comes a fierce-looking young woman in tank top and shorts, carrying a plastic deli dish. She's muscular and small, with dark bronze skin and a serpentine headful of black curls, not your ordinary Meals on Wheels. She looks more like a tough little heartbreaker from the Israeli army.

"Got some leftover turkey, Pap."

"Yum. McGuire, this is my girlfriend, Valerie. Mr. McGuire is down from New York City to interview me, sweetie-pie."

Her frank, hawkish eyes give me a once-over. "Yeah, he's obviously from New York. New Yorkers all have that mad ferret look when they come down here."

Pappy slaps his knee. "*Hee-hee.* Fair warning, McGuire. She'll tell you what she thinks."

"Well, it's true, Pap. Three quarters of my clients are New Yorkers who can't unwind."

I clear my throat frumpily. "What kind of clients do you . . . serve?"

She draws a business card from her hip pocket and flips it across the table to me. It says:

GIFT OF HAND

SWEDISH MASSAGE, SHIATSU, SPECIALTIES (ASK)

OUTCALLS ONLY

LIC. PHYSICAL THERAPIST, VALERIE RIGGS

Pappy squirms. "Yeah, okay, fine, you don't need to advertise in here."

"I'm not advertising. He asked me a question, I'm answering it."

"Nobody asked for your calling card."

"Well, excuuuuse me!"

"Val, we're busy. Mind if we get on with it?"

"Hang by your thumbs, I don't care. I'll just give the kitchen a few licks and hit the road."

"Do that."

Slipping behind his back she makes a devil sign over his head and twitches her torso in a kind of voodoo dance parody. I wonder about the mechanism of attraction here. A fetish for old men? Possibly it's his shaved head.

"Let's go, McGuire. What do we need now?"

"Well, background, I suppose. Context."

He throws his head back. "*Hee-hee*—context! McGuire, I'm so full of context we just might never get back to Hemingway!"

"Let me worry about that. Talk about yourself. Start way back. Tell me what kind of childhood you had."

"Childhood? Very, very brief. Born on the frontier, 1895. Mother dead—scarlet fever. Father beat shit out of me. Pop was a retired Indian fighter turned federal marshal. Cleaned up my home town of Farley, Montana. He had a great life gunning down drunk cowboys and humping bar girls until my mama died and he got religion. Then he turned into a Bible-thumping old pickle and beat me even harder. So when I was seven, I built a shack in the backyard and went out there to live with my dog. I told the old man I had a pistol and if he came near us I was going to shoot him. He left me alone."

"So you grew up fast."

"Fast! McGuire, by the time I was fourteen I had lived forty damned lives already. My life was like Hemmy's fantasy of the boy's life he wished he had had. I had my first hangover when I was eight, screwed my first woman when I was nine. By the time I was eleven, I could outfight any man or boy in Farley, including Pop. I almost killed him in a bare-knuckle scuffle the day I turned thirteen and that's when I decided to leave home, me and Roscoe."

"Who's Roscoe?"

Pappy pats his crotch. "Right here, pal."

"You mean— Oh."

"Roscoe is, shall we say, uniquely long and broad in the beam. He got to be known by the vaudeville girls who used to pass through town and stay in the hotel where I washed dishes. 'Tell Roscoe I've been missing him,' they'd say. One pretty little Irish girl came through and said she had heard tell of Roscoe back east and wondered could an introduction be arranged. Only problem was she had also met my pop and arranged to do a little free-lance work with him. The old fool had never given up the girls and used to meet the incoming trains and chat up the talent. So, me and the little colleen were on our third or fourth go-round when the door flies open and it's Pop. He sees me and goes berserk, drags me out in the hall by my hair. I couldn't put up with that so I knocked him downstairs. I can still hear his head hitting the steps like somebody dropped a bowling ball. 'Who is he?' the girl says from behind the door. 'My pop, the marshal.' At that she panics. 'Oh, Jesus and Mary, I'm done for. They'll tar and feather me for sure!' But I calmed her down and to make a long story short, we got dressed and left town on foot, walking at night and sleeping by day, until we crossed the state line to Cheyenne, where nobody gave a hoot who we were. Well, we didn't have a cent, so she taught me how to pimp and turned a few tricks. That got us some clothes and a room at the railroad hotel, where we stayed in bed for forty-eight hours and then took a drawing room on the first train east. Oh, Jesus, you should have seen Hemmy's eyes when I told him this stuff. He was almost crying. 'You were thirteen?' he'd say. 'Thirteen?' "

"Don't let him fool you," Valerie says from the kitchen. "He wasn't ever thirteen."

"Aw, put your hat pin away and sit down with us."

She brings a chair from the kitchen and joins us, smoothing Pappy's nonexistent hair in a daughterly gesture. Incredibly, they make a rather handsome couple. His eyes are all over her as she bestrides the chair.

"So," she says to me, "you're the guy that's going to write Pappy's book?"

I glance at him. He nods back.

"Think it'll be a best-seller?"

"Hard to say. There's certainly a lot of interest at the publisher."

She looks at me piercingly. "And what about you?"

"Me?"

"Yeah, what's your interest level? Do you believe Pappy's stuff?"

"That's not exactly my function, of course, I'm just here to help him get a book written."

"Mm, diplomatic. You ought to be in the State Department or something."

"Well, do *you* think he's telling the truth?"

Pappy's eyes flick back and forth as we rally.

"Of course. Does he sound like a liar to you?"

Good point: there is a feverish candor in his presentation that would most likely jam a lie detector.

"I can always tell when somebody's lying," she goes on. "And there's something else, too." (She rests a hand on Pappy's shoulder.) "I used to work in Santa Monica Hospital—I've seen a lot of movie stars, TV stars. Look at him. Can you see it? That's star quality. He radiates it." Her eyes flare as she strokes his cheek. "Look at him real hard and turn on your star meter."

This girl knows how to massage more than muscles. It's as if she has snapped on a five-thousand-watt Gro-Lite: Pappy is positively swimming in it, a slow star-grin creeping across his face.

He stands up.

"I've got to pee," he says, his gaze going sly on me. "You got to pee, McGuire?"

As a matter of fact I do, but something tells me I'd better hold on to it.

"No thanks."

"No? What are you, Superman? You been sittin' there all morning drinking coffee and you're telling me you don't have to pee?"

"That's right."

"Bullshit. C'mon and pee with me."

"I don't have to, okay?"

He snorts. "Okay, hold out. Pee in your pants for all I care."

He shuffles out the back door, where he urinates loudly into some bushes.

"Listen to that," says Valerie. "I stopped trying to keep a garden back there. He just pissed all over it."

Pappy shouts from the backyard: "Always like to air the old boy in the morning."

"Silly ass." Valerie mutters and goes to the sink to run some hot water. "Hey, Pap, when's the last time you had a total immersion bath, huh?"

He shuffles in. "Don't give me that crap. Any time you want to do the immersing you've got an open invitation."

"Let's do your head, anyway," she says, bringing in a steaming bowl which she sets on the table alongside a straight razor and a shaving mug.

Arms dangling gorilla-style, Pappy settles into his chair. Valerie lathers him up, then strops the razor and pulls it across his head in quick, deft strokes. The whole ritual has the look of habit. She must do this every morning.

"Hold still, funny man, or you're going to have razor tracks in your scalp."

"Listen to that, McGuire. What a pistol!"

Valerie slaps at Pappy's shiny skull with a warm washcloth and then rubs it down with witch hazel. His eyes droop and close.

"Going to put me down for my nap, sweetie-pie?"

"Nope, I'm working this afternoon."

"You're awfully quiet, McGuire. You want your head shaved, too? C'mon, be a big boy."

"Not today."

Pappy laughs. *"Hee-hee.* Not today—a real laugh line. Hey, we're gonna be some comedy team, McGuire! We're gonna be the goddamn Sunshine Boys, right?"

"So long, Pap."

Valerie is out the door.

"I'll level with you, McGuire: you'd have to be a hell of a man to keep that one interested. You got a girl like that?"

"I've . . . got a girlfriend."

"Oh yeah? I bet my girlfriend could lick your girlfriend. Let's throw 'em in a Jell-O pit sometime and see who gets out alive."

"Oh, come on."

"Only kidding. What does yours do?"

"She's . . . an artist."

"An aww-tist. Well, lah-de-dah!"

It occurs to me that this is the first time I've talked "girlfriends" in about twenty years. It doesn't feel right. And what the hell *is* all this aggressive small talk, anyway? "Excuse me, but can we continue?"

He straightens up and smiles as if he's skunked me in some arcane game. "Go right on. Ask me something."

I unpause the tape recorder.

"Okay, so you were thirteen—whatever anybody says to the contrary—and at some point back then, you began to write a page a day, correct?"

"Correct."

"What was your attitude toward what you were doing?"

"Didn't have one."

"But you must have. You were becoming a writer."

"Writer? That's hardly the word. I was just a compulsive scribbler. A freak. I didn't know what a writer was. It took me till years later in Paris to realize there wasn't anybody else like me, never had been. I was a unique animal."

"Can you elaborate?"

"Well hell, I taught myself to read and write when I was five. That's pretty unique. While other kids were drawing stick figures on the wall, I was making word pictures. Just for fun. From six on I kept a journal, and by the time I was eight you could hardly call it a journal anymore. I'm telling you—every time I wrote something I was creating the world. It wasn't poetry, but the achievement was to take a moment's worth of experience and make it new every time you would come back to it. 'Make it new.' I used that phrase with Pound the first day I looked at his sonnets. Those were my words."

"Pound?"

"Ezra."

"You knew Ezra Pound?"

"Sure I did. Long before I ever met Hemmy."

"Let's get into that."

"Okay, it's 1908, I'm going on fourteen, living in New York, by that time making a living as a boxer, a part-time bartender, and still pimping for Essie, the Irish girl, all the while writing these one-page prose pieces. Ezra walked into the picture just as he was leaving for Venice. He'd been fired from his teaching job and was exiling himself in a huff. He didn't know beans about Europe. He had a headful of academic fluff and a flair for the word, but so far you couldn't call him a poet. He knew how to scribble a sonnet, but the one he showed me sounded like mush."

"Ezra Pound showed you a sonnet in 1908?"

"Oh sure. We were living in Hell's Kitchen, near the waterfront, me and Essie. We used to work the steamship passengers coming and going for quickies. I spotted Pound down by the Cristoforo Columbo; it was a cold day, middle of the winter. He was peering around with that unmistakable hungry hawk look I'd come to recognize: a fellow on the loose looking for a woman. We exchanged a few words and he followed me back to the house where Essie was waiting. He was kind of brash and showy but I noticed he was shaking. Turned out he was a virgin. But Essie took care of that. Afterwards we sat around and he kind of announced he was a poet, started pulling out sonnets, triolets, like a parlor magician flaring decks of cards. I said, 'You sit here, I'll show you something.' I went and got some of my stuff and as he read it his mouth dropped open.

" 'By thunder, you show me one thing—the poor ol' prose paragraph can deliver a two-ton bomb. This beats all!'

" 'Wrote 'em yesterday,' I said, and without another word I lit a match and up they went. 'And I'll write some more tomorrow.' "

"You burned them?"

"Well, of course. I never kept anything I wrote. In those days I never looked back."

"And Pound?"

"Well, off he went to Venice with his brains scrambled by me and his ashes hauled by Essie. Almost missed the boat— they had to drop a rope ladder for him. And the last thing he said was, 'Come to Europe, for God's sake!' That was young Ezra, vintage 1908."

"And did you follow him? To Europe?"

"Well, we're getting ahead of the story, but—yeah, I turned up over there."

"All right. We're back in 1908."

"That's right. And about that time I started to get serious about the fight game. Promoters were after me and I started making good money, better than I ever made as Essie's pimp. So a few months later I sailed off to England for a series of fights. Ezra was in London trying to find a name for the kind of way I wrote. I told him I called them 'compressions.' No, he says, it's got to end in 'ism.' He didn't like 'Compression-ism.' Sounded too much like 'Communism.' All right. I give him another label: 'Imagism.' Now he's jumping up and down. 'That's it, that's it!' He takes the name and goes out to save the world with it. One thing I can say for Ezra, by the by: he never stole my stuff. Hemingway—oh, Jesus, that's a dif-ferent story, we'll get to that! Now let's see, where the hell am I? Oh yeah—so Pound wanted me to contribute to *Des Ima-gistes*, but I said, 'The hell with you, I'm no *imagiste*, I'm a prizefighter and don't let me see my name in any of your damned propaganda for that matter!' Ezra and Amy Lowell had a bunch of little poets walking in lockstep. You had to be an *imagiste* or you fell off the face of the earth. Ezra wasn't ever happy unless he had everybody lined up in rows, flashing little *fascisti* salutes. He went to military school, you know. And you see where it got him. . . ."

Pappy gives a weak little wave of dismissal. He's out of gas.

"Time for my nap, McGuire. Let's call it a day.

EIGHTEEN

I'M SUDDENLY IN the best damned mood!

Who in their wildest fantasies would have thought that right over here on Gruntbone Alley we had the very progenitor of Modernism?

Eric "Pappy" Markham, the man who taught the Lost Generation to write!

There are some real virtues here: imagination, verve, a sort of screw-history attitude that makes for good gossipy tall tale telling.

The Hemingway vignette is riotously in character.

Pound's lost virginity—delicious!

No sign yet of murderous obsessions, just a curious stress on his killer dong, which does seem a bit overdone—but let's face it: to father modern literature you would have to possess, at least symbolically, a pretty heavy-duty phallus.

Could some of this—even just the tiniest fragment—be true? Craig has a shred of a point: *nobody saw it happen.* Who's to say . . . ?

I'm back in my hotel room watching TV. The idea was to get comfortable, but my air conditioner isn't working, so I'm lying here with the ceiling fan kicking up a zephyr of sorts, but it's no match for the sweltering island heat. They've promised to move me to another room but so far it's all talk. I suppose I could have spent Pappy's afternoon nap time in the shade of the huge vine trees that shelter his backyard; I could have sat there listening to him rattle the bedroom shutters with his great sonorous rootings and slobberings, but I wasn't in the mood.

My feet are insufferably hot. What I need is to buy sandals—some fresh air, a stroll, a cold beer. Yo, Key West—crazy little place. Most likely, the moral danger here is sunlight making you lazy and sybaritic. Places like this, according to Yugo, you oil up and lie around until one day you get up for a beer, look in the mirror, and you're fifty-five. This is Yugo's standard quip about why he hasn't moved out to L.A. with the rest of the TV business. "Your whole life slides by while the sun shines," he says. Of course, I need hardly add, it will slide by anyway (on my honor as a biographer) so why blame sunlight?

Actually it's not so bad once you get outside. Right now, mid-October, there's a trace of a breeze, a hint of a future. But here's something curious: all up and down the street I keep sighting big-boned, white-bearded Hemingways, strolling along in Banana Republic safari gear. What's this all about?

Outside Sloppy Joe's Bar, I let a hulking street craftsman in a do-rag measure my feet and cut me a pair of sandals. He is a sullen churl. Probably learned leatherwork in the slammer.

"Why so many Hemingways?" I ask him.

"Look-alikes. One of them contests tonight." With a snort of contempt, he indicates Sloppy Joe's over his shoulder.

My sandals are going to be too big but somehow I don't want to argue with this guy. I pay him and flap-flap into the cavernous afternoon darkness of EH's legendary haunt.

Like the rest of the bars down here, Sloppy Joe's facade is wide open to the Key West outdoors. Of course they're working the Hemingway angle to death, but that's okay, so is the rest of the island. There is a special sales booth for Hemingway T-shirts. The bartenders and waitresses all wear them, marked STAFF. Pictures of the Master dot the back walls. Frozen drink machines keep churning up an endless supply of rum runners and *papa dobles*, Ernie's favorites.

I crawl onto a barstool and light a Camel. The bartender, a sweaty, big-breasted woman in a pink EH tank top, pauses in front of me.

"What can I get you?"

"What's a good local beer?"

"Budweiser."

"Quaint. Bring me a tall one."

Sitting—or hunkering—beside me is a skinny Adonis in a black leather jacket (cultish, the motorcycle variety, worn over bare chest), young, truculent, in his cups. He is tanned an angry mud-red and has his hair gathered back into a greasy swoop. Not my kind of drinking companion, it seems to me, but how wrong we can be. He's a writer, of course. And jolly company, it turns out, although he has an odd affectation: he talks straight ahead, never once looking at me. He's a feature reporter from *US*, on leave to research a book on celebrity impersonation, which he says is the halcyon mark of our failing times. His working title is "Wanna-be's." He's in Key West to take in the Papa contest, which he says is the major phenomenon of its kind for people over fifty-five.

"You wouldn't believe what I've seen," he says, fixing his hopeless eyes on a vacant spot across the wide expanse of horseshoe bar. "Everybody knows about the Elvis impersonators. But how about the Willard Scotties, the Rothies—"

"Rothies?"

"Philip Roth impersonators."

"No."

"Yes! Yes! The Rothies gather at a certain deli in Newark. Some of them come all the way from Arizona. Supposedly even Roth himself shows up, but no one can figure out which one he is."

"Roth impersonating a Roth impersonator. I hear you."

I begin to see, beneath the grease and the hoodlum's slump, a fallen preppie. His name is Renwick Thorne and he went to Pomfret and Princeton. Impersonation fills him with fear and loathing. He's a Jeremiah, writing about it to warn the rest of us: things are out of hand. We are impersonating remote giants instead of transforming ourselves into legitimate self-creations. We are pygmies. We are giving away the store. He still hasn't looked at me but senses he's got me hooked. He doesn't realize my mind is racing along on a tangential sidetrack:

Impersonation as purloined LifeForm!

Egad, why have I never picked up on this? I could get a whole new chapter out of it: The wanna-be tries to reconceive his formless LifeForm by "grafting" onto it the symbolic trappings of an Elvis, a Marilyn Monroe, an Ernest Hemingway. I agree with Renwick: it's sick. In terms of my theory it's a LifeTrap, a parasitic act in which you end up devouring your own LifeForm potential. It explains Pappy's horror of the EH impersonators: to Pappy, it's *Hemingway* who's the impersonator, an Eric Markham wanna-be!

Suddenly Renwick snaps bolt upright, blinks twice, and

makes a lurching dash for the street. As I finish my beer I can hear him retching forlornly into the gutter. He is a lost soul, struggling but lost. His LifeForm shows in the willowy crook of his spine. But N.B.: Renwick Thorne could give LifeForms a major boost by weaving it into his book (which, he says, has already been targeted as a Book-of-the-Month Club alternate selection). I settle his tab and follow him into the street to continue our discussion. He has already set off, striding aimlessly across Duval and plunging into a cross street. I follow him and catch up as he rounds the corner into Whitehead.

"Everything okay, Renwick?"

"I don't wanna talk about it."

"Where are we going?"

He shakes his head and pushes on, nose into the wind. I don't believe he has yet looked in my direction.

Up a few blocks the street starts to look seedy. The possibility crosses my mind that they might have crack slums in Key West and we're headed into one. Maybe I ought to steer him back toward Duval. There's a questionable housing project across the way—we could be mugged, a couple of drunk tourists—

Here comes a cab. I wave it down and shove Renwick in.

"Where to, guys?" asks the driver.

"Just drive. Something'll come to me."

"How 'bout the grand tour? I give a good one."

"Fine, but make it silent."

"Silent?"

"We're professional thinkers. We want to think."

"Ah. I see."

Renwick's head slowly drops to his chest, then he jerks awake. I really doubt he'll make much sense at this point. But my mind is humming like a top. *Impersonation as purloined LifeForm* . . . what a kick! Let's give him a try—

"So Renwick, where does it all end? I mean what if we start to value imitation over creativity?"

"That's not hard to predict—just a minute." He rolls down the window and spits. "If all you have to do to be somebody is be somebody else, no one'll be anybody anymore. Pretty soon we become a society of mimics. Hemingway imitators. Elvis imitators. John Kenneth Galbraith imitators. Nobody forges any new images. Pretty soon a century goes by and we're still imitating the same old heroes, except it's passed over into ritual now: everybody has a period look. This opens up the other periods. We start to get King Charles II imitators, Grover Cleveland imitators, Madame Curie imitators, Beethoven imitators, and so on. To be and to wanna-be become inseparable, synonymous. You are what you ape— Driver, stop the car!"

He opens the door and dry heaves into the street.

"Where can I drop y'all?" says the driver, hinting now that he'd like to see us safely out of his cab.

"The Hemingway House," I say, wishing instantly I'd bit my tongue. But why the hell not? I never did see it, not once in all my days as a Hemingway scholar.

The cabbie circles back through the slum where he picked us up and all of a sudden here's a familiar vision looming up on the left, a big ugly green house with wrought-iron frippery and a shoulder-high brick enclosure. I recall the smudgy old black-and-white snapshot of the place reproduced in every book on Hemingway. I must have seen it a few thousand times in the old days.

"I want to take a tour," says Renwick, and while I fumble to pay the cabbie, he stalks up the walkway.

It's quite a place, this rambling compound, lots of space, with a swimming pool and a garage cum pool house. Our tour guide is a chatty black woman who repeatedly ignores Renwick's obscene footnotes and raucous yawns. What she has to say about Hemingway is mostly legend rehash but I'm interested in the details about the pool, which had to be gouged out of the coral by hand (blasting is prohibited in the Keys). And how Pauline replaced the ceiling fans with trendy Venetian chandeliers, causing the house to swelter in the tropical heat. This is something Astrid would do. The property is overrun with cats, all alleged descendents of the original Hemingway felines. They have names like Gertrude, Pablo, Sylvia, Ezra. The tour guide spends too much time on their lineage.

"Who cares about the fucking cats?" blurts Renwick, his breath reeking.

"Watch your language!" says a large father of two humiliated teenagers. Renwick ignores him grandly, but settles down.

I think I've seen enough. Renwick's insufferable rudeness is stretching everyone pretty thin (I'm standing as far away from him as I can). Now he's taken a seat on the lawn, where he intends to stay, arms folded, in a pout. Let him take care of himself. I'll discuss LifeForms with him when he's sober. I'm out of here—

On my way, I check the gift counter book selections. Mostly the eternal standards, overpriced, plus some local "I Fished with Papa" vanity press items— Incredible! A copy of *Hemingway on the Terraces!* You might think it would feel nice to know I'm still in print in the House of Hemingway, but here's the sad truth: the very sight of it depresses me. It reminds me of youth, my poor burdened youth—of sodden betrayals and unspeakable acts, naked aggression, surrender to my weakest impulses, sexual confusion, nuclear family holocaust—in short, my old LifeForm, a mashed potato. It reminds me why I'm here: one more sleazeball assignment involving an old man with a story to palm off.

Bogus.

And even if it were true—a legitimate testimonial narrative—who the hell cares anymore how many brandies EH had with James Joyce in Michaud's? Here I am, the creator of LifeForms—perhaps a prophet of the new fin de siècle—still peddling my services as the gun-for-hire that I always was.

Question: Would Einstein have ghosted a book on flat-earth theory the year before he came out with e = mc²?

Answer: I'm not being paid to make judgments. Just get on with it. As Robert Mitchum used to say, "You clean the chicken feathers off your teeth and go on to the next scene."

—but excuse me, *who's this?*

I don't want to make a big thing of it *but* . . . Tour Guide Number 2, just leaving with the group following ours, is none other than the raven beauty I encountered that first day at Pappy's, "from *Vanity Fair*" (in a pig's eye), a.k.a. Lynn Bowen!

She recognizes me just as her group rounds a corner into Hemingway's kitchen.

"Hemingway liked to clean his own fish," she is saying, "but he had a bad back, so he had extra-tall counters installed . . ."

Without missing a beat of her patter, she winks in my

direction and shrugs a private shrug, as if to say: So you caught me, so what?

Since arriving in Florida I think a lot about sex. Could it be the weather? the pregnant cloudbanks? this misty moisty low-pressure system?

So? Am I that different from anyone else?

My sexuality is, shall we say, standard—except that, for a single guy, I make very few new conquests and can go months, years, without sleeping with someone—which I've always attributed to modest appetite. There's nothing wrong with modesty, is there? I mean, am I that much less a man because I don't walk around trying to jump every woman I meet?

Yet on the head level it happens a lot: I persist in wondering . . . what would sex with certain people be like?

For example: Lynn.

I find myself running through it in my mind—I'm doing it right now—stopping, starting over again, elaborating, elongating, running variations, making changes. As I cross over to Duval Street I have to affect a stiff-legged limp to hide my shame.

And when I talk to Astrid, from the corner phone booth that looms just ahead, I will have to hide my guilt.

"Astrid?"

Across satellite pathways, we exchange our standard greeting pattern.

"Hi, sweetheart."

"Darling!"

I'm outside a grocery story on Truman Avenue. From the phone I can see the headline in one of the tabloids: DWARF FROM SPACE SAYS TIME WILL END.

"I miss you, sweet. When are you coming home?"

Time will end . . .

"Oh, a week. Two weeks. What's going on in New York?"

"God, don't ask! I just tied three hundred and fifty-seven little knots and I'm coming out of my skin. It's for the *Mental Shimmer* piece and I think I've got it sold already. Meanwhile Sophie's getting her opening ready. Will you go with me?"

"If I'm back."

Time will end. Then I won't have to go back. Everything

will just simply . . . stop. Whatever it is, it won't matter: none of us will ever meet again, Pappy's book will never be written, Sophie Luxembourg's gallery show will never open, there will be no need for LifeForms. Wouldn't that be a twist? A superior race of aliens stops time. History tossed away like a used Dixie cup. Judgment Day—

"Elliot?" A note of suspicion. She sounds suddenly far, far away. "Are there women down there?"

"Women in Key West? What a laugh."

"Don't tease me. You sound oddly opaque, that's all. It's threatening."

"Honey, I've only been here a day or two. You give me more of a workout than I can handle, you know that."

"Mm. Mmm, I wish you were here right now."

"*C'est impossible.*"

"You know how I get after tying so many damned knots. If only I could nap or jog it away."

"Try a cold bath."

"Oh, shut up."

"I'm serious. Cold water works your hormones over and causes blood chemistry changes."

"Never mind."

Isn't it ironic how the most intimate conversations between lover and lover turn inevitably into shams of duplicity and evasion? Throughout the call I've been flashing Lynn (assuming that's her real name) across my mental screen, turning her image over and over like a 3-D simulation. Did Astrid stumble onto my secret frequency and take a direct hit?

"I'll be home soon, darling. Everything's going to be all right."

"Hurry please."

But first—let's trot on down Duval Street toward the Blue Conch. I must remember to check my message machine: have I been evicted? Have my winter things been confiscated? This money shortage is wearing me down. So many ships out—but the cash won't flow. I may be billing W&D for time and expenses, but this gig is only a temp—and I have to produce a finished manuscript before I'm in line for Pappy's seventy-five thousand. God knows how long that'll tie up my head.

On the brighter side: so far at least it isn't quite the night-

mare scenario I expected. No monster attacks of Hemo-phobia. I could conceivably live with this project for a while—
Let's take a good hard look at my attitude: am I going native? That's the occupational hazard implicit in biography: in the bio biz you suspend disbelief, you "go along." Either that or you end up fighting the material.

But there's something else here, something unsettling about this bizarre meta-world of Pappy's. This is no Myron Skolnik, after all. He is monstrously persuasive, he compels genuine belief. Before you know it I could be up to my elbows in this craziness, although exactly what that would mean, I'm not quite sure.

Confusion.

At the desk a fax: "Scribble, scribble, scribble, Mr. McGuire. Love and kisses, Craig."

Scribble?

Has he figured out my scam? Does he care?

NINETEEN

"WHAT ABOUT A *Moveable Feast?* Did he get it right?"

Pappy looks like he needs to spit. "I want to be fair, okay? I don't want to say it's one lie after another cooked in senti-mental vomit. So I won't say that. But you can read between the lines. He wrote me out of it. But I was there before he was. Like I said, in those days I had a room in the rue Descartes. Hemmy lived down the hill on Cardinal Lemoine. The room he talks about working in, with the little wood stove, that was mine. I told him Verlaine had died in it, which was bullshit. 'Really!' says Hemmy, quite impressed. He used to come over and drink with me when he was pissed at Hadley, then I moved on down to the Mouff and let him take it over. He was writing these long, rambling tales in dialect and so forth. Copycat versions of other writers—Ring Lardner, Sherwood Anderson. He was a leech. He looked at my stuff and was amazed—'How can ya do that in four or five lines?' Easy. I told him to give me some odds and ends he had lying around—newspaper stuff, things he had clipped and so on—by next day I'd turned them into tight, powerful little pieces. 'Compressions.' He tried it himself, but it didn't work. He always left in some phrases, a line or two that jangled, ruined it. I took what he tried and rewrote it. Those early years in Paris I literally rewrote everything he later published. I don't mean 'edited,' I mean *rewrote*—and in some cases *wrote*. I worked with him. I got him to strip down to the bare image. The basic building block. I turned him on to my notion of compression. I told him compressing a story for the news cable was one thing, but making what I called a compression was another. I took a few of his pieces and showed him what I meant. I compressed 'em. He took them away to study what I had done. I forgot about them until later, when he published them, my versions, word-for-word. I was his silent collaborator—out of the kindness of my heart. And how did he repay me? With a dagger in my back. But that part came later."

"I want to get into that. But let's set it up. How did you, this Montana hick, this yahoo from nowhere, end up in Paris in the first place, hobnobbing with the literati? Was it on the force of your youthful dreams?"

"What dreams?"

"Well, to be a poet. Or whatever. What were the dreams that propelled you?"

"Pfah—" He waves that idea away. "I wasn't interested in being a poet. I had no dreams. I was a boxer, a pug, a jock. I liked to fight and go places and that was the extent of my dreams, if you could call them dreams, to fight and travel. Scribbling compressions was just something I had always done, a habit. I had no concept of literature or of myself as an artist. Oh, I knew about such things as poets and painters, but they lived in a different world from mine. That is, until I met Gabrielle."

He speaks the name with several underlinings, as if I should know who we're talking about.

"Gabrielle who?"

He's quiet for a moment. He swallows hard. I realize he is fighting back tears. Finally he steadies himself and speaks with a thick rasp.

"Gabrielle, my . . . wife."

Well, well, well. This is an unexpected wrinkle.

"I didn't know—"

"Forget it. She's gone." He swipes at his wet cheeks. "See, most of my life I wrote one page every day, no more, no less. I didn't have a reason, it was just something to do, like working a crossword puzzle. One page. It had to be substantial enough to fill the page, compressed enough not to spill over. This was the technique I eventually taught Hemingway. But I used to throw them away. Why save your old cigarette butts, was my attitude. But Gabrielle got hold of me with a whole new idea—Art, with the capital A. She took what I was doing and showed me how I ought to make it last. She saved my stuff and wouldn't let me burn it or throw it out. She took me as I was, a wild animal, and had me half tamed before she . . . before she . . ."

Pappy stops again and stares off into the morning, choking on a hairball of grief.

"Tell me about her."

He clears his throat and resumes, in a low mutter.

"She was part of the group over at Sylvia Beach's. A country cousin of Adrienne Monnier's. Only she wasn't left-handed like all of them, so she was trying to figure a way out from under Sylvia's thumb when one day I walked in with Pound. Pound liked the girls when he was in the mood but he had just met Olga Rudge so he had his hands full. There was Gabrielle, fixing something. I thought she was the most heart-breaking little thing I had ever laid eyes on. Sylvia was making a big fuss over Pound so Gabrielle and I had a chance to eye each other and chat a little, just enough to know we were the true ticket. She told somebody she was going out for a coffee and that was the last time they ever saw her at Shakespeare & Company. Gabrielle and I were a perfect pair of lovers. I never had to coax her. She had thick glasses and she was always reading, always a book in her hand. But she got pregnant right off the bat—and she was devout, see, no tricks for her, she was going to have the kid. By this time I was twenty-seven—it was the winter I met Hemmy—and so far as I knew, I'd never been a father, so I said, what the hell, let's be Mr. and Mrs. A priest married us and we got a room for an hour and made love a few times. She said, 'This is so like dying,' and her eyes closed. A few months later I buried her."

Gloom fills the room. Pappy gives me an accusatory look,

then attacks. "You think that's a cheap scene? Huh? Live through it, sonny, live through it. The cheaper it is, the more it hurts. You want refined pain, go curl up with Henry James."

"Now look—"

"Forget it. I don't need sympathy. Let me go on. I'm just . . . I'm not used to this, okay? The only reason I bring up Gabrielle, see, is to make an important point, which is this: she taught me to make the connection between what I was doing and her world—books, publication. I was a primitive. I didn't care if anybody read what I wrote, I wasn't out to cut a figure in the literary world, I wrote for the pure need of the act. But listen carefully: after Gabrielle everything changed. From the moment I put the last spade of dirt on her grave, I wrote to exist between the covers of a book. Now whatever I wrote would go in that book, the book of my life. It would all be for her. And that's about when I first met Hemmy."

"Who not only stole your stories, your gifts to your dead wife, he even published stories of his own that you had rewritten."

"Oh, those! You could hardly call 'em stories. They were strictly experiments, practice. Hemmy was desperately looking for a way to bust into art. I said I'd help him on one condition—that whatever we came up with would stay in his files under 'examples—not for publication.' My big mistake was to give him stuff of my own to learn from, things Gabrielle had loved and said were worth saving. If she had lived, she would have published them on her own press. . . ."

Pappy stops to snuffle, then wipes his face and goes on, under control.

"So—I had this parcel of finished work and I loaned it to Hemmy. 'Study these,' I said. He studied them. He made copies of them. And they got into print all right—in Hemmy's first goddamn book. God knows where my head was—he had been circulating them around for months as his own work. Pound, Gertrude Stein, they'd mentioned what a find this kid was and all the while I was too unconcerned to ask 'em what the hell they were reading. It was my stuff! The balls of him! He knew he'd catch hell from me eventually. But he had such a desperate need to make it and he knew he wasn't getting there fast enough. He needed good work, not those little dialect features he'd been doing, but real monuments. He couldn't build them himself so he stole them from me. Stole my work. Mine."

"Okay. Supposing he did—they were just his first steps. Hemingway wrote a lot more than those early pieces. What about later? *The Sun Also Rises? A Farewell to Arms?*"

"Oh, give him credit, he was a quick study. Put it this way: he finally learned how to apply the basics of the lessons I was teaching him. He was a one or two trick pony and he went a long way on those tricks. But the work that would be considered 'for the ages' was already done. By me. He knew it, too. Sure, he stood on my shoulders and did some fair work later on. But without the early stories, he would have slid into history without a trace. He would have been a replay of Sherwood Anderson, a Gertrude Stein in pants, just like a lot of other writers from those days you never hear about now—they did good work, but not good enough for history."

His eyes have frosted over. He blows his nose, a sad honk. "I'm tired of talking. . . ."

TWENTY

"HEY, PAP! TAKE a break?" calls a man's froggy-sounding voice from the front yard. We have been sitting for nearly twenty minutes in the waning light, Pappy snoozing in place, chin bouncing on his chest, me gazing intently at him, trying to penetrate his stubborn mystery.

"It's Roland," he says, jerking awake. "Must be the cocktail hour."

He's ready to roar. First a pee in the backyard (I use the bathroom toilet—which doesn't flush), then we pile into Roland's pickup truck and head for Sloppy Joe's.

"Slow down," Pappy orders, spotting a Hemingway impersonator window-shopping on Duval Street with his wife. Roland slows the truck to a walk.

"Hey, you!" Pappy yells out the window. "You dropped your face!"

Falling for it, the Papa clone stops and looks down at his feet.

"*Hee-hee-hee.* Ah, these creeps! Take a look, McGuire, and you'll see what it all came down to for Hemmy."

"Notoriety, you mean? Cheap celebrity?"

Pappy makes a fart with his mouth. "Bullshit! If Hemmy could see this, d'you know what?"

"What?"

"He'd be creaming. He loved himself so bad even this would do. This would be top of the world for Hemmy, seeing these god-awful joyboys trying to out-Papa each other."

Tonight the inside of Sloppy Joe's is looking like the Hemingway Room at Madame Tussaud's, peopled with all the standard image variations on EH, time-frozen, swilling *papa dobles*, arm-wrestling, thumb-wrestling, head-butting, sniffing under each other's tails. Pappy leads us to a vacant table. "Just take a look," he says, squirming around in his chair. "I feel like a grief-struck daddy watching his sons parade in drag. Except it's me they're impersonating. And they don't even know it! Every look Hemmy ever tried he took from me. Well, okay, fuck 'em all. I just come here when I want to feel bad, when I want to make myself puke. And you know the worst of it, McGuire?"

"What's that?"

"It's my own damned fault. I spawned this layer of scum. That breaks my heart. To think I loosed this on the world—"

"Now, now."

"It makes me want to make 'em all fucking *vanish*. You ever feel that way? Like you want to eat your young?"

"Not exactly."

Pappy folds his arms and rests his case. "Get us a drink, Mr. Warren and Dudge."

"Elliot! Elliot McGuire!" a voice booms.

Somebody here knows me. Who? Jesus—it's Ernest Hemingway coming this way! Can I avoid this? No, we're on a collision course with not one but three Hemingways, big ruddy white-haired bears with draft beers in their mitts. One of them is gawking at me with recognition.

"Elliot! It's me, Howie Ritz. Remember me?"

"My God, Howie." Of course I remember him: Howard

Ritz, the only Hemingway scholar I ever really hung out with.

Howie and Pappy stare back and forth at each other like fun house mirror images. An odd look of crypto-recognition passes over Pappy's face. Howie wiggles a jaunty finger at him. Do they know each other? It is an altogether strange moment.

"Howard Ritz, Eric Markham—" I mumble.

Howie holds out his fat pink hand. Pappy pushes it aside with the back of his own.

"See you in the morning, McGuire," Pappy says, tottering to his feet. He tugs at Roland's shirt. "Smells like we walked into a ladies' underwear hamper."

We watch them stalk off into the street, noses high.

"Don't mind him, Howie. He's just an old grouch."

"Sure, sure. Well, jeez, Elliot, it's been a long time," says Howie Ritz, beaming anew and pumping my hand. I keep staring at the Papa part of him, remembering a clean-shaven mousy Jewish guy with little or no flash. Now he's all bulked up and sports the full white Papa beard and safari wardrobe to match. He introduces me to the other two Hemingways, high school English teachers from somewhere else in the Keys. Then he is telling me about his life as if showing off a new car.

"Had a little crisis, Elliot, left Ann Arbor, bummed around Paris, got a nice job down here at Florida Southern. Hey, this is paradise, man. Lots of fishing, a new wife. What are you up to in Key West?"

"Long story, Howie."

"Uh-huh. Thereby hangs a tale, I bet. Elliot, you're looking at me funny. It's the Papa thing, right?"

I make polite demurring noises.

"Sure it is. Well, you're looking at last year's Hemingway Look-alike Champ and these boys were pushing me damn close all the way."

"Almost caught yer ass, too," says one of the others, spilling some beer on the floor. All three of them are pretty swacked.

"Listen, Howie," I say, suddenly hungry for a civilized evening with someone outside Pappy's world. "I'd love to catch up with you. Can I buy you dinner later? I'm at the Blue Conch."

"Well, sure. These boys'll be heading back up to Key Largo. My wife's out of town. Sure I could do dinner, that would be nice."

I keep marveling at how much louder Howie is, and certainly heavier and more jowly, than I remember him some ten or fifteen years back.

"Let's meet in the raw bar," he booms. "After the contest." We shake on it.

Renwick is perched alertly at the bar. He seems to have leveled out a bit. He even refuses when I try to buy him a drink. There's a stenographic notebook in front of him, in which he occasionally scrawls a line or two of shorthand.

"I had a good steak dinner, a few cups of coffee. Now I'm working." Indeed, his eyes are flicking back and forth, catching every detail in the room. He even looks directly at me, perhaps for the first time. His eyes are milky brown.

There's been an interesting development: he's fallen in love (as he puts it) with Lynn, the tour guide/reporter who inflamed my own imagination. After they made him leave the Hemingway House (threatening to call the cops) he found a spot outside the compound wall where he could watch her from afar.

"I'm very obsessive in my infatuations. She has something that makes me want to drown in her. So I clung to the wall and wouldn't budge—"

I want to hear the rest but the contest is beginning. On the stage, a skinny male emcee in a Panama hat excuses the band and announces the prize for tonight's winner—a case of Johnny Walker Black, Hemingway's favorite Scotch.

"And let me add that we've got the national media with us tonight—*Time* magazine and NBC are here." Assorted cheers and boos from the bar, which is suddenly spilling out into the streets.

One by one, the phony Hemingways are introduced and called to the mike to make a brief statement. Four or five of them bear an uncanny resemblance to EH until they open their mouths—as though they've been dubbed by bad actors. One sweats buckets in a thick, cable-stitched sweater, trying for the Northern Michigan look. Another one carries a cat. Most of them are well oiled. One stumbles on the way up. He looks more like Mickey Rooney and is a dentist from Biloxi.

Howie acts in an emeritus capacity, watching from the judges' table (the other judges are a Hemingway scholar from Purdue, a local used car dealer, and Hemingway's distant cousin Egbert, a high school football coach from Santa Rosa, California). Howie has a few clear favorites, including his two chums from up the Keys, but when the winner is finally announced, it's the cat man, a looming double for Hemingway circa 1952—

Congratulations Wayne Moffit, retired petrochemical sales representative, from Bernardsville, New Jersey!

Renwick has declared his workday over and is drinking as hard as he can.

"Hemingway," he muses, between double swills of a boilermaker. "What do they all see in the guy?"

A perfect opening: while he's still sober I want to work on him. "They think they see an almost perfect LifeForm."

"Mmm." He stares straight ahead and flicks at the booze in his shot glass.

"What do *you* think they see?"

"Oh, power and fame, power and fame. Star wash like this is always about power and fame." He slumps into his drink, then frowns a bit, looking directly at me again. "What was that word you used?"

"LifeForm. There's a theory by that name. My theory, actually. Understand your LifeForm—master your life."

"Ah."

Don't push, plant the seed. Then steer lightly away. "So tell me about the ravishing tour guide."

"There's not much to tell. I'd slay my firstborn for her, that's all. If she hadn't let me go home with her I'd have taken cyanide."

"If she—*what?*"

"I'm stuck with this ridiculous tendency toward obsessive love just like other people are stuck with psoriasis or chronic malaria. It's my cyclical adolescence, coming around again like Halley's Comet. I just can't seem to change my . . . what is it? Life-what?"

"LifeForm— You slept with her?"

"I didn't say that."

"You implied it."

"No, no, no," says Renwick, sucking on his drink. "When she saw I was nothing but a sick puppy, she took me home and fed me a meal. When she saw I was hopelessly in love with her, she let me kiss her. When she saw I wouldn't stop kissing her, she said, okay, with this glistening serenity, and put me to bed. No sex, she just left, disappeared for the rest of the day. My mind is blown. I'm here forever if I can stave off New York."

"But don't you have a deadline?"

"Yeah, but I could do the work down here. The biggest complication is a personal commitment."

"A woman?"

"No, a dog. I left an eighty-pound Doberman with my mother."

TWENTY-ONE

HOWIE AND I have a drink in the raw bar and watch the moon set spectacularly into the Gulf. Howie is a little drunker than I am and gets on a subject that I usually try to avoid, my past.

"Yeah, Elliot, I would've thought by now you were the one who'd have the full life story out, the Big One, the one that would put everybody else in the dust. I always pegged you for the high road—as opposed to me, say, a genial duffer."

"Please, you're too kind."

"I don't mean to put myself down, mind you, I've done good work. It's just I never had the desire, the big burn. I always wanted to do my little piece and go fishing. But you, man— You were in with Baker, you were having lunch with Mary Hemingway, you were in the fast lane."

"Well, Howie, we all know what happened, don't we."

Howie pushes his tongue through a gap in his teeth and rubs at his beard, remembering.

"Don't I know it. I was there."

"Could we talk about something else? Let's get out of here and find a restaurant."

We dawdle up Duval and take a cross street, reading menus

as we go. Finally we find a quiet little restaurant with a garden and a fish special. But first, another round of drinks.

"I have to ask you the obvious question, Elliot. You down here on some kind of Hemingway project? Coming back to us?"

I shake my head. "This is personal, mostly a vacation."

"Mm. Married yet?"

"Not so far." I want to get it back on Howie. "Tell me about your new wife."

"Ah. She's a ball of fire. Teaches school, runs the *Key Breezes* advertising paper, four hell-raising boys. Some family I married into, Elliot. It's like living on the deck of an aircraft carrier. I just stay out of their way. Esther, that's my wife, she always wanted to meet Hemingway. She was a Papa groupie—even went to Cuba once when she was a teenager and hung around the *finca*. Miss Mary shooed her off. She has a shrine to Hemingway in the bedroom. You can believe what happened when she saw me." Howie looks around, full of rum and mischief, and erupts into jiggles of laughter. I grin along.

"Howie, I have to ask you something."

"Oh jeez, I haven't laughed like this since I donno what, go ahead."

"The old man I was with—"

"Yeah, the chrome-dome. Pappy, they call him."

"What do you know about him, anything?"

"Not much. He's a local eccentric. A bum, really. His hobby seems to be bad-mouthing Hemingway. But you'd expect something like that these days, wouldn't you?"

"He claims he knew Hemingway."

"He's the right age, it's possible. What if he did? A lot of people knew Hemingway."

I feel myself dangerously close to wanting to talk about the whole hustle.

"You're down here on assignment, aren't you, Elliot?"

"No."

"*Esquire* or something?"

"No no."

"You know, I always wanted to write up Sloppy Joe's for the *New Yorker*. Get the mood of the place when a Papa party's going on. I suppose I'll never get around to it."

"Does that ever bother you?"

"What?"

"The thought that you'll never do it."

"I don't know why it should. If I had a nickel for everything I never got around to—"

"That's not really it."

"But that's the way I feel."

Sure, sure, but why is it that you can't even follow my drift, Howie old boy? Why am I tortured by the thought that there is something, so many damned things, I may die without doing? Why are you not? I wonder if Pappy would relate to this nasty little existential quandary? I bet he would.

What was it, I'm trying to recall, that made me like Howie Ritz in the first place? Perhaps it was just that, his lack of anxiety about the future, his modest little mound of ambition. He was comfortable to be around in a period when I was engaged in a high-intrigue love affair with my future. He is still comfortable as I go about mounting another amphibious attack on the Slough of Despond. But now I see him more as a clown with a saggy LifeForm, a moral munchkin twittering away in his lost blandness, never having known what life was for but, unlike *moi*, never having let it bother his head. I decide to turn up the voltage on him a notch.

"Howie, did it ever occur to you that you might be the Messiah?"

"Huh?"

"You heard me."

He gets a touch defensive. "What kind of messiah might you be referring to, guy?"

"The One, the Chosen One."

"Jesus, you mean?"

"Come on, Howie, we all know Jesus was only a contender. I mean, if you're a Jew you have to believe that, right?"

Howie sighs. "Elliot, I'm not too big on Jewish concepts. What do the Episcopalians say?"

"I don't know, but the Jews say any Jewish boy can be the Messiah. What about you?"

"To answer your question, no. It never crossed my mind. I hope it never will, either." He stuffs some fish into his mouth, wipes his lips, and looks around for the emergency exits, but I'm not going to let him off the hook.

"Hemingway was Jewish, you know that."

Howie laughs. "Here we go, silly time."

"No, he was. The latest and most extensive textual analysis has shown that he was a Sephardic Jew, born in Latvia and smuggled to Oak Park to the Hemingways, who had been told by an astrologer that they wouldn't be able to conceive a male child."

Howie squints at me, uncertain. I've got him going.

"What do you mean textual analysis? This is bullshit."

"Listen, I put a computer to work on the entire EH corpus, a big one, a Cray-3 supercomputer, using some new software called TextTELL that makes sophisticated informed arguments based on minute cybernetic operations, millions per second, performed on every bit and byte of a massive data base, in this case the complete works, including letters, of Ernest M. Hemingway. I focused on biographical angles and this is what the machine came up with. Startling revelations. Like he was gay, had an affair with Jean Cocteau. He didn't commit suicide, he was murdered, assassinated. And do you know who did it?"

"Eleanor Roosevelt."

"No."

"I don't know, who?"

"Me."

"Bullshit, you were too young—"

"Thirteen years old, it's the best possible age for patricidal bloodshed. Sullen angry teen, driven by blind homicidal adolescent rage. It happens every day. Read the papers."

"Try your shrimp, you haven't touched them."

"Hemingway was a self-hating Jew. Why else would he write a whole novel around torturing one poor innocent Jewish guy whose only crime was to be boring, so they flay him alive—kike this, kike that—everybody in the book shits on Robert Cohn because he's a Jew."

"Elliot—" Howie is sneaking glances around the garden, afraid some real Jews might be eavesdropping.

"Howie, I don't mean a religious Messiah, I mean this: didn't you ever feel that you could do something that contained such power in it that it would change people, make them think a whole new way, raise them up, make them better? Didn't you ever have that thought in your head for one second?"

Howie looks back at me, unshakable, and wags his head. "Nope. It's all yours, guy. You can have all that crap. I'll be out on the boat." He grins. "I'll look up and wave when you fly by."

I have a choice: I could say something like, "I'll tilt my flaps," and move along to a softer subject. But something is putting me into a foul and combative mood. I feel like an angry linebacker dying for a punch-out. Something in Howie, this tenacious Wonder Bread aspect of his personality, is irritating the hell out of me. I want to push it back in his face.

"Well, I believe you really are the Messiah, Howie. I've come to that conclusion. I think it's people like you, hero imitators, clones, you people are going to be the ones who change history and make something of the human race."

"Elliot—"

"Shake my hand."

"Elliot, cut it out."

"You won't shake my hand?"

"Come on, settle down."

There is no animus in Howie's tone. I could never pick a fight with him, damn it, he wouldn't let me. That's the way he has always been. That's why healthy pink glows through the relaxed tan of his cheeks. This is a happy man, only momentarily flummoxed by my tortuous behavior, only a wisecrack away from restored contentment. Here is a man untroubled by his baggy LifeForm, unaffected by it in the extreme, as he sits face-to-face with this angry spider from his past.

We shake hands.

I suppose it's time to tell the story of my flaming downfall as a Hemingway scholar. Or my comeuppance, as some would have it. The headline reads like this: AMBITIOUS BUT FOOLISH YOUNG ACADEMIC SHOOTS SELF IN FOOT. Or, as Sven might say, "his unconscious contrived his undoing." In any case, as you might expect, booze plays its role, its wormy little walk-on of a role, as does weariness, false hilarity, a weird pseudo-camaraderie with my "colleagues," and oh yes, the fact that my mother had just died, painfully and hopelessly.

The occasion was the so-called Hemingway Dinner, an annual affair held somewhere in the country every January by the Hemingway Association (or HA). The attendees are EH scholars come to schmooze, politic for jobs or grants, mix with the guests of honor, usually old Hemingway pals and sycophants—and this being 1974, plenty of those types were still alive. The dinner was held at the Waldorf and was black-tie. I was hot: *Hemingway on the Terraces* had just come out and I had them talking with this enlargement on Hemingway's recreational life in the bistros and cafés of Paris. So, it was kudos to Elliot McGuire. Yvonne Scudder Vinson, the Dragon Lady of Hemingway studies, past president of the organization, had taken a shine to me and was going to recommend me for a major grant. Her husband, Ronald Vinson, the late-Hemingway specialist from Northwestern, was hosting the dinner and asked me to make a toast. I was walking on Olympus.

But a crosswind was blowing: a few days before—and only weeks after Mom's funeral—my dad had legalized his liaison with Kristin. I took the happy couple out for drinks and blacked out, a bad sign. I was between apartments, sleeping on Yugo's daybed, but that couldn't last since he was obsessively hustling women in and out and getting tired of introducing me every time. Temporarily I took a room in the Hotel Gilmore, in Murray Hill, and tried to enjoy what was happening in my professional life. But the more I drank—and God did I drink!—the more I stared in the mirror and asked myself things like, "Who do you think you are?" and "Who cares about the goddamned Hemingway business anyway?" It was a true late adolescent (or early mid-life) crisis and happening at precisely the wrong time.

Add to it all the fact that I had begun work on what would turn out to be my close-out project in the Hemingway field: *Papa Among the Piranhas: A Study of Hemingway's Attitudes Toward Biographers.* That's right: the ultimate nihilistic project for a Hemingway biographer—a study of how he hated, feared and despised us all. Certainly a great way to psych yourself up for delivering a toast at the Hemingway Dinner. "Here's to a bunch of worms and parasites—Fenton, Young, Baker! Oh, and here's to the rest of us!" But I wasn't concerned with the irony. The entire day of the dinner I spent locked away drinking Scotch and writing a rambling short story about a young blind man who walks away from a train wreck with his sight restored, then is run over by a truck. I had never written fiction before. It wasn't half bad.

By the time I had dressed myself and lurched up to the Waldorf, I was feeling slick and dangerous—as when you know you are about to drive recklessly, jump into water fully clothed, make a pass at someone's wife. I don't even remember the preliminary speakers or the dinner itself, but my toast was unforgettable. For me, that's where the movie will always begin and end.

After Ronald Vinson's avuncular few words—I believe he raised a few chuckles by calling me the "Nick Adams of Hemingway scholarship"—he pointed his flinty old nose in my direction. I rose and somehow managed to stay on my feet.

"Thank you, Ronald. Y'know, I'll be damned if I remember how I got here tonight, but let me just say it's a rare pleasure to be so feted and fed and watered and so . . . so *called upon* by such a legend as yourself"—I saw Ronald twitch involuntarily as I misused the reflexive—"so here's first to you, Ronald, Kemosabe! Then of course—can't forget old You-Know-Who, the Great Boo-hoo, without whom et cetera et cetera—but you expected that, didn't you? Sure you did. Okay, so relax, it's out of the way. Now . . . Simon says let's make a real goddamn toast of it, shall we?"

The faces waited above their starched collars and pearls, still as stone. I lurched earnestly forward.

"I mean, don't you actually get sick of it all after a while? Of it, of him? Sure you do. I know exactly how you feel, God only knows I'm feeling the same way most of the time, so let's just see, mmm . . ."

My mind was sailing through the blackness of space. I had no earthly idea where it would touch down.

"Well then, well—here's . . . to *fiction!* How about that?" I thrust my glass high in the air. "Here's to fiction, the kind of work we'd all rather be doing, eh?"

In my own defense, I think what I had in mind, assuming I had a mind at that point, was a pat on the back to prime stuff, the literature, the work itself, without which ipso facto we had no jobs. Reasonable enough. But it slithered out of my mind another way altogether.

A few timid hands raised their glasses. Everyone else remained frozen. Yvonne Scudder Vinson tensed visibly, and then I remembered: she had written four or five unsuccessful novels before turning to Hemingway studies. I had flipped through them—all written with stolid correctness, a dead hand, something vaguely distasteful about the narrative voice. Kind of like Mrs. Vinson herself. Howie Ritz had once said she was "hard to like." Everyone loved Ronald Vinson and marveled at his deplorable choice of a mate.

So what did I do? Sit down? Oh, no. Living dangerously and loving it, I decided to repair the damage on the spot. Gesturing toward Mrs. Vinson with my glass I continued:

"And what better exemplar of the state of the art than *il melior fabbro*, you, Yvonne. God help us if fiction is left to fester in lesser hands than yours."

She winced. What had I said? No matter. I refocused and addressed the crowd.

"God bless Yvonne for giving it a whack, five novels, let's give her a hand." As I gestured her way, some champagne slopped over the side of my glass and went down the front of her dress.

A few hands splattered together in either horror or embarrassment. Mrs. Vinson's eyes were jammed shut and she seemed to be willing herself to disappear into her chair. Someone was tugging at my jacket.

"Thank you, Elliot," said Ronald Vinson with infinite sadness as he rose to cut me off.

The rest of the evening flew, pixilated in my memory. I remember ending up in one of the hotel bars with Howie Ritz, who was telling me I ought to remember to call Mrs. Vinson first thing in the morning and mend fences. I did, of course. But here's how the call went.

"Yvonne, it's Elliot McGuire."

"Oh."

"Yvonne, about last night—"

"About last night?"

"Yes, the toast and all. You know, all that."

Silence. I plunged on.

"Well, I hope you know that, tired as I was—oh, and I had a little mix-up with some medication for my, ah, my back, you know, one drink on top of that and I was, well, the awful truth is that I was—"

"Elliot McGuire. Oh, yes. You know I was about to get in touch with you."

"You were?"

"Yes, the Zinzenthaler Grant."

"Ah, yes."

Her voice sweetened a tone or two, placing it somewhere along the scale between hungry Siamese and forlorn sea gull.

"I realize now that there was a misunderstanding. I certainly can't recommend anyone for a grant unless I know them better than I know you. Or your work for that matter. I understand you've done a paper or two that Ronald has read but I'm much too busy at the moment to read them. Is that terribly unfair?"

"But you read them—remember the symposium in Minnesota?"

"I read so many papers. There must be a mistake."

She was quietly, deliberately slashing me in long bloody strips.

"Yvonne, this is a sincere apology."

"Excuse me?"

"No, excuse *me*. I beg you. I'm sorrier than you can imagine."

"I'm sure I don't know what you mean."

"Yvonne—"

She hung up without saying anything so I suppose you could say I had had the last word. But as of that moment I was finished as a courtier in the palace of Hemingway studies. Oh, I could go back to the provinces and work humbly away, like Howie Ritz, but the writing on the wall said to drop all thought of major success. I had offended the dark queen. My cachet was suddenly polluted. The banshee Yvonne Scudder Vinson was loose, drinking the blood of my infant reputation. Let's face it, I was rat bait.

One thing I have never told Howie Ritz is that I, too, am a Jew. Surprise. Why else would I be so pissed at Hemingway for trashing Cohn in *The Sun Also Rises?* WASPish as it all looks, I am half Jewish, and the half that counts: my mother, out of an old Savannah Jewish family, might have been Robert Cohn's niece. He might have been my great-uncle. Is it any wonder that, professional distance notwithstanding, my stomach never fails to tighten in anger and shame as I encounter Jake Barnes's underhanded contempt for his "friend," this kike Cohn? Or that back in the old days, Howie and I argued time and again about it—Howie Ritz, Jew, all soft and squishy over Ernest Hemingway, Jew baiter, finally one day to stride out of the closet as a full-blown Papa dragster? Astounding.

"What do you care?" Howie used to wail at me in bemusement. "You fuckin' WASP! You're an Episcopalian."

I never told him why I cared. The argument itself was more important. The principle. Not that I was a secret Jew or whatever. You shouldn't have to be Jewish to take offense at Hemingway's anti-Semitism—this was the essence of my position. Revealing a Jewish parent would have softened my argument. But it didn't matter anyway. I couldn't get Howie to care. I can't get him to care now.

And who should care anyway, I'm thinking, in this leafy old grotto of brick and moss and white linen. Who should care about anything but good food and good drink? And who am I to be taking stern moral positions about anything, come to think of it? The unseen penurious hack behind *I Killed Hemingway.* A conspirator. A swindler. Worse than that, a double-crosser. Proud of yourself, Elliot McGuire?

Howie and I are having trouble getting out of here. It's not the bill—thank God for plastic, I'm too blind drunk to handle real money—it's that the tables—are arranged—in this zig-zag— Oh shit, we've done it! We've both fallen over the same table. Howie, as you might expect, is laughing, unable to rise off the floor. I've at least made it to my feet, but I'm shimmying back and forth as if I were on a skateboard. Our waiter is joined by the bartender, and within a few seconds we are out in the deep green dark frangipani jungle of lower Whitehead Street.

"I hope you wrote the sonofabitch a good tip."

"I probably wrote him into my will."

"Jeez, this is fun, Elliot!"

And he means it. He's wheezing with laughter and fellowship. My old friend. My buddy, Howie Ritz. All of a sudden I want to cry. He *is* my buddy, I realize in a boozy flare of consciousness. And when he heads back to Key Gumbo or wherever it is, I'll be without friends again. But Jesus Christ, man, it's no reason to weep publicly!

"Want me to walk you back to the Blue Conch?"

"No." *Snuffle, snuffle, honk!* "No, I can make it. Thanks—"

Howie throws his fat arms around me and pounds my back. "Hang in there, Elliot, you're gonna be okay, boy. You're going to make it!"

He doesn't know what he's talking about, but I believe him, goddamn it, I believe him.

TWENTY-TWO

IN THE MORNING it is Dueling Hangovers over at Pappy's. Mine glares across the table at his like a sullen attack dog. His stares back, a Gila monster guarding its hole.

We sit.

"Well?"

"Well, what?" he growls.

"Are you up to it this morning? You don't look so good."

His jaw stiffens. "I'll hit anything you pitch. You don't look so damn good yourself."

"I feel rotten. But all I have to do is listen."

"I can talk. Just get me going. Where do you want me to start?"

"Where we left off, I guess. Where you showed him how to write."

"Exactly."

"Led him out of the woods."

"And more than that, too."

"Oh?"

His eyes spark as his memory machine heats up. I turn on the Sony.

"As a matter of fact I did one thing that saved him for the ages. Saved his life, literally. Made a goddamn man out of him, too, as a writer anyway—although the whole thing came damn close to killing him—and again I mean literally."

"Go ahead."

He leans back. As the story gears engage in his head, his face crinkles into a smirk. "Hemmy came to Paris with a satchelful of crap. High school imitations. It makes me laugh to think about it. Kid stuff! A few stories from that lake up in Michigan, a chunk of a war novel, some phony Montparnasse sketches—none of it worth spit. I did the biggest favor I could for him under the circumstances: I cut him loose from his juvenilia."

My gaze sharpens.

He beams back, nodding with manic speed. "That's right, McGuire. You know what I'm talking about, don't you?"

I certainly do. . . .

In 1922 Hemingway's wife Hadley gathered up every piece of fiction he had written up to that point in his young life, including (for some inexplicable reason) the carbon copies, and stuffed them into a valise for a trip from Paris to Lausanne, where Hemingway was waiting for her. What happened next is familiar to every student of Hemingway lore: in the the train station, the Gare de Lyon, Hadley took her eye off the valise and it was never seen again. Gone without a trace, Ernest Hemingway's early work, every scrap of it lost.

"Hadley's valise?"

Pappy's smirk widens into a sunny grin.

"The theft . . . it was you?"

"You get a gold star, sonny."

"Tell me about it. Tell me the whole thing."

"*Hee-hee!* It's a hell of a story, all right."

He's up now. He tangos toward the fridge, pulls out a beer, and pops the top. "You know, I should've been a goddamned teacher. I would've been a pip. I was teaching this boy how to write. Compress, I'd say. Get to the point and get out. I told him to throw his early stuff away. It was inferior trash. Imitations. I said his career as a real writer would begin the day he wrote his first compression. He bucked, of course—he'd put a lot of himself into this high school stuff, he'd even thrown some away—he thought he had a body of work. I let it ride. I knew what I was going to do. Sometimes you have to go outside the law to do good. You put on the mask, the cape of Zorro. You ride at night to screw the guilty and strike your blows for the innocent. You go outside the law to make changes in the axis of the spinning universe. That's what I did."

"Go on."

"I waited for the opportunity and one day it came. I was at Hemmy's visiting Hadley just as she was getting set to go meet him at Lausanne. It was almost Christmas. She was stuffing the manuscripts into an old valise and all of a sudden it came to me what to do:

" 'Maybe you should take the carbons as well,' I says.

"She stopped and gave me a blank look. 'Whatever for?'

" 'Well, that way he can work on them at the same time somebody's reading them.'

" 'Oh,' she said.

"And that was that. Hadley wasn't one to give a man much of an argument. She stuffed the carbons in and I walked her down to the street and we found a taxi. I rode over to the station with her and helped her on the train with her stuff.

" 'Thank you, Ricky,' she said. 'Now I must visit the loo so please don't wait. Let's say good-bye here.' She gave me both cheeks and kissed the air, French style.

"As soon as she turned her back I had my hand on the valise. She went one way, I went the other, it was easy as that. I walked away whistling, bouncing on the balls of my feet, thrilling inside when I thought of Hemmy's reaction on the other end. He'd never know what a favor I'd just done him. I had that feeling you get when you've helped a blind man cross the street. You glow a little bit with your own righteousness. You've done more than just help one guy, you've served a higher order. You've done your little bit to correct the cosmic wobble.

"I went home with the damn thing and it got heavier and heavier on the way, like something dead, a corpse. I should have burned it all, of course, but some perverse notion—like a necrophiliac's desire to keep a dead lover—made me shove the valise under my bed.

"Then that night Hemmy showed up, off the return train from Switzerland:

" 'Ricky! Ricky! She's murdered me!' he was yelling out in the street.

"I came to the window and said, 'Hemmy! Jesus, you're supposed to be in Switzerland.'

" 'I'm not supposed to be anywhere or anybody or anything,' he bawls up at me. 'I'm a dead man, I'm a rotten, blown-up, drifting, stinking corpse of something that was once a man.' And he sits down on the curb with his face in one hand and starts moaning. Very dramatic. You never saw Hemmy this way.

"By the time I got down to the street he had picked a fight with the concierge, and her husband had rolled out—a big mean character who worked on the river. It was Chinese poker, the three of them circling each other, until I came out and pulled Hemmy on down the street. He was so drunk all his natural grace was gone. He stumbled, he kept focusing and refocusing his eyes. Those two would've made hamburger out of him if they didn't stick a knife in him first.

"I said, 'Look, Hemmy, nothing's so bad as all that, I say we get you into bed—'

" 'Dead men don't go to bed!'

"And off he goes, stomping up the Mouff, over the hill and down Cardinal Lemoine toward the river. Every time I tried to steer him toward home he took a swing at me, so I kept a few feet behind and just followed along. Over by Notre Dame he went out on a bridge, out to the center, and I started to feel edgy.

" 'Ricky,' he said, calmly now, and bone-tired, as if he had pedaled a thousand-mile bicycle race and lost by a foot, 'everything I ever did is a pile of ashes in some rag picker's stove.' He plucked a cinder out of the air. 'Look, pieces of me floating all over Paris. . . .' This wasn't like him, this kind of self-dramatizing crap. He had to be drunker than I had ever seen him. He looked down at the river, then up into the dark sky, and shook his fist at where the stars should have been but weren't.

"Of course, I knew what it was all about, but I played innocent. This was all part of what I knew he had to go through. Death comes to the spirit, then first light and rebirth. Nobody ever said cauterizing a writer's ego doesn't hurt like hell!

"I saw him as writhing under the white heat of the surgeon's knife. But he saw something else: he looked over that bridge, and in the darkness of the river he saw the big black wings of death unfold and make a place for him. He was ready to quit. I realized it as soon as he made his move—one foot on the side of the bridge and into the air. He made a flying arc and fell fast, hitting the water like a bomb. It was cold—you know how bone-chilling Paris can be around Christmas—but I threw off my coat and shoes and went right in after him. Jesus, if he died it would be on my hands! Here I had hatched a plan to make him a real writer and where was it going? Straight to the morgue if I didn't turn it around fast!

"He didn't fight me when I reached him. He let me pull him to the quay and we staggered out, frozen. Some bums were gathered around a brazier warming themselves. One of them had my jacket and shoes. I realized we were both in for pneumonia if we didn't get someplace warm, so I put Hemmy's arm around my neck and walked him back up the street to find a cab.

"Well, I assumed he was back on his feet, so to speak, when out of the blue (as if a dive into the river wasn't enough for one night) he threw himself in front of a car. The driver slammed on the brakes and skidded to a stop against a curb, knocking over a market stall and making some horses rear up and scatter a pushcart full of fruit. Everyone was jabbering at the driver, who kept pointing at Hemmy and crossing himself.

"I couldn't put up with it. I did what I should've done a lot sooner: I slugged him, knocked him cold. Now he was just a wet sack of potatoes that I could sling over my shoulder and hope the gendarmes wouldn't give us a hard time.

"I realized we were only a few streets from la Maison du Paradis, which was a high-class bordello where I knew the bartender and the cook and several of the girls, although the madam took a dim view of me because I never paid. So I approached from an alley in the rear and banged on the kitchen door.

"When they saw me, everybody was running around yelling 'Zut!' and pouring hot rum and tea and stripping off our stuff. Madame was gone, said the cook, to the opera and someplace after that, so we were in the clear. The bartender ran us up the back stairs and a couple of the girls who weren't busy took over, pulling me into a gilt-and-velvet room that was so warm I could see the river water steam off our clothes. The girls seemed to get a kick out of the whole thing, a change of pace for them. One was a strawberry blonde with a trim figure and freckles; the other was dark and plump, like a Renoir, with big ripples of flesh under her robe. They couldn't stop giggling. They stripped Hemmy down and giggled at his little blue button of a penis, shriveled by the cold. They giggled when they saw the scars on his trick knee. I threw some coal on the fire while they pushed and pulled and finally settled him between the satin sheets and covered him with a quilt. Then the big one crawled in with him.

" 'He needs his mama,' she said with a pout. She went to work and it looked like a squirrel had been set loose under the quilt. Hemmy's mouth cracked open and he grunted.

" 'Who is this man?' said the other. 'You never brought him here, M'sieur Eric.'

" 'He would not come before.'

" 'He is beautiful. Your brother?'

" 'He is a writer.'

" 'Is he a good writer?'

" 'He has written some bad poetry and some early stories of no distinction. The stories have been lost, which is good. He will have to do them over. With my help he is writing several very good short pieces.'

"The girl pretended to be fascinated but she wasn't really listening. With a dreamy little smile she was undoing the front of her gown, showing me how nicely her freckles cascaded down over her young breasts. This same girl had told me once that she'd had dreams of Roscoe in which he rode a wild horse and burst through her window and bloomed like a big purple rose and so forth. She wanted to get down on the rug with me and she didn't want to wait.

" 'Mm. Oh. *Oh, yes*, M'sieur Eric.'

"I never really trust them when they call out your name but in a minute her eyes were rolling and she had started to drool. That's about as real as it gets.

"By this time Hemmy's bed looked like a pup tent in a storm. His girl, a fleshly mountain of a thing, had risen up and settled herself square on his loins, making like the avalanche that crushes the comatose skier. Hemmy had a thing about avalanches so I hoped he wouldn't wake up too fast.

" 'His little man is awake enough but Monsieur is sleeping through it all,' said the girl.

" 'If the little man stays awake, who cares?' said the other girl.

" 'But if he gets lost there will be no one to go searching for him.'

"That got them both to giggling again. The big one began to snort so hard she lost her balance and rolled off of Hemmy, crashing down on the mattress beside him. The bed made a noise like a capsizing lifeboat and heeled over on the floor. The girls were in hysterics now and Hemmy picked this moment to open his eyes and rejoin us, amidst the shrieks and clutter and the warm velvet room he had seen only in the private erotica of his Boy Scout's mind. And he panicked.

" 'Get away from me,' he says and starts backpedaling on his ass until his back's flush against the wall. He looks from one girl to the other, bug-eyed, then at me, then down between his legs to make sure his equipment is still there—which it is, barely. Then gradually he comes around, with a tough, sullen look on his face, like a guy who knows the joke's on him and he's trying to figure out whose chops he's going to bust for it.

" 'Whose idea was this?'

" 'Whose do you think? It was either here or stumble home with a case of pneumonia, you didn't give me much choice.'

" 'Get my clothes.'

" 'Why don't you relax. We could drink some champagne.'

"They were still wet but Hemmy insisted on beating it, so the girls went into a closet full of whips and harnesses and found us some satin pajamas, building an ensemble on top of that. I thanked everyone and we shoved off for my place, me talking nonstop to perk Hemmy up, him stuck in a black cloud of a mood as he thought about what it was like to be out of control—which was worse to him than having a hot poker up his ass.

"He said, 'Jesus, Ricky, Jesus. I can't stand it.'

"Then all of a sudden he was weeping into my shoulder.

" 'Can't stand what?'

" 'It's like a Chinese torture. Every nerve in my mind is being ripped loose and drawn out and set afire, one by one. Like goddamned birthday candles.'

" 'Come on, Hemmy. Chin up. Don't be scared.'

"All of a sudden he straightened up, like someone just shot him in the butt. 'Scared? I'm no fucking coward. I've never backed down in fear in my life, you snake-eyed son of a bitch. You take that back or I'll make you choke on it. Take it back right now!'

" 'Aw, Hemmy—'

"*I'm no goddamned coward!*'

" 'Well fine.'

" 'Take it back.'

" 'All right, you're not a coward, Hemmy. I just meant when you feel that way, remember your courage, old pal. Remember the war, remember how we could feel calm with the bullets whipping right past our ears and all that. Fear is like trapped gas. You wouldn't shoot yourself over a gas pain, would you? Just go ahead and pass it.'

" 'You don't get it.'

" 'Sure I do. I just see it different. You think you're dead in the water because those stories are gone. Well, you know what I think? I think you're a free man. You've been walking around with chains on, eighteen chains or however many stories there were, and now you're set free. You can skip, you can dance, you can take off and fly. Come on, let's go somewhere!'

"Then all of a sudden he had his arms around me. 'Jesus, Rick, you're my pal. You're my only goddamned pal in the whole world.' And, I swear to God, he kissed me on the mouth."

"Hemingway kissed you on the mouth?"

"What's the matter, you hard of hearing?"

"No, it's just—who ever heard of Ernest Hemingway kissing a man on the mouth? Just momentary disbelief, that's all."

"Believe it, kid."

"So then what? Are you implying he was gay?"

"I never said that. I'm just recounting an event precisely like it occurred, no more no less. There's no judgment involved. Maybe he aimed for my cheek and missed, I don't know. History'll sort it out."

History, of course. Let history do the job.

"By the way, what happened to the valise? The manuscripts?"

He shoves a toothpick into his mouth. "I dropped them in the sewer."

So much for history.

TWENTY-THREE

"WELL, WHAT ARE you thinking?"

"Just static. Nothing. Lots of things."

"You think I'm queer."

This makes me laugh, the old homophobe. "Yes, and I want to hold your hand, you dear old thing."

Pappy chuckles. "Get away from me."

I believe this is the first time we have shared a laugh. For some unaccountable (and probably treacherous) reason, it feels good. It is one of those moments where the busy fabric rips and a sliver of eternity pokes through. It is déjà vu upon déjà vu, I have been here before. Sun washes the room, making prismatic splashes of color. Somewhere down the street a screen door slaps shut. My mind is spinning in the moment, waiting to re-engage, and Pappy is grinning at me as if he knows, as if he drugged my coffee and is watching me turn on.

"You're something, McGuire," he says finally.

"How's that?"

"You come down here and grill me like Perry Mason—what're you trying to do, trip me up? We're in this together, aren't we?"

"Can't deny that."

"Then why don't you lighten up, son? Tell me this: how is it going to help you to make a liar out of me?"

He has a point. A pleasant weariness makes me plead no contest. I flap my arms out in a shrug.

Pappy cocks his head to one side, studying me. He could almost be my therapist. "Let's just rest it a while. Let's talk. Tell me something about yourself."

I switch off the recorder. "There's not all that much to tell."

"Oh, I bet there is. I bet there's a lot more than you let on."

"Not really."

"Why be coy with me, McGuire? What's your real game?"

"I'm a writer. Isn't that real enough?"

Pappy's head bobs up and down soothingly. "I know, son. I know, but not *this*, right? Not ghostwriting. You do this for the beans, but what's the real game? Plays? You a thespian? Poetry?"

I break into a half-grin. "You know, you're not as foolish as you seem."

"Do I seem foolish?"

"Sometimes. Not now."

His eyes narrow. "You're an idea man. That's it, ain't it? You're working on an idea."

"Well . . ."

"I knew it," Pappy declares. "You had that air about you. An idea man. I respect that, McGuire. I respect that about you. You just went up in my estimation."

"Why? You know absolutely nothing about my idea."

"I know you can think. I know you can put two and two together. I read *Hemingway on the Terraces*. I even stole a copy."

"Oh, but that's not thinking. That's just writing. I gave a slant to some biographical material—so what? People mistake writing for ideas all the time. The average jerk thinks Hemingway was an intellectual—but he never had an idea in his life."

"Amen to that, brother."

"Don't be so smug. Neither have you."

He laughs. "Touché, touché—but hey, I don't have to. I've got you for that. I can tell how good you must be. You've got a fine irony about you. That's the number-one requirement for an idea man. Irony. I thought you were a damn snob at first, but now it all falls into place. You're not a snob, you're an ironist! Tell me what you're working on. What's it about?"

A long hesitation, a sigh, a sinking sensation. "It's a way to use some of the techniques of biography to make a better life for yourself."

"Doesn't sound like you want to talk about it."

"Well, mm—"

"You trying to keep it under wraps or something?"

"No, not at all. It's just—" Just a funny premonition that if I let him in on LifeForms, sooner or later he'll find a way to make me choke on it.

"McGuire. Elliot. Tell me, look around the shack, look at this life of mine. Maybe we're not best friends, you and me, but we're sharing a foxhole here, and you tell your foxhole buddy things you'd never tell your best friend. Here we sit, in the grime of war, shells whistling by overhead—"

Trying to chase the metaphor I begin to realize why he has trouble writing.

"You don't hold out on your foxhole buddy, McGuire. So c'mon—what's your spin?"

"It's not really a spin. It's more what you'd call, vulgarly I guess, a message."

"You mean something like—fear the wrath to come?"

"No no, not a Christian message. It's definitely pagan."

"Oh, pagan. Sacrifices, fertility, naked above the waist—"

"Not that kind of pagan. Secular is more like it. It's a way of replacing religion. When your life, or LifeForm, as I call it, runs out of steam, you don't bow down to an unseen higher power—you turn to LifeForms therapy. You change the form of your life. And that takes care of it. You're renewed, you're whole, you're ready to live again."

"Whew. Way above my head. Lemme see if I get it: I have a life, my life has a form, my form goes poop, I blow it up again with . . . LifeForms therapy!"

Do I trust this, is this sincere interest? Or is he leading me through some elaborately subtle put-down routine that is destined to go off in my face like an exploding cigar?

"That's a way of putting it."

"And what's the therapy?"

"Well, it's very technical. Therapists would have to get training and all that. Basically the therapist would help you conceive a new form, bring new energy and vitality into your life."

"Mm. Like what we're doing here, right?"

"Well."

"Well, what? Hemmy stole my life, I'm stealing it back. This is part of it—we're giving me back my LifeForm, right? You're helping me. You're my therapist. Right? Right?"

"In a way."

He studies me hard. "But . . . not quite."

"Not quite," I allow. "But I don't think you need a therapist. You're doing pretty damned well on your own."

He looks back at me with a small grin playing at the edges

of his lips. "I imagine you're writing a book about all this, ain't you? To launch it on the world?"

"Oh, sure. *LifeForms*, it's going to be called. And once it's out I wouldn't be surprised if it made quite a noise."

"Sounds like a barn-burner."

"You'd have to read it, I suppose."

"Written much?"

"It's almost finished."

Liar. I don't even have a finished chapter. There have actually been a few miserable paragraphs and pages here and there, and an overview for the Warren & Dudge proposal. But deep down I see everything on paper as a series of false starts, the tone never quite right, something dismaying about every try. In my darkest moments, I look at geniuses like Freud and Jung not as my familiars but rather creatures from another planet— powerhouses of brilliance, energy, desire, efficacy—and what the hell am I? A struggling hack, a nowhere man, a middle-aged neurasthenic with nothing to mark the best years of my life—gone without a trace, forty years and nothing but these scraps to show for it!

Oh calm down. Doesn't success often come late, and with no visible preparation? Of course it does.

LifeForms has been a long time on the boil. You have to live through plenty just to know what "a life" is. What does it matter now that comparing my own mushy start with Hemingway's flawless early career had me depressed for years? I am about to come out of nowhere and make Ernest Hemingway look like a Bic lighter in a storm. In LifeForms it's called a "LifeNova," a sort of Big Bang–ish act of great achievement in which a universe comes into being out of nothing, nowhere. . . .

I am determined not to lose stride. I've got to work my way out of here and back to New York. LifeForms is turning slowly, slowly in the wind. Without strict discipline there is no telling how long I'll be stuck in Key West with this charming psychopath. I snap on the machine.

"Where do we go from here?" he says.

"Okay: Hemingway. Let's zoom in on the man himself. What was he like? Your personal view of him? Start with anything—what were his habits, how was he hung? Whatever."

A smile freshens his face. "How was he hung, that's a good one." Interest beams through his slouching limbs like tracer fluid.

"I told you A *Moveable Feast* was bullshit. Expert on penis size—hah! His own dick was normal, but that wasn't big enough for Hemmy—it drove him nuts that it was the one muscle in his body he couldn't beef up by working out! Not that he didn't try: some quack told him that stretching it in traction would elongate the cells. I went with him the first time, tried to talk him out of it. We stopped by the Louvre and I showed him the dongs on the statues, just like he shows Fitzgerald in the book. I says: 'See, it's as big as it has to be, Hemmy.' Nope. This doctor's gonna make a regular stallion out of him and so on. So he put himself through that for a few weeks until he realized it wasn't making his weenie any bigger."

"You mean Fitzgerald and the statues, it never happened?"

"A lot of things never happened, at least not the way Hemmy wrote it later. He did a lot of that—taking situations where he was the fool and turning them around so that somebody else came out the butt of the joke. Of course I didn't know it yet. He was still my buddy, I would've fought the Foreign Legion for him."

"Let's get into his head. What was Hemingway's fuel, what made him run?"

"That's easy: the big D. Anything dead got his wheels turning. He used to swat a fly and stare at it for twenty minutes."

"Okay, Hemingway and death, sure. But what was your personal view of it? How did you see death working in his head?"

"Oh, shit, it was everywhere. You could always get his attention with a story about a horrible death. I made one up once about a skier in an avalanche. He used it, of course. One time a woman was chopped up by her lover. Hemmy used his press credentials to get into the morgue and look at her—what was left of her. He stared and stared. Then he took some snapshots. Later on, whenever he wanted to make a woman feel funny he'd whip 'em out. He had an extensive photo collection of what he called 'deads'—had 'em organized by war, missing heads, missing limbs, interesting facial mutilations, et cetera et cetera. Sometimes he'd follow a disfigured vet down the street. Surreptitiously, you know. Pretend he was occupied with something else.

"He got to know an undertaker somewhere east of Montparnasse and he used to drag me over there to watch the guy working on a stiff. Of course, it took Hemmy five minutes to be an expert mortician. He knew just where the slits are made to drain the body fluids, how you have to keep the throat open so the body won't belch in the middle of the wake, how you have to clip certain muscles so the body won't sit up. The mortician was an old guy. He used to pay Hemmy to help him pick up bodies. In those days they didn't have adjustable stretchers to roll them out, you had to dump them in a handbasket and carry them downstairs, and it took muscle. He told me one time they went to pick up a fat man who had died of a heart attack and got wedged into his bedroom door so bad that, with rigor mortis and all, he was stuck. They tried every possible way to jimmy him loose, but nothing doing. So Hemmy got a sledgehammer and beat the body to a pulp, softened him up so they could slide him out. When he told me about it he broke into such a fit of giggles I couldn't get him to stop.

"Not a very pretty story."

Pappy scratches at his chin. "Not a very pretty man. I'll tell you this, for instance: he loved talking about how he'd kill certain people if he had the chance. He'd impale Ford Madox Ford on a spit and roast him over a barbecue pit. He'd keelhaul Bob McAlmon. Do you know what keel-hauling is? An old naval punishment: you tie the wretch up and drop him over the stern, then with a rope you pull him under the ship, end to end, all the way to the bow. If he isn't drowned he's cut to ribbons by the barnacles. And to continue the nautical theme, he'd dip T. S. Eliot in pig blood and set him adrift in a nest of hammerhead sharks. He told me once how he'd kill his mother: hang her from her ankles and dunk her in eau de cologne, a little longer each dunk, till the final one he'd just leave her under—"

"Pappy? You up, Pappy?"

"Come on in, honey. Dan Rather is here."

She drops in with the slim grace of a lingerie model—the goddess of sweet chaos, Renwick's *belle dame sans merci.*

"McGuire, you remember Lynn."

"Of *Vanity Fair.* Of course."

She lights up with a hesitant smile. She has a nice one.

"Oh yeah, that—" Pappy huffs. "Well, you have to understand—I didn't know who or what was coming down here from New York. I was just stacking the deck a little bit in my favor."

"I understand."

"Did I pass?" she says, her voice full of good humor.

I look at her: she would pass anywhere. No wonder Renwick is in such a frenzy.

She dangles a small wicker basket under Pappy's nose. "Good stuff this morning, Pap."

"What you got?"

"Leftover apple pie, baked carrots. Val's coming with some potato salad— Hey, Pap, you don't look so good."

"I'm improving as the day goes on, honey. Soon as I get my nap I'll be fine—"

"Yo, Pap!"

It's Valerie with the potato salad and a bag of fried chicken. I take this opportunity to slip into the toilet for a pee. But rats! the recalcitrant old commode is now off its moorings and lying sideways.

"Out back, McGuire," Pappy calls.

He is waiting in the yard, apparently holding off until I arrive. A pissing contest?

"Go ahead, I'll wait."

"Wait, hell. Let's do it together. Pull yours out."

"Never mind."

"Come on. I have to go, you have to go. Jesus, McGuire, you aren't afraid to piss with an old man like me, are you?"

"Oh, well . . ."

I unzip and let fly into a small bush, trying not to allow a comparison test between my medium-sized member and Pappy's horsy giant. The sound of his gush drowns me out.

"Can't hear you, pal. That's an awfully tiny bell you're ringing there."

"Oh, come on, now—"

"Well, it may just qualify. Let's put 'em together and see."

This is absurd! I would turn around and walk right back into the house except that Lynn is in there, and anyway I'm only halfway through my pee. Pappy, on the other hand, has dumped his load and is standing beside me, ready to compare dongs.

"Lynn, Val! Come out here and bring a ruler—"

"No!" I bleat. "Stay where you are!"

Turning, I catch a glimpse and—okay, I am definitely outclassed, as if such a thing should matter. It shouldn't, of course. But for some reason I am steamed up over this whole damned thing, this penis chauvinism of his. What right has he to make a competitive spectacle out of our plumbing? "Great—now I've sprayed my pant leg!"

"Don't worry. Things dry fast down here."

Valerie is peeking out the back door. "Pappy, Elliot, dahlings, we're going over to the graveyard for a little picnic. Coming?"

"Hell yeah! Come on, McGuire, zip up and let's go."

Oh, why not? It's fun time. To the goddamned graveyard— let's go tease the dead!

Pappy brings along a jug of what looks like lawn mower fuel but turns out to be muscatel. As soon as we sprawl on our sides among the raised slab mausoleums, Pappy goes semicomatose and curls up to sleep.

"Is he okay?"

"Sure," says Valerie. "He goes out for five or ten minutes, it's like a night's sleep for him."

"He looks like a baby, doesn't he?" says Lynn. "A little baby old man."

Valerie sloshes some wine into her mouth. "Hey, Lynnie, don't you think McGuire is a handsome man? Kind of an intellectual Burt Reynolds—?"

"More like Abraham Lincoln."

"Oh, God no!"

"But Lincoln was very sensitive, very soulful looking. I always had a crush on Lincoln."

Valerie burps delicately. "Well, come to think of it, when my dad took me to the Lincoln Memorial I was pretty awesomely impressed. I mean, have you ever been two feet tall and stood between Lincoln's legs looking twenty feet up to his crotch? I almost fainted."

The women are getting silly.

In the midst of it, Pappy comes slowly back to life, not particularly interested in what's going on. Two or three long pulls at the wine and his musculature seems to have returned, along with his skin tone and the rude sparkle in his eye.

"What the hell's so damn funny?"

Valerie says, "Well, McGuire here, he just reached over and laid a big sloppy kiss on me—"

"That's not true," I whine.

"What?" She turns on me. "Why the hell not? What's so hard to believe about that?"

The women break into a fresh round of laughs. I've decided to maintain a good-natured grin until this is over.

Pappy screws up his face at them, glances back at me, and draws a small pistol, a nickel-plated Saturday night special, from his back pocket. Oh, Jesus, here we go. What an argument for gun control! I mean, what kind of place is this, where ninety-three-year-old assassins can stalk the streets armed to the teeth? He waves the gun at the girls.

"Shut up."

They simmer down fast.

"We're going to play a little game."

"Pappy—"

"McGuire and me. You girls watch."

No. A fist slams down in my mind. "We're not playing anything. Put that thing away—*put it away!*"

"What say?" He swings the gun on me and suddenly I'm in a very bad way: sweat sprouts on my back as I reconceive that what we have here is an ambulant psychopath, an authentic danger.

A weak grin slinks across my face. "Never mind. What's the game?"

"Russian roulette." He spins the revolver. "One bullet. Who gets it?"

The women, who have seen a lot more of Pappy than I have, are visibly uneasy.

"Hey, Pappy, time for your rub," says Valerie.

"Later." His eyes seem to be looking for something in my face. "You first?"

"This is ridiculous—"

"You first?"

"No."

He puts the barrel to his temple and, looking straight into my eyes, he pulls the trigger.

Click.

"My lucky day. Your turn." He hands me the pistol.

What in the name of God's bicycle have I gotten into here? For a few lousy bucks I really have hooked up with a nut. Would I compromise my LifeForm by stepping in front of a truck?—well, what about *this?* BIZARRE RITUAL GRAVEYARD SHOOTING CLAIMS NEW YORK GHOST WRITER. Thus history remembers Elliot McGuire. I snatch the pistol out of his hand and throw it as far as I can. It clatters against a gravestone about thirty or forty feet away.

"What the—?" Pappy's mouth flaps and his eyes sphere out at me. "My gun! That's my goddamn gun! You know what that piece cost me, you stupid fuck?"

"I don't care—what kind of idiot do you think I am to play suicide games with you? I'm going back to New York City. You can write your own book."

"You're shaking, pardner."

"So what if I'm shaking!"

"Look at my hand." He holds it up motionless. "That's the difference between you and me."

There is a bouquet of distant laughter from the girls, who have gone off to retrieve the pistol.

"Guess what?" Valerie calls. "No bullet."

Pappy rolls out his big flannel laugh and sits down on a grave. *"Hee-hee-hee!"* Again the laugh is on me.

"Now see there, McGuire? You got all hot over nothing. You got scared. Simmer down now. Look at the sky, feel the breeze. Look at the girls. You're alive, you're okay." Suddenly he lowers his voice to an obscene whisper that sounds like it's inside my head. "You ought to take a crack at Lynnie."

"Come again?"

"Lynn. She's your style. You think she's Jackie O and then

she eats your lunch. Wouldn't you give up eternity for a few minutes with that?"

Is this another form of pissing contest? What's unsettling is that, yes, as noted, I *have* been thinking about sex. How can you hang around with these women, these lookers, and not have occasional thoughts? He knows it, too. He's going to torture me with it.

"Didn't I tell you I have a girlfriend in New York—?"

"Oh, how *could* I forget?" he croons with high sarcasm. "We're all taken care of then, ain't we? Girls, just imagine— he's got his own lady friend back in New York City!"

"Rrr, I'll rip her eyes out," Valerie says, making witchy faces.

Suddenly Pappy claps his hands together. "Okay, fun's over. The gun, please."

Lynn hands it back and he jams it into his pocket. He rubs his old meathooks together and beams. "Who's going to put me down for my nap?"

Valerie points a finger at Lynn. "You, baby. I've got a gig."

"Come on then, Pappy," says Lynn, affecting the husky tone of the dog trainer or professional nurse. "Time for Lilly White's party."

We walk back to Pappy's in a dull silence broken only by Valerie, who sings to herself in a breathy soprano.

"Coming in, McGuire?" says Pappy at the door. Beside him, Lynn slips her arm lazily around his waist. She seems oblivious to his big paw as it cups her rear.

"No, I'm not coming in, thank you."

I'm still in a snit. And why not? I am being increasingly abused by this bullyragging old fart, and one thing I can do without at this point in my life is more humiliation.

"Aw, c'mon—you can snooze, too. Then we'll up 'n' at 'em."

"No thanks, I've had it for one day."

Here comes the big, disarming grin (eerily crooked, like Hemingway's) and the squeeze of his hand on my shoulder. He's right beside me again, and this time it's all gentleness and warmth. The man does have a load of charm when he chooses to pull it out.

"Listen, son, no hard feelings, okay?"

"No feelings at all. I'm just through for the day. We'll start again tomorrow."

He looks at me as though waiting for something else. When it doesn't come, he nods and gives my shoulder a pinch.

"Fair enough." He turns to Valerie. "Give him a ride. Where're you going, McGuire?"

"The Blue Conch."

"The Blue Conch it is, sir," Valerie says. She opens the car door for me like a chauffeur.

One more glance back at Pappy. Lynn tugs at his belt but he lingers in the doorway, his face radiating reconciliation. He waves.

"Tomorrow, son."

I'm dismayed to find myself thawing, wanting to go back to him and make it up. He does lay down the mood, all right, and plays right to my weakness, old men with desperate tales to tell.

Valerie guns the engine and we're off.

"Tomorrow," I mutter.

TWENTY-FOUR

WE RIDE IN silence through the heavy tropical air.

"Pappy can be such a pain in the ass," Valerie says. "Like, sometimes he makes us take him to the beach. You have to lead him around in the surf like an old dog. I don't mind a lot of things, but senior recreation—that's too much like work."

"How so?"

"I used to be a geriatric physical therapist. That's how I met him."

"You met Pappy through physical therapy?"

"Yep. He had a broken leg two years ago. Didn't want to go to the hospital, but Social Services came and took him away in an ambulance. He went totally bullshit. You would've thought they were taking him to the electric chair. They put me on him and I had him calmed down the first afternoon. But that's how I lost my job."

"By calming him down?"

"Well, it's more like *how* I did it." She checks out my reaction with a sidelong glance. Her lips curl. "You know Pappy by now, you can guess. They caught us one night and that was it, I was bounced. It was okay, though. I was ready for a change. I was a registered physical therapist so it was easy to get my massage license. I've been free-lancing ever since. Don't look back—three little words I live by."

Watching Valerie drive, watching the flow of her soft mounded places, one into another, makes me realize I should settle things for good with Astrid. I can't continue this pretense of couplehood, not and spend time like this around other women.

Of course Valerie isn't really the issue. The real threat is the other one, the quiet one, the dark thin exquisite one, the one who hangs back in her perfumed mystery and makes me think thoughts that would send Astrid screeching out into the night to find me and cut my faithless throat.

"There's a guy down here named Renwick Thorne," I say. "Do you know him?"

"Sure. The guy who's after Lynn. She won't sleep with him and it's driving him crazy."

"Oh." That's what I wanted to hear.

"What do you mean, oh?"

"Nothing. Just oh."

She grins. "There but for the grace of God, eh?"

"Eh what?"

"Goes you, Mr. McWired. Goes *you*."

"Not following you."

"Lynnie. You're wondering whether you've got half a chance."

"Oh, come on."

"Hey, McGuire: I may not be tall, but I'm smart. I walk through the world like a radio antenna, picking up the waves. Don't bullshit me, you can't. That lady back in New York, she better pull on her foul weather gear."

I settle back into a protective shrug. If you can't beat it, fold. I fold my mouth.

We zip down Simonton and jog over to Duval.

Looking at Valerie makes me want to have a drink.

Normally, as I said earlier, I don't run around in a state of hormone fever. (There was Kristin, of course, the notable exception—but wait, didn't that peculiarity have more to do with the unspeakable thrill of incest and—oh, screw it, I hardly want to think about that now.) I mean, really, I'd prefer not to let something as cumbersome as reproduction obtrude into a relationship at all. This is part of my problem with Astrid. Frequency. She wants things on an everyday basis, which is too much for me. Not just sex either, involvement, complete involvement. A classic problem.

We stop at a light near Sloppy Joe's and I unhitch my seat belt.

"I can take you to the Blue Conch."

"That's okay, I'll get out here."

"Well, g'day love," she says Aussie-style. She purses her lips and kisses the air (mocking me, I suppose).

I open the door and hit the street.

Minutes later I'm having a drink at the bar with Renwick, who seems to have leased a stool in Sloppy Joe's. To be precise, I'm having a double and God knows how many he's had.

"So lemme try it again," he slurs. "You're saying wannabes are biographical failures who try on somebody else's life?"

"LifeForm. Right, they appropriate a whole new Life-Form."

"Like a suit of clothes."

"Well, if you need a metaphor."

"But Elliot—this whole thing of yours, it's metaphor-driven! I mean, isn't it?"

A shrewd observation. How can he think when he's drunk? "In a sense, I suppose."

"I mean, wineglasses, cornstalks—"

"Yeah, yeah. But only in the sense that form, when applied to something that moves through time, like a life, has to be either mathematical or metaphorical, one or the other. And let's face it: for the average person, metaphor is infinitely more useful."

"I see. You're saying that LifeForms *really* has a mathematical basis, but you're just,"—he waves a limp hand—"teasing the public with its metaphorical face?"

"No, no. There's no math involved."

"Mm, I rest my case."

I don't exactly seem to be grabbing him with LifeForms. Let's get his take on Pappy's wanna-be version of literary history.

"Listen, Ren, suppose you were researching a biography, the life of a famous author, say, and you turned up a source—someone who claimed to have known the author—and that source kept coming up with great stuff, only it contradicted the official story."

"Great stuff?"

"Yeah. Colorful anecdotes, irresistible little historical asides, personal notes, details, marvelous stuff."

"But not true?"

"Well, one wonders."

"You mean it *might* be true?"

"Not really, but sometimes it seems so . . . convincing. And then, if you've ever written a biography, I mean, you come out with an altered view of what truth is anyway. What the hell is it? Absolute objective truth—there's no such thing in biography."

"Hm. That's interesting. No such thing as truth. Okay, if you can't have truth, what do you do? What becomes the criterion for good biography?"

"Oh well," I mutter into my Scotch. "I guess you just do the best you can—"

"*Entertainment!*" he shouts suddenly, rising off his stool and pointing toward the ceiling. "Whatever gets you off, man, whatever gets you off! Right? Am I right?"

Conversation stops all through the bar. We're over the top. Surely this is an example of a good mind poisoned by pop culture and too much booze.

Or is it?

TWENTY-FIVE

MORNING AGAIN, IN the mottled backyard sunlight behind Pappy's. Tape rolling.

"Blood sports. What about bullfighting?"

"Ah, the bulls—that's one I was never interested in. He

wanted me to come to Pamplona with the rest of those doo-doo-heads. I never liked Spanish things, I don't even like the sound of the language. But the Spaniards were much more affectionate to him than the Parisians. They kissed his ass. He liked that. Later on he told me he was eating bull balls for strength and potency and courage. Some Spaniard had sold him a bill of goods. Back in Paris he'd go down to the stockyards and buy 'em by the quart like oysters. Next thing you knew he was drinking bull blood. Well, it was just too far out for me, I couldn't see eye to eye with him on that."

"Why should you?"

"He tried to convince me. Hemmy never felt good about something unless he had a whole crowd dancing to the tune. 'In East Africa the kids drink cattle blood like Ovaltine.' 'Yeah,' I says, 'So let's all get G-strings and go live in the jungle.'

"There was crackpot medical theory his father had told him about—if you want the properties of some organ you eat the meat of that organ. Bad heart, you eat heart. Bad prostate, you eat prostate, and so on. Hemmy enlarged on it—you want brute ferocity, you eat bull balls. You need courage, you drink the blood of a hero. He told me he was at some *feria* in Catalan and a matador named Rivas took a goring. Hemmy had his *Star* press card and followed everybody into the infirmary and bribed the surgeon to save him some blood. While they were stitching Rivas up, Hemmy slipped out with a half-pint of his blood and downed it. Within a minute, he said, he felt more courage than he'd had in a lifetime. It was pumping through his veins like a drug. I said, 'Jesus, Hemmy, it's a metaphor! Don't you know you'll never amount to anything until you can lay off the metaphors?' The thing that escaped me altogether was that this was a guy in the early stages of vampirism. That part of it just never occurred to me."

"Wait a minute, wait a minute." We have definitely crossed a line here. "Let me get this straight. You're saying Hemingway was a vampire?"

"I'm saying that he drank blood and he had his reasons for it. You can draw your own conclusion."

Suddenly Pappy is going through one of his little instant meltdowns into age and infirmity. The defiance melts and he's a puddle of sagging flesh and spidery limbs; his voice wavers.

"I'm tired. I'm through for this morning. Maybe there's a beer in there. . . ."

He rises painfully and shuffles into the house. I hear him rasping at Lynn, and Lynn's girls-school inflections in response. I hear the remarkable noise of my own brain buzzing on the subject of Ernest Hemingway, vampire. I don't know what he was getting at, but what a twist. How can I use it? Metaphorically, of course. Hemingway sucking literary sustenance from the raw pumping veins of the innocent Pappy. But literally as well? I mean, the memoir *is* one lie after another, why not just kick ass? Pappy Markham, fearless vampire killer: VICTIM TURNS TABLES ON BLOOD-LUSTING PERSECUTOR!

Or did Hemingway ever bite Pappy? Let's find out. Would this make Pappy a vampire, too? Come on, now—leave it alone.

Inside, Valerie has joined the party. Pappy's face appears at the back door.

"Going down for my nap, McGuire," he says, all pink and revived.

I stay put, watching two black lizards chase each other through the vines. It's times like this that I realize how hooked I'm getting on this junk assignment. Delusions can have the power to infect; I should move more cautiously. In practically no time, I can feel myself making a distinct shift toward believing every word out of the old fool's mouth. I can chart my slide: from "This is bullshit" to "This is entertaining bullshit" to "This is *convincing* bullshit."

Take a deep breath. Hemingway the vampire—absurd! Let's examine it logically. The guy was out fishing for weeks at a time. No vampire could spend so much time in the sun, right?

Right?

Q.E.D.

Pappy is exhausted; he beds right down, but not before he extracts Valerie's promise to return later for a massage. Lynn and I can hear the pleading and bullying through the bedroom wall. Then, silence. Then Pappy snoring. Valerie is out of his room almost as quickly as she went in.

"That was easy. I just patted his back and he went right out. What's next? You working today, Lynnie?"

"Nope." Lynn looks at me. "We could all have lunch at my place. I've got some great leftovers."

The three of us stroll over to Lynn's tiny, immaculate cottage on the far side of the cemetery. I wonder how she can afford this on part-time pay from the Hemingway House.

At the front gate, Valerie balks, announcing that she won't be coming in after all. Her antenna is up. Something has been going back and forth between the two women, a wordless cluster of messages. Val knows exactly what the score is.

"See you guys later. Four feet on the floor, okay?"

"Sure, Val."

"She's my pal, Elliot. You be good to her."

Lynn gives her a push. "Go on, Val."

She opens the door for me and suddenly I am in her world—sparsely furnished, a place of hanging plants, a gold leaf mirror, an Oriental rug. Across one wall is a single shelf of New Age books. The air is tinged with the smells of dried fruits, spices.

She takes my hand and pulls me in.

"Are you really her pal?" I ask stupidly, needing to find something to say.

"We're friends, I guess. We hang around together. She's fun. I knew her back at the hospital."

"You worked there too?"

"Yeah, I was an ICU nurse. She was—" She laughs. "Well, she was unbelievable."

"How?"

"I shouldn't."

"Sure you should."

"Well, she and Pappy—"

"I know about that."

She looks surprised. "You do? Since when?"

"Since yesterday. She's very forthcoming."

"You can say that again. She's got a lot of confidence. She's always trying to pull me into things."

"What kinds of things?"

"Oh . . ." Long pause. "Things."

I let the silence stretch. Finally, she breaks it.

"Like Pappy. I mean—I really love Pappy, but at first, with

Val it was like, let's get into this old guy, the two of us—sexually, that is."

We're both quiet for a minute, standing there, thinking our thoughts about that. Valerie and Pappy. And Lynn.

"She's very persuasive. When we first met she wanted me to try all kinds of things. She'd find out things I'd never done and convince me to try them."

"Like what?"

"Like—I don't know, I can't think of anything."

A long pause. Then:

"Like sex with women. With her, actually."

Another pause.

"Did you enjoy it?"

"At first. She knows a lot, she's a woman, after all. But a man can do everything she can do and other things besides. It's just, most men don't know how to, or won't . . ."

She trails off, checking me with a glance. I am blushing to my toenails.

"Well, anyway, we got into something with a guy, both of us, and I realized I wanted just the guy, not her. She took it pretty well. She stimulates me. Only, sometimes I can get overstimulated. I have to watch that. I mean, normally I'm kind of a stick-in-the-mud, I stay at home, I just kind of recede."

Silence grows around us like a jungle. I hear a voice that I hardly recognize as mine. "I'd . . . like to get to know you."

She smiles and seems to drift toward me. She sits me down by a little damask-covered table and opens a photo album. Wordlessly she guides me through it. She is a baby, then a little girl. She sits behind a birthday cake as her father cuts. She is awkward, braces on her teeth. Then she's bloomed into a shy, bikinied teenager. College and after: she is posing with various men. Then she is married. She is on a vast front lawn, a snazzy parvenu Florida mansion behind her. At that point the pages go blank. I look up at her.

"What happened?"

Renwick has told me what he knows: a bad marriage, husband made her quit nursing. Indolent life in the slick set, too much to drink, not enough to do. One day some unspecified calamity drove the husband over the top and the screen goes blank.

Her face is numb as she closes the album. My gut urge is to reach out and touch her, but instead I close my eyes: maybe if I quick-read her LifeForm, if an image rises out of the soup, maybe I can devise some instant therapy.

"What are you doing?" she asks.

"Just looking for something. Inside my mind."

She doesn't say anything. Then it appears. A broad open chute plummeting like a ski jump, fanning out as it rises, and then dropping off into a darkness so black it is like a blank wall, or an infinite night. My eyes pop open.

"What?" she says.

"Your life till now—it's like a giant launching pad. There's an incredible future component. I've never seen anything like it."

"Elliot, what are you talking about?"

Let's back up a few squares. First, try a quick thumbnail sketch of LifeForms—I give her my thirty-second version. She seems to stay with me.

Now: a careful (infinitely careful) description of her Life-Form. "Are you interested in space travel, that sort of thing?"

"Space travel?" She looks back at me bleakly.

"I only ask because what I see suggests that kind of apocalyptic vision. Like the end of history as we know it, new beginnings, second chances on a cosmic scale." As she stares, uncomprehending, I realize this must make as much sense to her as the Dead Sea Scrolls read backwards. "Like, imagine a ski-jumper: he's going down, down, down—and just at the nadir of his arc, he elevates and takes off—new energy, new speed, soaring off into space, as it were."

"Space travel?" Her face has drained white. This is getting arduous for some reason. I'll try something else.

"Look, Lynn. I want you to do something. It's a LifeForms exercise. I want you to close your eyes and tell me the story of your life, starting now, and then extending off into the future."

"But how do I know the future?"

"You don't. But when you close your eyes and start, you'll see: it seems to come to you."

"What's the point?"

Careful, now. "Future potential. The more you tell, the more familiar you get with the process of sending probes out into your own future. It's the beginning of reconceiving your LifeForm."

She sighs and closes her eyes.

"See it. Visualize it. Then tell . . ."

After a long silence, she hunches forward and begins to sob. Something has gone wrong. Now I touch her. We touch. I hold her. I feel her.

"There's nothing out there," she says desolately. "You don't know. This is awful. Nothing like this can work for me."

"Lynn, start with this very moment and go forward. Just one minute. Two minutes. Five."

In a stricken, whimpering voice, she begins. "I . . . I'm here with you. I'm crying. It's all a mess. You're helping me. I look up at you. I . . . start to feel, sort of, better. I . . . we . . . we—I can't say this."

"Yes. Go on. You can. Say what you see."

"We . . . kiss each other and, and—"

She tells it right.

I can't stay for more of this future. There is an endlessness here that frightens me. A drop-off into the subnight of her scary LifeForm. One kiss is as close as I dare come to it. She seems to know it all with an ancient ruefulness. We're breathing hard. This is the time to go.

She nods as I break away and head for the door.

TWENTY-SIX

BACK AT THE Blue Conch, breathing chaos, I snap the TV on (it's Yugo time) and fall into my tousled bed. I light a Camel and watch my breath fume and billow as the ceiling fan spreads it through the room. A kiss. From the future? No, don't think about it. Just keep smoking, get into Yugo. Yugo, the pro, the LifeNova—my benchmark, my intimate connection to success. Love doesn't threaten Yugo. He is all fame, money, wherewithal. From deep inside the plague that riots through his soul, he can reach out and goose the world and the world will say "Ahhh." I must learn to do that.

"Today our guest is Brantly Swann, the New York sci-fi writer who claims he was an interstellar abductee. He's written two best-selling books about it and here's one of them."

Close-up of book cover: *Into Infinity.* I've read it. I've read his other book, too, *Lessons from Infinity.* I'm actually interested in this stuff—from a LifeForms point of view anyway. Again, it's all about apocalypse. If there were anything to it, I would have to adjust LifeForms to account for sudden intercessions, interstellar deus ex machina factors that could play hell with conventional theories of history—the sort of thing I have to keep a sharp professional eye on.

Brantly Swann is a bookish-looking fellow with honest horn-rims and a breathlessly sincere manner.

Yugo prods him: *"Let me get it straight, now, Brantly—these little creatures, or whatever you say they were, they carried you up to their spaceship, their flying saucer, whatever—?"*

"That's right."

"Brantly. Brantly. Look out there: that's America out there, Brantly. Do you think America is buying your story?"

Am *I* buying it? Crazy as it seems, nothing has tripped my shit detector yet. No bells, no sirens. He's convincing. I kill the sound. I'm sorry, this is giving me the creeps. Little belief-impulses are scuttling up my pants like so many crabs. To his credit, Yugo was mounting at least a mock challenge to Brantly Swann's nicely crafted tall tale—although his audience certainly wasn't treating it as fiction. Brantly is actually quite credible—I'd have real trouble disbelieving him if he were telling me his story man-to-man over a couple of beers.

But this blind predisposition to believe, is it simply a given? A biographer's occupational hazard? Each day down here, I feel mounting awe at Pappy's raw claims, his chutzpa, his creative lying powers—the ability to create new reality, if that's what it is.

Dear Abby: To be honest, I'm becoming engaged by the whole thing. Little by little I'm coming to tolerate Pappy's version as though it were essentially true. But I really ought to go on record here: it's bothering me. I'm dismayed over it, over my growing attraction to this ridiculous rendition of history. Signed: Confused.

Dear Confused: You need a breath of fresh air, a change of pace, you need—

A knocking at the door. Oh shit, the maid. I forgot to hang out the Do Not Disturb sign.

"Come back later, please."

"McGuire, let me in, quick!"

Now this is intriguing. I immediately recognize the voice— Valerie's. But what's she doing here? I swing the door open.

"Thanks." She slips past me, a massage pad rolled up under her arm. "I'm hiding from a client."

"Hiding?"

"Yeah, he wanted a little more of me than I was willing to part with, so when he ducked into the bathroom, I ducked out."

"To my room?"

"I figured it was the last place he'd look."

She looks flushed by the chase, in her running shorts and lacy tank top. She throws her pad onto a chair and sits on the edge of the bed, crossing her legs. "Is that Yugo?"

"Yeah."

"Mm, I adore Yugo." Her eyes bore in on the TV screen. "It's like seeing a man look back at me from the mirror. He's my incestuous twin."

"Interesting point of view."

"How come you're watching Yugo, McGuire? I mean, like instead of *Masterpiece Theater* or C-SPAN or something?"

"Yugo's a friend of mine."

She straightens up. "What? You know Yugo? Since when?"

"High school. College."

"My God, you're telling the truth, aren't you? How come the sound's down?"

"Actually I was watching the guest, Brantly Swann, and . . . oh, it's too hard to explain."

"Brantly Swann. Looks like an animal activist."

"He claims he was abducted by space people and taken away in a UFO."

"No kidding? I wonder if Lynnie knows about him."

"Why should she?"

"She didn't tell you?"

"Tell me?"

"Oops." She covers her mouth cutely, feigning embarrassment.

"Tell me what?"

"Well, she doesn't like a lot of people to know, but . . . see, she has this fear that something like that's going to happen to her."

"Something like what?"

"Like with this guy Brantly. They would sort of come and take her away. Guys from space. Or so she says. Who really knows about things like that? I just go along. She won't go out of the house sometimes."

"How long has this been going on."

"A few years, I guess. It's why she came down here in the first place—she feels safer in the Keys, don't ask me why. She still has spells. When it's real bad she just obsesses. Can't do anything. It broke up her marriage and everything."

So that's it: the unspoken calamity, the marriage-buster. The shadow. Everybody has a secret.

"Hey, don't say I told, okay? Personally, I don't think people ought to hold anything back, but Lynnie's very private about her little quirks."

I look back at Brantly Swann's face on the tube. Yes, the same shadow. Let's try something: I close my eyes and concentrate. Before I see it, I feel it in my gut—as though I'm being pulled forward by a multiple G–type force. It's his LifeForm: a roller coaster with a single mountainous precipice, a catastrophic dip and a flying leap into black infinitude.

Smiling, Valerie sits back and pulls in her legs. All of a sudden I'm noticing a cuddly self-awareness in her movements that I wasn't picking up before. I think she's about to come on to me. But what could possibly be the aphrodisiac? My ineluctable sexual modality? Not likely. The connection to Yugo, I guess. Or perhaps some competitive weirdness over Lynn.

"How was lunch?" she says.

"Fine."

"You didn't stay very long."

"Long enough."

She looks down and waits a beat. "Did you guys have sex?"

I don't answer.

"No, right?" she says.

"How did you know?"

" 'Cause you weren't there long enough. Lynnie takes a long time. Once she starts."

"I see."

She rubs her lips with a forefinger. "I make you nervous, don't I?"

"Yes."

"Does Lynnie?"

"In a different way, perhaps."

"She's got—mmm, a hidden personality. I'm not saying you shouldn't get involved. Just be ready. No matter how much you like what you see, there's a lot more to Lynnie than meets the eye."

"You, on the other hand, are easy as pie."

She laughs and raises her shoulders in a graceful shrug. "What you see is what you get." Or what I *could* get, is the implication, as she moves closer, brash, mischievous, impervious to rejection. She leans against me and whispers: "And I bet Yugo has an unlisted phone, huh?"

"Sure."

"Well?" She shifts slightly, brushing me with her breasts.

"Look, Valerie, if you ever get up to New York, I'll make sure you meet Yugo, okay? Now, I think we'd better stop there."

"Okay, fine. So much for that great adventure." She retreats to the other side of the bed and sits in a cross-legged slump, like a summer camper. "So look, McGuire, do you mind if I just hang out here a few more minutes? Till the coast is clear?"

"That's fine."

"Pappy's expecting me of course. Let him wait, the old tyrant." The hawk's eyes flutter at me impishly. "Hey, imagine what Pap would think if I told him about this—me and you, Val and Elliot, alone in a hotel room."

"Let's not find out, okay?"

"He's awfully cute when he's jealous."

"Really? Somehow 'cute' doesn't quite capture the Pappy I've come to know, if not love. Contentious, maybe. Warped, deranged. But I have this silly problem with grandparental figures who carry guns, so let's not depend on my judgment. Can I ask you a question?"

"Sure."

"You and Lynn—what's going on? What's the attraction to a ninety-some-year-old wreck of a body?"

"Ah. I knew you'd get around to that at some point." She smiles. "Weird, huh? You probably think it's like being turned on by shoes or dogs or something. Well, I like youth-ful bodies, too, I like all kinds of bodies. So does Lynnie. Men never understand that old bodies aren't such a huge stumbling block, even to sex. I mean Pappy's got this total connection to other things, big things—he just pulsates. Young guys don't have his kind of spiritual energy. He's tapped into a primal source of karmic jet fuel—you know it, too, don't you?"

"We-e-ll—"

"Well what? Admit it: he's got hold of you too. I watch how you react to him. Come on, confess."

"He's got a certain . . . enthusiasm, I guess. Charisma. It's there—"

"Well, that's what I'm turned on by, just like you. Only I'm not afraid to make it physical. I can get hot for that old bag of bones. So what if he's no fun at the beach or he can't do fifty push-ups? When it comes to the essentials, old age just turns up the burner for me."

I button my lip.

"Oh golly, we're making you nervous again, aren't we, Mr. McGuire, and we haven't even mentioned Roscoe yet, have we? Incidentally, I bet you call your little guy something too, don't you?"

"Valerie—"

"You call him Valerie? Aww, that's sweet."

"Look, it's been a long day—"

"Never mind, never mind, I'm going. I'd rather take my chances in the hall than stay here. Anyway, I've got gigs the rest of the afternoon." A line of weariness appears in her forehead as she gathers up her things and traipses toward the door. "By the way—everything I said about old guys?—forget it when it comes to Yugo, you got that?"

"Sure. Got it. I'm sorry, Valerie, but—good-bye, okay?"

She's almost out the door. But not quite—here comes the parting shot.

"You know, a guy like you, McGuire, you sort of throw a challenge in the world's face. It's like you're saying *noli me tangere* all the time—you know what that is? I learned it in this Christian commune my parents parked me in once. It's what Christ said when he came back from the dead so pure and all.

Don't touch me. Don't touch me. You ought to think about that."

"I'll think about that."

I don't want to think about that or anything else that comes out of her twisted head. Jesus, no wonder she and Pappy get along! As the door clicks shut, all I want to do is smoke, stare at the silent screen, and merge slowly, thankfully, into unconsciousness.

TWENTY-SEVEN

IN THE DREAM, my penis grows like Pinocchio's nose with every glorious lie I tell. I am skimming through the ocean shouting lies into the sky. It's ten or fifteen feet long and growing. EH wants to reel it in and hang it up, back in port, from one of those heavy display chains, like a thousand-pound prize silver marlin. He is towing me from the rear of the Pilar and shouting through a megaphone. He helps me make up more lies, he knows some whoppers. "Sharks!" he roars suddenly. Enough lies, they are circling. They will chew me down to size. Ashore, there will be nothing to hang up. Then: gunfire! EH is on tiptoe, balancing perilously on the stern of the Pilar, firing a Thompson submachine gun through the blue exhaust smoke. One of the sharks is hit. The others turn on it, tearing it with their teeth. The ocean roils with blood. EH reels my big fish in. . . .

Key West must be the land of dreams. God knows I have them here! In therapy my problem was just the opposite. No dreams. To me the reason was simple: my kind of dreaming was done while awake. My dreams were conscious creations, they were *out there*. No need for nocturnal mental events. But Sven said no, I actually produced more dreams than I could ever handle in therapy, if only I remembered them.

Wouldn't you know it—now that I don't need dream material, I'm flooded with it. Giant penises—ten, fifteen feet and up! I wake from these horrors in terrible shape—heart racing, head jangling. Isn't there something I could take, a dream suppressant? Let's go, pharmaceutical geniuses, get creative—I need a new drug! Besides booze and pot, bad TV is the only one I have (just about anything on the Fox Network will do).

After Valerie left, several hours of sleep produced four or five howlers (including the one above), the themes, as always, clear enough: sexual confusion, anxiety about getting on with *LifeForms*, domination by elderly males (I wonder who?). I killed half a bottle of Scotch but it didn't help. Turned on Fox. Started to panic toward midnight as I felt the margin wearing thin between waking consciousness and these internal horror featurettes.

Now I need a reality check.

Out of bed. Into my clothes. Into the night. What time is it? The streets are swarming in the moist heat. The bars are full, band music blaring, sawdust, sweat, pool tables, hanging ferns, hungry-eyed men and women, take your pick. I don't want any of it. It's very simple. I want peace.

I want Lynn.

In the muted inky-green of the street where she lives, I take up vigil across from her house. There is a soft light coming from her bedroom window. It flickers slightly. Candlelight. Is she praying? Meditating? Talking to the other side of the universe? Do I dare knock?

"Oh, hi."

"I'm sorry, I know it's late—"

She puts a finger to my lips and pulls me in by my shirt. The smell of her place—so sweet, so full of health and eternity and luxury—almost makes me swoon.

But it's not going to be as simple as it ought to be. I look at her and see the beginnings of new complications, webs and snares yet unknown, networks of roads untaken, mystery tours, journeys to the end of things, the dying fall of love and desire, I see it all in a second. To say nothing of complications from space. Little men. Swarming figures of dismay emerging from her mind like clowns from a kiddy car. Am I up for this? Can I stand more strangeness?

"She told you."

"Told me what?"

"About . . . my problem. She told you, didn't she?"

"Yeah."

"Goddamn her."

"It's okay. I wish I had known earlier. I wouldn't have gone into that song and dance about . . . space travel and all."

She jerks open a drawer and pulls out a pack of Merits. "I only smoke when I'm mad. Want one?"

"Thanks."

She unbolts a set of French doors that leads to a tiny deck off the back of the house. We go out into the darkness. Looking skyward, she blows a wary column of smoke at the stars.

"It's not so bad," she says after a moment. "I live with it. I just don't like a lot of people knowing, that's all."

"What do you think it's all about?"

"You don't want to know."

"Yes I do. I really do. It's only a problem, after all. Everybody has something—delusions, phobias—I'm afraid of flying. I'm afraid of Ernest Hemingway, for God's sake."

She takes two or three long drags and crushes the cigarette out. Then she lights another one. Her voice, when she finally resumes, is pitched so low I can hardly make it out.

"I know it's stupid. I'm not like one of these nuts you read about. I know things like this don't really happen. But that doesn't help: in my gut I believe they're going to take me."

Almost imperceptibly, clouds are moving in. In a while they will cover the black dome of creation like fairy cotton. I feel a mood akin to grief. Right now I could be convinced that I will never see the sun again. But wait, don't be absorbed by this miasma, make a theory, think it through. Could it be, for example, that the worm of apocalypse lives coiled within the apple of every soul? If so, perhaps Lynn's worm has just broken forth, swollen to full snakehood, and temporarily wrapped itself around her mind. So prod it, challenge it.

"Why you?" I say, breaking the long silence. "You of all people?"

She shudders softly. "I don't know, maybe they'd want to breed me in a cosmic zoo someplace. Who knows? But I can't seem to shake it off. On good days it's hardly there. Bad days I can't even get out of bed because it's like . . . they're on their way. And—"

"And . . . *sayonara*."

She glances up sharply. "That was inappropriate."

"You're right, it was. I'm sorry."

Her eyes search me for hints of treachery. "I know you wonder about me. Men always do. Who is she really? Why does she hang out here and live *this* life? Well, do you understand now? I just have to keep everything simple, you know. Really, really simple . . ."

Jesus. No wonder Renwick came up empty. But what about me?

She stubs out her cigarette and flips the butt into the darkened yard. "Let's go in," she says. "I don't want to be out here anymore."

"Should I leave?"

In a gesture of distraction, she takes hold of my shirt again. "No." Her eyes take me in, inquiring, beseeching. "Stay."

She leads me back into the house.

Miraculously, like the weather down here, her mood begins to shift. Everything is softening, her eyes, the lines of her body. Safe inside, she seems animated by a need to be close to me. We can feel each other's heat. Desire and curiosity are taking over. What *would* it be like to make love to Lynn, with real feeling, rich caresses, exquisite delight? We're breathing heavily again. This is my pornography—I share this with Renwick: put a hand on me and I explode into festoons of romanticism.

And she reads me like a cheap novel. Her eyes narrow, with quickened interest, as if I had just stood up and quacked like a duck. She takes me to the daybed and sits me down. She settles in beside me—rather, she puts next to me her complex of softness, body heat, delicate scents, enigmas. She looks my face over carefully, searching it for something, and leads with her lips, kissing me once, twice, then a long, slow, undulant third time.

"Listen, Lynn—"

She shushes me. Sliding her things off, she leads me slowly and sweetly to first base . . . second base . . . third. I struggle to free my spunky little pal, passing him from my hand to hers like a relay baton. She guides him toward home—

But . . . oh, no, no, no!

We are malfunctioning. A hot sweat breaks out across my back. He is receding, cringing, a swooning protoplasmic noodle.

"No good."

"Let me just—"

"No, it's . . . forget it."

We lie there for a moment, then get up and begin to dress.

"It's okay," she says, with a sweet grin that almost convinces me it is—but it's not, it's not okay. Something is terribly, horribly wrong. I know a thing or two about failure, but this—this doesn't happen, not to me, not like this.

No. I can't accept it.

I sit there sticky with sweat, unable to look at her.

TWENTY-EIGHT

SEE HOW MORNING always comes after all!

Here I am, up at eight, on the balls of my feet, singing. I feel fantastic. Fan-fucking-tastic!

But how can this be? The man is fresh from a shocking sexual breakdown. He *has* to be depressed, suicidal. Yet here he is, light on his feet, fluttering in the promise of the morning like a new butterfly. How? What's the secret?

The secret is LifeForms!

Why do you think I'm so excited about the damn thing?

Look at the power of it: after drooping at perhaps the most crucial sexual juncture of my life, I save my manhood, my ego, my sanity, my life, by nothing more than ten minutes of LifeForms self-counseling. Did it all by myself. Came up with the answer, and it was so simple (yet so elusive) I almost blush to speak it.

Oh, maybe there was an embedded message or two for me in the TV that ran all night, but whatever the case, I awoke knowing just what to do.

Dump Astrid.

That's right. End it. Cut my losses. *Our* losses, for God's sake—she's no happier with it than I am, she couldn't be.

The bald fact is, my love affair with Astrid was always a garden full of weeds: a wild unproductive thing, choking off the possibility of love. To say nothing of its capability for deadly mischief—look what it did to me last night. No, Life-

Forms says, counterfeit devotion can cripple the love machine: do the honest thing with Astrid and you will be opening the door to endless love with Lynn.

So much for last night. Today the future contains no dread—far from it. The very sidewalks seem to sing in the morning light as I cruise Duval Street looking for a paper, a good healthy cup of coffee, a cozy breakfast nook.

Suddenly my attention is diverted by the sight of an erratic white stretch limousine as it makes a 180-degree swing and inches to a halt at the curb across the street from me.

A gunmetal-gray window slides down and a bony wrist emerges. A finger beckons.

It's Renwick. "Yo, I'm going to the airport, want to see me off?"

I skip through the traffic and hop in. The limo reeks of booze and cigarette smoke. The TV is blaring a daytime soap. Renwick mixes drinks at the bar.

"I got a call from *US* yesterday. An interview with Kim Basinger. Can you imagine? To be three feet away from her. Like, to *touch knees* with her! My God, man, doesn't it fry you to think about it?"

The limo drops us at a low-slung bar on one side of the airport terminal. We drink beer.

He seems to have gotten over Lynn. There is not a word about her and I'm glad. I don't want to hear it—anyway, I've got other fish to fry with Renwick:

"Listen, Ren, remember what we were talking about the other day—a new standard of truth and all that?"

"Yeah."

"And you said something like, it should be entertainment, or whatever gets you off?"

"I did?"

"You did."

"Okay."

"Well, I'm interested in pursuing that. I mean, refining it a little, perhaps."

"Mm."

"Like, suppose the gold standard for truth became something like 'convincing?' If you *believe* it, it's true?"

"Sounds fine to me."

"A little careless, maybe—but bold."

"Robust."

"And don't you think that's exactly what biography needs now?"

"Sure, a bold theory. Robust. Full-bodied."

"Otherwise it'll languish."

"A bastard cross between truth and fiction."

"Exactly. Until someone—*someone*—invents a theory that lifts it right up there with the great disciplines."

"Convincing," Renwick enunciates, letting the concept roll across his tongue. "I like it."

I like it, too. Suppose Pappy really *is* telling some form of "the truth"? Then so what if I can't stop believing him? *If I'm convinced?* That just means he's registering high on the truth meter. You could even go so far as to say he's spinning a major correction to the Hemingway canon. The fucker is rewriting history!

My head is buzzing.

We drain our beers and step out into the bright sunlight. The last I see of Renwick, he's waving good-bye, in dirty shorts and moldy sandals, his motorcycle jacket open to the navel. Good-bye, pal. Thanks for the stimulation. I need a good swift two-handed mind game every now and then.

I hail a cab and give Lynn's address. But as we cruise by, I can see that her shades are still drawn. It's not yet noon, let her sleep. I direct the cabbie on to Pappy's.

TWENTY-NINE

ALL RIGHT: *convincing* is going to be the new standard, so be it. But let's not be fainthearted: let's apply the damned thing rigorously to everything that comes out of his mouth. If it's not convincing, it doesn't get in.

This morning, for instance, he is leading off with a tasteless yarn that combines two of his favorite themes, Hemingway the fatuous snob and Hemingway the relentless brute.

According to this one, Hemmy is infected with such a hopeless case of anglophilia he even puts on an English accent, saying things like "I say, old boy" and "Thenks awf'leh."

Drinking in the Dingo one day, Pappy challenges him: "Who the hell do you think you are, the Prince of Wales? You're about as English as a hot dog with sauerkraut and mustard!" A small drunk Englishman down the bar pipes up: "Good point. You're not, are you, Hem? English, that is." In a diabolical fury, Hemingway calls the unfortunate little Englishman out into the alley, where he beats him mercilessly.

"That's a pretty ugly story. Too ugly, perhaps. I'm not sure I'm convinced."

"What?"

"There's too much of the stock villain about it. And even though Hemingway may have been something of an anglophile, it would be unlike him to affect an English accent."

Pappy lifts his chin and sights me fiercely down the bridge of his nose. "Well, none of that's my fault. I'm only telling you what happened. I'm a witness to history is all—and I'll tell you something else: there's a hundred big-bully stories like this about Hemmy, they just never made it into the holy writ. Mary Hemingway got 'em all squashed as rumors, and Carlos Baker didn't have the guts to print 'em and there you are."

I hold his gaze. "No. Sorry. Whether or not you say it happened, it has to be convincing or it doesn't make it. You've been pretty convincing so far, but this one smacks of apocrypha. Plus I'm sure an incident like this would have been written about elsewhere. You say there were witnesses. And everybody knows Hemingway was no angel, there's some pretty rough behavior even in Baker."

"Don't argue with me, smarty-pants. I've been living with this stuff more years than you've been alive. Who does it have to convince, anyway? You? What kind of special talent do you have for being convinced or not?"

I maintain elaborate self-control. "You're talking to a professional biographer, that's all."

"Oh yeah? Biographer, huh?" His eyes are small and cold. "You're no biographer, you're a New York hack who's gone all squishy around the edges, that's what *you* are. Don't try to kid me."

Something clutches at my innards but I won't give him the satisfaction—I stare back evenly.

"In any case—this story has to be more convincing to overcome its absence from the canon."

"Canon?" He stands up, smiling wildly. "Your problem is you forget who you're talking to."

"Not at all, you just strain my credulity, that's all. But it doesn't matter, I'm here to do a job, and I'm doing it. Just don't insult my intelligence."

"Intelligence! *Hee-hee-hee!* You wouldn't know intelligence if it walked up and snipped your tie." He looms over my chair and for a moment I think he might just make a fist and punch me. "You want to know the difference between you and me, McGuire? We live on different sides of the mirror. I operate in the world. My actions cause things to happen—they make a difference—they make *history*. It doesn't matter whether you believe what I tell you or not, because you operate in the shadow world. Nothing you've ever done or ever will do is going to leave a fucking trace!"

The door opens and Lynn and Valerie peek in hesitantly. Pappy immediately turns on them.

"What the hell's going on with you two? You, Val—don't play the idiot with me. Where were you yesterday? I waited all afternoon."

Valerie looks quickly at me. "Well, Pap, I had a bunch of gigs that came up real fast. If you had a phone here I could've called you, but a gig's a gig. I have to make a living."

"And I've got to stay alive, honey," says Pappy, voice cracking like an old tragedian's.

She hugs him. "Oh, Pappy, Pappy, Pappy. Well, come on in the other room, darling, let's get you fixed up. Come on, babe."

Appeased by the body-to-body hug, Pappy goes docile and allows her to lead him into the bedroom. Before closing the door, she glances back at Lynn and me with a wink and mouths the word *later*.

Lynn puts some food in the fridge and starts making sandwiches while I sit and play with my coffee.

Pappy's words, so penetrating, so honed to kill, reverberate in my soul—which, if given form, would resemble nothing so much as a crushed fedora.

"What was that all about?" says Lynn. "Pappy was pretty riled up."

I concoct a lame analysis of what the shouting was about,

but it makes me tired. I don't want to think about it now. I end up shrugging it away and we lapse into silence.

A car passes in the alley, stereo blaring, and fades away.

"I'm quitting the Hemingway House," Lynn says.

"Really?"

"Yeah. I knew I would eventually. I'm tired of telling the same old stories."

"Oh."

"Tending bar is more my kind of job. I'm working a shift at Sloppy Joe's starting next week."

"I see." With every exchange the canyon that separates us widens. All I can think of is shame. To her it hardly seems to matter.

"If I were really into Hemingway it might be different."

"But you're not."

"Not really. He doesn't grab me."

"You might try the early Hemingway."

"You mean the stuff Pappy wrote?" She says it with a straight face. Or is it a mask? I'm not sure who it is I'm talking to anymore. We hear Pappy moaning through the bedroom door. Then Valerie, breathless and chirpy, in a series of mounting *ooh*'s ending in an orgasmic glissando. I steal a glance at Lynn. She laughs softly and smooths back her hair.

"Roscoe," she whispers, wrinkling her nose. It's an attempt at levity but we both instantly make all the wrong associations. I feel my face light up with a schoolboy's blush. She sees it too.

"I didn't mean to embarrass you."

"I'm not embarrassed."

Pappy comes with a great roar.

"Oh, shut up," says Lynn. She darts a nervous glance at me and goes back to making the sandwiches, as if we had heard nothing more than a dog barking in the yard.

THIRTY

COMING OUT OF the bedroom, Pappy is in a bawdy mood, the funk of the morning forgotten. He wants to eat and talk, he wants to drink beer and schmooze with the ladies. Now he even wants to be my friend.

"Come on, McGuire, cheer up. I didn't mean it. They were just words."

Words indeed, but with malice aforethought. Hard to wave off. Maybe I ought to tell him how his half-pint inamorata was all over me yesterday, although it might kill him, literally, to know how close he came to being outcocked by the medium-sized McGuire. No, let it go: I'm in no mood for a pissing contest.

"Let's just get on with it."

The women decide to move into the sunshine out back. They take a six-pack and Pappy's old radio and strip down to their underwear in the blast of solar magnificence that plunges through the frangipani.

"Lookit that Lynn," says Pappy, ogling them through the window. "She's your type, McGuire, sleek, reserved, classy."

"Come on back to the table, let's get started."

"You and her would be a real twosome, you know? What do you think? We could have a double wedding."

"Sit down, will you? I want to start."

"Jesus, son—okay." He eyes me like a fish. "How about a drink, you look like you could use it."

"Yes, thank you."

All he has is a pint of blackberry wine, but I don't care. I would gladly drink shoe polish at this point. I snap on the Sony as he bends creakily to sit. Several gulps of wine, a shudder—I'm ready.

"Look, let's have a laugh. I'll tell you a funny one—"

We settle in around the kitchen table.

"You know that story he put out about stumbling into

Gertrude Stein's and overhearing Gertrude and Alice B. going at it? You know—'No, Pussy, don't'? Well I'll tell you about that one. Because I knew the real story and he damned well knew I knew—and it drove him crazy. It was actually me that was dropping by Gertrude's, she had some compressions of mine that she was going to show one of her chums. Usually if you dropped by there you did it late afternoon, but that day I went early, just after lunch. God knows where Alice was but Hemmy had sniffed out that she was gone and had gotten in there like a dog to the garbage. It was just like he writes except instead of him dropping by it was me. And me standing there hearing Gertrude in the back go 'No, Pussy, don't, don't' just like he says. Only then I hear Hemmy, kind of thick-tongued, mooing over and over again: 'Mommy, mommy, mommy—' like some big baritone of a talking doll you might find under the Christmas tree!"

Pappy leans back, savoring the meta-reminiscence.

"I knew it was Hemmy's voice, even though it was kind of full-throated, and it cracked me up, but here's what I did: I ran upstairs yelling 'Hang on, Gertrude, I'll save you!' like I was going to chase out an intruder or something, and right into her bedroom. Jesus, you wouldn't believe the sight! There she was, piles and piles of her, like a great temple of flesh, and right there at the portal of her inner sanctum, there's Hemmy having his goddamned moveable feast! He turns, his eyes all scared and beady, like a skunk ready to fire, and when he sees me he goes white. Can you imagine? He sees me, grinning down at him— What a sight! God, if I had only had a camera! And I'll tell you something else: it's a good thing Hemmy didn't have a gun, because my guts would've been spread out across Gertrude Stein's bedroom wall. As it was he struggled to his feet and swore at me and you could tell he was going to try to snuff me with his bare hands but Gertrude yells out 'Hemingway, Hemingway, Hemingway!' very clear and very under control, and he pulls up. Then to me she just waves her hand—you know, be off, like I'm a pizza boy who came to the wrong door. She was as cool as an afternoon breeze, got to hand it to her. I got in a wink at Hemmy and beat it—I had more than what I'd come for—and on the way out I heard her say, 'No one will ever believe it. Not in a thousand years.' "

"For good reason," I say, but rather feebly.

"Aw, come on, here we go again. Get off the rag, McGuire, this is history. You're a fool to let the real thing pass you by."

"The real thing." I can't help but stifle a smirk.

"Well, people believe what they want to believe—you're walking proof of that. And what they don't want to believe, there ain't no possible way to convince them. I suppose there's going to be those that don't want to believe a story where Hemmy goes down on Gertrude Stein—yet the same assholes'll take the things he said about Scott Fitzgerald for straight gospel—like darts in the poor guy's corpse. See what I mean?"

"It doesn't matter."

"What doesn't?"

"Whether or not I believe you. I'm doing a job."

"Yeah, I believe you've said that before. But hell, McGuire, what kind of a job is it going to be without good faith on your part? Jeez, it's like having a lawyer that thinks you're guilty. What a mess!"

But, to tell the truth, he doesn't seem so broken up about anything at the moment as he beams around the table, sipping his beer.

Valerie bursts into the kitchen, dripping wet. "Pappy, Lynnie's spraying me with the hose!" she shrieks.

I realize how young she is. She has no history. She hasn't yet begun to drag her past around like tin cans on a string. Every casual sin evaporates in the clean white-hot vapor trail of her youth.

Pappy snaps back to the playful present and suddenly, for the moment, he has no history either. Snuffling with suppressed laughter, he leads Valerie to the other side of the shack, where they turn off the spigot, and round the corner to attack Lynn with a high-powered squirt gun.

Left alone, I ransack the place for some secret stash of booze—no luck, of course—and before I can rise from hands and knees, Roland walks in the front door.

"Oh, hi, dude." His eyebrows bounce up and down. "Need some help?"

I decide to be honest. "Yeah, quite frankly I'm looking for a drink."

"Right here," says Roland, sliding a curved half-pint of peach brandy from his back pocket. His eyes widen and his lips smack as he watches me draw a gurgling mouthful. I hand it back and he takes a swig. We are two bums sharing a bottle.

"Ah, Mama! That's good," he says. Then the ruckus in the backyard draws his attention. His mouth drops open as, through the window, he sees Pappy cavorting with Lynn and Valerie. He chuckles. "Look at that old fucker. Ninety-three and he plays with more snatch in a week than I'll ever see in my life."

"So? You think that's happiness?" My voice slashes with contempt. "Dogs in the street see more snatch than any of us. So what? Don't kid yourself, Roland. He's in hell."

Roland blinks at me, his mouth blustering silently, then looks away, embarrassed. I can guess what he's thinking: *Whoa*, where did *that* come from? I wonder myself. I mean, hey—can't these fancy New York writers recognize simple happiness when they see it out the back window? Apparently not.

Let's face it: if anyone's in hell at the moment, it's me. But at least I'm one step ahead of Pappy because I *know* it. And knowledge is power. Right? Right . . . ?

THIRTY-ONE

ROLAND HAS DROPPED by to announce some kind of illicit private barbecue at the Hemingway House, hosted by Big Murray Jacques, who lives in the pool house.

"Murray's half in the tank already, but he got this big box of frozen New Jersey corn by Federal Express this morning, so he's having a corn-eatin'-steak-'n'-brew-and-music party."

Murray is a portly bear of a man who plays elegant cocktail piano somewhere on Duval Street. Roland says Murph "the Surf" Barnett, the reclusive rock star, is coming. There's bound to be plenty to drink. All right: the sun is well over the yardarm, Pappy is wheezing, I'm half smashed myself, neither of us is good for any more work—let's call it a day.

Our procession to Whitehead Street must look like something out of Hieronymus Bosch. Roland and Pappy, with their collection of limps, ticks, and jerks; the two women, disheveled and alluring in their damp T-shirts; and the morose, stoop-shouldered intellectual, stumbling along behind in a silent haze of alcohol and depression.

All we need is a robed monk flaying us with a whip.

Steaks are sizzling on the barbecue when we round the corner of the house and disperse into the backyard. Big Murray, who is operating from somewhere inside a haze of alcohol, greets Pappy with a hug, almost wrestling him to the ground.

"Papouli! My good man, dig the music? Dig it?"

Something by Murph the Surf is on the stereo, jacked up loud and aimed out the back windows of the Hemingway pool house.

"Who the hell is Murph the Surf?"

"Oh, come on, Papouli. Lead singer and guitar player for Space Oddities? Won five Grammies?"

"Hm."

"Quite a character, Barnett," Murray chatters on, turning to me. "Burned out, retired at the height of his fame. Now he lives down here, cooks, paints, practices calligraphy, seals his letters with wax, makes one album a year, never tours, never parties."

Over by the barbecue there is a big tub full of ice and cans of beer. I grab two Buds from the cold slush, chug one like water and sip on the other. Murray is everywhere, lumbering hither and thither in a state of hyperactive euphoria. As he moves he veers to one side or another, like a bear on skates. His girlfriend, Jill, stays nearby, keeping a cool eye on him. He'll be on ice by sundown.

Pappy is dancing, at first alone, Greek-style, then with Valerie, who squirms up to him and helps him do a geriatric stomp. There's a beach bum look to the guys around the beer tub—shades, beards, long hair, baseball caps. The women are thirty-something and have weathered faces and weary eyes. Everyone wears a T-shirt, which seems to be the national costume of Key West.

Stumbling into the house I look for a place to drain my bursting bladder. Upstairs the music is so loud I can't hear the sound of my pee rushing into the toilet, but I can feel it, and relief surrounds me in a glow of momentary well-being. I close my eyes. The world swivels slightly, but I'm doing fine. When

I open them I notice a scrawl over the commode: YOU COULD CHOOSE PEACE. Is that true? Could it be that easy?

Suddenly the insistent whomp of the stereo is silenced. From down in the yard below come natural sounds: birds, people talking, guitars tuning, a fiddle, a mandolin.

"Oh!" says somebody. "Murph must be here."

Down in the yard, I go for another beer. The musicians are sitting around in bare feet, drawing everyone's attention with a shimmering background of pickings and lickings—which one is Barnett? The one with the guitar. He opens his mouth and sings: "I want to live fast, love hard, die young . . . and leave a beautiful memo-ree . . ."

Something is tugging gently at my senses. Something that doesn't love the vacuum in my soul and wants it filled—with music, food, companionship, endless afternoons, soft breezes, the love of children, dogs, women. Something that couldn't care less about Elliot McGuire the once and future cosmic White Rabbit, the 50 proof LifeForms Messiah. Something that wants me lost in the music.

Now Barnett is on to an old Bob Dylan song, the one about Queen Jane. Then it turns into something I never heard before, something about Joseph and the coat of many colors. Barnett stares ahead mournfully, as if he were blind. He seems not to know or care what he'll do next but moves seamlessly from song to song in a cocoon of sound. It's good music, top-notch—I may have a tin ear, but I can recognize professionalism. The songs sprout like flowers from within flowers. I am fighting back tears. Everything is making me feel like this is the first and last afternoon in the history of the world. I want to have a guitar in my hand. I want to join this brotherhood of the moment. I want to embrace somebody—

There is a gigantic belch from Murray, who has slumped into a chair, crippled by drink, and keeps dropping and picking up a cob of buttered corn. His girlfriend whispers to him and he shakes her off angrily. The music ends in a modest dying fall and everyone claps.

It is Lynn that I want to embrace.

I plunge my hands into the ice again and come up with another beer. Two of Barnett's musicians are right behind me. We get into a spirited discussion about brewing beer (about which I know nothing). I scan the yard, looking for Lynn. She seems to have just disappeared around some corner. The feeling, that little chunk of eternity that had me for a moment, is disintegrating.

Across the yard, Pappy is chasing after Valerie, enraged by something. He aims a scowl at me, a clear meaningful laser blast from fifty feet, and I know instantly what's happened: she's told him something—God knows *what*. She's dropped something on him like, "Oh yeah, well guess what? I was with McGuire yesterday, chump, and if you want to know what happened, use your imagination." I wonder if he's carrying his gun.

Murph Barnett is holding court in a corner of the yard, all gangly and Mediterranean-looking, with his dark eyes and phony dreadlocks and the rings in his ear. I drift in that direction, looking for a reason to avoid Pappy. Roland has captured Barnett and is yammering some drunken litany of blind praise into his ear. He sees me and tugs on my wrist.

"Murph, this is McGuire. McGuire's a New York writer."

Barnett nods and appears to want to shrink into the bougainvillea.

I raise my hands. "Not that kind of writer."

He smiles and relaxes a bit.

"Well, y'know, the word *writer*—"

Sure I know. Writer: synonymous with lush, leech, parasite, paparazzi, introvert, and so on. I look at this kid, this retiree. He has earned ten or fifteen million dollars and is in seclusion at age twenty-eight. I persistently refuse to be impressed by fame—but the LifeForm . . . his LifeForm is so strong it surrounds him with a neon aura. I must talk to him about this.

"What kind of writin' do you do?" says Murph. I can see he is trying to be modest and homespun.

"Biography."

He makes a sour face. "We've had a couple of those done, unauthorized. They got everything wrong."

"Maybe you should have helped."

He looks at me as though I've told him he should be nicer to little old ladies.

"Well, it's all behind us anyway."

I want to ask him why it is that famous folk refer to themselves as "we." Do "we" go a little cuckoo from overexposure, is that it? I'm about to lurch forward into that subject when Murph decides he wants to elaborate.

"Yeah, all this attention isn't healthy, you know. When you're a walking version of everybody's weirdest fantasies you're at risk. People come out of nowhere. They want to kill you, fuck you, worship you. We just had enough."

"But what a platform!"

"We didn't see it as a platform. We saw it as a disaster waitin' to happen."

I can't resist: "Tell me something. Who is 'we'?"

He looks at me and slowly curls into a ball of blank composure.

Pappy blusters up.

"McGuire I'm going to tell you this once. One time only. You touch Valerie in the wrong place ever again—you so much as rub up against the chair where she was sitting—and you're dead meat, you get it? Dead meat!"

Barnett steers himself deliberately off to another part of the yard. My head is revolving in half turns. I have to keep resetting my eyes. I manage to locate Pappy at the center of my field of vision and glare back at him in a sudden fit of rage.

"Look here, don't threaten me. She came to my room, uninvited." I could tell him that nothing happened. But why give him the satisfaction? He deserves some squirm time. "Whatever went on was none of your business."

"It was too, you turd."

"Oh hell, what's the difference? Since when have you become such a paragon of virtue, you and your monster wang?"

"You're walking the line, son."

"Well, you've been walking the line all week. A lot of people wouldn't take what you've put me through, waving guns in my nose, subjecting me to ridicule, abusing me to my face. I've just about had it with you, understand?"

Pappy steps back and studies me. This he didn't expect.

"You're drunk, ain't you?"

"You're drunk too."

"But I can hold mine. You can't. You're ruining the barbecue. Look, look around—"

And I realize that they've all quit doing whatever they were doing to watch our little scorpion dance. Pappy's face crinkles into a hideous grin.

"*Hee-hee-hee!* You don't even know where you are, do you? You want me to remind you? The side of the mirror where nothing happens, right? You're a stenographer, a clerk to people like me and Murph and people who live real lives and make things happen. You know what happens to people like you, McGuire? One day they wake up and they know it's all over, they're through, it's rat scratchings from here on out— and they blow their brains out across a wall."

I can't believe the cruelty of the speech. I have no words. I rush forward and shove him hard, a pointless, uncoordinated thrust. He recovers, arms flailing, and his eyes burn back at me with surprise and hatred. We're both wheezing with emotion.

"Take out your gun and do it right, why don't you?"

"I don't need a gun for you, son."

He settles loosely into a boxer's crouch. Later they will tell me that it was a left hook. I don't see it. And then I don't see anything at all.

THIRTY-TWO

ITEM: PUNCHED OUT by a ninety-three-year-old. Out cold. How about that? I wish I could laugh about it now, but I can't. Sober as I am, painfully hung over to boot, I take the full impact of the reflection: I was creamed by a doddering nonagenarian, a near-derelict wreck of a human being, a bum.

This must be the nadir of my LifeForm, it has to be.

Item: Lynn. Can't perform with her. Dr. Masters, Dr. Johnson, what the hell is going on?

After the KO I slept for eighteen hours in her bed. Waking was like being stillborn into bald sunlight. I smelt coffee, felt the coolness of a sheet. I heard a dog bark somewhere, a screen door slap in the distance.

Welcome to the world, Baby McGuire.

All right, there's no need to overdramatize a poke in the jaw and a hangover. I have a royal headache and I've obviously puked my guts out a number of times. Big deal. I'm safe in Lynn's little house on Eaton Street. Someone is hammering a nail in a backyard. A radio is playing. I hear voices downstairs. Life goes on. I'm going to be okay.

Then I sense another presence, *hers* as she leans down to kiss me, a sweet wet touch on the cheek, like a new mother would kiss her birth-ravaged lump of an infant.

"You hungry yet?" she says.

"So far."

"Want to try breakfast?"

I nod and she goes away.

No, I'm never going to drink again. At least not for a long, long time. What do I want out of this life, anyway? I want health, self-respect, forgiveness, peace. Besides love and money, what else is there?

She returns with toast and coffee, and as I watch her bending to place my tray on the bed, I feel blood flow back into my dead places, like spring water to the desert.

Every place but one.

As I look at her, as I ache to make love to her in the same way that Jake Barnes must have ached for Lady Brett, as I munch on a humble bite of dry toast, I come to the inevitable conclusion: *take action.*

And instantly, I know what the action must be.

"Lynn, I've got to go."

"*Go?*" Her eyebrows fly up. "Go where? Relax. You're in no shape to go anywhere."

Rising: "Oh, yes I am."

I check my pants. I've got my wallet. I've got my keys. I have all I need.

"Where are you going, Elliot?"

"The airport."

A quick cab ride, a dash to the ticket counter while they hold the Miami flight for me (checking me point-by-point against the official hijacker profile)—and I am up, up, and *away,* launched like a missile to New York, a surgical strike aimed at the guilt-source of my phallic distress.

THIRTY-THREE

HER FINGERS, THOSE luxurious pampered fingers, twist un-characteristically as she talks. The hands wave elegantly this way and that, but always the fingers resume torturing each other, as if she were actually trying to will arthritis into her joints.

I can't remember every step of the journey, but here I am, in a plush SoHo tavern, safe amongst the knurled oak, the frosted glass, the wicker and comfort, a beer in front of me, listening to Astrid complain.

"It's just . . . the damned strings. I mean, I'm so exhausted by strings, by tying knots, hundreds of knots, tying them and retying them, knot after knot after knot. And for what? I get no encouragement. No one seems to care half a damn whether I do it or not. And I look at someone like Sophie and what she does—how easy it is—and all the attention she's getting. It just makes me want to park myself in front of my TV set and smoke pot for the rest of my life."

"Got any?"

"That's not the point."

Astrid has a very penetrating voice and tends to let it rip as she warms to a subject. At the next table, a woman is enjoying a solitary brandy and trying to read. Every so often she lifts her head and glances malevolently our way.

"I mean sometimes I just wonder why I'm torturing myself. Who ever told me I had to be an artist anyway? Why does anybody have to be an artist? What does it matter? You could probably blow up every sculptor in New York and no one would even notice!"

"Do you have to tell the whole bar?"

"Was I shouting?"

"Let's drink up and get out of here."

"That's fine with me. If you want to know the truth, I'd

much rather be on the street where I can smoke a fucking joint."

"I knew it. Do you want to leave?"

"I want to go to Sophie's fucking opening. Then I want to go home and cut my fucking wrists."

She's lowered her voice a touch but it can still be heard all the way to South Ferry; every head in the bar has now inclined in our direction. The woman at the next table slaps her *New York Review* and sighs theatrically.

"Well, you've certainly got everyone's attention. Do you really want to go to the opening? If you're so down on art why not take a break? Let's go somewhere else. Anyway I have to talk to you."

She withers me with silent contempt and walks out. I feel rooted to the chair. Let her go, a devilish voice yammers in my brain, to hell with talking to her, write her a letter. Stay seated, order another beer. But no, Astrid's left her purse, plus she's got the pot, so I hastily throw some of her money on the table and follow her out.

The joint we share is from a stash she has kept in a humidor for two years, ever since her ex-boyfriend brought it back from Humboldt County. By the time we roll up to the Poets Gallery on Wooster Street, I am going, going, going . . .

"Sophie, darling—!"

"Astrid!"

They embrace lightly, touching cheeks. Sophie Luxembourg is all in studded black leather, her fortyish face discolored with splotches of red. Her hair is dyed vivid blue and chopped in random bald places, leaving the rest to spill over one ear. She's standing in what could only be described as rubble, moments after a bomb blast. Apparently the ceiling has just fallen, spilling heavy chunks of plaster to the floor.

"This has got to be the wrong day," I whisper to Astrid. She looks at me oddly and goes back to greeting Sophie.

"It's just stunning, stunning."

"Oh, I'm such a wreck, Astrid, nothing's right, I'm full of Valiums—"

A mixed crowd of bearded tweeds and New Wave-y slicks in black shades and smeary hair stands around gazing at the mess, swilling Perrier and munching cheese and crackers. I pour myself a Dixie cup full of red wine and toss it down. Drinking, as I've drunk today, makes me feel dangerous. Pot makes me careless and stupid. I am primed for disaster.

"Elliot, I want you to meet Sophie— What's wrong?"

A fit of helpless laughter strikes just as Astrid pulls me forward into the presence. Sophie's particolored face congeals into an expression of tentative greeting, then a suspicious pout.

"What's so laughable?" she says.

My arms reach out in a gesture that takes in everything— the rubble, the people, the event, the entire universe of Sophie Luxembourg. "This! *This . . . !*"

Sophie blinks once, turns without a word, and is instantly on the other side of the room.

"Now you've done it. Couldn't you see how much she needed support? How could you be so cruel?"

A monster is running loose in my brain. I slide into my Sidney Howard imitation.

"But darling, isn't it perfect! I mean, that this is where we end up—in the midst of this *va-a-ahst* wasteland of art, this stylish heap of bomb-blast. Don't you see the justice in it, darling?"

"Don't you dare mock my accent. And stop that ghastly giggling. Stop it right now! You're going to ruin the whole event for Sophie."

Anger spurts like a column of oil up my neck and gushes into my brain.

"Screw Sophie. I just don't care."

"That's it, isn't it? You genuinely don't care. You've never cared about my friends, have you? You think they're all just silly characters in some dumb SoHo soap opera, don't you? Don't you? And me, too—"

"No."

"What? I can't hear you."

"No. Not exactly."

"Ah, but close, isn't that right?" She drops her voice to an intimate hiss. "Well, if that's the way it is, you can just pack it in and find someone else, someone you can respect."

"Yes."

"I mean it, why don't you?"

"I have."

She blinks. Her head snaps back. "You what?"

"I have. Done what you say. Found someone else, I mean. Someone in Key West."

She observes me intently, shrewdly, radioactively. Slowly she nods. "It's true, isn't it."

"Yes."

"You bastard, you stinking shit."

"Her name is Lynn—"

A sudden roar: "I don't want to know her wretched name! Can she fuck you like I can?"

"Let's not ruin Sophie's opening."

But Astrid has forgotten Sophie and is preparing to go toe-to-toe with me in a grand coda of (don't we both know it?) farewell.

"Can she? Can she pull it out of you like I can?"

"I'll let you know."

Her voice can now be heard in Shea Stadium. *"I hope your useless prick falls off!"*

"Astrid—"

Conversations are sputtering to a halt. Sophie half falls into a chair. Astrid reaches down and picks up a chunk of rubble. With a tomboy's guileless grace she swings at my head and connects, just below my left ear. Then she drops her hands to her sides in horror as she watches me (stunned but essentially unhurt) dig up two handfuls of plaster dust and let it trickle helplessly through my fingers.

Outside, where I find myself dumped to the sidewalk by a hefty skinhead buddy of Sophie's, I listen to my heart beat frantically in my ears. Let's get a handle on this: nothing more than a momentary episode of LifeBlast, a judicious use of moral dynamite to jar open the road to freedom.

Wounded as I am, I rise from the pavement and leap for joy. I'm free!

A quick stop at the apartment. A message: *"Elliot, darling."* Astrid's voice, from earlier in the day, probably about the time I was on the airport bus from La Guardia. *"It's around noon, sweet. Just listened to your message. What a wonderful surprise! Sophie's opening is today, did you come back for it? Anyway, see you soon, darling. Mmmmwah."* Our last kiss.

THIRTY-FOUR

BACK IN KEY West there are notes for me at the Blue Conch.

A fax from Craig: *"Are you there, old boy? Please check in, Sir Harry is champing for news."*

A laborious scrawl from Pappy: *"McGuire, please forgive and forget. I am a foolish old man. The girls have set me straight and all I want now is to regain your confidence and good feeling and get on with it. After all, we've got a job to do, don't we? There isn't that much left. Let's just forget our differences and grind on. Pappy."*

"Shake?"

I let him take my hand in both of his monster paws. His face is stretched like parchment and filigreed with wrinkles. There is worry and confusion all through it.

"You got my note?"

"Yeah."

"I've been a damn fool."

"So have I. But not anymore. I don't need to take the kind of abuse I've been getting here. I have other options."

He bows his head, all submission, all humility. He won't give me any trouble.

"Beer?"

"No thanks. Let's just get started." There is new starch in my manner. Pappy defers to it.

"Anything you want, just let me know."

"I want to get started."

"Righto." He sits and waits with hound dog eagerness. "Where were we?"

"Let's go right to the heart of the matter."

"Which is?"

"The betrayal. When did you find out?"

"Find out what he was up to? Not until the first book came out."

"But these things had come out separately, in literary magazines, long before the book."

"Aw, I never followed all that. I wasn't interested in who was publishing what. I just didn't pay any attention."

"But when the book came out—"

"That was different. It was all my stuff. Things I had dreamed up for him to work on. Pages of mine he had taken home to study. Pieces of journalism he had brought me and I had rewritten as compressions. Some of it he had written himself, but only the crap, like 'My Old Man,' which I had told him to throw away—it should have been lost with the other 'lost' manuscripts—or 'Up in Michigan,' which is the kind of story a horny college student writes. But then I saw 'Out of Season.' He had brought me a few notes and said, 'Here, how good are you? Make something of this?' "

"You wrote 'Out of Season'?"

He nods. "I started with his notes—a page or two of scrawl, dear diary stuff about some snit Hadley was in—and I put it on a thing I remembered from the war, when a girl and I went fishing in Switzerland, and the little Swiss rummy who thought he had hooked a rich American. That part was all mine."

"Which part was Hemingway's?"

"The bickering between the man and the woman. I never had problems like that with women."

"I see."

"Hemmy looked at it when I was through and just shook his head."

"Speechless."

"In a word."

"All right. So the book came out, *In Our Time*. You realized you'd been had. What did you do?"

"I went bullshit. He had raped me. He had lifted my work and rushed it into print, he had trashed my spirit, turned my generosity into so much dogshit. I had saved the man's life and gotten the Judas kiss in return. I tell you, he's lucky he wasn't in Paris. He had gone off to Canada because Hadley was pregnant and didn't want to drop the kid in a French hospital. If he had been in Paris I would've gone looking for him with my fists and it would've been an awful business. I was just as big as he was, I was in better shape, and when it came to boxing, unlike him I was the genuine article. You had a taste of that—"

"Never mind."

"I would've torn him apart. I might have killed him right then and there."

"But you didn't."

"No, I had to wait, and while I bided my time, all my heat turned to ice. Pretty soon he got back from Canada with his new baby. Pound was off in Rapallo for the winter so they squatted at his place for a few weeks. Then they moved around the corner to the place above the sawmill on Notre-Dame-des-Champs. He used to work at the Closerie des Lilas because nobody went there. I had thought a lot about how I was going to handle this. At first I wanted public revenge, knock him on his ass right in the middle of Vavin, right out in the traffic between the Dome and the Rotunde where all the gossips would see it. But I kept rethinking and every time I did I lost heart for a gesture like that. I didn't want to humiliate him. I didn't even want to hurt him that bad. So one day I came to the Lilas and didn't say a word, just sat down at his table. He looked up and there I was, like Banquo's ghost, not saying a word, just looking at him. He started to drip sweat but at the same time he turned on the big grin.

" 'Rick! Goddamn, what a wonderful surprise—!'

"He held out his hand. I just looked at it, then at his face. I never even spoke to him. I poured out my drink on his pants and stood up. His grin kind of froze and then turned into a scowl.

" 'Are you going to tell me what's eating you?'

"I turned and walked on down the street without answering him. He knew. He knew."

"He was eating you—"

"Chewing me, digesting me. Bit by bit. He took my enthusiasms, my style. He took my work. He tried to look like me, talk like me. The Hemingway man, the man he wanted to be, was me, and he studied me until he got me just right. The way I held my head when I listened to people, the way I stood at the bar, the way I laughed. Piece by piece he worked out a carbon copy of me. Then he took his version of me out into the world, wearing me like a new coat, and before you knew it people would say to me, 'Oh you got that from Hem, didn't you?' or 'You must be going around with Hem.' He had gotten away with it. He had pulled off the perfect crime. He had stolen my image so perfectly that now it looked like I was the thief. This is something Hemmy was good at, acting out the big lie. And once he'd done it, you were cooked. Ask Harold Loeb, or Scott Fitzgerald, or Chard Smith, or anyone else he ever blindsided. He ran you over from behind. He took your dignity and chewed it till it was like old gum that you'd stick under a theater seat. He took my future, my chance to be more than this ninety-three-year-old nobody you see here. He stole my life away. *But by God I'm going to get it back!*"

He slams the table with both hands. His eyes are bugging out and his lower jaw juts at an absurd angle. He whacks the table again.

"Easy, Pappy. Let's get back on the track. Hemingway's back in Paris, you've confronted him. What next? Did he retaliate?"

"He didn't dare."

"You must have run into each other around town."

"Yeah, but like strangers. After we stopped speaking, I watched him for a while. We frequented a lot of the same places, but now he was climbing the social ladder. I saw him whoring himself, becoming more spoiled, more dandified, chasing after people he thought were stylish, people with affected manners who collected flashy literati like him. I saw him shed Hadley for a rich little piece who dressed him like a doll and trotted him around the rich idler circuit. This was the beginning of Hemmy's big slide."

"What about you?"

"At first it was just a hole in my spirit, a kind of sadness. Then the real anger bubbled up. I realized there were times when I wanted to finish the job and kill him. It wasn't a clear, thought-out kind of thing; it was craziness, an obsession with seeing him dead, seeing him lying in a coffin with mourners filing by. It wasn't healthy. I stopped writing completely and went back to boxing because I knew boxing would absorb some of the anger. I was still young enough to make a living at it. I fought under a French name, Marcel d'Amboise. One day Hemmy showed up as a sparring partner. I knocked him out. He came to see me fight once and sat ringside. He had Archie MacLeish with him. I spat a mouthful of water on 'em.

He never came back. After a while I was about to fight a contender. I had developed a big following—they thought I was French. Then one day it came out I was an American. Hemmy had snitched on me—I got that from a French sportswriter who knew the inside story. The fans turned on me—they'd been had. There was a lot of pressure on the Commissionaire du Sport to punish me. They took away my license to fight.

"The night after that happened I decided to kill Hemmy. I climbed up on the roof of his flat and jarred the bathroom skylight loose. I waited. Finally Hemmy came in to take a piss. He looked up, I looked down . . . and I pushed the goddamn skylight so it fell on his head. It almost worked. Almost. The next morning I was sick about it and I made a decision: I would never again attack another human being like that, in cold blood. Hemmy included. Write him off! Let him die in my mind forever."

"So you tried to kill him and he knew it. Did he do anything about it?"

"Not publicly. He would never admit to fear. But I had spooked him. In his guilt, he saw me everywhere. I was the friend that had helped him get somewhere and he had paid me back with multiple knives in the back. He knew what he had done, but he still couldn't understand my behavior—the silence, the unpredictable gestures, like throwing a drink on his pants, spitting on him from the ring. I guess he thought I'd get it out of my system and come back for more, which is what most people did after being screwed by Hemmy. But after the skylight incident—he got the message loud and clear. I tried to banish the thought of him but he haunted me. I was in a bad way: I found myself standing in his street at midnight, looking up at his window; or calling his number from a phone booth and hanging up when he answered. Things like that. He knew what was going on and it panicked him. He was great in situations where he could size up what was going to happen. But now he thought I was a psycho—unpredictable. He knew I had killed men in the war, so he looked on me with awe and still more fear, the fear that if I was crowded too far toward the edge, I might turn and kill like an animal. I'm not saying he went around wetting his pants every time he saw me, just that a big clump of anxiety had lodged in his guts, and he was sweating a lot and drinking more than usual and having trouble writing and sleeping. It messed up his marriage. It made him vicious to his friends. He was fouling his nest all over the place, so finally it all added up to a single message: get out of Paris, far away, go where I wouldn't go. So the fool set off for Key West.

"I knew when he was due to sail. I knew everything that was going on in his life. I followed their car to La Rochelle. Hemmy was in a great mood. He thought he had shaken me forever. They got on the boat and a while later I saw him at the railing in a crowd of passengers. He had a ridiculous hat on. He was grinning and waving. I stood on the quay, staring up at him, sending him a silent message. Sooner or later his mind would pick up that message like a radio signal. And sure enough, it happened—his eyes found me and when they did, he slumped like a prisoner does when he hears the gate slam shut behind him. Then you could almost see an invisible line connecting our eyes, and across that line I sent him the message: Go on, asshole, try to run away."

Pappy's face is set in a curious mixture of pain and grim pride. His look goes around me, through me, over me, back sixty years to the day he drove Ernest Hemingway out of Paris in ignominious retreat. This is not the look of a man acting out a sham, it is the face of memory.

"You'll never run far enough," he whispers.

THIRTY-FIVE

"PAPPY . . . PAPPY?"

Across the table, his mouth is ajar; his spirit has left his body and is wandering, a phantasm of revenge.

"Pappy, come on back. Let's finish it up."

"Where'd we leave off?"

"Hemingway was gone. Left France with his new wife. You watched him sail."

"Watched him sail, yup." His head bobs up and down. His eyes hunker in. He needs a jump start.

"So you had Paris all to yourself."

"Mm . . ."

"Paris without Hemingway?"

"Not much to say." He takes a deep breath and sits up a little straighter.

Suddenly he brightens. "Y'know, I proposed to Valerie."

"Proposed what?"

"Marriage, you dope! We're getting married as soon as her divorce comes through."

"She was married before?"

"It was just some kind of hippie arrangement, she never sees the idiot."

"Mazel tov," I say. "But let's stay with it, shall we?"

He shrugs, gone blank again, empty.

"C'mon, Pappy. You pick the subject. Just start talking, whatever comes to your mind, okay?"

"World War Two."

"Go."

He drains his beer with a sigh. "I saw it coming, but what the hell could I do about it? When the Germans walked into Paris I was going with a rich Parisian widow who wanted to hang on to her lifestyle so she dumped me for a kraut officer. One night I saw 'em in a nightclub and before I knew it I had walked over and punched him in the face. This threw the place into an uproar. The lights went out. Somebody was singing "La Marseillaise." I walked out of there knowing I had about twenty minutes to go underground before some SS gorilla put a Luger to my head and tumbled my ass into the river. And that was the beginning of my career as a Free French undercover agent—but let's do that some other day, that's another story altogether."

"No it isn't," I snap at him. "Tell it." I won't permit any slack today or any other day from now on. I'm going to wrap this up if it kills me. "Keep going. The Germans wanted you. What did you do? Where did you hide?"

He sighs heavily.

"I went to the old Maison du Paradis, which was catering mainly to Germans now. Figured that's the last place they'd look for me. I went in the back, with a dirty tradesman's apron on and needing a shave. Georges, my old pal the bartender, was the kind of guy I knew had underground connections. He set me up with new papers and I got involved with his maquis, which was about twenty guys, mostly bartenders, who pretended to tolerate Germans, then passed stuff they heard into an intelligence network. I grew a mustache and cut my hair and got some phony spectacles and before long Georges put me behind the bar. We'd alternate. Whoever wasn't tending bar was bicycling around from café to café picking up scuttlebutt. Sometimes a kraut would hear me talk and look at me funny. I'd tell him I was Quebecois. Most of 'em had never seen a real American, except in the movies. I never had any trouble that way. Toward the end we got into sabotage. I killed a few *milice* and hung up their bodies. It was good for morale. The fact that I was middle-aged made me less suspicious. Just before the Liberation everybody knew the Germans were pulling out. Our maquis went after snipers. It was crazy. You had to be careful not to get shot by our own guys. I was working the roof of the Ritz when Hemmy's private army came rolling in.

"Now, I had no idea he was back in France, much less that he was riding around with a bunch of resistance fighters pretending to be the Lone Ranger. Anyway, downstairs our people had rounded up a few prisoners and Georges was questioning them. I was feeling good. I had the roof secured so I strolled downstairs to liberate the bar. And that's where it all came to a head, at the Ritz. That's where I saw author and humanitarian Ernest Hemingway commit mass murder."

"Mass murder?"

"You heard me right."

"Who did he murder and why?"

"Lemme back up. See, me and my maquis boys had captured some Germans who were trying to burn files and stuff upstairs in the Ritz. Then, like I said, I went down to the bar, which was empty, and I was crouched down behind the bar looking for an olive when in comes Hemmy and a bunch of Free French crazies. 'I liberate this bar,' he says in his pidgin French. Then I rise up from behind the bar and you should've seen the look on his face—like someone had thrown dogshit in it. 'You,' he says. 'Shall I shoot him, Papa?' says this skinny little zit, same one that wanted to shoot Andre Malraux later, same kind of twerp that Hemmy always attracted that would've shot himself in the knee if Papa told him to. So I pulled the oldest trick in the book: 'Jean-Pierre, cover me!' I yelled, looking past them. They turned. Nobody there. When they turned back, I had the bartender's shotgun in my hands, aimed at Hemmy's face. 'Sure,' I says, 'shoot me. And watch your Uncle Ernie's face go up in smoke.'

" 'Just a minute,' says Hemmy. 'Just a damned minute.'

"Suddenly there was machine gun fire from outside the bar and we all hit the floor. This time when I raised my head somebody swung a gunstock that caught me broadside. When I came to I was tied up in a hallway upstairs. You ever been in the Ritz? All gold leaf and filigree. A silly place for a war. But Hemmy had things organized. He had set up some kind of staff headquarters in a suite. One of his flunkies dragged me in there. A bunch of German prisoners were sitting against a wall, blindfolded and tied at the wrists. Hemmy was sloshed on brandy. Roaring at the krauts in German, French, Spanish. The flunky pulled me over and stood me in front of Hemmy's desk—it was like a scene out of a war movie, Hemmy playing the Otto Preminger part. And we looked at each other.

" 'Well, Ricky,' he says after a minute.

" 'Well what, Bozo?'

"Hemmy couldn't stand somebody talking to him like that, especially in front of his French joyboys.

" 'So you think this is a clown show?' he says, clenching his teeth and puffing up like a blowfish.

"He takes his pistol, makes sure I'm watching, walks down the line of prisoners, pumps a bullet into each German. In the head. One by one they slump over, five of them. Five little krauts hardly old enough to shave; five little flunkies in the High Command who never saw a day of combat, caught trying to clean up after their bosses. And there was Hemmy at the height of his overblown vitality, showing me his *cojones*."

"And you were next."

"The gun was at my head. Then all of a sudden somebody sticks his face in and yells, 'Papa! What the hell—?' An American reporter. This was my chance. 'Look here,' I yell. 'I'm a Yank and he's about to put a bullet in my head.'

"Hemmy holsters the gun and pinches my cheek with a big grin.

" 'You passed the gut test, kid.'

" 'Then untie me, fatface.'

"Hemmy forces a laugh and looks at the reporter. He's young, just a kid. I can see he idolizes the Great Man and there's no way in hell he's ever going to put two and two together and get four. All he wants is for Papa to set him straight. Whatever it is he'll believe it. Hemmy's dying to finish me off but he knows he's on thin ice. He laughs this creepy laugh and starts to cut me loose with his commando knife—"

"Yo, Pap? Pappy?"

My heart jumps. It's Lynn with an order of fish 'n' chips from Sloppy Joe's. Gratefully I leave Paris behind. Her mere presence is all I need to bring me down from the slaughter at the Ritz. There's so much I want to tell her, but can't in Pappy's presence. More than anything, I want to be alone with her somewhere; I want to know if making my break with Astrid has done its work.

"Hello, Elliot." She speaks with an odd lack of nuance, as if mildly bored, nothing more, to find me here. As she clears Pappy's mess of a table and washes his festering dishes for him, I try to project my new phallic readiness, but she, on the other hand, seems to have almost forgotten who I am. Not that she's hostile (I get a polite smile the few times her eyes meet my obsessive gaze), just maddeningly detached. I wonder in a paroxysm of suspicion: is this really Lynn? Can there be a twin sister?

I glance at Pappy. He looks back and forth between us, curious, reading the invisible ripples. He senses mischief. Like an old lion, he has picked up a telltale trail.

"Well, well, well."

"That's a deep subject, Pappy," Lynn remarks, slipping into a chair midway between us. We eat. She avoids my eyes. The heat is overpowering. Pappy nudges her with his knee. "Everything okay in Lovebird Land?"

My spirit plummets. He knows something. He's going to wipe my nose in it.

He yawns theatrically. "Well, now, nappy time, wouldn't you think, Lynn, honey?"

"Okay, Pap."

"Now, you sure things are okay with you and Sir Galahad, here? You kids don't have any love troubles, do you? I mean some of those pesky little hang-ups that even healthy young folks get every now and then? Lock and key problems, y'know? Little boy-thing mishaps, maybe? *Hee-hee!*"

Lynn's jaw tightens but she says nothing. She doesn't have to: she's obviously done her talking already, betrayed me to him, thrown the slops of my manhood to this old shark.

"Nobody gonna talk?" Another stagey yawn. "Okay, okay. Lead me in, babe, I need a good rub today. Oh me, you never know about these things, do ya—come on, Roscoe, it's beauty rest time, *hee-hee-hee!*"

Forever it seems the heat of the day drifts by and I have infinite time to lie still and contemplate this unutterable blackness, but I don't. Every now and then I can hear a groan of pleasure issuing from Pappy. My imagination runs riot: she is stroking him up, sucking him, striding him, sliding dreamily up and down his old monster of a pole. No, thinking is too hurtful. I let the blackness hollow out a hole in my mind and I fill it with nothing. More *nada*.

At last she appears, glistening with light perspiration but otherwise clean and unmussed. Her clothes cling to her so crisply I realize she never had them off.

"He's asleep," she whispers, with a finger across her lips. Again her eyes regard me with a dull lack of empathy. This is not the Lynn who nursed me back to consciousness, it has to be Lynn's twin, the body double. We stare back and forth like strangers.

"I heard," I say.

"Heard what?"

My head goes stupidly up and down. "Never mind, I heard. And by the way, thanks so much for your discretion, your consideration, your loyalty—"

"What, Elliot?"

"You know what. Do you think I'm stupid? He knows, he knows about us."

She doesn't react. In fact, the moment is characterized by what she *doesn't* do. She doesn't dissolve into denial, doesn't rush to comfort me, doesn't burn with guilt. She simply looks back at me, from inside her mystery.

"I have to go," she says finally, not freighting it with subtext but making it a simple utterance, like "Hot, isn't it?" She waits a moment for me to respond and when I don't, she shrugs and, with a wave, is gone.

Jesus, what have I gotten myself into?

THIRTY-SIX

"WELL, WHAT'RE YOU so foul-faced about?"

Nap over, he beams with vitality, all set to pick at my liver like a playful hawk. The stray thought flits across my mind that I could leap forward and break his neck in seconds. I shove my hands into my pockets.

"Nothing."

"Nothing, eh? You sure about that?"

"Absolutely positive."

"Why don't you have a beer, McGuire?"

"No thanks. Can we get started?"

"Goodness, we're pushy! Give us a minute, okay? I've gotta give Roscoe a little air, I'll be right back." He stands, patting his crotch, and saunters into the backyard.

The insolent, innuendo-laden twinkle, the ironic smirk—what next? What further humiliations do I have to endure at the hands of this rapacious old tartar?

No, I've got to get back on even ground with him. Press ahead, put on blinders, stay sober. Forget about the debacle of Lynn for now. Deal with the dreck another day. Get this thing moving. Get it that much closer to over.

"Pappy." My voice rings with command.

"Yah?"

"Get back in here. Now."

"I beg your fucking pardon?"

"Get in this house now or I'm on the first plane back to New York."

He sticks his head in, puzzled. "Now hang on, hang on, no need to—"

"Let's understand one thing. No matter how much humiliation you think I can take from you there's a limit, and as of now, you've exceeded it. I'm very tired of you at this moment. I'm tired of your face, your voice, your murderous fantasies. I can and will walk away if you don't sit down instantly, finish this day's work and prepare to wrap the project up tomorrow."

"Now wait just a minute—"

"No!" I shout, in a voice he's never heard out of me before. "You sit, damn it!"

He gives me a long measuring look and skulks back to the table.

"Sit *now* or I am out this door!"

The blood vacates his face. Slowly he lowers himself into his chair.

"Right: back to work."

"Okay, for Christ's sake, where were we?"

"We were at the Ritz. He was about to put a bullet in your head."

"Yeah, yeah—"

"Or we could proceed directly to the assassination and get the whole damned thing over with—"

He squints at me anxiously. "We'll get there, McGuire. I can't just jump it. There's a few more stops along the way, just . . . just hear me out . . ." He trails off, his eyes pleading with me not to bolt.

"Right: Hemingway wanted to kill you. Why?"

He scratches at a patch of scalp and slumps down low in his chair.

"Well, that's easy enough: I'd seen way too much. The murders. The ball of fear behind the strut. I knew Hemmy's real story and he knew I knew it."

"So your decision to kill, to rid the earth of this unrelenting nemesis of yours, was based on self-defense."

"Partly."

"But you waited over fifteen years? It doesn't make sense. Why the hell did it take you so long?"

"Hold your horses, I'll tell you if you give me half a chance. We're getting ahead of the goddamned story."

"Just answer the question, please: Why did you wait so long to carry out the assassination?"

Pappy squirms in my authoritarian grip. "Well, the . . . I don't know, the thought of it came slow."

"How slow is slow?"

"Truth is it never even occurred to me until years after the war. I'm not a natural murderer. I don't think in terms of killing people."

"I see."

"Well, it's true: when I thought back to the Ritz, where we came face to face and I began to realize I had almost blown Hemmy away right then, I didn't like the idea one bit. I mean, hell—who wants to think of himself as a killer, no matter how many good reasons he has? I was so upset I blocked the whole event out of my memory. On the street in Paris people would ask me, Did you see Hem at the Ritz? I'd say, Nope. But later, much later, things began to come back to me. The look on his fat face when he stood in the bar, my finger brushing the trigger. I should have done it then. I would've done it if I had known what was coming."

His eyes clear up. He coughs a few times and spits. As much as I long to wrap this up, it's not over yet. He holds me with his glittering eye, his ham of a hand. Up ahead the final gun blast waits, but for now we must keep toiling up this endless mountain of a story.

"When the war ended I wasn't young anymore. It was like a rerun of my situation after the first war: stuck in Paris, not a penny to my name, having fought the good fight, exhausted, back to square one. But let me tell you, square one is a bleaker place at fifty than at twenty-three. You look around and see a different world. It's not morning anymore. It's late afternoon in the deep of winter with darkness falling early and you're a long way from home. I decided to get back to the States. I had had it with Paris, with the French, free or otherwise.

"So I drifted home to New York with a plan. I would write my page a day—and by the way, through it all I had never stopped writing, always did my page a day, did it, threw it away. But now, for the first time in my life, I'd write it to publish it. That's what Gabrielle had always wanted—now I'd do it, and dedicate it to her. I'd write my memoir of two wars and the years in between. I'd get an agent, I'd get an advance. I sat in a coffeehouse down in the Village and saw the whole vision shape up as I wrote, piling up more and more great stuff with each cup of Viennese roast. Why not grab my rightful place in the world? Why not stand up like a man and take credit? Eric Markham, the man who did his bit to push the balky jackasses of literature in the right direction, toward clarity, toward the perfection of simplicity, the fall of a single leaf, the perfect circle?

"But an odd thing: as I tried to make connections with the literary people I knew who were back in New York, I kept striking out. Harold Stearns had got married and was living in the country. Wouldn't answer my postcards. My phone calls never got through to people. At first I didn't give it any thought—people get busy after a war. Look at me! But when six months had gone by and no one, I mean no one, had given me the time of day, I began to wonder what the hell was going on.

"I had written three chapters of my memoir, and I knew it was hot. I began to circulate it to old friends. Nothing. Sent back without a word. A young agent asked me in. She raved about it, said she'd put it up for auction, we were going to be rich, and so on. I went home and slept good for the first time in weeks. Next day the package was at my door, by messenger, with a note: 'Sorry. On further consideration can do nothing with this.' She wouldn't take my calls. I dropped in and told the secretary I'd wait all day if I had to. Next thing I knew the cops were putting me out in the street. What the hell was going on?"

He pauses rhetorically. He knows he's got me going.

"Well?" I say after a moment. "What *was* going on?"

"Hemmy again. Another knife in my back. And I'll tell you how I found out. I'll leave out the years of scrounging and torment, the wasted years at what's supposed to be the peak of a man's achievement, the downward spiral of my spirit and the near-wreckage of my health. I'll leave out the humiliation of that wall of silence and rejection, the disintegration of a mature man with energy, future, and a story to tell into a reclusive wreck of a has-been who never was."

"All right, all right—"

"I'll skip right to 1952, when the bolt of lightning struck and the curtains fell from my eyes. Thank God for insanity. Because of all the people I had known in Paris, there was one, only one, who was immune to whatever force field had been spun around me making me untouchable—and he was crazy. Thank God for crazy old Ezra Pound, the leper, the Jew baiter, the other untouchable American genius. Thank God for Ezra, because he alone was able to give me what I needed, the master key to the whole stinking puzzle."

And here he brings back Pound! I'm practically on my knees to the audacity, the sheer gall of it!

"Please tell me about it."

"I wrote him one day. It was about 1952. I was at the bottom of my dive. Living on the Bowery. Eating at soup kitchens. Drunk most of the time. A fifty-seven-year-old ex-nothing. No future. No dreams. The boy who saw the universe in a grain of sand—gone. One day I picked up a *Daily News* in the trash and there's Ezra's picture. TRAITOR POET LIVES GOOD LIFE IN GENTLEMAN'S NUT-HOUSE. The gist of it was indignation that the poet who sold his country out should be in comfortable circumstances instead of dangling from the end of a rope, which is where the *News* thought he ought to be. I don't know what possessed me at that moment—I started out for Washington. Grabbed a bus. I just knew somehow that Ezra had the answer. I got there and started walking. Past the Capitol. Past the Washington Monument. Up into the hills. And finally I was on the lawn at St. Elizabeth's.

"There were Ezra and Dorothy, sitting in beach chairs and looking older than God. Ezra was feeding the squirrels and a couple of pimply adolescent poets or junior *fascisti* sat in the grass picking up the pearls of wisdom as they fell out of his old crackerbarrel of a mouth. They were all sipping tea and munching chocolates. I walked up and stood there for a minute. They looked right through me. Then I realized they thought I was one of the resident nuts. 'Ezra, goddamn it, it's me, Ricky Markham!' He screwed up his face. Dorothy looked like she was going to faint. I wondered what the hell it was about me that put them off so.

"Finally a big grin came across Ezra's face. 'Wall, round up the missionaries, Mother! Polly, put the cauldron on, we'll all have stew!' "

"What did he mean by that?"

" 'Ezra,' I says, 'don't play games with me. I'm tired to my bones. Nobody'll touch me and I don't know why. What is it? Don't turn me away. Tell me what's going on.' "

"Ezra jumps up all of a sudden and makes a flourish with his arm in the direction of the ward.

" 'Come on with me.'

"We stride past the trees, past little groups of gibbering nuts, into the ward, past the blithering TV sets, and into Ezra's room. He goes through a stack of letters and pulls one out.

" 'Read this.'

"It was from Hemmy. He let me keep it. I've still got it."

Pappy roots around in a dresser drawer until he comes up with a mangled piece of paper. He waves it in the air.

"Read this."

I unfold it, careful not to let it fall apart in my fingers. The message is short, in somewhat rickety typescript.

Ezra:

Warning you and anybody else that Eric Markham survived war and may turn up stateside. Don't show him any exposed flesh or dire consequences sure to commence. Remember Justin d'Antoine, the naif who peddled wispy poems around Vavin? Have late bulletin on his final moments. Rick cut his throat and feasted on various body parts to indulge cannibal fascination. This is the true gen. I got it from d'Antoine's old mistress who cleans rooms now at the Ritz. Ricky stole a stack of the kid's poems and tried to pass off half-assed translations as original work. Someday I'll get the whole story down, how a big pretty boy with promise manages to fuck his life to shreds and ends up in the dark, with a taste for human flesh. Can't beat his peers so eats them instead. How do you like it now?

Hem.

I look up, straight into Pappy's fierce eyes.

"You see that? It wasn't enough for him to take away my identity and steal my work. Not enough for him to poison my name and leave me drifting, cut me off from any possibility of publication. He had to finish me off good. *I knew too much.* I knew he was an undead, a killer, a drinker of blood. And trying to smear me with cannibalism when *he* was the cannibal, I knew it and he knew I knew it. So what did he do? He took up where he'd left off in Paris. You saw the letter—only now I was contaminated everywhere, there wasn't a patch of ground on the entire earth where they didn't spit at the sound of my name, chase me away from the fire, grind me into dust."

"So what did you do about it?"

"I sent Hemmy a cable, demanded a meeting. I said I'd been to see Ezra and I wanted a face-to-face explanation. He didn't answer back so I sent him another cable: *'Unless I hear from you, expect me at the finca and God save us all.'* That got through his thick skull. He cabled back he was going to be in New York and would meet me at the Stork Club, gave me a day and a time. It was early morning. The place was closed. Hemmy was in the Cub Room at a table all by himself, nervous as a hamster. Sherman Billingsly, the owner, walked me back there and sat down at a discreet distance. He let me know he was packing a gun.

" 'What's this craziness, Rick?' says Hemmy.

"I handed him the letter. 'I want a retraction.'

"He reads it and holds his hands up, innocent as a lamb.

" 'Jesus, Rick, you can't think I stirred up this snot, can you?'

" 'If you didn't, who did?'

"He proceeds to tell me somebody's out there going around claiming to be Ernest Hemingway, charging up hotel bills, seducing boys, and pulling pranks like this. He was going to personally break the fucker's neck if he ever laid hold of him, but in the meantime I should disregard it whenever something strange turned up with his name on it.

"I almost believed him.

"We had some drinks and started talking about old times, the old days in Paris before things got so complicated. He started blubbering about his ex-wife Pauline, who had just died, and before you knew it his arm was around me and he was apologizing up and down for everything he'd ever done to me. He wanted to make it up to me, he said. He was on his way to Europe, but he wanted to do something that would set me up for the rest of my life. He pulled a key out of his pocket.

" 'I've got a place in Key West, it was Pauline's. There's a small house behind it, out by the pool. The best stuff I ever wrote I wrote in that house. I want you to live there, Rick. For as long as you want. Here's the key . . . it's all yours.'

"Well, to make a long story short, fool that I was I took him at his word. I was exhausted by New York. Maybe at long last he was going to do right by me. I packed a bag and bought a bus ticket to Key West." His mouth curls in futility.

"And when you got here?"

"I walked up Whitehead Street until I saw the mansion. There it was, Hemingway's Key West palace, built on my flesh and bones. Nobody home there, windows boarded up and all, but the house by the pool, the one Hemmy mentioned, was open. I used the key and walked right in. Everything was nice, just what I had in mind, except for one thing—a woman standing in the middle of the living room screaming her bloody head off. And before I had a chance to tell my story the cops drove up and wrestled me out to the squad car. She was Hemingway's tenant, they were telling me, and you can fill in the rest. Having a key only made me look like a thief as well as a prowler, so I spent the night in jail, hung out to dry by the nuts in Key West, Florida, with Hemmy off in Europe having screwed me again. To round it off, I made a new decision right then and there that Ernest M. Hemingway would answer to me once and for all. I moved into an old burnt-out shack and stayed on. Key West was going to be my last stop. That was 1952 and I haven't been farther than Stock Island since—excepting once."

"When was that?"

"July 1961. A little trip to Idaho."

"Ah. And let's get on to that, can we?"

Pappy's eyes widen unevenly. "All right. We can and will get to that. How he knew I was coming, how he had my mind on a beam. And about the several rings of protective black magic he developed to try and defend himself—"

"Wait a second— Magic?"

"Very heavy magic. Hang around, McGuire, it's only starting to get good."

"You're saying Ernest Hemingway was—what, a magician? A warlock?"

"And why the hell not? It fits. He couldn't stand the idea that he might die or especially that something—or somebody—might kill him. He was drawn to expert knowledge, because that was a form of power over uncertainty. Black magic was just one more step along the line he lived on. It started with eating bull balls and drinking hero blood. That

168

moved him into epicurean cannibalism. Now, when you operate in that area you naturally keep certain company. One thing
leads to another with those people and before you know it,
you meet a vampire. Well, that's interesting, you say. You
experiment a little. And presto—you're on the other side of
the wall, you're an undead. I believe it. Cuba is full of that
kind of power. Jesus, man, look where he lived—out in the
country in the middle of nowhere surrounded by people who
drink chicken blood and make rattles out of snake balls. This
man had to kill animals again and again and again. Why?
Everybody gives psycho reasons, but what about the other,
more practical reasons? Animals are a source of blood. It was
peacetime, he couldn't keep killing humans—not and get the
Nobel Prize, too, right? Animals had to do. And he remained
undead—read my lips: *undead*—he went through shit that
would've killed ten horses. The final proof was the airplane
crashes, two of 'em in a row, *blam-blam!* He walks away from
both. That's when I knew. That's when I knew he would never
die unless I made it happen. Then he won the goddamned
Nobel Prize and I couldn't stand it. Jesus Christ, every time I
opened a picture magazine there he was with his goddamned
fat mug—!''

"So you started thinking about killing him."

"I was thinking a lot about it, yeah. I would daydream it.
And wherever he was, he knew it, too. There are ways of
killing an undead, of taking away their power, and he sensed
that I could do it to him. For the rest of his miserable life, he
sat there across the water in the *finca* sucking up my vibes like
radiation. Two years later he won the Nobel. After that I guess
he figured he was too big for me. A Nobel winner—I couldn't
lay a finger on him."

"His mistake."

A stark laugh. "One of the many."

"What else?"

"He should've left me alone. I might've let things slide. Like
I told you, I'm not a murderer. I've killed men in war, but
otherwise, look at me—a man of peace, a pussycat. Life in Key
West wasn't so bad, really. I had women, good weather, I was
healthy. Maybe things hadn't worked out the way they would
if I had my druthers, but it didn't matter—I could still write,
I could write my page a day, just like when I was a boy, I could

make wine from the ordinary grapes of life, and brandy from the wine, so what did I care?"

"Well? Something pushed you over the edge. What was it?"

His face goes dead. "Right then he made the biggest mistake of all. The fool used his magic to preempt control of the right side of my brain, the place where my mind opened into eternity, and shut that side of me down. He crippled me as sure as if he had cut me off at the knees with a hacksaw. That was the turning point."

"You realize what this sounds like, don't you?"

"I don't care!"

"Listen, mental wards are full of people whose minds are quote-unquote *being controlled*—"

"*I don't care! He took my voice!*"

"Well—I mean, how did he do it? What was the mechanism?"

"Damn it, I told you. Magic. He made me a blind mute with an abcess where my imagination had been. Listen here, do you want this story or do you want to walk? You keep threatening to go back to New York—okay, why don't you? Just butt out! You think you're dealing with some kind of a nut? Take a fucking walk—"

My hands go up. "No, it's okay. Never mind. Let's go on."

He puffs and pouts, cooling down. "No more of that, y'understand?"

"No more, I promise. So. The last straw—control of your mind. You were a killing machine. At last, you would stalk and eradicate him, cold-bloodedly, without mercy."

"Would you show mercy to a dog who's tasted human blood? He was a killer. He was on the side of death. Why should I have had any more pity on him than he had on the rest of us? Do you forgive a killer just because when his brain chemistry permits he can dance and sing and cry and kiss a baby? Do you? Do you?"

I have no answer.

"MAGIC IS LIKE an information system, you know. You mess around long enough with magic and you learn to pick vibes out of the air, just like shortwave radio. Ordinary people don't know when somebody's stalking them, but all that time Hemmy had a notion I was coming. This is what crippled him those last years. They thought he had fried his brain with too much booze. Bull. The man was scared, petrified, and you know what?—he never told a soul. It was the one thing he couldn't confess to. I mean, what's he gonna do, roll over in bed one day and say, "Kitten, I think Ricky Markham's on his way to blow my head off and it's got me so spooked I can't think straight"? He was like a rat inside an electrified box. Zapped and trapped. He had screwed with my head and now his own precious mental instrument was shut down."

"How did you know this?"

"I knew."

"But how?"

"He sent me a letter . . ."

He takes another tattered yellowed typescript from his bureau drawer. As he hands it to me I notice his hand shaking with an uncharacteristic palsy.

Mayo Clinic, Rochester, Minn.
June 20, 1961

Dear Rick:
   Awfully glad you liked Key West enough to plunk down. I called that one right, didn't I? I know you're on your way to see me and it's a free country so don't know what the hell I could do about it anyway. It's hardly worth it now, though, with what they've done to me. Blood pressure is down to 140/70 but now have trouble remembering (which never

had). In particular, Paris days gone, which is painful because we were all of us so damn young and it was so good. Trying to do something with it has me on the ropes.

Have good claret here anyway and I think there will be quail once am out. Remember Roosevelt and fear itself? That's the key. You never know when the fear will hit. But we don't ignore it as well as we did when we were young. It's an undiscovered country, isn't it?

Stay away, Rick.

Wish you luck with everything but what you have in mind. Wish I could write good letters and say like you what a man's mind can say in the night without words. The words do not line up right for me anymore and that is miserable.

Sorry but can't release my grip on you. Have one punch left I can keep throwing and will throw it till the bell and on beyond so come if you are coming and bring your own best punch. Fear itself is not enough to make a man let go. Not until you smell my shit. You think I would let you go? I would sooner go on Ed Murrow and tell the world you wrote my stuff, and you know how soon that will be.

I will be in le Trou from 2 to 4 on Saturday and Sunday afternoons and if anybody wants to shoot me they should come and do it or else for christ sake stop talking about it.

Best always,
Hemmy

"If I had any second thoughts about what I was going to do, they were gone when I read that. He was damaged goods, and I was damned if I was going to spend my golden years under the spell of a brain-sick old fraud."

"You killed him to lift . . . a spell?"

"Let's just say it was my summary judgment for all the accumulated wrongs he had piled up against me. This mental block thing, it was just the final straw in the lifetime of abuse I had taken from Hemingway. Hemmy's bell was tolling. And I was pulling the rope."

His eyes cloud up. I realize he is going to sit, motionless, stalled, like a sickened toad, until I prod him.

"So you went to Idaho."

"I wrote this once."

"Yes, you did."

"Do I have to go through it again?"

"Let's hear it again. There might be new details. Come on, don't die on me. How did you get to Ketchum?"

"Bus. Nothing particular to say about that. It was a bus trip."

"All right. Pick it up wherever you want. What do you remember?"

"Here's what I remember: I remember the sound of my feet slogging through the mud on the way to his house. I remember the house sitting there quiet as a morgue. I remember how I circled the place like an Indian, figuring out the best door. It was dawn so I knew he'd be wide awake. And I knew something else: I knew he knew I was out there.

"He opened the door for me. Didn't say nothing, just held it open and grinned at me, or rather his face parted like a cut wound and his eyes wrinked. I had a pistol in my hand. He just ignored it. Held out his hand. Acted like he was actually glad to see me. I said to myself: *The fool—here I am to kill him and he's grinning at me.*

" 'I was expecting you,' he says.

" 'I know.'

"Two choices: I could start blazing away, or I could let the moment ride. I was curious. What did he have in mind? I motioned to him to step back into the house, then I followed him inside.

" 'I've been working on a book about the old days in Paris,' he says. 'And I'm putting in a whole chapter about you.'

" 'Bullshit.'

"The grin starts to fade. He can't read me and it's bothering him. You know the way it is with executions—I've seen my share in both the wars and you never know how somebody's going to go. But there always comes a time when they know it's all over, all the preparations, the little time-wasting details. There's no way back. And this is when the bowels open, the sobs erupt, the body throws itself to the floor pleading for mercy. I was afraid we were going this way with Hemmy. He wanted to chat, show me things, take me around the house. He was struggling, like a little kid who doesn't want to go to bed: just five minutes more, one minute more . . .

"One time, once only, he begged: 'Please, Rick, for old times' sake, let me finish the Paris book.'

"I shook my head. I wasn't about to set myself up for another double cross. I knew there wasn't a single true story he could tell about me and him and Paris. And I'd already had a sample of the kind of beauties he would tar me with, given half a chance.

"I had brought an old Timex watch and I kept looking at it. I had to get a move on. There was no telling who was staying in the house. Any second George Plimpton or somebody might stroll in. I felt cool and removed. No emotion, just a little irritation that he was holding me up.

" 'Kneel down,' I told him.

" 'I won't die kneeling down,' he said, looking back at me. In another mood I would have taken that as a challenge and forced him down, but right then I had no feelings about it one way or another.

" 'Suit yourself.'

"I raised the pistol with both hands and aimed for his heart. But something made me hold up: he was staring at the pistol, wrinkling his nose like he smelled dog poop or something.

" 'Not with that!' he yelled. 'Do it right, do it grand!'

"He motions to the shotgun cabinet. Why not? I sidled over and grabbed one . . .''

Here Pappy drops his gaze. I notice he's looking at one of the snapshots he once showed me, the headless Hemingway, blown (as he put it in the vastly superior written fragment) onto the cover of *Life*. And what the hell happened to that fragment, by the way?

"Bang-bang," he says, his eyes wide as he imagines the scene. "Both barrels."

"And you were free."

I can barely hear his response. "And I was . . . free."

Now he's looking at the other snapshot, the old black-and-white one: the buddies pose, Hemingway and "Rickie" Markham, youthful, arms draped around each other's shoulders. We should certainly have that for the book. The gory one too, I suppose.

"What are you thinking?" says Pappy suddenly, looking up from the snapshot.

"Remember the fragment?"

"Of course I do. What about it? You want to know why it's different, right?"

"Sure. Not that it really matters. I mean, we'll use the most compelling version. But yes, why the divergence?"

Pappy's eyebrows arch into a semicircle of pain. His head waggles pitifully. He is going into his now-familiar shrinking man act, at the close of which his sinewy body will collapse into a pathetic little bag of ancient wrinkles and bones.

"It didn't work."

"What didn't?"

"I should have known, see. When you're as far along as he was, when you're an undead, death isn't the answer."

"The answer to what?"

He takes his time, finally draws himself up and gives me the eagle stare, all prickly defiance.

"The fragment, that scene I wrote . . . was *his*, the one piece I saved out of all that juvenilia I dumped in the sewer. Nick Adams comes home from the war and shoots his old man. It was fantasy, a piece of masturbatory crap. Hemmy never even finished it. But I used it, I adapted it. What else could I do? He still had his hands wrapped around my mind—" The voice is getting hollow and raspy. He pulls up and swallows, fighting for control. His eyes are sloppy with tears.

To my horror, I catch myself thinking: Does he still have it? *How can I get my hands on the original?* A patricidal fantasy— Hemingway actually penned one! The old fire dog of a Hemingway scholar inside me is salivating.

Suddenly Pappy's arm lurches out in a crooked arc that takes in the whole of his physical existence.

"Damn it, do you think this is all I'm good for—this dire mess of a chicken shack? This last-ditch dump of a Florida key, this aimless barren turtle race you call a life? I'm a bum because of him. And he keeps me a bum, day by day, minute by minute, squeezing my head like a sponge. Alive, dead, it doesn't matter. He can do it from this side, he can do it from the other side. So I diddle with the girls and read some and drink and kill time waiting in the sun to die. But write? Make something of myself? Never. *Nyet.* No way."

"He controls you from the other side?"

"What does it look like to you? I blew his head off, I scattered his brains, I gave him the final punishment for crimes against my spirit. But what did it all come to in the end? I still can't write. Twenty-five years without a page of my own. Do you know how long it took me to redo that assassination fragment of his? Five months. And why? Because he was out there. Out there in the dark reaching into my mind. Aw *Jesus* . . ."

He breaks off, moaning, shaking, sobbing. Why the hell do I feel such sorrow for him? Not just simple pity but a rush of profound sympathy bordering on grief. Why do I want to comfort him, to assure him that he has so much to be grateful for: love, strength, a big healthy putz—?

Yet part of me withers in horror: this man is a certifiable maniac, a menace to society and—

Oh, God, here it comes, I'm taking him in my arms, with such a mixture of repulsion and love that I haven't felt since my father reached out for me (unprecedented) in the hospital, minutes before he crumpled into a pile of sheets and nothingness. Pappy is crying into my shoulder as I hold him, the old lizard, as I do my best to comfort his inflamed spirit, hurting as it must like an angry tooth, a white-hot ball of indescribable woe—

And then the trapdoor opens. Images that for years have remained stored in the cellar of my own mind wriggle out into the light.

The letters.

A boy's letter to Hemingway. EH getting back to me in good faith—but how was I to know he was on his last legs? My stupid arrogant answer to his answer (oh, the oblivious self-righteousness of a thirteen-year-old!) and his answer to that: double barrels against his forehead.

For a moment, rocking Pappy, I relive the full shock of the obituary headlines. My fault, my doing? Could *my letter* have witlessly pushed him over the edge? Feckless Elliot McGuire, the most destructive horse's ass since Beethoven's nephew! Literature wants to thank you, Elliot: you were such a prideful young bungler that we lost Ernest Hemingway a good ten years before we had to!

And here I am giving comfort to his mortal enemy, this old wreck of a fantasist, letting him blubber away on my neck, with his hopeless stubble and his insupportable breath, merciless reminders of where we all end up no matter what shape our fucking LifeForms take. Are you satisfied, Elliot McGuire?

But wait. Wait. Let's *think*. Let's try to make something decent out of this awful epiphany. Could we possibly, possibly swing it in a positive direction?

Let's struggle. Let's get creative. How about something like, "Killing the Inner Hemingway: an evolutionary step along the path to self-realization"?

Or: "Don't we all have to 'kill Hemingway' to open up some space for ourselves . . ."?

Yes. Make a note of this: *Killing Hemingway: the ultimate breakthrough—*

Jesus, I'm blind with tears.

Part Three

NO MATTER WHAT it looks like, I am not a complete fool. Let's be clear about that. I'm perfectly aware that I drink too much. I know that for days my behavior has bordered on the pathological. My sensors are in working order. My various alarms have been calibrated, set, reset, and management has the situation well under control. I can safely say that I'll be decreasing my alcohol intake in the very near future. That's a pledge.

Actually, I went on the wagon for a few hours today, but postponed it when I arrived at Miami International and suffered a minor phobic attack, nothing much, just a strong odor of death surrounding Gate 23B, mental images of entombment, cremation, that sort of thing. Silly, now that I sit here in luxurious stillness, twenty thousand feet above the smooth Coke-bottle green of the sea below. I've had a few therapeutic Scotches—so what? I know my limits. Just watch me turn it off when the time comes to get serious.

"Another Scotch, sir?"

"Thank you."

Judge how clearheaded I am. Even before leaving Key West,

I had the presence of mind to call the *Times* (on Craig's dime) and place an author's query in the *Book Review*:

> For a 'Lost Generation' memoir, any information about Eric Markham, American expatriot of the '20s and '30s in Paris, contemporary and friend of Ernest Hemingway etc. etc. . . .

Why not? It certainly wouldn't *hurt* if there's some linkage out there between the Convincing and the Objectively True. Let's just see what some old-fashioned traditional methodology churns up.

Ah, me! What a moment!

Maybe it's just that life can seem like such a simple trick when you're riding in majestic stillness over the clouds, free of fear, a brand-new Scotch in your hand—*but I'm actually having fun!*

And this: who'd have thought I'd be headed home from this tawdry gig plotting a major promotional boost for LifeForms? Well, believe it or not, the way I feel right now I'd put my name on *I Killed Hemingway* in a second! I'd write a preface linking Pappy with everything from the American tall tale to the literature of paranoid schizophrenia—then wind up with a LifeForms analysis not only of Pappy, his bizarre vision and brazen retelling, but of *Hemingway himself*, the great Front-loaded Pooh-Bah who set such a blistering pace on the front nine, then withered and collapsed.

Yes!

Humming like a top, I barely notice as gravity reclaims me and we descend and land.

Ah, New York! Jolly old town. Savor the foulness, the trashiness of the airport, the blunt surliness of the cabdriver. But my mood is starting to slip. Everyone in the streets suddenly resembles some mildly threatening form of wildlife—fanged lizards walking their dogs, crocodiles slithering into Gristede's. Today the afternoon reeks of that nutty smell—you know the one—is it garbage incineration? Bad chestnuts? Urban body odor?

I really ought to cut my drinking back.

"Seventh Avenue and Tenth Street," I enunciate to the cabbie, twisting my lips to fit the Plexiglas slot. "Right side," I specify.

"Right side, right side, *right*, damn it—!"

He swerves left across several lanes of traffic, halts, and waits sullenly for his money before flinging me out into the avenue beside St. Vincent's.

What about this craving for a drink? Maybe an infusion of sweets will help. I dodge and toil and limbo my way across Seventh, then Greenwich and into the Korean deli for drying-out supplies: a massive Cadbury with hazelnuts, a Toblerone semisweet, a Sarah Lee carrot cake, and for good measure, a pack of Pepperidge Farm molasses crisps . . .

I duck out of the deli like a thief and round the corner into Bank Street. There is no sun in the sky here. Madmen go racing past on their way to the river. You could cut the hysteria with a wok chopper. This is New York. I am home.

The high that jangled me on the plane is now definitely gone. My jaw still aches from the punch I took the other day. I try not to think about it but demonic images of Pappy keep wriggling through the crevices of my awareness. In the foyer, mail is jammed into my box, dunning notices, emotional cheap shots ("Will you adopt this wounded bird?"), an invitation to a publication party for a new novelist (let him go hang himself). I trudge up the old spiral staircase, which creaks in all the familiar places, and let myself in. Something has been putrefying in my absence. I go, by long-established habit, straight to the answering machine to listen to my messages while I decide how to get on with the show.

"It's Yugo, big fella. Hey, catch me on 'Saturday Night Live,' this week, okay? I'm guest hosting. You want tickets? I'll see what I can do. Call me at the office."

I've never understood why Yugo keeps pushing our friendship. There was a time, just after he got famous, when I didn't hear from him; he was "associating with his peers." But now that he's got the talk show I guess he's too busy to run with the showoffs. Or maybe he thinks of me as some kind of moral beacon from school days, ha ha. Who knows?

"Yugo again, guy. Hey, you gone underground or something? Well, 'Saturday Night' was a gas and I've got it on tape, so let's have lunch and taste the highlights . . ."

"Yugo redux. Hey schmuck! What's the matter with you? Don't you check your messages? You make me puke, you intellectual. Call me."

The one object I maintain in full view, after redecorating this creaky old floorthrough in bold white-on-white, is a snapshot of my mom and dad taken by a roving photographer. They are nightclubbing. He's in black tie, a broad grin ripping across his big jaw. His eyes stare beyond the camera. They are wider than eyes should be, as though he's in pain, trying to laugh an ulcer away. Mom looks directly into the camera, her fingers curled sweetly around a cigarette, which she holds at a voguish angle. My parents.

My decorator was Astrid, recommended by Craig. I had moved in the week after my great-aunt Esther died.

"You can't live here," she said. "This is an old lady's place. Let me turn you on to white."

White-on-white-on-white. The kind of pad that instantly shows abuse. A coffee upset here, a mustard accident there, a layer of yellowish neglect. White is unforgiving; it reflects confusion, sagging morale. Did I think an endless prospect of white would cheer me up? Well, think again, sucker. Even Astrid's body, so white you can see right through her skin to the blue blood in her veins, even this ultimate white was destined to snag on my gray scale.

I rip open the Toblerone and bite off a chunk of the rich dark chocolate. No, no good. I pour a tumbler of Scotch and draw a hot tub, scalding, hot enough to kill microbes, at least the ones that infect my mind. Pretty soon I'm pleasantly gaga and only the memory of something I read about "hot tub deaths" keeps me from drifting off. I dry myself, groggy, and fall into bed, sheathed in layers of white terry cloth.

It's the purple hour and night is stealing in. I will be a good boy, God, just don't let me die too soon.

Tomorrow and tomorrow and tomorrow—

Shit! Tomorrow is my birthday.

THIRTY-NINE

"HAPPY BIRTHDAY, YOU old cud!"

Yugo's eyes are flashing. Everyone in the Russian Tea Room knows him. Loves him too.

"Andrei, Grishenka—c'mere a minute. Say happy birthday to Elliot McGuire. Very big writer, world authority on Hemingway."

He goes on like that to the nodding employees, one lie after another: I won the National Book Award, the Pulitzer Prize, the Bronze Star. What the hell, let him rave. I just watch him. Fame has made his face look bigger. And something else about it, too—what?—it seems to radiate twenty or thirty watts of bulb power. If you turned off the lights in here Yugo would burn with fleshy iridescence.

Eventually, the ordering done, the palavering over with, his face settles into a web of anxious creases. Over drinks, my Scotch, his Perrier, he decides it's time to graduate from small talk. We're going right to what's on his mind.

"You don't know how isolating all this has been." It's a different voice altogether, a worried sotto voce rasp.

"All this what?"

"This . . ." He waves a hand around the room. As he does, a film actor, whose name escapes me, waves back. "See what I mean?" he says between his teeth, returning the salute with a bright grin. "I don't mind being recognized, mind you. The fame part is fine. I wanted that from the beginning."

"Then what's the problem?"

He widens his eyes, a schoolboy blanking on a test question.

"Pain." He grips his heart. "Pain in here—no, down here, more like in the gut."

"Have you seen a doctor?"

"No no, not that kind of pain. Fear is more like it. Fear."

"What are you afraid of?"

"I don't know, it's like fear without an object. Everything's great. But I hate it. Wouldn't that scare the shit out of you? I've got this show by the tail. I go around and around and around inside it like a hamster on speed. I've got a staff of thirty-five people. I've got the most important people in the world coming and going. It's working. The train is rolling and I can't stop it." He grins jauntily at a passing fan. His voice drops to a rough whisper. "I'm fucking miserable, Elliot."

"Hughie. Have a drink."

His hands go up in protection. "No no, I can't. I can't drink and do the show. Nor Valium or anything like that. See what I mean?"

"Maybe you need a vacation."

"No no, Jesus, no."

I look around. The room is full of stars, punch-through people. I recognize Woody Allen, staring into his soup. The late Carlos Baker, or someone like him, is in the rear of the room gazing back at me.

"Jesus, if I took a vacation I'd never come back."

"So quit."

All the fear and pain flow into his face at once. "Oh God, Elliot, no—it's everything I ever wanted, don't you get it? I can't let it go, if I did there'd be nothing left but a black hole with wind whistling on the other side and if I fell into *that* . . ."

He waits. I grope for the right thought and come up empty. "You know, I'm the wrong guy to talk to about this. Absolutely wrong. Especially at this particular moment."

"That's not true. Of all of us you're the one, guy. Don't fend me off. I couldn't talk to a shrink, I couldn't talk to a woman, I couldn't talk to my family—Jesus, don't you know who I am? I'm Yugo! How does fucking Yugo go up to somebody and say, 'I'm scared, friend, I'm scared'? Nobody understands the worm that poisons success, not unless they've known failure, right?"

"Right." Sure, anything. I signal frantically for another drink.

"You, Elliot, you're . . . intimate with failure. Your feet are in the rocks. You know what it is to bleed. Believe me, you're the only one I can talk to. . . ."

Let's get it straight: here's Yugo sitting there across from me, *the* Yugo, face on every supermarket slick, just bought a two-million-dollar pad in the Hamptons (so I read)—and he's asking me for emotional guidance because I'm "intimate with failure."

"Talk then, go ahead."

Something in my tone pushes his alert button. He repositions quickly, the adroit talk show host. "Now look, Elliot, I'm not casting aspersions—I'm looking up to you, up to your depth, your experience, your mind, you always had a better mind than I did. You're like a big brother to me, guy—" He actually wipes tears from his eyes. "You're my weather vane, that's it—I'm fucking storm-tossed, guy. And I'm looking to you for direction, for which end is up."

I put a hammerlock on Andrei (or is it Sergei?) as he floats by: "Another Scotch."

My problem is twofold: not only am I the last person in New York who should give advice to the confused, I am also profoundly unsympathetic to Yugo's complaint. And it's not just that he's rich, successful, impactful, masterful; there's something else. I'm mad at the sucker. Yeah, mad. It's been simmering for six months, ever since I approached him, at his own instigation, with an idea for a show. Just then I was struggling to get LifeForms off the ground and I pitched it to him this way: assemble a panel of lifestyle experts, psychologists, some examples of early achievers, Roman candles, flameouts. And me, the author. Call it something catchy like "LifeForms of the Rich and Famous." So what if it was a work-in-progress? After a featured appearance on *Yugo*, I'd have a contract within a week!

And how did Yugo respond to my pitch? A smile and a weird, uncharacteristic silence. I recognized the smile: it's the one he uses when he didn't catch what you just said but doesn't want to admit it. I call it the Denial Smile. A toothy wall signaling a warp in his rhythm.

I waited a few minutes and made the pitch again. Again, the smile and no comment, nothing—

"You going to answer me?" I said after a minute.

"Hm?"

"I just pitched you LifeForms. Twice. What is this, are we in the Twilight Zone?"

The smile dimmed. He squirmed. "Okay, I didn't want to

have to say this, but here goes: I have this problem, Elliot—
I'm in the big leagues. *Yugo* is not a local chat show. I go
head-to-head with Donahue, Oprah, Geraldo. If I get caught
off base I'm rat bait."

"LifeForms is off base?"

He shrugs miserably. "Unless you publish it, I'm afraid so.
Elliot, whatever it is you're selling, you have to make it exist
in the world. Otherwise I can't consider it. When the book's
coming out, then we'll talk, okay big fella?"

Big fella.

And this from the friend of my youth, Hughie McDonough, who, without me, would've flunked fifth form.

Yes, I admit it: to this very millisecond, I'm still nursing a
monstrous grudge.

The food has arrived. I ought to throw it in his thirty-watt
face right now. Oh, later. Later for my fury.

No, now.

"I have an idea," I say.

"What?"

"Do a show on your problem."

"Oh, come on—"

"No, I mean it. Come out of the closet. Bring on a couple
of shrinks, experts on fear of success, get hold of some stars,
corporate high flyers, people who had unaccountable nervous
breakdowns when they got what they wanted."

"Hm." He's taking the bait.

"Then bring me on as perspective, an old friend, known
you since the flood—yeah, your old pal, author of *LifeForms*,
a work-in-progress—"

"Please, Elliot—" Clearly he had forgotten the whole affair—these lightweight extroverts can't keep an idea in their
heads for more than ten seconds—but now it has returned to
splatter on his head, the wet pancake he flipped into the
stratosphere six months ago. "Elliot, don't do this to me."

"To you? To you?"

"I've come to you, I'm vulnerable—"

"Oh, give me a break, you're indulging yourself in vulnera-
bility just like you're buying new houses, fucking new
women. This is spiritual materialism. Tomorrow you'll be
trying out manic depression, next week it'll be impotence."
(Said with a shudder.)

"Cool your voice, will you?" He grins around the room. A waiter misinterprets the grin as a summons.

"Yes, sir?"

"No no, everything's fine."

I can't seem to make a drink last. "Bring me a Scotch and one for him."

"No, not for me."

"Bring two, do you understand?" I bellow.

The waiter looks at Yugo.

"All right, all right. That's fine." Yugo winks broadly and flashes the Denial Smile until the waiter is gone. "Simmer down," he hisses at me. "You trying to get us thrown out of here?"

"I'm trying to send you a message."

"Okay, I get the goddamned message. I owe you one, I know I do. I owe you a fucking show. You name it. Only please please don't shit on my head, not today, I can't stand it."

The Scotches arrive. I drink both of them. I try to stop shitting on his head, but from the look of numb horror that has settled into his face, I'm not so sure how well it's working. I'm thinking I really should turn my attention to blotting up some of this booze with food when an arc of electricity licks at my central nervous system and I am suddenly alert. Yes, there is an odor of danger here, no mistake about it—someone is in here, somebody who has a bead on me. I can feel it in every follicle. Someone has tracked me to the Russian Tea Room and intends to do me harm. Absurdly, the thought reels through my head that Pappy is lurking, probing me with his telepathic death beam, the one he chilled Hemingway with. He is jamming my mind from somewhere in this very room—

I stagger to my feet. No, the beam is coming from another source. I raise my arm and point stiffly toward a table in the rear.

"You, Baker, stop staring at me!"

Looking remarkably alive, Carlos Baker focuses on neutral space as he rises and retreats toward the men's room. A few tables away Woody Allen gathers up his book and slinks toward the door, soup half finished. Yugo covers his face with his hands.

"That's it," he says to his lap. Forcing a grin, he looks up and waves a finger at one of the Russians. "We're outa here," he mutters through his teeth.

"Wait a minute. What about lunch? Didn't we come here for lunch?"

"I've lost my appetite. Check, Andrei?"

I don't remember exactly how I got from there to here, all I know is I'm on Seventh Avenue, pacing autistically back and forth in front of a newsstand near Carnegie Hall. A repetitive annoyance is piercing my brain space. It's one of those pay phones that rings and rings and rings with hopeless persistence until someone, in this case me, has the balls to pick it up. "Hello?" I hear nothing, then a cackle (a *hee-hee*?) or is it simple static, a momentary burst of sunspot interference?

"Get off the fucking line!" My savagery resounds in my ears. No wonder Yugo drifted away without saying good-bye. "Excuse me," I mumble to whomever or whatever is out there. "Sorry, didn't mean to be so abrupt." But nothing is on the line but the crackle of empty space.

Softly, so softly that, with luck, not even God will hear, I hang up.

FORTY

IT'S ABOUT TIME to get into my relationship with Ernest Hemingway. Oh yes, I had one, too, and mine was real. As real as it gets by mail, anyway. It was the spring of 1961; I was thirteen, a dangerous age, and (as I came to understand, after five years of therapy) trying to deal with the fact that I despised my father, who was a florid show-off of a professor, a Lit Crit bombast artist at my own school, Columbia, a bludgeon of a dad with a perverse streak that led him to undermine me with countless sophisticated tortures that I don't care to go into here. Something in Hemingway's affable, bearish looks reached out to me. This (therapy revealed years later) was the dad mine might have been; one who beamed on his offspring with kindly forbearance, took them hunting and fishing, told them secrets. I wrote him a letter. I have the copy here in my hand. I reads:

Dear Mr. Hemingway:
I have read and loved your book, The Old Man and the Sea. *I would like to be a writer myself someday. My dad has said it is a stupid idea and that writers don't live very long and other disparaging things. Obviously you are an excellent example of a writer who has lived a long time. Do you think you could send me some advice about how to be a writer? I am working on three novels called* The Bronze Hammer, In Silver Service, *and* Ages of Gold. *They are roughly about the history of mankind. Would you read them when I am finished? I am thirteen years old. How old are your sons? Would it be possible to meet them and perhaps visit you next Christmas? I wonder if it is worth it, after all those years, to have spent so much time alone with your writing. Can you tell me? Also: is there a special season of the year when you get your best writing done?*

Yours truly,
Elliot McGuire

The projected trilogy, of course, was a bald lie, I was working on nothing of the sort. What I really wanted was for EH to be impressed, extend a fatherly hand, tell me I was a terrific kid with the future written all over me. What came back two weeks later sent me into shock:

Dear Elliot:
What you describe is not impossible but roughly equivalent to sending yourself off Niagara Falls in a pickle barrel. Your dad is correct in that a writer's life appears stupid to 90% of the rest of us and appearances count for realities, practically speaking, at least in American life. You will be assumed to be a dolt. You may be a dolt. I don't write anymore because I am tired of living like a dolt. Although it may be too late for me, you have time: go to medical school, law school, take a flyer in business. If I could do it

over I would choose the world (as it is, have ham-strung
myself trying to have both, but that's a shaggy dog story and
I can't remember things long enough these days to get to the
end). Elliot (that is your name, Elliot?) don't write me
again; nothing personal, just that your letter made me sad.
Sadness is all over things in this place. There is a fine
spring dryness in the air and the mud has thawed just
enough for good walking. But sad. Do you have a gun?
Gun safety is very important. Obey your father. Honor your
mother.

Best always,
Ernest Hemingway

All the signs were there: the horror to come was etched into every line. But I knew nothing about the hospital, the shock treatments, the slow dimming out of that miraculous machine, the Hemingway brain. I knew nothing of *nada* and the endless final darkness of death. Damn it, I had written from my heart to Papa Hemingway, the delightful roguish whitebeard who lived in the pages of *Field and Stream* and *Life*. And I was stung by his reply.

I waited almost two months before I wrote back:

Dear Mr. Hemingway:
I don't think you have a right to say, "obey your father."
You don't know my father. I am a writer. It is my destiny
to be a writer and you should not stand in the way of
destiny. You think it is a mistake to be a writer, well that
is your mistake, not mine. I think it is necessary to know
yourself and know when it is time to take action. Some
writers perhaps are "dolts," but why should that keep me
from fulfilling my destiny? Do you know what your destiny
is? You ought to; maybe then you would choose the world,
if that's what you really want, and stop giving bad advice
to hopeful young writers like me.

Yours truly,
Elliot McGuire

Three days after I mailed the letter, EH shot himself. *How do you like it now, gentlemen?*

And what did it feel like? Even now, nearly thirty years later, my heart sinks and my face burns with guilt and shame as I reread my petulant little outburst. Only later, when I was sure Hemingway hadn't kept it, was I able to relax my fear that someday I would be exposed (a Hemingway scholar, yet!) as the teenage egomaniac whose snotty letter pushed Papa over the edge.

Letters.

I'm sitting on my living room floor, sifting through the wreckage of my early life. Paper piles high and overflows— relics of college days, my years as a young Hemingway scholar on the make, my analysis. It's all here, too much of it. Too much evidence of a life sputteringly misspent, a flatulent Life-Form, a dribbling away of the choice years of youth and early maturity.

Today I plan to burn it all, every last scrap.

Oh, I know exactly what I'm doing. After Key West, I put myself through a little course of LifeForm analysis and reached the obvious conclusion that I was overdue for a Life-Spurt. LifeForms protocol dictates that, before you move on to Act III, you strike the set of Act II. Everything must go— this is according to my own authority. Physician, heal thyself! Purify! Cauterize! Thrust that unsightly stump of a life into the fire!

First, however, I am taking one last look—and it's been going on pretty much nonstop for three days now. There's a lot to sift through. Stacks of letters. Shoe boxes of three-by-five notecards from projects that go all the way back to the first firecracker I ever set off in the literary world (I was still an undergraduate), my article in *Fitzgerald-Hemingway Review*. It was "Hemingway's Phallus: Life Imitates Form," the paper that first attracted Carlos Baker's attention and got me "tea" with The Widow. (Baker was avuncular and laudatory, Miss Mary was helpful but standoffish—after all, I was writing about her dead husband's plumbing!)

There's my (yuck) fiction—six or eight stories, plus an aborted novel, written in the heat of youth and powered by a vision of beating EH at his own game. It's all here: tough, weary young main character plagued by unspoken family se-crets, the irresistible lure of blood, the plague of infinite knowingness. The novel follows the adventures of a doomed and disaffected male college student who wanders to Spain in search of his soul and is taught bullfighting by a suicidal ex-matador. Sound familiar? Into the fire . . .

There are the card files from my more recent hack period—mostly pseudonymous biographies (I wrote as "Wilfred Redfield"). There's Cuthbert Forbes, founder of the International Congress of Good Will . . . dog trainer Rod "Buck" Thorne . . . Lt. Col. Jonathan Lipsky, astronaut and tomato grower . . . lumber king Everett Greene . . . Joey "the Plumber" Palumbo, the mafia don who stiffed me . . . The list goes on and on. Author Redfield certainly was a prolific son of a gun!

But there's nothing here worth saving. The past may have its uses, but this crap is tugging backwards on my spirit like a web of carnivorous tentacles. Let's burn it all! On to the future—

Ah! An early obituary draft. Sven started me on this sort of thing (Sven the Jungian). I used to do them in the subway instead of crossword puzzles.

Writer and thinker Elliot McGuire died today at his South Hampton, Long Island, summer home, age ninety-two. Author of twelve novels (this is definitely dated!) *McGuire rose to equal rank with Mark Twain, Henry James, Herman Melville, and Ernest Hemingway, as a voice of unsurpassed power and originality in American letters. . . .*

Yes, there's no time like the future!

Here's a little fantasy magazine feature (a LifeClip) from the end of my life.

Nobel laureate Elliot McGuire is his own best example of maximum achievement in the second half of life. After an abbreviated career as a literary scholar, McGuire toiled anonymously for 15 years as a corporate historian, ghost writer, and private biographer. Then, at age forty, he electrified the publishing world with his monumental LifeForms.

McGuire's intelligent eyes mirror his struggle to accommodate the "lost" period of his life. "I was in a descending retrograde vortex—living in reverse, if you will. NOT getting on as a scholar, NOT having a family, NOT undertaking adventurous projects, NOT forming friendships with my peers, NOT establishing a foothold, a beachhead, NOT, NOT, NOT! The one thing I did do was learn the craft of biography, and this led me to what we now know as LifeForms. Once LifeForms was off the ground I was a different person. I soared."

I think I'll save this. I like the soaring image. Flapping like a giant duck, rising from my own ashes and all that. The Phoenix is my signature myth after all—Sven pointed that out years ago. I'm always setting myself ablaze along with everything around me, a sort of LifeForms arsonist, then transcending obliteration into some form of new life. Although N.B.: speaking as a biographer I do feel obliged to ask—is it really possible, even remotely, to isolate the essence, the fine wine, the sine qua non of "a life"?

Whenever I go on like this, Kristin, my ex-stepmother (or whatever the hell she is at this point) reminds me that I'm only a pretend intellectual and shouldn't try to sound like the real thing. Professional philosophers like herself, she says, handle matters like this all the time; what seems like the absolute World Riddle to me could be dealt with in a few quick strokes of killer logic by her or any one of her colleagues.

The first time she threw this at me was the night of my father's memorial service (a lapsed Catholic, he disdained funerals). She had handled the arrangements with her customary precision and, when it was over, invited me back to the apartment for a glass of sherry and to tell me she had set me up with a chunk of Dad's money—generous, considering she didn't have to give me a penny (the old man certainly hadn't). I stayed on, drank a couple of bottles of wine, and we ended up in bed. Even though Kris was younger than I was, she had always played the stepmother and I had fallen into the complimentary role of balky son. Now with the Oedipal theme acting on me like an aphrodisiac I took the big risk and opened my mind to her. There, naked in my dead father's bed, in between ravishings of the widow, I unveiled a very early, very meek attempt at a theory of life-as-form—and got more or less the response noted above. Since I was still suffering through my flameout as a Hemingway scholar, you can imagine what Kris's disdain did to my confidence level.

Practically speaking, of course, my intellectual Waterloo was that long-ago Hemingway Dinner, the night I sloshed my career, as well as Yvonne Scudder Vinson, in cheap champagne. Without that particular disaster I might well have gone on to be, as Howie Ritz says, one of the leading Hemingway biographers. But I would also have been a psychological wreck. In fact, when I stood up to make my toast that night, I was already demolished goods, already seared by venturing too far inside Hemingway's danger zone. Thank God for the infamy! By now I would certainly be a walking mass of scar tissue.

In any case, for a while after the memorial service, Kristin and I lived on as roommates in the rambling old apartment, not caring what anybody thought about it. She occasionally craved my services, enjoyed my companionship, but wanted nothing to do with my mind. When I finally quit the Oedipal nest, it was because my mind, after years of abuse, struck back. I simply stopped being able to maintain peak performance with Kristin. This, she realized after logical analysis, was unacceptable; she started seeing a man (that is, another man) and I was more or less reduced to the status of a lodger. Then the other man moved in, a tall Hungarian émigré with legs like telephone poles, a classicist. He and I treated each other with exquisite consideration but a ménage à trois was out of the question. I found my own place.

About that time an old prep school buddy of Yugo's and mine offered me a ridiculously large amount of money to write a corporate history of Dyno Computers, a rival of IBM in the personal computer sphere. This piece of work led to a vanity bio of Dyno's founder and CEO, Chester Wu—and I was made. The assignments continued in an unbroken line leading right up to (and presumably ending with) Hemingway assassin Eric "Pappy" Markham.

And what was so wrong with that? Couldn't it have sufficed? Why are one percent of us driven to grace the world with a Great Gift while the other ninety-nine couldn't care less? What was the matter with me? Why couldn't I give up my One Percent Club membership? Just go to a job in the morning, then relax and consume, watch the best TV, see the choice movies, cuddle with my wife, play with my kids? Look at Howie Ritz—no desire to be the Messiah; that's the way! Then look at me: "Excuse me, excuse me, I have a message for humanity."

All kidding aside, I've begun to wonder if this could be a sickness, this message business.

And if so, how to heal myself?

Self-immolation? Then start the fire.

First, however, there's a job to be done. Lay in some provisions. Lock the doors. Bring on *I Killed Hemingway.*

FORTY-ONE

WHEN YOU WRITE an entire book in what amounts to a single three-month sitting, it does funny things to your perception of time. Whole uninspired stretches of calendar fly by as unmarked non-instants, while the fiery twenty-minute breakthroughs seem to extend into eternity. On the macro scale, you hardly even notice major seasonal changes. The present recycles so subtly that any distinction between "now" and "then" is impossibly blurred. So, just as you're getting used to your warm-weather things, snowstorms are raging in the parks and streets and, damn it, you have to admit that, unbeknownst to your slipping and sliding inner time scale, a strange new season has taken up occupancy outdoors.

Obviously I didn't get at it right away. Excessive boozing had a lot to do with that. What was the problem? Multiple: LifeForms on hold. No up-front advance money, thanks to the stupid deal I negotiated with Pappy. On top of that, I saw the end of my per diem from W&D—even my "editing" fee wouldn't be payable until I submitted a finished manuscript.

I also drank because of what I could only call a relapse of Hemo-phobia. Symptoms: threatening dreams, ugly reveries, waves of paranoid anxiety associated with any old man who happened to resemble Hemingway (or Pappy).

But no matter—I had to get moving.

I woke up one morning and poured out all my booze. It was time.

Strategy: treat it like any other project. Jump in and go at it with both feet. That morning excitement began to flow back into it for me. I realized that, as a radical theorist, I was breaking new ground. Everything was grist for my mill.

My neighbor upstairs, Magdalena, has for some time been working on an encyclopedic cookbook which she figures will clock in at seven hundred pages and take six years to complete. She's in the "chicken" phase now—meaning she tests eight or ten chicken recipes a night up there and since she lives alone too, needs help dealing with the leftovers. Thanks to Magdalena, not once during the winter was I short on animal protein.

By then I was transcribing my tapes, reliving the weeks in Key West, an unexpectedly creepy experience. At first the very sound of Pappy's recorded voice would throw me into a kind of Hemo-phobic panic. But by Thanksgiving (chicken à la turkey up at Magdalena's) my mood had shifted. I was no longer suffering sweats, sleepless nights, nightmares of Pappy drawing my blood or whatnot. I was, in fact, in a state of high excitement over the material.

My working view was this: we had entered a new era of intellectual history. Bottom-line veracity (whatever that had been) now paled before *evident* biographical verisimilitude.

If it quacked like a duck, by God, it *was* a duck!

Renwick was right: biography *was* entertainment! Go with the story. Help the story. What the hell, *embellish* the story!

By Christmas I was working with the transcripts, paraphrasing, positioning the material, sketching in transitions, waking every morning clearheaded and full of enthusiasm for the weirdest twist of all: my own personal creative additions to *I Killed Hemingway.*

It began innocently enough: I remembered Pappy mentioning a shooting in Ezra Pound's flat and I realized he had never got around to telling me about it. He had no phone, of course; what was I supposed to do, fly back to Key West? Skip it altogether? Certainly he couldn't write it himself—not with Hemingway's hand on his brain. But there was another alternative: sketch it in, re-imagine it, *write it myself!*

That's all it took to turn me into Pappy's literal co-creator. I found I could easily mimic his voice on the page:

> *"This le Chat character looked skinny and girlish, but if he got mad, his eyes widened and he seemed to grow two or three inches. He was yelling at the dealer, who had apparently burned him, and before you knew it he had a*

*pistol in his hand and would've killed the bastard right
then and there but Ezra did something so crazy, so beautiful, I could've kissed him. He stepped in front of the gun
and said: 'Listen here, if you want to spill blood, spill the
blood of a poet!' Said it in French, pointing at the ceiling.
Le Chat. What a dude! He raised his pistol like a duelist
and walked around Ezra, right up to the dealer, and shot
him in the butt, point-blank . . ."*

By the time I was through, I had added so many anecdotes,
so much wordage, that I had virtually lost track of whose
story was whose. It didn't matter. They all fit. They were
appropriate. Most of all they were *convincing*. I had stretched
biography to its ultimate limit—the flashpoint at which fiction, events imagined by an author alone, became truth.

Around Christmas I decided to take a break—a mistake, of
course, since as soon as I had time to be lonely, I was swamped
by a paralyzing depression. Rereading my stuff I could see that
though it was certainly adequate, it lacked the verve, the pul-
sation, the sheer living presence of Pappy's. It was inferior, in
terms of gut creativity—even in terms of my own standard,
convincing. Let's face it, once again the old goat had outcocked
me and I knew it.

On a howling Christmas Eve I decided I wanted a tree. They
were selling them on the sidewalk up on Fourteenth Street, a
huddled bunch of evergreen survivors. I took home a
scrawny, table-sized fir that was as lonely and discarded as I
was. I dried it with a hair dryer, trimmed it with some plastic
balls and tinsel and a thin strand of blinking lights, talked to
it until I could see it was feeling better. *Noël.*

It wasn't long before I was back on the job. The actual
catalyst was a New Year's phone call from Craig, who had
spent two tortured hours in Sir Harry's private jet en route
from Chicago and had just that moment deplaned, stinging
from a tongue-lashing. "He's absolutely seething," he shouted
at me through an airport phone. "Elliot, if you value my job,
my life, our friendship, I beg you—*finish up!*"

All right. I hung up the phone and got down to it.

As I've said before (and Hollywood knows it well) nothing is more deadly dull than a writer writing, so let me put it in a short-form version with some punch.

MONTAGE: Writer humps at the word processor. Days without shaving, eating, bathing. Erratic sleep patterns. Binges of feverish performance followed by dying falls into bed, spells of blank unconsciousness waking into day or night. Before long, Writer is hot, bumping and grinding in orgasmic fits. Whole paragraphs seem to splatter onto the screen like hunks of human seed.

> "Hemmy said, 'C'mon, let's go to Gertrude's in drag.' So we went over to the rue de Rivoli and bought a couple of cheap frocks, the biggest we could find, and a girl I knew made up our faces. Then we had a few drinks and took a cab to Gertrude's. Alice Toklas didn't know what to do with us—little beads of sweat popped out of her upper lip, and as she led us up to Gertrude, her eyes were like hub-caps. 'Deux Mesdemoiselles, Gertrude—' she said, so shook she forgot the phony names we had given. Gertrude reared back and gave us the once-over several times over. 'Well, my dears, what do you do—write, paint?' Hemmy kept an absolute straight face: 'We're Greco-Roman wrestlers, Miss Stein, and we'll take on any bitch here, the dirtier the better. How 'bout yourself, want to pull up your skirts and get down in the mud with us?' "

But always there, coming and going like an intermittent ache, was the truth: Pappy's stuff had more zip to it, more creative reach and energy than mine. There was no way around it: the harder I tried to match him, top him, the clearer it showed. Pappy Markham, nonwriter, bum, was beating me at my own game.

Occasionally there were interludes. A Christmas card from Lynn turned into a flurry of full-blown correspondence.

Okay, sure I was glad. Except that, after she had zoned me out that day at Pappy's, I had pretty successfully put her out of my mind, and now she was back there, haunting, lovely, available (she told me), mine if I wished, if I could . . . and the letters made it tantalizingly palpable.

We could try again if that's important. Any number of times, I don't care. . . . And I'm sorry I was so cold to you but I saw how needlessly tortured you were by the purely physical part of it and wanted to do something, anything, to get you off the hook. So instinctively I just did what I always do—pulled back, went into noncommunication mode, retreated. Sorry, Elliot. I mean that.

I answered that it hadn't really affected me that much (a lie). Anyway, I explained, I was shy of commitment to just one woman, relationships in general, needed my space to myself etc. and had been working on this with my therapist for years. Impotence was not my style (I wrote), and if I ever made it back to Key West (doubtful) I'd be myself again and would be sure to make it up to her tenfold.

This last bit of swagger led her to respond with an open invitation and prompted the following: ". . . tell me (and I'll tell you back) some kinds of things you like to do or have done. . . ."

Soft-core wish lists flew hotly back and forth but the novelty died pretty quickly and we both seemed to realize that, given who we really were, something else was going on here, something other than common smut.

She told me more about her extraterrestrial fantasies. I challenged her on logical grounds (good therapy for phobias, even Sven, the Jungian, says so)—why, for instance, would they always mess with people like her, just plain folks whose stories would never be believed? If they're really out there, why not reveal themselves to a George Bush, a Nelson Mandela, a Ralph Nader? Even someone like Carl Sagan?

Of course she had chewed extensively on that very question. The answer—obvious, once I thought about it—was that high visibility would blow their cover. They were anonymous researchers, not diplomatic emissaries. (The name Carl Sagan, by the way, was apparently a surefire laugh out in space. Brantly Swann had said it's the punchline of an intergalactic knock-knock joke that defies translation.)

In her last letter (I never answered it), she fired this shot across my bow:

Elliot, I wonder if I would be half so afflicted with this thing if I were in love. I mean real, spiritual, two-way love, giving and receiving. I used to have sex a lot because I thought it would keep them away—like the old Hindu belief that you can't die while in a state of deep meditation—but, like suppose I had a man who loved me and I loved him back, and we hung out together and slept together and that sort of thing? Doesn't it seem logical to you that they might steer clear of happy people? When I'm bad I keep thinking it's misery itself that might draw them, like blood draws sharks, and that sends me into a panic. I mean, when it's like that, I'm putting out incredibly strong signals—you know, take me out of all this, I'm dangling, disconnected, ready to drop off the earth. It's the times I'm most miserable that I'm most afraid of them. I mean, what if you came back, and you lived with me, would they still want me?

I had no answer.
I didn't dare answer.

So the winter passed, a rich brew of private events, as *I Killed Hemingway* struggled to be born, survived infancy, and grew into a whopping handsome stack of sizzling pages. Then one day it was done. I printed out two copies, boxed one, and set off through a snowstorm to hand-deliver it to Warren & Dudge.

Then I came home, sat down with the other copy and read it, start to finish.

It was trash.

FORTY-TWO

SO, DONE.

Done now for nearly a month and still I'm suffering from the crash, the spreading bruise, the let-down. Black bottom, EH called it. As soon as the goddamned book was out of my hands my spirit took a dip. When I reread it at home the dip turned into a dive. Now I'm nosing the bottom and it's awfully cold and dark down here.

Oh yeah, I'm in terrific shape. Debts. Still no money. Nothing but big black clouds on the horizon. Surely the advance from W&D for *LifeForms* (when they finally decide to kick it over) will help, but my guess is it won't go far enough. I need a substantial grubstake, something to maneuver with, to give me some running room.

Yugo, with all his bucks, would certainly come through, but after that disastrous birthday lunch, I don't have what it takes to approach him for spare change. Astrid is rich too, but I'm not about to creep back to Astrid, hat in hand.

This is one of the ways I torture myself when old Black Bottom comes around. I spend whole days, like today (a stunning Currier & Ives kind of day, a day to be out ice skating, brunching, driving to Vermont with skis on the rack) worrying about money.

In the old days, whenever I needed temporary funds I could always turn to Kristin. We've been out of touch, but perhaps that's good: I turn up out of the blue with a breezy request for a few bucks to tide me over. Nothing outlandish about that—as long as she doesn't make me squirm. And this way I'd be keeping it literally *en famille.*

I'm watching an attractive couple make their way up Bank Street, languidly, playfully nudging each other every few steps. They are young, in love. At the corner, they step into a spiffy little Porsche and start to neck. They are rich. I have to do something about my situation. I pick up the phone and dial, rehearsing mentally what I'm going to say.

"Look, Kris, the problem is cash flow—I mean, checks are being cut for me all over town, but the time element's all screwed up. So it's temporary, a bridge loan—would you like me to pay interest?"

That's always a good move—offer to pay interest.

Only, her response is not as smooth as I had hoped.

"Elliot, this is not going to work. We have to talk."

A whiff of ancient mortification has me suddenly upset. "Kris, don't put me through this."

"Come over, we need to sit down and have a talk."

"We can talk, fine, but don't make the money conditional, that's all I ask."

"Forgive me, but where do you get off, Elliot, asking for unconditional money? Why should you, with your record, get money without conditions?"

Why? Because it's mine, damn it. Because it belonged to my own blood mother. Because it was my future, my patrimony, before you were ever even born. Because we're all the family that's left, Step-mommy Dearest. Or because I fucked you faithfully for as long as I could. Reasons, reasons, reasons—do you want an argument? I'll give you an argument.

But why waste the breath? "Okay, half hour. Will Lazlo be there?"

"Lazlo is . . . Lazlo has moved. Justin will be here."

"Oh."

There's a long silence. Justin, whoever that is, is obviously in earshot.

"I get it. See you in a half hour."

FORTY-THREE

IT'S ALL SO familiar. The half-moon curve of Riverside Drive; the polished brass and fancy alabaster of the lobby; Augie, the old doorman, who remembers me in all my phases, sweet little boy, smart-aleck kid, Oedipal motherfucker.

"So you a professor now, Elliot, lika you dad?"

"That's right, Augie." What the hell, he's an old man, I know what he wants to hear: everything turned out all right.

"Where you teach?"

"The New School, NYU."

"Atta boy!"

The elevator door opens. I almost expect to see the ghost of my mom, dark and pretty again, herding my own small self through the lobby and out to the street to walk me down to St. Hilda's and St. Hugh's. She never really cared if we were late. Sometimes we would even hook over to Broadway for a "second breakfast"—coffee for her, a cherry Danish for me.

I hear the peephole click, then a moment later Kristin opens the door and there she is, shapeless in her trademark white sweats. She's aging, too, I realize with a shock. There's gray in her hair and her glasses seem thicker. When she smiles, little networks of wrinkles appear. *They all go into the dark.* . . . She gives me a kiss on each cheek and a quick hug, hunching forward so our bodies won't come together.

"Hello, darling."

She's most motherly, as she leads me into the living room, which has undergone a complete change of decor since the last time I was here. In the years after I replaced my dad as Kristin's lover, the rambling apartment remained pretty much as it had always been in my childhood. It was an academic's den in those days, full of pipe smoke, oak paneling, books everywhere. A calculated slovenliness was cultivated by my dad, who never did anything without calculation.

Now minimalism reigns: everything is black, the exact opposite of my place on Bank Street. There are no curtains, no rugs. Here and there a chair, a chrome end table, a skinny Italian lamp. A black leather sofa dominates the living room. My bedroom is now a workout room for the new boyfriend, Justin, who climbs off one of his Nautilus machines long enough to crush my knuckles with sincere fellow feeling. As Kristin plunks me down on the sofa and goes for coffee, my memories flow away in a river of black. Only the view of the Palisades hasn't changed.

"I'm glad you met Justin," she says, pushing her glasses back up her nose.

"He seems like a nice fellow. What does he do?"

"Astrophysics. Just came to Columbia from Berkeley, the NASA Mars program. Let's see: astronaut trainee, does triathlons, lifts weights, also a rock climber, a little rugby, a little polo. Races power boats." She reels it off with restraint, but clearly the balance of youth, brains, and brawn turns her on as she contemplates the swamp of her forties. No more white-maned lions for Kristin—she only needed that when she was an ambitious kid—now that she's a lioness herself (with tenure at Barnard) she does her own hunting.

"What happened to Lazlo? I liked Lazlo."

She shrugs as if to say, Who knows? Ask Lazlo. "Chemistry is mysterious. He began to lose his."

"Mm. Interesting, isn't it, how chemistry translates into structural engineering? Lose your chemistry and all of a sudden your buttress won't fly."

"Elliot's little joke."

"You know why I'm here, Kris. Please, let's talk."

"What is it you need? Precisely."

"Fifty."

"Fifty dollars?"

"Fifty thousand dollars."

Long pause. From my bedroom comes the sound of Justin pumping iron—loud grunts and great thunderous whomps as the giant barbells hit the floor. I remember our neighbors, the Goldsteins, who used to bitch and moan from the apartment below when I rolled as much as a single marble across that floor.

"Fifty thousand dollars!" She can hardly mouth the words. "Are you kidding?"

"For one month. That's all, one lousy month."

More groans from Justin. Kristin looks vaguely in the direction of the racket.

"One month."

She's up now, pacing back and forth in front of the picture window. "No. It's not a month. Even if it were, there's a larger principle at work here."

"No, there isn't. Don't intellectualize this. I simply need to borrow some cash—"

"No. Absolutely not. Try to remember that I'm not your stepmother anymore. We ended that phase. Nor are we lovers. We never talk, never see each other. We have no relationship, none. Now: I was very generous with the money I got from your father because I didn't agree with him that you were a wastrel and weak-willed and all that—or if you were, much of it was his own damned fault. I set you up. I gave again and again. I've shoveled it out to you on many occasions, but that phase is over, too. I'm not giving you any more money."

"Kris, it's not for me, it's for LifeForms."

She tosses off a laugh. "LifeForms—that piece of pseudo-intellectual trash."

"Don't start."

"All right, I won't, but please—don't try to cast me as some sort of a white knight for LifeForms. God, I might somehow end up on your letterhead and get my tenure revoked."

"Thank you, I do love sarcasm."

"Well, what do you expect? I've watched you for years: you're a sweet guy, Elliot, but let's face it, you weren't even able to hang in there as a serious biographer. I mean, *biography*, for goodness sake! Is there anything more brain-dead than biography?"

"I'm working on that."

"With LifeForms? Give me a break."

"Not with LifeForms. With something way beyond Life-Forms—something that's going to blow biography sky-high and have reverberations right on through historiography, philosophy, critical theory, across the board."

"Should I sit down for this?"

"Never mind." My voice is trembling. "I'll tell you this much, though: it's based on something awfully damned close to one of your own pet notions."

"Mm, which one?"

"Truth as rhetorical persuasion. Only I take it much, much farther—"

"Oh, spare me, Elliot."

"Kris, I need money! Desperately!"

"No! You need a brain!"

"Why? Why, goddamn it? LifeForms isn't Relativity Theory, it's self-help. You have no moral right to turn me away. I'm helping people! Unlike you, I'm using intelligence to turn people's lives around and make them live better, longer—"

"Listen, sweetheart, there are two things about your life you ought to accept: one, don't try to play in the intellectual big leagues. And two: you are not guru material. I'm awfully sorry, but there it is."

"Don't, Kris, don't do this."

A red stain of rage is spreading across my sight lines.

"I mean, don't come here looking for flowing nipples, Elliot. I've dried up for you and you ought to be grateful, because you know what? This is the only way you're going to become anything more than a moral paraplegic."

Suddenly, like something out of one of Myron Skolnik's slasher pictures, I leap up from the sofa and spring at her, pinning her against the picture window. Her glasses slide down to the end of her nose but she can't push them back because I have both her wrists gripped tight. I see her eyes widen with animal fear. Through the sweats I feel her body, plumper than I remember it, her heavy breasts flattening against me.

What now? Push her through the window? Send her flying eight stories to the street below?

"Justin—!" she half pants, half shrieks. "Justin, my God! He's, he's, he's—"

At that moment there comes a yowl of shock and anger from the exercise room, accompanied by a double-whomp and silence, then stunned groans. Justin is in what sounds like excruciating pain.

"Unnh! Kristin—"

As quickly as it came, the rage deserts me and I let go, rocking back on my feet. Kristin pulls free and runs to Justin in horror.

"Oh God, he's crushed himself!" she shouts from the exercise room.

I compose myself as best I can and stroll after her.

Trapped on the bench, the astrophysicist is writhing on his back, pinned under what looks like half a ton of blue iron. One arm is apparently useless; with the other, he paws ineffectually at the massive barbell, which lies across his neck.

"I think one of my pecs snapped."

Kristin glares at him. She struggles to lift the barbell. Not a chance.

"Elliot, for God's sake help us, please!"

"I don't know. I'm not at all sure I could even attempt it—moral paraplegic that I am."

"What?"

"Fifty K will do."

She blows a tangle of hair out of her face. "You complete shit—"

"Never mind, call nine-one-one, I'm leaving. No amount of money is worth the verbal abuse I'm getting here."

"Wait a minute, wait a minute, Elliot. Wait, okay?"

She trots heavily around the corner to a small desk in the hall and I can hear a fountain pen scribbling. While we wait, Justin and I exchange manly grins, mine sympathetic, his tinged with agony and bemusement.

"Here, here, take it," Kristin whimpers through her teeth,

as she flaps the check at me. "One month, Elliot. One month."

I take it and examine it carefully. "Wait, this is only twenty."

Through gritted teeth: "Take it or leave it."

Fair enough. I fold it slowly into my wallet and turn my attention to the barbell—it's not easy, but I put my whole body into it and manage to raise it an inch or so, high enough for him to slide free. He rolls off the bench and hits the floor like a side of beef. There is a steady banging from underneath the floor—the Goldsteins, I imagine (still alive?). In a diffuse fury, Kristin picks up a five-pound dumbbell and starts banging back. Justin nods at me from the floor in wordless gratitude. I've done my thing, I'm getting out of here.

In the elevator I wonder how close I came to murder. Second-degree murder, of course, but still . . . Unthinkable. Yet I'd better try to think about it, I'd better check myself out thoroughly. Back to Sven? But I can't afford him. LIFEFORMS AUTHOR WOUNDS ASTRONAUT, THROWS STEPMOM FROM 8TH FLOOR WINDOW. *Incest triangle ends in bloody death . . . !* Yes, it could have happened. I was just a synapse away and she knows it. The elevator door rolls open and there is Augie, beaming. My knees are shaky, I want to sit down, but not here, not under the gaze of this failing old keeper of the shards of my past.

"You wanta cab, Elliot?"

"No thanks, Augie." I keep my legs moving, out the door and around the corner toward Broadway.

No, I think it was just the illusion of attempted murder. I never actually tried to break the glass. The window just happened to be there, that's all, it was just a surface, something to push against, it might as well have been (should have been) a piece of solid wall. I'm no murderer. Let's not run away with this thing, let's keep it in its proper perspective. Sit down and think about it. Sit down before you fall down.

I slump onto a bench in the middle of Broadway, scattering the pigeons, moving the bag ladies over, sending a momentary ripple of suspicion through the crackies, the junkies, the off-duty whores.

I close my eyes and try to get a fix on Kris's LifeForm.

Nothing. I take a deep breath and try again. A blank screen. This is very disturbing. It's as if someone or something has been tampering with my head. An unseen hand has reached in and knocked my plug out of the wall—

Shit, my mouth is moving again.

Am I becoming one of these people, one of these New York crazies who thinks with his lips?

Once, on a fine spring day in Paris (this day burns in my memory) I stood up tall at a café table and announced to all Paris, all France, and especially to the French girl across the table from me, that within ten years I would be a major American novelist. I believed it. So did she. I could tell by the way her eyes widened and her mouth curled into a smile.

Well, naturally I wanted to be a novelist! When you peel away everything else, that's all I ever wanted.

That's what my fumbling attempts to connect with Hemingway were *really* all about—making that vision real. Even as I slipped and slid into Hemingway scholarship, the notion never completely drained away that I would jump ship at some point, go over the top with a work of fiction ("Here's to fiction").

When I read Hemingway, it was to mine him for his secrets.

What never occurred to me was that EH—in his mania for expertise—Hemingway, the great perfectionist, dead and gone though he was, would find a way to trash my attempts, freeze them in their tracks, choke them word by word.

So: nothing I ever wrote could be good enough. My fiction came out wooden, imitative, without style, stillborn. I was like a shy child struggling to improvise a secret poem in front of the Supreme Court. It got so bad that whenever I sat down to write I would break out in flopsweat. If a few words limped out onto the page, they were exactly wrong. Day after day, I choked.

Finally, I decided to hang up my skates for good. I didn't need this abuse. I would take Hemingway on some other day, some other way.

But this day in Paris, I forgot. And for that one moment (with EH's implacable ghost off napping), the rest of the world forgot too.

Some days are like that: a smell of spring, immortality in

the face of a girl, and suddenly you can do whatever it was you had given up on forever. Suddenly it's easy. How could it ever have seemed even remotely difficult, much less impossible?

It was a good day. A world-class day. In fact, if today (right now, sitting here mumbling to myself among the flotsam and jetsam of upper Broadway), if today someone offered me the chance to go back in time and die on that day, I would have to give it serious consideration.

But the offers aren't coming. So home, Elliot, home. Snow is threatening.

A day like today can only get worse.

FORTY-FOUR

IN THE MAIL here's a copy of a memo from Sir Harry Taymore to the Warren & Dudge sales force:

Prepublication response to Eric Markham's I Killed Hemingway *indicates we have a potential best-seller on our hands! Here is just a sampling:*

A LITERARY BOMBSHELL! *(Kirkus Reviews)*

FASCINATING NEW REVELATIONS . . . DESTINED TO TURN HEMINGWAY SCHOLARSHIP ON ITS HEAD! *(Publishers Weekly)*

IF YOU READ ONLY ONE BOOK THIS YEAR, THIS SHOULD BE IT! *(Variety)*

I Killed Hemingway *is shaping up to be one of our strongest titles in years. Sales support materials are in preparation and you are advised to pitch it strongly, starting now. Believe me when I say I fully expect it to run, not walk, out of the stores. You can quote me on this, chapter and verse!*

The production schedule has been hastened drastically,

on an initial print order of 100,000! The rest is up to you.
Tally-ho!

Sir Harry

P.S. I am proud to announce that we shall enjoy an oppor-
tunity to MEET THE AUTHOR at Spring Conference!

Clipped to the memo is a note: *Good show, Elliot! Sorry no*
royalties, but we'll make it up on LifeForms. Meanwhile, you've
got a champagne dinner coming to you, your choice of menu and
venue. Love & kisses, Craig.

Meet the author? Not Pappy, for God's sake, that would be
ridiculous. They must be plotting some way to stir me into the
soup. But then who besides Pappy even knows I wrote it? I
certainly haven't leveled with Craig. Well, in any case it would
be interesting, and a solid opportunity for LifeForms. I suppose I would have to go on TV, sign books in stores, perhaps
even tour with Pappy—a dicey prospect. But how would I
ever explain the genesis of the whole thing, the sleazy double
cross that led to my ghost authorship?

No, tempting as it seems, best to stay undercover.

Anyway I don't have time. Too busy pushing LifeForms.
Today I'm having lunch with PBS producer MacKenzie
Broadfoot. "Mac" is one of the can-do guys in public TV.
When he signs onto a project, money rains all over it. He
produced the *American Blood Feuds* series with Vincent Price
and *Concert Hall America*, with Dudley Moore and Chet At-
kins, and so on—the man never strikes out. Allegedly he's
seen my proposal; he took a phone call about it from Yugo
(who has been feeling guilty as hell ever since our lunch).
According to Yugo, he even bought into the notion of me as
the on-screen host.

The cab lets me out in front of Broadfoot's gilt-edged old
building, just across from the Metropolitan. The fact that
we're meeting here in this splendidly expensive piece of old
New York strikes me as a positive sign: clearly Mac wants to
talk terms—no office phones ringing off the hook, no fires to
fight.

After what seems like an interminable delay, he answers his
doorbell, an aging Erroll Flynn type, peering at me from his
puffy, hung-over, mustachioed face.

"McGuire?"

"Yes. Good morning." It is past two in the P.M.

He shows me in, mumbling something about the maid's day off, which is meant as an apology for the appalling mess—rumpled clothes everywhere (women's and men's), half-empty glasses with engorged cigarette butts floating next to lemon rinds. A wall of glass displays the museum across the street.

"Drink?"

"No thanks."

MacKenzie Broadfoot is about thirty-five, beefy and raffishly good-looking, rumpled as he is. After a brief coughing fit, he pulls a pack of Kools out of his bathrobe pocket and lights one up. He has the habit of exhaling through his mouth and sucking the smoke back in through his nostrils. We stand in his living room for a moment, awkwardly silent. He seems disoriented.

"Forgive me, McGuire," he says, "but I've forgotten why you're here. I mean, I knew we had a meeting. I guess. But the substance . . ." He trails off, making circular motions with his hands. I hear a toilet flush somewhere.

"LifeForms."

"I beg your pardon?"

"My proposal for a series."

"Ah. Sure, of course. What was it again?"

"LifeForms?"

A light layer of sweat sprouts across my face as the gravity of the situation dawns: I am going to have to tap dance my way in here. Desperate, I grasp at a straw. "Yugo? Didn't Yugo call you?"

"Oh, Yugo! Right, right, right, I've got it. Now things are falling into place." He laughs, coughs, motions toward a giant leather sofa that looks like it came from Bloomingdale's that morning. "Sit down, won't you? What can I get you? Coffee?"

"No thanks."

"You don't mind if I just nip into the kitchen and brew a cup for myself, do you? I can't get started in the morning without it."

He's back with his coffee in about five minutes, during which time I've gone to hell and back fighting the impulse to glug from the liter of Dewar's that sits on the coffee table an arm's length away. At one point a pretty woman in a rumpled

213

silk robe pads through the dining room on her way to the kitchen, ignoring me. I hear what sounds like an argument in spits and hisses and she pads back, reversing her route.

Broadfoot reappears, somewhat pulled together after his coffee. Whatever the argument was about, he's still pissed off from it. Irritation has replaced befuddlement in his manner and he wants to move this thing along.

"Okay, now, Yugo said—I forget what he said. Why don't we start from the beginning, okay? LifeForms is . . ." He extends a hand, palm up, and sits back, giving me the stage.

"Well, Mac, basically what LifeForms is, is a comprehensive life-reckoning system, kind of Platonic in character, that allows you to draw on the energy of your progress through time by determining your own unique life shape, or 'form,' and connecting that knowledge with a systematic appraisal of the major archetypal LifeForms, as I call them, that I've isolated and identified in my twenty years or so as a biographer." Pause for breath.

How are we doing? Not so good.

Broadfoot's face has frozen into a quizzical trance. He shakes his head as if to clear it. "I'm sorry. That went right by me. Let's try it again. If you had ten seconds to impart that information, what would you say?"

"I'd say that wouldn't be long enough."

"Oh, really?" One eyebrow flies up.

"Well, it is a series, after all. The idea has a richness to it that takes some time to, you know, develop."

"Hm." He puffs on his cigarette and glances at his watch. "Yugo spoke very highly of you, so I have to assume this is a solid idea, if we can just get to the root of it. Melinda—!"

"What," snaps the woman's voice.

"Come in here a minute."

Melinda stalks into the room and throws herself petulantly on the sofa beside him, momentarily flashing her rather considerable breasts as she regathers her robe.

"Explain it to Melinda. I'll just listen, okay?"

"We-e-ll."

"Go on. If she can figure it out, we may have a go here."

Melinda wraps her arms around herself and glares at Broadfoot. "What kind of crack is that? If I can get it, any idiot can get it, is that what you're saying?"

He shrugs. "Well, we're not making closed-circuit shows for neurosurgeons here. Somebody out there has to get it."

Furiously she turns her gaze on me and starts to tap the floor with her foot. "Go on."

"Well. Mac, this is obviously a bad time to—"

"No it isn't. It's perfect. This is the perfect time."

"Please go on," the girl says, her voice suddenly reassuring. Her gears have shifted so smoothly I realize where I've seen her before: on TV; she's an actress. She leans forward to take a cigarette and lets her robe flap open again. With a quick withering glance at Broadfoot she sits back and beams at me as though I were a crippled child. "Please, please," she coos, firing up the Kool with a fat sterling silver lighter from the coffee table.

"Okay. Okay. Sure." I feel my spirit start to belly over, like the *Titanic* on its way down. "Well: every life has a shape. It's like people. Every person has a shape—fat, thin, wasp-waist, stubby legs, whatever. The shape of your life is just as identifiable as the shape of your body."

"Okay." She's frowning with concentration.

"What LifeForms says is: you can literally alter the course of your life by changing that shape, that form. You can become more successful, live longer, be happier, by first understanding what your form is, and then by taking steps to improve it."

"Like breast implants," Broadfoot kicks in.

She glowers at him. "Shut up. Okay, I'm with you. Know your form. That's terrific. I love that."

"LifeForms would illustrate that basic idea by looking at the lives of ten or twelve famous individuals each of whom personifies the ten or twelve basic LifeForms. Shakespeare, Leonardo da Vinci, Oscar Wilde, Mozart, people like that."

"Good, good."

"Then we'd show how ordinary people exhibit these patterns. Then we'd follow a group of contemporary individuals as they go through the process of learning how to change their LifeForms for the better."

Broadfoot stubs out his fag and sits forward. Something is beginning to hook him.

"Hm. I get it. Self-help couched in a kind of highbrow

historic approach. Kind of a combination of *The Ascent of Man* and Richard Simmons."

"Sure." Whatever, whatever.

"And we'd have an on-screen host, of course."

"Of course—"

"Yes, of course. Somebody with a foot in both worlds. Cavett, perhaps. Or George Plimpton. Or—Jesus—*Mailer!*" He turns earnestly to Melinda. "What about Norman, honey, didn't he say he was looking for something the other night?"

I hear my voice rise. "I don't believe he was looking for this."

They both turn and blink at me.

"I mean—what I mean is, the host business, that's all taken care of. That's all set. Isn't it?"

"It is?"

"Yeah, didn't Yugo, didn't he . . . go into that?"

"I don't understand, you've got a host attached to the project already?"

"Well, yes. . . . Me."

"You."

"Mm-hm." There is a silence here during which I could read the Gettysburg Address.

"This is negotiable I would assume?"

"We can talk about it."

FORTY-FIVE

"THAT'S WHERE WE left it. That host business—the moment it came up, I could tell he was going blank. Yugo specifically said he had already run it by him. You figure it."

It's my champagne dinner in the Grill Room at Four Seasons, only it's lunch, and since I've decided to stay on the wagon, I'm watching Craig swill off the champagne while I guzzle miserably at a lime Perrier.

"You saw Melinda Watson's tits?" is all Craig can say, wondrously, over and over, as he munches his salad.

"Listen to me, damn it, I'm telling you about these people.

She's a manipulative ball buster and he's a stuffed-shirt vulgarian. And as for Yugo—"

Craig swabs his mouth with a big shiny linen napkin. "Oh, Elliot, haven't you learned what a short attention span people like Yugo have? When they don't remember things, they make up something, they fake it. Listen to Uncle Craig, my boy: don't ever try to pull off a key move based on something Yugo told you."

"Thanks for the advice. But it's too late now."

"Well, the point is . . . mm, this is great champagne. The point is—what?"

"The point is, I probably could have wrapped up a deal with Broadfoot on the spot. Now he's put me on hold over this."

"Who else do we know at PBS?"

"No, Broadfoot is my one big shot because of his clout. I can't afford to waste three or four years going through ordinary channels."

Craig stops chewing. "You realize I've been selling *Life-Forms* to Sir Harry as a spin-off from a high-culture TV series."

"Well, okay, but ultimately it stands on its own. I mean, it's a thought system, who needs TV? Look at *Passages*—that wasn't a spin-off."

"Different era, different situation. I'll do my best for you, that's a promise. If Broadfoot bails out it just makes it a harder sell, that's all. Meanwhile"—he brightens—"*Killed* continues to roar like a lion. We're all so thrilled."

"Mm. Say, what's this crap about 'meet the author'?"

"Oh, that. Just a little dog-and-pony show for the sales force."

"Yeah, well nobody asked me."

Craig's face goes blank. "Asked you?"

"Well, sure. I feel really ambivalent about being identified with this book. There's a possible tie-in with *LifeForms*, but it would have to be handled just right. A public appearance—I don't know. Where's the conference going to be, anyway?"

"Atlanta."

"Forget it. There's no way I'm going."

"Have no fear. You're not the author of this book, no matter how heavy an editing job you pulled off."

"You mean—?"

"Of course. We've lined up the assassin himself, and believe me, it wasn't easy. First he made us check with the authorities in Idaho to be sure they weren't interested in reopening the case—what a laugh! Then he insisted we go to the Feds, just in case they had in mind to bust him for violating Hemingway's civil rights. Then we had to agree to put up his significant other, and guarantee them a limousine, et cetera, et cetera—the man should have been a Hollywood agent! Oh, by the way—" He reaches into his fat Gucci shoulder bag. "Check this: an advance copy."

My spine freezes.

I cradle it like the dead body of a small animal.

In all fairness, I must say I'm seized by grim admiration. It's really quite a package. On the cover is Pappy, all grizzled and naked from the waist up, in his sporty new Papa Hemingway beard and thatch of snowy hair (the aging Hemingway would have killed for hair so thick). Balanced against one hip, rising from his loin area like a cartoon enlargement of Roscoe, is a double-barreled Boss shotgun, presumably (the cover implies) the one that ripped Hemingway's head off. The title slops across the top in dripping letters: *I KILLED HEMING-WAY.*" On the back, heading up the parade of prepublication blurbs, a come-on line: "The Shocking Truth About the Assassination of America's Greatest Novelist—Told Now for the First Time!" No, we are beyond even revulsion here and into awe, simple religious awe. This is tastelessness raised to a power so high you want to kneel down and kiss its ring.

"Jesus."

"He blew into New York for a day to strut his stuff for the editorial board. Absolutely knocked 'em dead with a choice selection of howlers from the book—like his version of the "Don't, Pussy, Don't" story—and the revised Scott Fitzgerald penis-anxiety episode—great stuff! So right on the spot, Sir Harry moved up pub date once again and penciled Pappy in for Atlanta."

Blew into New York . . .

Paranoia is suddenly frizzing me like radiation. "Listen,

Craig, tell me something: is *LifeForms* in any kind of problem
state with Sir Harry?"

"Not a chance, old boy. As I've always said, it's a monster,
and everybody at W&D knows it— Wait a sec: isn't that Ann
Beattie over there?"

"Where?"

"At the bar. Ann? Ann?" He arches his eyebrows in a mask
of hilarious greeting. "Hi, Ann . . ."

The woman swivels on her stool and is not Ann Beattie.
Craig recomposes his face, all business, calls for the check (a
bit prematurely, it seems to me) and we're out of there.

FORTY-SIX

INCREDIBLE HOW FAST twenty thousand dollars can flow
through the cracks of your life!

After paying off my credit cards, catching up on my rent,
my dry cleaning, my cleaning lady, various personal balances
long overdue, I'm practically broke again.

He was in town . . .

Lately it seems that two voices are vying for dominance in
my mind. One says, "Relax, Elliot. You're almost there." The
other says, in a rasp of derision, "Put yourself out of your
misery, jerk. There's nothing on the other end for you."

He's found my frequency.

And he's sitting on my seventy-five grand.

FORTY-SEVEN

"MORTIFIED. DEFLATED. HOW about stunned?"

"Stunned?" Sven leans forward wearing his listening look.
I'm in for what he calls a "tune-up."

He is very professional, very adept at zeroing in on me, even
though it's been nearly a year since our last session.

He isn't buying stunned. "You say you're stunned that he's going to make a speech?"

"You're goddamned right."

"But how else would you expect them to promote it?"

A good question—he always manages to skewer the essential. How else *would* they promote it? If Pappy didn't exist they would hire an actor. So why am I stunned?

"Well, to address the sales force, usually it's an established author, someone presentable at least. This man is a murderer."

"Do you believe that?"

"Who cares? Everyone else seems to."

Sven nods a rueful Swedish nod. "Yes. That's stunning in itself. But I have a sense you are feeling more than just shock and amazement at the folly of publishers."

"Maybe." Suddenly I feel like I want to vomit. The urgency passes, but I remain queasy.

"Well . . . ?"

"Fear, I guess."

"Mm. And the fear is of . . . what?"

I close my eyes and try to verbalize the lump of dread I've been carrying around for days. "That somewhere in Pappy's craziness is everything I'm not and never will be."

Sven squints and waits.

"All right," I proceed, "I'm working on a theory that biographical truth is no more, no less than the sheer creative power of the story. Pappy has that. He has boldness, the power to create—everything I need right now but can't seem to get my fingers around. The fact that his book is about to punch through— It's just intolerable to me. I can't stand it. Jesus, I have to calm down—"

"And LifeForms?"

"LifeForms has shrunk to a tiny dot in my mind. I talk a lot about it, but it's like I can't find it. This scares me, too, it scares me more than anything. To lose it like that. To be somebody's victim."

"Victim?"

"Oh sure, things like this don't just *happen*. Somebody's on the other end." My head bobs up and down. Sven waits. "And you know who that somebody is, don't you? Guess who is out there doing the shrinking?"

"Oh, come now—"

"Yes. He can play with minds, long-distance. He's done it before."

Sven stares at me for a long time. That must have got his wheels turning! I can almost see the smoke curling out of his ears.

"What kind of thoughts do you have about him?" he says finally.

"Thoughts like that. Or that he's powerful and I'm not. That he's part of the structure of things and I'm just filler. I mean, look what he's done."

"But it's all lies."

"Not if my theory is correct. Listen, I didn't believe his stories at first, but I'll never think about Ernest Hemingway in quite the same way again. Will you? Even if it's fantasy it's had the same effect on me as new truth would have had. I've been *convinced*. And what does this say about biography? Maybe truth is so unreliable you just have to write it off. As a matter of fact, hasn't this always been biography's dirty little secret?"

Sven stiffens ever so slightly—I suddenly recall he once attempted a biography of Erich Neumann. "So much for any distinction between truth and fiction," he mutters.

"Well, so what? It's a classic debate, it's a legitimate question."

"Not the way you're framing it. Biography must have standards. Truth has standards."

"Yes, but a performance like Pappy's stands them right on their head, that's my whole point."

"No."

"Yes."

Sven is upset. "All right. So Pappy is a persuasive storyteller. That doesn't mean he's controlling your mind."

"Well, he's doing something strange. He's a Lifeform destroyer, that much I've experienced. He drains off LifeForm energy. He did it to me in Key West. I was okay when I went down there, now I'm a shambles. He sucked me dry and he's still doing it. He's a long-distance vampire, a mind cannibal—"

"Elliot."

"You think I'm crazy, don't you?"

"No, of course not, you're under a lot of stress—"

"Damn it, stress is not what this is all about!"

"Don't shout, Elliot."

"I'll shout if I damn well please!"

Some tune-up. On the subway ride home, the train lurches to a halt between stations, the lights go out, and I have a panic attack. These things are contagious: as chance would have it, I'm sitting in the claustrophobes' car. One whimper out of me and the darkness is full of gibbering and shouting from all directions. This keeps up until the lights pop back on and the train hobbles into the next station and we all turn back into ordinary sober human travelers. The doors open and I scamper out of the ground like a chipmunk, screeching for a cab, and ride the rest of the way home slumped in the corner. Inside the apartment, I draw a hot bath and plunge in, desperate for warmth and containment.

Now let's just sit here and soak.

But I can't make my mind quit. *He's addressing the sales force!* What's going on? How was it arranged without my knowledge? I'm supposed to be W&D's man in Key West, aren't I? Who's Pappy been talking to? Shit! I'm boiling—

Sorry, out of the tub. I'm going to have to do it; I'm going to call Lynn.

Rising like a whale, I towel off quickly and slip into the old raincoat that I use for a bathrobe. . . .

FORTY-EIGHT

I CATCH HER on her shift at Sloppy Joe's. There's a lot of bar noise, but her voice comes through like a blast of sunlight.

"Elliot, it's you—I can't believe it!"

"Well, this is really more in the way of a business call."

She deadens. "Oh."

"Pappy was in New York, did you know?"

"No."

"Listen to me, Lynn: he's trying to stiff me. He was in town and he didn't call."

"He's pretty busy these days."

"He's making a speech at the Warren and Dudge sales conference. Did you know that?"

A sigh. "I guess I did. To kick off the book tour."

"*Book tour?* What book tour?"

"Didn't you set it up for him?"

"No way! I had absolutely nothing to do with it."

"Wow." She pauses. "Okay, here's what I know, Elliot: he's grown out his hair and beard, he's got new teeth, he's going to Nautilus three times a week. He spends all morning at the library. He's quit drinking and Valerie has him on some kind of colon-cleansing diet."

"My God."

"Want me to tell him something for you?"

I'm reeling. "Just . . . tell him to call."

"Okay." Pause. "What's it like up there?"

"Chilly."

"Why don't you come down? I miss you."

She had to do that. She had to add those last three words.

"Why don't you come up here?"

"You know I can't travel, Elliot. If I so much as set foot off Key West I'd be a basket case. But couldn't you come down? I really do miss you."

"No, no." I hear my own sigh blatting in the earpiece. "You know, now that you mention it, I think I must have developed some kind of phobia about Key West. Like a premonition that I'm going to die there or something."

There's a pause. Her voice takes on a husky intimacy. "I love those letters we used to write. I read them over all the time."

"Mm."

"Listen: if you come, surprise me."

"Surprise you?"

"Yeah, you know." I can hardly make out the words. "Come when it's dark. I'll open the door and we'll . . . get into some of that stuff. I can see it. I'm pre-visioning."

"Lynn, I can't."

"They're waving at me, I've got to go now."

"So do I."

"Listen, I'll find out everything I can and write you, okay?"

"Thanks. I don't think I'll be calling you again. It upsets my system."

The elegance of her silence is lacerated with bar noise. "Well. Write me then. I've got to go now."

"Me too."

Out my window, over the rooftops—is that a cloud bank I see, that massive passing presence, that solid black boat of a thing that just slid majestically by? Now it's gone without a trace—

"Elliot?"

"Hm?"

"Surprise me—"

Outside the sky is clear; I can even see stars now through the amber penumbra of the city. My finger presses the button, breaking the connection, and Key West bursts in my mind like a phantom soap bubble.

FORTY-NINE

THERE IS A book tour, a big one.

Publisher's Weekly writes that Pappy will hit fifty-six key bookstores nationwide, signing *Killed* at every whistle-stop. There will be segments on "60 Minutes," and "20/20," a serialized excerpt in *People,* and guest appearances on all three network morning shows, plus Donahue, Geraldo, Oprah, Joe Franklin, Larry King, and (you guessed it) Yugo.

Should I die laughing at the irony? This bum, this illiterate babbler, *punches through,* makes his grand entry by the front door while I cool my heels around back?

No. I'm not in a mood to inflate or romanticize the situation. He owes me seventy-five grand. I simply want my money. Let's take a trip to Long Island. . . .

Wonderbooks is the biggest bookstore chain in the universe and the Long Island City outlet is known in the trade as a litmus of average reading taste, a classic test market. It is laid out like a gigantic suburban hardware store: instead of Plumbing Supplies, Garden Center, Power Tools, or Automotive, you have Best-sellers, Cookbooks, Travel, New Fiction, and so on, in endlessly receding nooks and crannies.

And there he is, at a raised table back in New Nonfiction.

Even though I'm prepared for Pappy's new look, it's still a shock to see someone so like Hemingway back there signing books. The Mr. Clean pate is indeed gone and the bottom of his face is bushy and white. Valerie sits next to him, looking cat-slick in a splashy satin sheath. There is a stack of books on the table and next to that a life-sized cardboard cutout display from the book's cover: Pappy and his Boss shotgun.

Four or five people are waiting in line. I join the autograph hounds and wait my turn, watching Pappy play the role of author-in-the-world as if he were born to it. Like EH, he affects small round wire-rimmed glasses and keeps pushing them back up the bridge of his nose. The elderly woman in front of me is confused.

"Mr. Hemingway, I've waited thirty years to meet you."

"Well, ma'am, I've waited my whole life to meet you. What's your name?"

"Bernice Platt—oh my, this is better than the time I met Burt Reynolds!"

"To . . . Bernice Platt, a finger-lickin' mouthful—"

"Watch it," Valerie says, through her teeth.

"—for a hungry man's mind."

"Oh, sweet! That's priceless!"

So far, neither Valerie nor Pappy has noticed me. I shove my copy of the book under his nose.

"Sir, I have a meaningful quote I'd like you to use."

"What is it, pal?"

" 'To Elliot, along with the money I owe him.' "

Pappy's chin jerks up. He looks at me hard. "What're you doing here?"

"What do you think? You never called me. I'm here for my seventy-five thousand dollars."

"I don't have it yet."

"You're full of shit."

Quickly he scans the room—no W&D people in sight, I made sure of that. Valerie, who went blank for a moment, now has her wits together. "Elliot, don't make trouble."

"This is no trouble. Let's have a little ceremony. Did Pappy bring his checkbook?"

"I told you, I don't have it. Val, go get somebody."

Valerie slips off her chair and trots toward the front of the store. No one is behind me in line. Pappy puts his face close to mine and whispers furiously.

"Listen, punk: I'm telling you I don't have your portion yet, you're saying I do. Who's in a better position to know?"

"I am. I talked to Joanne in Accounts Payable. The check was cut six weeks ago and went out to you three days later. You're trying to stiff me."

A sudden pitiful tone enters his voice: "It's spent."

"I don't believe you."

"Believe it, McGuire." He jerks his head in the direction Valerie disappeared in. "That woman soaks it up like a blotter. We're married now, you know."

"Congratulations."

"See that dress she's wearing? Pure silk. We got a new house—everything in it's got to be just so."

"Come on, she's a hippy."

"No, no. When she married me she said, Pappy, I'm growing up. And to her that means spending money."

"Do you honestly expect me to sympathize with you?"

"I don't care if you do or not. But that's where the money's gone. Along with my soul."

No. There is something in his eyes that doesn't match up. A watchfulness. He's measuring me with each word. This is pure performance.

"Stop bullshitting me. You get me seventy-five thousand cash and I'll be out of your life instantly. Or else."

"Or else what?"

"Or else . . . I go to court."

A bluff, but why not try it?

He gives me a heavy-lidded stare. Then he breathes and puffs, breaking into a tight grin.

"I can't. I'm telling you the truth. I just don't have it. Go on to court if you want."

"Pappy, this is for real. As soon as I get to a phone, I'm going to call my lawyer."

He shrugs wearily. "More power to you. What can I do? I've got a book tour going here, I'm scheduled up to my neck night and day. You're right: we made a deal. Go ahead. Go to it."

Out of the corner of my eye I can see Valerie returning

with—oh, Jesus, it's Craig, looking very pale and corporate and frazzled.

"Elliot, what in the name of God are you doing here!"

"Just a personal matter between me and Pappy, that's all. And it's all settled."

"No it's not!" Valerie snaps. "You're threatening my husband."

"I am not."

"He is—he's going to do something to him."

"Val, honey, shut up."

Craig gives me a wild look, as though I were a bull elephant on a rampage.

"Craig—it's me, Elliot. Who are you going to believe?"

Craig glances toward the front area with a frantic, cringing expectancy.

"Sir Harry's plane has landed, he's due over here any minute, damn it. I don't want any fuck-ups."

"Well, get rid of Elliot then," Val screeches.

"Wait a minute, wait a minute," roars Pappy. "I'm taking a goddamn break. C'mon, Elliot, come with me, let's go outside."

He hooks me around the shoulder and we leave Craig and Valerie bobbing in our considerable wake as we break through to the street.

For a moment, neither one of us has anything to say. We walk slowly, heads down in thought, like an old married couple.

"Coming down to Atlanta?"

"Why the hell should I?"

"Maybe you haven't heard." Pride throbs in his voice. "I'm giving a talk—"

"I've heard enough talk from you."

He spews a sigh and tries a lopsided Hemingway grin. "Well damnation, Elliot, at least let me buy you a drink!"

"I don't drink anymore."

"I don't either. Val's got me on a health regime—"

I cut him off: "I don't want to make small talk. You know how to reach me if you want to."

"Elliot, don't be bitter. Life's too short."

"Not yours apparently."

He crows with laughter, then takes hold of my shoulders with genuine affection. "Hey, listen, son, in spite of all, don't forget I love you."

"Come off it."

"Pappy loves you, y'understand?"

"No, I don't understand."

"Some day you will." He stands off a ways, beaming at me, and holds out his hand. "No hard feelings? Come on, shake, damn it."

"I'll see you in court."

I must say I'm feeling better having gone out and stood up for myself. As my train clatters into Penn Station, I'm actually a bit encouraged. Battle lines have been drawn. I'm carrying my life in my own two hands. Self-reliance—it turns quicksand to marble, makes anything seem possible. As Thoreau said, "Simplify, simplify, simplify" (did he have to say it three times?). Go out there, find a Walden, get naked—weave a grass skirt, build your own log hut. Well, why not? That's what a good dose of higher morality can do for you. It's so simple: do the right thing. Just say yes. Don't tell me you don't know right from wrong!

Back at the apartment, I pencil up a list of celebrities from all eras who have one thing in common: vivid and basic Life-Forms. These are textbook examples of FrontLoaders, Repeaters, TransFormers, LongRunners, FlameOuts, Ripplers, BottleNecks, and BlackOuts. Here's what I have so far: "Mozart, Jesus, Jane Fonda, Charlie Parker, Elvis Presley, Ringo Starr, Elizabeth Taylor, Bertrand Russell, George Burns, Marlon Brando, James Dean, John Lennon, Greta Garbo, Cher, Sonny, Claude Pepper, John F. Kennedy, Martin Luther King, Van Gogh, Lord Byron, Jimmy Rodgers, Keats, Bartok, Chopin, T. S. Eliot, O. J. Simpson, Sting, Colonel Sanders, and—sure—Ernest Hemingway." Get the drift? We learn by example, and the more gestaltishly familiar the example, the quicker we learn. By the time I'm through, any reader with average intelligence will be able to grasp the hierarchy of LifeForms instantly, just by connecting each distinctive form with its famous exemplar.

I'm on a roll. Struggling for money and pride is producing interesting side effects: lust for independence, renewed *amour propre.* Here's a key thought: even when I burned it up, I never rejected my past—I simply *e*jected it. I pushed the button and let it drift into oblivion. I don't need it anymore—but God knows, it served its purpose; it got me as far as here, ground zero, this bracing moment, and so I send love back to it, across time, across the pain of it all, an affectionate caress to the other end of my LifeForm. Young Elliot, I love you. Let us now choose peace!

FIFTY

THERE IS A message on the machine from my agent, Jerry Bronstein. I've been playing it over and over, trying to hear some hint of reprieve, something, anything, in Jerry's tone of voice.

"*Elliot—Jerry. Bad news on* LifeForms, *W&D kicked it back. I'll be in the office today and tomorrow.*" Not the merest breath of hope.

Something has always interested me about suicide, namely, what keeps me from trying it? I'm never tempted, no matter how horrible things get. Now, for example, watch as I reach for a kitchen knife and hold it to my carotid artery (or jugular vein, I'm never sure which is which). I could press just a *leetle* bit harder than I'm pressing, give it a jerk, and my *LifeForms* problem would go away forever and forever. W&D would simply collapse into the vortex of my consciousness and drain away for all eternity.

But I can't.

Unlike the Hemingways, who kept suicide around like a familiar old family toolbox (item: four self-exits in the same nuclear family), I seem to be suicide-proof. Not that I'm afraid of it, it's more elemental than that: I can't kill myself in exactly the same way that I can't wiggle my ears or roll up my tongue; for me the necessary muscle group doesn't exist. Self-death just isn't part of my wiring plan. So I'm safe in a moronic sort of way—even as I now press, press, *press*—

Ouch! Jesus Christ! What the fuck am I trying to prove? Get a Band-Aid, idiot!

I'm all right now. I'm relatively calm, I'm ambulatory. I'm up and out on the street, I'm clean, well-dressed, and I'm taking the high road—straight to Jerry Bronstein's office.

It's a small, thriving literary boutique on the ground floor of a brownstone over in Murray Hill. Jerry has been my agent for fifteen years. I was one of his charter authors back in the days when we used to drink together. Now, of course, he has over two hundred clients, and since he married Nina Rienzi-Furstenberg, the editor of *Millennium*, he spends a lot of time running with the fast horses. We don't socialize anymore, but he looks out for me—which is why I'm astounded that this W&D thing was allowed to slip through the cracks. Marie, his assistant, buzzes me in and sits me down with a cup of coffee and the latest *Publisher's Weekly* while Jerry finishes a phone call in his office.

"How much?" I hear him saying (there are no doors in Jerry's suite). "I can get you at least that . . . Mm-hm . . . Darling, listen: all I have to do is *appear* on Sixth Avenue and they are positively chasing me down the street to get to you. No, it's true, I don't have to sell you. My only problem is to get creative enough to structure your best deal. And that's what we'll talk about on Tuesday. . . . Yeah, well, how's this: four books, five years, five million bucks? Hm? No, I'm not kidding. You're hot, this is the time to spring it. I've got at least five houses breathing heavy and when we're through there's going to be blood on the floor. Just a minute, darling—" He sticks his head around the door. "Ah, Elliot. Be with you in a second." He covers the phone with his hand and whispers impishly, "I've got Evangeline Welles on the phone here—Jesus, what a monster!"

Evangeline Welles, syndicated columnist, author of *Blame It on Bullwinkle, Excuse Me Mrs. President, Let Them Eat Graham Crackers*, and other inexplicable best-sellers, and listen to the kind of deals getting bounced around out there! I don't know, maybe it's a blessing that W&D passed. There's no telling what Jerry might be able to engineer out there in the lunchtime jungle. I was probably a fool to take the package directly to Craig in the first place. So much for going around your agent.

"Elliot, Elliot, sit down, you look great." No eye contact.

His voice is perfunctory as he ushers me in. He still has Evangeline Welles and five million bucks on his mind. "Now let's see, where are we . . . ? Oh yeah, *LifeForms*, *LifeForms*. Yeah, bad news. No TV series, and then Warren and Dudge, that's a blow."

"No TV series? What about MacKenzie Broadfoot?"

"You didn't know? He just announced he'll be working the next five years on 'Rod McKuen's America.' "

"Okay, *force majeure*—but Warren and Dudge, that was a sure thing, what the hell happened?"

He stares back at me, exaggeratedly blank. "What do you mean, what the hell happened? They passed, that's what happened."

"Yeah, but how? I mean, how was it allowed to fall through? Craig Vandermeer is one of my oldest friends. All you had to do was reach in with one hand and close the deal."

Jerry very deliberately smooths some papers and looks at the ceiling.

"Elliot, there was no deal."

"But there *could* have been."

"If what? Don't kid yourself, man, there was no enthusiasm at all, not one ounce, not even from Craig."

"You don't know that—"

"I know. Listen, Elliot: first of all, you made this move yourself. You submitted a package that I never even saw."

"Granted. Maybe that was unwise. But you might have kicked a little bit when it came back. I mean, I was given every assurance by Craig that—"

"That what? Elliot, don't ever go naked into an editor's office, even if he's your best friend. What do you think I do all day? I save authors from themselves. I position projects like yours in such a way that when I walk out, it's sold, they've got to have it. No, this was yours, Elliot, from start to finish. I won't accept one scintilla of blame."

"All right. All right. Warren and Dudge is out of the way, we'll call that my mistake. Now what?"

"Now what? You tell me."

"Well, you've seen the package. Where can you take it?"

"I can't take it anywhere."

"Didn't you read it? We're talking about *LifeForms*—"

"I know what we're talking about. I read it. I have to be

frank, Elliot: the proposal sounds like one of those weird religious fliers they hand you in the park. The sample chapter—I have to confess, I don't get it. I can't try to sell something when I don't get it."

"You don't get it? But we've talked about LifeForms, you were enthusiastic. Now you say you don't get it?"

"It doesn't come together for me. I mean, sure, I comprehend the basic idea—every life has a form, you can change your form, change your life—but there are missing pieces. I'd have to see it fleshed out. Your outline—it's provocative but it doesn't answer any of my questions. No, I can't sell this."

"Don't shit me, Jerry. You could pick up the phone and have an auction going in half an hour. What's going on here, are you trying to ease me out? Is that the message?"

"No, Elliot, no, no—"

"Then what the hell is going on? I don't know what the problem was at W&D but I know this: I'm about to launch one of the great thought systems of the century. Do you want to be on board or not?"

"Look, Elliot, I'm not saying it's not going to be great. All I'm saying is this: so far, you don't have enough on paper to get it launched. I think that was the problem at W&D and it's certainly my problem. I need to see a full draft."

"A full draft! Do you know how long that's going to take me? I'm broke, Jerry. I was counting on an advance from W&D."

"All right, that's another bone I have to pick with you. You made a deal with Craig to edit I Killed Hemingway for a flat fee, now it's a best-seller and you won't see a penny in royalties. Do you think I would've cut a deal like that? Again, what do you think I do all day, play with steel balls?"

"That started as a few days' work and then—there were complications—let's not talk about I Killed Hemingway, okay?"

"Why not? It's getting a lot of attention, a lot of critical interest. That's something we could turn to your advantage. Your name's not on it but you obviously helped him with it. I think I could use it as a lever to get you some good work."

"What kind of work?"

"Well, like Rolly Riles, the old commie folksinger, wants a collaborator for his life story. I had a call just this morning from Elmer Yancey's office, you know, the ninety-seven-year-old congressman—"

"No!"

"Hm?"

"Three things: One, I don't want to be identified with *I Killed Hemingway* on any terms but my own, and I haven't worked them out yet. If anyone brings it up just let the subject drop. Two, no more ghostwriting. The best years of my life are going by while I help every rich illiterate over sixty-five tell his life story. And three, the time for *LifeForms* has arrived. Whether you connect with it or not, we're living in an era of obsession with other people's lives. Biography is to us what theology was to the Middle Ages. *LifeForms* is going to be the flower of this obsession and it's going to grow right out of my head."

"You may be right. So do it. Go out there and do it. Write the book. If it's all you say it is, then I'll get you a million dollars and that's a promise, okay?"

"But Jesus, don't you get it, Jerry? I need the money now. A million dollars in two years is pie in the sky. I need something to live on *now*, this week, today—"

Marie is at the door. "Excuse me, Jerry, it's the Aga Khan on oh-four—"

"Oh, shit, I better take this. Elliot, I'm sorry—"

"Forget it. I'm leaving."

"Oh, Elliot, c'mon."

"No, I don't think we have anything more to talk about. Everything's quite clear."

"Elliot, don't you dare leave. Marie, give Elliot some more coffee and take him out to the sculpture garden. I'll be off the phone in five minutes."

"No, I'm leaving. Which way is out?"

"Which way is—? Elliot, are you okay?"

I'm not sure. I have to say I'm having a little trouble with up and down. Also right and left. My vision is going. What else? Dizziness, cold sweat, weak at the knees—aside from that I'm fine, fine.

"Make him sit!" Jerry is shouting. "Put his head between his knees!"

That's all I remember until I come to, much later I fear, stretched out on the couch in my sock feet. Marie's worried face hangs above me like a paper moon. I come to a sitting position and accept a glass of orange juice. It's just like giving blood.

"Where's Jerry?"

"He had an appointment, but he said for you to stay as long as you wanted to. Are you sure you're okay?"

"Never better."

"I'll call a car for you."

Is this it? Is this the clunk of bedrock under my feet at last, at long last?

Analysis: Do as the man says and get the work done. Go home, McGuire. Fire up the word processor. Be a man, clean off the chicken feathers, lower your head and push. *Excelsior.*

The work, the work is all. Do the work and something is bound to turn up. . . .

FIFTY-ONE

"AND THIS IS *the chandelier—I told Pappy the place lacked something and then when I saw this beautiful hunk of glass, I just had to have it.*"

"*Anything she wants she gets, you'd better believe it.*"

Pappy and Valerie are showing off their new trailer for a few million folks at home, and if you've never seen a crystal chandelier in a mobile home, I feel sorry for you. Obviously Megan Swift (the female co-host of *Sunday Morning Journal*) is impressed with Mr. and Mrs. Pappy and their tiny elongated American paradise—which comes across on TV as an Ethan Allen showroom stuffed into an aluminum condom. This is what my portion of the advance money has bought.

Now we're relaxing in the backyard as Megan's partner, Bob Lansing, gathers crumbs at the foot of the distinguished author.

"*Pappy, tell us what success means to you at this late stage of your life.*"

"*It's sweet, Bob, real sweet. I mean, you figure it: you go for years living on nothing while the man who stole it all from you is up there getting his Nobel Prize—*"

"*Pappy isn't getting a thing he doesn't deserve,*" Valerie butts in, spilling cleavage as she leans over Pappy to plant a kiss on his head.

"The fuck he isn't!" I shout at the screen.

Meanwhile we are getting a look at Pappy's "writing room," which is either a tiny garden shed or a chicken shack, I can't tell which, outfitted with a table and chair.

"*This is it, Bob and Megan. Every morning I just sit here with a pad and pencil and pray for a good day. Writing is like fishing or hunting ducks: you have to know how to wait—and, of course, you have to know what to do when the waiting's over.*"

Now Bob is on screen, full face. "*The waiting is over for Pappy Markham, a man who's been waiting for over sixty years to tell his remarkable story. Now, with the publication of* I Killed Hemingway, *Pappy is getting the literary attention he feels is long overdue.*"

Cut to an affable dude in a white beard—oh my God, it's "Hemingway Scholar" Howie Ritz!

"*He's actually redefined the Hemingway legend, he's put new twists on all the familiar stories, he's offered a new set of facts, a countertext, if you will, even down to the death itself. And no matter what you think about it, that's quite a feat. I'd say—with an ounce of caution, perhaps—but I'll say it anyway: the author of this book has literally stolen a place in the annals of literature.*"

Gag.

"*When we return,*" says Megan Swift, "*We'll take you on a tour of Pappy Markham's Key West, led by His Honor himself, the honorary mayor of Duval Street.*"

I'm glad I'm taping this; I can't believe what I'm seeing. Mayor of Duval Street, my ass. Might as well make Lyndon LaRouche Queen of the May. And can you believe Howie Ritz—the annals of literature!

Now there's a beer commercial on the screen and I want one so bad I'm almost on my knees. Why am I still on the wagon? It's not advancing my cause. It's been days since the debacle at Jerry's office and what have I been able to accomplish? *Nada.*

No, I take it back, I managed to borrow a thousand bucks from Astrid. I'm not proud of this. She didn't want to see me. I didn't want to see her. She dropped a check in the mail. *Nada.*

Craig, that worm, crawled out of his hole long enough to offer me an apology (abject, embarrassing) and some work. Prompted by Jerry, no doubt, he came up with a real dog, which he ventured to toss my way over the phone (most likely so I wouldn't be able to throw a coffee cup at his head): "It's a new edition of *Death Parade*, Elliot. We want to bring it up-to-date. A lot of terrific people have passed on in the last twelve years and we want them in there."

Death Parade. The coffee table encyclopedia of deathbed stories. The final moments of over three thousand prominent personalities from every era. The pain, the indignity, the struggle, the mess, the horror. Revised. Elliot McGuire, editor. I hung up.

Nada.

—And we're back! With "I Shot the Sheriff" on the sound track, as we drift down Duval Street, all jerky and hand-held, with Mr. and Mrs. Pappy. Everybody has a good word for Pappy, a slap on his back, a pat for Valerie's ass.

As the camera turns into Sloppy Joe's, I realize we're going to see Lynn behind the bar, and sure enough, there she is looking wry and tolerant of all this brouhaha. And what does she think of Pappy Markham? Megan Swift, holding a mike in her face, pops the very question.

"He's such a hunk. If I could pick my own daddy, it'd be that man."

Oh, sweet! Then we cut to the old polar bear himself, live on stage, with a mike in one hand, a drink in the other. What now—do we have to listen while he croons "My Way"?

No, what we get is more like a secular Jim and Tammy show: Pappy introduces Valerie, who bounces up on stage, hisses something at the band, and breaks into a quavering, off-key rendition of "Proud Mary." During the guitar break, she and Pappy boogie around the stage. As the tourists give out a collective roar, Bob Lansing's voice drones that "in so many ways" Pappy is the kind of "senior" Ernest Hemingway might have wished himself to be.

Then it's Pappy, voice-over, as we watch him at his desk, scratching feverously in a composition book, describing his "new book." It's a novel this time, and the plot: *"A man decides to change his life by starting all over, like a newborn baby, and imagining a new shape for it, what I'd call a new 'life-form'—"*

"Shut up!" I'm screaming at the screen, "Shut up, shut up, SHUT UP!"

The segment wraps with one last quiet image: at sunset, Pappy, pants rolled up, taking a meditative stroll down Smathers Beach with soulmate Megan Swift, who ventures: *"Pappy, about the assassination . . ."* (Go, Megan! Hit him with your best shot!) *"There's all this publicity, and your own admission of guilt . . . do you ever fear arrest and extradition?"*

"Megan, the more my story gets out—the more the people get to know me and know how Ernest Hemingway made me suffer—the less I worry about any action being taken by the good people of Idaho. I just decided I was going to put my life, my future, in the hands of the literary public. I feel secure."

I'm choking. I've got to get out of here, out into the casual innocence of Sunday morning. I erupt into my hallway and stagger down the stairs. In the foyer I notice a letter taped to my mailbox. Something is scrawled on it in hot lavender: "Received this by mistake. Love, Magdalena." Glancing at the return address I see it's from a Frank DeForrest, Litchfield, Connecticut. I rip it open—

Dear Elliot McGuire:

In answer to your query regarding Eric Markham, yes, I knew him in Paris in the early twenties. Although I have given a number of interviews to scholars researching the "Lost Generation," no one has ever mentioned his name to me and I most likely would have gone to my grave never having thought of him again were it not for your "author's query" and his recent succes de scandal, *the deplorable I Killed Hemingway.*

In those days certainly no one took Eric Markham seriously as a figure of any future importance; at best he was regarded as a colorful, if hapless, young rogue. To my knowledge, he arrived in Paris in 1923, at the age of about eighteen. (This, by the way, makes him not ninety-three but eighty-three at most, a number of years <u>younger</u> than Ernest Hemingway, not older, as he claims in his book.) He was

*then a strapping, handsome, energetic, ambitious boy, and
for some inconceivable reason he gravitated toward the
literary life. God knows, he had no talent for it and was
perceived by the American literati in Paris to be something
of a pest; but his personal charm opened a number of doors
that would otherwise have remained shut. Hemingway, for
instance, liked him at first and took him on as a kind of
apprentice whom he could lord it over in a big-brotherly
way, one of the many roles that man played to the hilt. By
the way, I should say that, despite his many faults, so well
documented at this late date, I had great respect and
admiration for Ernest Hemingway. He did turn savagely
on Ricky Markham, as he so unfairly turned on many of his
other friends, myself included. However, he was justified in
this case. Ricky submitted several plagiarized works to
Hemingway at the* transatlantic review. *Hem, so pleased
to see a protege do well, planned to include the works
(several tightly compressed prose poems, I believe) in an
issue he was putting together in Ford Madox Ford's
absence. When an erudite sub-editor recognized them as
translations of a young French poet of the Quarter who
had just died of starvation or consumption or whatnot (an
appropriate bohemian death, certainly) Hem immediately
yanked the work and refused ever to speak to Ricky again,
causing him to be generally ostracized by everyone else as
well.*

*Now: this brought out a dark streak in the boy, who took
to standing in the street outside Hem's at all hours and
haunting the cafés where Hem drank. A showdown of sorts
occurred outside the Dome one evening when Hemingway
asked Ricky to accompany him down an alley where they
could talk in private. Of course a fight broke out. I was one
of the only witnesses (the others are long dead). Ricky, who,
like Hem, was a proficient boxer, knocked Hem down
several times and seemed to have won the battle, when
Hem came up with a table leg from a nearby pile of trash.
Wielding it as a club, he stunned Ricky with one blow, then
tossed the table leg aside, beat him mercilessly with fists,
and walked away.*

*That was the end of things for Eric Markham. As the
story of his plagiarism spread he was shunned, a pariah.*

He may or may not have continued trying to write his own rather pitiable prose poems, I have no idea, but his personality underwent a distinct transformation—from ebullient "kid" to intense cynic in the Robert McAlmon mold, always with a sneer, always a bit frightening physically in his readiness to take violent offense at some innocent gesture or remark. He merged into the demimonde of the Quarter. I believe he became a paid "escort" catering to adventurous married women. I later heard he had married scandalously, a young Negro heiress from somewhere in the Caribbean. They lived splendidly in the avenue Wagram, and as the decade drew to a close, were said to have withdrawn to her family's estate in St. Croix or wherever it was.

In any case, once he was gone I thought nothing about him again. Like many young Americans in Paris in the twenties, I returned home after the stock market crash. I was certainly no artist and it was time to do something with one's life. I entered the family business in New York and that was the end of it.

My story has a curious postscript, however.

Once, while traveling in Florida, I cruised to Key West as the guest of my wife's cousin. As closely as I can reckon, this would be just after the Second World War, perhaps 1948. As we approached the mooring, I was astounded to recognize one of the men who was helping haul us in. Twenty years had gone by but it was unmistakably Eric Markham, now an imposing hulk of a man in his forties. He stopped frequently to drink from a pocket flask and staggered a bit. When I called out to him, "Ricky!" it was as though I had fired a shot next to his ear. He looked from face to face with panic in his eyes. Something in his look silenced me—I'm sure he didn't recognize me anyway. He drained his flask and beat a rather quick retreat, all the while glancing back uneasily.

"Who is that man?" I asked one of the dock workers. I learned this: he was known in Key West as "Buster" Markham, and was considered a harmless "rummy" who spent his time either drinking, scavenging, thieving, or doing occasional odd jobs. I was left with the distinct impression that our boy Ricky had found his proper milieu.

I did not see him again until the other night, when—there he was, some forty-odd years later, on my television screen, hawking this horror of a book he has written. I have no idea why you wish to chronicle this rather insignificant individual, but in light of his more recent infamy (not so much a sin against Hemingway as slap in the face of history itself) I hope you intend some sort of exposé and would be delighted to assist you in any way my somewhat limited energies permit (I am eighty-seven years old).

Please feel free to call or visit me at my home at any time.

Sincerely yours,
Frank Bedford DeForrest

FIFTY-TWO

SURELY THIS IS what I needed. A break from the city. The peace of the countryside. Clear spring air and early vegetation reminding me that you can die and be reborn any number of times in a life. There was more than a hint of promise in the tone of the old man, who yesterday spoke to me over the phone with a faraway formal shout, as though reciting Milton through a hearing tube. "I'll send the car for you," Frank Bedford DeForrest said, and sure enough, as I detrain, a man in shabby chauffeur's livery is standing at attention holding a handwritten sign that says, MR. ELLIOT MCGUIRE. After a stiff little greeting, the chauffeur (who speaks with some sort of East European accent) settles into decorous silence. This is fine. I don't like small talk with drivers anyway; they should keep their attention on the road.

This whole trip has been a sentimental journey of sorts. I went to school up here in this corner of Connecticut. I even took this same train, coming and going from the Gunnery, my third and last attempt to stay college-bound (after flaming out at Exeter and my father's old school, Choate). I realize, as the familiar scenery goes by, that I recall the Gunnery days fondly. In a way I wish I were there now. Can we back up the tape to that point?

N.B.: life as tape. Explore.

The Gunnery was where I met Yugo before we went on to Columbia. Yugo was troubled. He set small fires, destroyed saplings, that sort of thing. He wet the bed. But he was popular, a big handsome guy with the voice and the verbal charisma that eventually got him where he is today. I have no idea whether he still wets the bed and sets fires (he seemed much improved at Columbia), but his attachment to me (at least the *idea* of me) as some sort of life purist began back then. We were inseparable. I weaned him off some of his bad habits and acquired some of his others. Give a little, take a little, that's the way it goes.

We turn abruptly off the main road onto a gravel driveway that snakes through a forest of rhododendron, then runs between a grand *allée* of trees, ending in an oval with a flagpole in its midst. The house itself is a vast rambling white clapboard colonial with black shutters. An ancient gardener is pottering around in a bed of towering delphiniums. The chauffeur stops near the barn, a huge lurching structure, and just at that moment, a riding mower roars out the barn door with a tottery old man bouncing on the seat. He wears tweeds, tattered but correct, a cloth cap, and sports a little white beard. This is what the ancient Freud might have looked like had he cut his own lawn.

Seeing the car, Frank (it must be Frank) pulls up and slides unsteadily off the mower. He toddles toward the car on his spidery legs, one hand outstretched.

"Mr. McGuire."

"Elliot, please."

"Elliot, of course. And you must call me Frank." It is the kind of patrician voice that is dying out quickly. It's old recordings of FDR, it's George Plimpton through a wall. In another ten years, the accent will no longer exist. Frank, I realize, is a walking piece of the past.

Certainly the house reeks of history. It is run-down, in the way very old people's homes are always needing new paint, new roofs, small repairs they are too old to do for themselves, too cheap to pay for. The walls are covered with prints, oils,

241

drawings that have obviously been there for half a century at least. The floors, made of foot-wide planks, lean every which way as we go from room to room in a quick tour of the downstairs. Antiques are everywhere, but not the sort of antiques that you go out and *buy*: they've been right here in the house since before Frank was born.

"This was our summer house," Frank is telling me. "Then I retired and my wife was ill, so we sold our Park Avenue place and moved up here. Then she died—"

"I'm so sorry."

"Thank you. It was eighteen years ago."

"Oh."

"It's rather a large house for me, I suppose, but I can't imagine moving. The children come, with grandchildren and great-grandchildren, and so on." Crickets twitter lazily in the spring heat while we sip tea and get the social chitchat out of the way.

"I have something to show you," Frank says, finishing his tea. He disappears into his small crammed study and returns with a tattered piece of what looks like parchment. "I had forgotten that I had this. I think you'll find it interesting."

At first, I don't. It appears to be a page of writing, badly typed and poorly spelled. He's not going to tell me this is another piece of purloined Hemingway—

"It's one of Eric Markham's attempts. No plagiarism here—you can tell by the almost total lack of any redeeming value whatsoever. It's a copy of something he submitted to my little publication, *The Exile*."

Context is everything. I refocus and go back to the beginning, suddenly fascinated:

Lament
by Eric Markham

Wasting away . . . Garcon! another fine a l'eau. *Tears slop my sleeve and the moon is whopping full. No, no! You're skin is a buttery feild of satiny-smooth silkiness to my Roscoe's raspyness. Run, then, flee from me, screetch and screem your way to freedom if you dare, my love. I am a snarly madman and will chase you ever in the crazy streets of the lost, lost city, my city, our city, my lost, lost*

love. In heaven aren't we jointed? Oh, oh stop your head-
long flight from the inevitible joining of our bones. Let my
rugged-raspy rake your silver-sheeny, let—

Let me off! I lift my eyes to Frank's weathered old monkey's
face, creased with merriment as he anticipates my reaction.

"A fetching lyric, wouldn't you say?"

So this is one of Pappy's "compressions"!

"You're sure he wrote this?"

"His plagiarized work was infinitely superior. Also, I
watched him whip this off, rather arrogantly, in answer to a
dare. He simply sat down at a café table and began scratching.
When I insisted that he submit a typescript, he went off to
Hemingway's newspaper office and was back within a half
hour. No, I believe it's authentic."

"May I have this? I'll copy it and return it."

"Please do keep it. I have no desire at all to have it back."

This Frank DeForrest is definitely a find. In the hour or so
before lunch he regales me with "lost generation" trivia—a
lunch with Ford Madox Ford, an auto trip and picnic with the
ravishing Kiki. As soon as tea is out of the way he offers me
a shot of bourbon, which I politely refuse. Finally, over cold
cuts and salad, he turns a long look on me. His voice is
suddenly a bit strained.

"Well, now. For your . . . biography, is it? Of Eric Markham . . . how best might I help you?"

"I'm not writing his biography. Not anymore."

"I'm so glad."

"Someone else may, someday, as a case history in galloping
schizoid paranoia. But not me."

"You, however, are here for a reason." He's speaking with
great care and his eyes have become piercing and analytical.
"What exactly is your concern with Eric Markham?"

A sigh, a falling glance. "I'm afraid I have to tell you something now that, that—" I break off, shaking my head. "I'm
Eric Markham's ghost."

He draws back. "His ghost?"

"Ghostwriter, I mean. His collaborator. I'm sorry to say
that even though you don't see my name anywhere, *I Killed
Hemingway* is an as-told-to. And it was told to me."

"Ah. I see now." Frank DeForrest has the finest old manners. Short of an infinitesimal quaver of one hair of one eyebrow, he will not shame his guest. He clears his throat and ventures forward amiably. "Tell me, I've often wondered how a collaboration like that works. I mean, who does what and when and—"

"Thank you."

"I beg your pardon?"

"Thank you, Frank, for not picking up a bullwhip and flaying me to ribbons on the oval in front of your house—"

"My dear man!"

"Yes, I'm being vivid—but thanks for continuing to treat me with respect after hearing what I just told you."

"Elliot, I've lived quite a long time. There isn't much that surprises me or even fires up certain emotions I haven't felt in ages—indignation, patriotic fervor, revulsion, all that. These days my cardinal emotion is curiosity, if you could call that an emotion. I'm curious. I believe that's what keeps me alive—intense curiosity. About tomorrow, for example—I'm curious what will happen tomorrow. I can hardly wait to know. So you see, all I'm feeling at this particular instant is 'What will he say next? Why is he here?' "

I take a sip of water and wipe my mouth.

"I'm here because I need your help."

Something comes into his eyes that tells me he knows, without my saying a word more, what I've come for. But I plunge on anyway.

"Something happened to me when I read your letter. Something like scales falling from my eyes—which actually glorifies it—I simply woke up, that's all. I reawoke in the moral universe after having snoozed for an indeterminate period."

Frank squints slightly and shakes his head.

"I'm sorry. It's actually very simple: I've done a tremendous wrong to Ernest Hemingway. I've wounded him. I've harmed him in the worst possible way, by poisoning his memory—"

"Oh, now, I think you're being a bit harsh—"

"No, no. You're the perfect host. I'm as guilty as Eric Markham. I sat down with his snake's nest of an oral history and turned it into a book with pacing, style, literacy and what have you. I made it a best-seller and in doing so, put a gun to the head of Ernest Hemingway the legend. I'm an accessory to murder—"

"My goodness, that's a bit much. Can I get you a glass of sherry? Hemingway was no moral paragon, you know—well, I needn't tell you. I believe the point you should focus on is that he spread a good deal of poppycock about both himself and other people. These fantasies of Ricky Markham's really belong there, in that netherworld of folderol that is essentially harmless—"

"But that's just it, it's not harmless. Look at what Hemingway did to Fitzgerald's memory with a few well-planted lies. Can you ever think of Fitzgerald again without his memory being twisted somewhat, given a clown's nose? I can't. And now the same thing is going to happen to Hemingway. Will you ever hear his name again without the image of this big mama's boy locked in cunnilingus with Gertrude Stein?"

"I believe that's not what would spring instantly to mind—"

"Oh, give it time, give it time. It's fully possible that someday, eons into the future, that's all that will remain of either of them in the mind's eye of posterity."

Frank stares at me like an amazed owl. Suddenly he bursts into a warbling laugh, so unexpectedly that before I know it, I'm grinning.

"What a notion!"

"Look, I know I'm overdoing it. The fact is simply this: I look with horror on my part in producing this travesty of a book. I want to perform a public service by destroying the book and the man who conceived it. I won't be able to live my life until I do. I've come to ask you to help me."

"Destroy?"

"Not physically. The book and the man just have to be put in their proper place. Nobody is doing it. Have you read the reviews?"

"Yes, I must say there's a great deal of tolerance for it. No one seems to want to dismiss it as rubbish. They like the book, they like the author. Do you know what it reminds me of?"

"What?"

"Years ago, a wealthy lady named Florence Foster-Jenkins used to rent Carnegie Hall and give voice recitals. She was a terrible singer, ludicrously awful and everyone knew it—even she knew it. Yet her recitals were great occasions, and the reviews, while a bit tongue-in-cheek, never actually took her to task for what she was—a poseur. They liked her and what's more they liked the *idea* of what she was doing, the creative audacity of it—"

"Exactly! That's it! He's getting by on creative audacity—sheer boldness. We have to step in."

"And do what?"

"Go public. Remind everyone involved, from Warren and Dudge to *The New York Times*, that in raising this book to the best-seller list, facetiously or not, they're all accomplices to the murder of Ernest Hemingway—"

"But wait—such a murder never actually took place. Aren't we agreed on that?"

"That's neither here nor there. They aren't challenging the assertion, so it's as if it had. Anyway, the real act of violence is to the public Hemingway, isn't it? And that's what we've all helped him perpetrate."

Frank's brow furrows in concentration. "What rankles me is the falsehood. It's a national disgrace that a falsehood is being tolerated."

I have him! "Exactly!"

"I'll do what I can. Do you want a letter? Shall I sign something?"

"I need more than that. I need your presence, on TV. I need you to stand up with me and testify. You've got tremendous natural credibility, Frank. Let's use it!"

"My dear man—it's all I can do to walk around my property once a day. You're asking me to go on television?"

"Yes!"

"I can't. I'm eighty-seven. I can't."

"Frank, remember Zola. He didn't think he could lead the fight for Dreyfus."

"Zola didn't have to go on TV."

In a panic I feel myself losing him, and for some reason the thought of it is intolerable. I want to throw myself at his feet. Descend to my knees in supplication.

"Frank, this is very important to me. At this moment it's my whole life. I'm trying to move from one sector to another, but I'm stuck in the bottleneck. Until the Eric Markham business is settled, I'm paralyzed."

"I can hardly comprehend what you're saying—"

"Help me, Frank. Help Hemingway. *Help the poor putrefying moral universe!*"

He rears back. His eyes are rimmed with white as he stares at me, trying to evaluate it all, struggling with his tired old brain to deal with a matter more forceful than anything he's faced in years. And knowing already (as I can see he does) that the answer, when at last it bubbles to the surface, will be yes.

FIFTY-THREE

COULD THE PENDULUM be swinging my way?

Since discovering Frank I've noticed a subtle restructuring in the bones of the thing: it's no longer one slap in the face after another. My step is bouncier, as if my shoes have been resoled in some magic material that turns ordinary slogging into a leaping bounding moon walk.

Example: just as I was contemplating my approach to Yugo—who, I read in *TV Guide*, will be the first national talk show host to give a full hour to Pappy and *Killed*, the phone rang and it was old glow-face himself, extending a personal invitation to join the panel.

"You're a natural for this, Elliot, Hemingway expert and all. And also I want to do something about that LifeForms mess—so we're going to flash it right up there under your name: 'Elliot McGuire, Creator of LifeForms,' or whatever you want."

"No need for that. 'Hemingway Expert' will do just fine. But listen: I have another panelist for you."

"Really?"

"A living link to the whole matter. His name is Frank DeForrest and he's eighty-seven years old. Knew Pappy and Hemingway back in Paris."

"Outa sight. How do we get hold of him?"

"Through me. He comes with me. We're a set."

"And what's he gonna say?"

"That Pappy is full of shit. That his stories are bald-faced lies. That he was a no-talent plagiarist and has it in for Hemingway for psycho reasons. That he ought to be either dead or locked up."

"He's gonna say all that? To his face?"

"All but the last. I'll say that."

"Elliot, what's going on, huh? You sound like you've got a personal case against this Markham guy."

"I do. He owes me seventy-five thousand dollars for a little job I did for him."

"Oh? What was that?"

"I wrote his book."

I'm gaining ground. Out of Donahue, Oprah, Sally Jessy, and Geraldo, three of them—all but Sally Jessy (who may drop the topic because no one from the Hemingway family will come on to describe the severe anguish and personal suffering this book has put them through) have gotten back to me with a tentative invite. A feature writer from the *Times* wants to have lunch. ABC is planning a segment for the evening news. And other ships are still out. I'm beginning to feel like a *Homo erectus* again.

W&D must have got wind of what I'm up to because Craig has left several messages asking for a lunch. But the kicker is another message, one I just played back for the half-dozenth time:

"Well now, aren't we the little backstage genius! Listen, little buddy, I'm going to be at a table by myself at the Regency tomorrow from nine to ten. Let's have breakfast. I've got a strong urge to save you from yourself."

His taped voice in the dark makes the tiny hairs on the nape of my neck stand and flagellate each other. This thing must be played out, played out to conclusion and beyond.

FIFTY-FOUR

"WHAT ARE YOU doing to me?" Craig half shouts, half mumbles, his mouth full of Caesar salad. I can always tell when he's profoundly upset: he attacks his food, jams it in his mouth, and talks through it.

And here we are, back at One Fifth Avenue where the whole thing started. The more things change . . . the more disgusting they get.

"I did you a favor," he slobbers. "I set you up, good money, a good piece of work, no hassles. Is this how you pay me back?"

"Craig—I'm sorry. You are not talking to the same guy who sat here six months ago."

Craig is evidently under considerable pressure to put this fire out. He eyes me glumly as several more shovelsful of salad go into his face. His normal mucoid charm is gone, replaced by whining asperity.

"Come on, come on," he says. "I've known you too long. You wax and you wane, inflate and deflate, but you don't change. You're always the same Elliot, always putting the corner on heaven as you leave a slight trail of slime—"

"Please. Do I have to sit here and be insulted?"

"Oh, Elliot, for Christ's sake, I don't want to insult you. I love you, I respect you. You've got more brains and imagination in your little finger than I'll ever have. But I just don't understand what you're up to. You're the enemy all of a sudden. I mean, going around to the talk shows, just to denounce this silly little book? What's it all about? What do you want?" One eye narrows, giving his face a comically shrewd tilt. "Is it money? We can always redo the deal. I always thought you should have a piece of the royalty action—"

"I want Warren and Dudge to withdraw the book."

Craig gapes at me in astonishment.

"And if not," I continue, "I'm going to do more than

impugn the facts in the book, I'm going to start talking about you, me, and Sir Harry Taymore."

Like a stroke victim learning to eat, Craig begins to chew, swallows several times, and wipes his chin with the big linen napkin. He signals the waiter.

"A double cognac for me and—tap water or whatever the gentleman is having."

"Coffee."

"Coffee, then." He watches the waiter tiptoe away and then turns on me furiously. "Are you out of your fucking mind?"

I shake my head. "Nope. Absolutely sane."

"Why, Elliot?" he says, voice barely audible. "Sir Harry is hard enough to work for when he's *happy*. Jesus Christ, the truth is, he's proud of this little monstrosity. He doesn't want it heaped with shit. He's told me to work with you. Convince you, buy you, whatever it takes. Elliot, can't you see the pressure I'm facing?"

"It's a lot bigger than just you."

"Oh fine, so I get lost in the dust of some grand pyramid of higher morality—great! Elliot, what do you think this is? We've got a cute little book by an insignificant maniac telling obviously silly lies about the Great Horse's Ass of American Literature—a cartoon! The public loves it, everybody's having a lot of fun— And here you are carting out the sword of God to blast us all to smithereens. It's overkill—don't you get it? You're making a fool of yourself!"

"No, Craig, there's more to this than you realize. The whole production is a literary forgery. He never put one word on paper. I wrote the whole thing, I even fabricated half the anecdotes. I was supposed to split the advance with him, behind your back, except that he ripped me off for it—"

"I forgive you, I forgive you."

"Well, fine. But that doesn't address the heart of the matter."

"Which is what?"

"The insult to history."

"Oh, for God's sake—"

"Sure it's a harmless little cartoon, but it's being played as real-life scandal. Everyone is saying, in effect, This is so outrageous *it could possibly be true!*" With a rush of nausea, I recall my enshrinement of "convincing," my own crippled justification for wallowing in this ditch of a project.

Craig is wagging his head ruefully. There is no more to say. I stand up suddenly, my stomach sloshing.

"Where are you going? Your coffee isn't here."

"I'm tired of arguing. I don't feel good. We're never going to settle this, we're too far apart."

"Elliot, one last time—"

"I've got to get some air."

I walk past the bar and toward the entrance, holding my breath. I can hear Craig raging at me, oblivious to the startled looks of the sleek downtown business lunchers.

"We're going to crush you, Elliot! We're going to break your neck."

I reach the outdoors and hold on to a lamppost, gagging and puking into the gutter. I try to imagine that with each convulsion a portion of the poisonous mash of my past flows out of me into the underworld of the city. Heave by heave, there go my equivocations, my self-deceptions, the ambiguous half-life I've lived ever since the day Ernest Hemingway read my petulant little foot stamp of a letter and blew his head off.

One last convulsion and I rise up, ready to walk away, stomach empty, head clear, certain for once who I am, where I'm going, what I'm doing. Hemingway, you old battler—this is a fate you don't deserve and it's gathering steam. Someone has to throw his body on the tracks and it looks like me. So be it. I owe you one.

FIFTY-FIVE

AND THERE HE is—the dream-stalker, the LifeForm vampire, the long-distance mind-suck—as he said he'd be, among the power-breakfasters at the Regency, scanning a copy of *Interview* with his picture on the front. This is a preening, wax-slick version of the old Pappy, even fatter, tanner, more bearishly formidable than he was at Wonderbooks. Celebrity suits him; he wears it like a rubber glove.

"Sit down. Did you see this?"

"No."

"I give a pretty good interview. We're trying to get hold of George Plimpton for a *Paris Review* shot—like a companion piece to Hemmy's that would set things straight."

I roll my eyes.

"Oh, you think that's funny?"

"No, not funny at all."

He tries to drill me with his eyes. A frisson of paranoia chills the base of my spine. Get it straight, McGuire, this is no warlock, this is a simple garden-variety hobgoblin—and what do we do with hobgoblins? We step on their little forked feet.

In any case, he's reading me accurately enough to turn off the rays. He settles into a morose pout.

"I can't figure you, McGuire."

"Oh, really? What could be simpler? To start with, you cheat a man out of seventy-five thousand dollars, he's not going to be your best friend anymore."

Pappy waves his hand impatiently. "No, that I understand. I didn't have any choice on that one—but, hey, the book is selling. Soon's I get royalties I'll be in a position to more than make that up to you—"

"Forget it."

"Ah! See, *that's* what I can't figure. I talked to Craig and he says you don't even want the money. What's going on here? Are we Ralph Nader all of a sudden? How can we get together on this?"

"We can't."

"Can't what?"

"We can't get together on this."

He grins helplessly and leans in a little. "Ah, come on now. Is it Lynn? Listen, McGuire, I think if you gave the girl half a chance—"

"Shut up."

"She told me she misses you, boy, no matter how your flag's flying." His face has widened with exaggerated concern, but he can't resist a half smirk as he watches me react to this brazen little dig.

"Let me put it to you this way," I say, fangs sprouting in my mind. "You used to tell me you were on the other side of the mirror, you and all the real people—"

"Oh that—" He tries to laugh it off.

"Well, first I'm going to shatter that mirror. Then I'm going to reach in and pull you out by your throat."

He's not laughing now. "Aw, c'mon. What the hell have I done to deserve that?"

"Plenty. You are in the degradation business and I am about to shut you down. Everywhere you go, you'll see me. Every show you're on, I'll be there too. Every paper you read about yourself in, you'll see my rebuttal. The whole literate world is going to know that you are a phony and the book is a complete fabrication, written by me, and that all you were in Paris was a no-talent pest, a snotnose, a plagiarist and no more Hemingway's progenitor than the hunchback of Notre Dame. By the way, do you remember Frank DeForrest?"

His eyes wrinkle around the edges.

"Yes, good old Frank," I go on. "He popped up with all sorts of fascinating stories about you in Paris—starting with your true age, moving on through your pathetic attempts to write, culminating with your plagiarism and how you were cut dead by dear old Hemmy. Want to see something? Here—"

I hand him his own sad little prose poem from sixty-five years ago—a copy, of course, I've learned my lesson. He takes it and reads, lips fluttering, hands trembling. Suddenly his eyes madden and he balls the paper up between his fists.

"Go on, eat it, I've got the original."

He flicks it into my untouched scrambled eggs. Then I see his eyes go from madness to mirth. He's laughing, laughing at *me!*

"Well, all *right!*" he crows. "This is war. Let's have a good one. You bring your troops—your Frank DeFaggots and anybody else you can run out of the closet. I'll bring mine—the American people! Because you know what? When this war's over, you're going to be flat on the battlefield and no one's even going to remember your name. There won't even be enough of you left to call you the Unknown Soldier. Oh, this is funny! You clown—you're going out to war and you don't even know who your enemy is! You think it's me, but it ain't. You're about to come up against the folks who put our little baby up there on the best-seller list, the ordinary American readers sitting at home in front of the fire chuckling away as they read—"

"No!" My chair tumbles backward as I stand. "They deserve better! They deserve to know they've been had, and that's what they're going to find out from me—every detail of the conspiracy, step-by-step. You, me, Craig, Sir Harry—"

The breakfast clubbers break off their wheeling and dealing long enough to give me a look.

"And what do you think they care? Huh? What do you think they're going to do, give you a medal?" His eyebrows arch into rainbows of hilarity. "They've got a good read and along you come to take it away from 'em. You think they're going to love you for that? Americans like to be tickled, McGuire, they like to believe what feels good. Doesn't make any difference whether it's *true* or not. You take away their fun and they don't like that."

I should just turn and walk out. Why do I stand here, staring back at him, boiling in the juices of my contempt? "I just realized something."

"What's that?"

"You never even *half* believed it, did you? You don't even have the excuse of borderline psychosis. You're just a simple crank, the kind of guy who confesses to a crime just so the cops'll make a big fuss over him."

Pappy sobers a few notches.

"I thought you were at least delusionary. No matter how ridiculous the stories were, I thought you believed at least some of them. But, no—you're just a common ordinary cockroach, aren't you?"

This is meant to be my parting shot, but something happens in Pappy's face that freezes me in my tracks. It's the rough visual equivalent of that place in all psychological thrillers where the killer's eyes start to roll, and spooky fright music swells up on the sound track. Just as I accuse him of sanity, I see his craziness billow up before me like a hot-air balloon. It is a scary sight. For a split second I wonder if he has his pistol with him. Then he slumps into a disorganized lump of cross-purposes.

"McGuire, listen: didn't you ever dream something and wake up and all of a sudden it was real? I mean, something's telling you you dreamed it, and something else just as loud and clear says it really happened, at a real place and a real time—and you don't know which is the truth so you figure you'll wait a few hours, a few days, and it'll sort out. So you do—and still you don't know. Weeks go by. Months. Years. Still you don't know. And you realize you'll never know for sure. But one thing: it's realer than any ordinary dream."

"To answer your question, no."

"It ain't a question, you fool. I'm telling you something. Be a smart boy and listen, because nobody's ever heard this—I've never told anybody before and I won't again. Sit down. Sit."

Against my will, as if there are strings attached to me, he pulls me back into my chair, back into the ring of his—yes, it is—his *power* over me.

"McGuire, let this run itself out."

"I can't, Pappy."

"Please, you've got to. Don't blow up the river. You'll kill all the fish."

"I don't know what you're talking about. You're a liar or a nut. Either way, you're a boil on history's butt and all you deserve is to be lanced and drained away."

"No, no, no. I'm telling you—my version deserves a chance! I didn't make it up any more than I dreamed my own dream. It's *out there*. Sometimes I believe it more than others, but one thing I never let myself forget: *it may be true.* Just as true as anybody else's damned story of who did what and why."

I watch him watching me from behind his eyes.

"McGuire, you'll never hear me say this again but . . . please. I beg you. *Please* don't make me out to be a liar. Let history decide."

I rise again, slowly. "Good-bye, Pappy."

FIFTY-SIX

YUGO CALLS HIMSELF "the Mick Jagger of Talk TV." He dances, jives, leaps in the air, swivels, humps. Unlike Donahue and Geraldo and Oprah, he rarely touches a mike: that task is handled by one of his "stick girls"—blond, quick-footed, big-breasted women who roam the audience ready to field questions at Yugo's command.

Shelly Rakoff, the producer who followed up my chat with Yugo, has told me to arrive an hour early to meet the other guests. She was very brisk, very Noo Yawky, offered to send a car, which I declined. I don't want to be early. The last thing in the world I need is to hang around the Green Room sipping coffee and munching doughnuts with Mr. and Mrs. Pappy! Nor am I anxious to hobnob with any of the other guests— dear Craig, an EH sycophant named Bernard Lyttle, and the ubiquitous Howie Ritz, who is making a name for himself as the only academic in the world (one hopes) outrageous enough to make the case for Pappy.

So I've arranged to meet Frank at the Stage Deli for a leisurely breakfast before cabbing over to the slums of Ninth Avenue, where Yugo's show spews live to the nation.

"I'm very nervous," says Frank after failing three times to raise his coffee cup to his lips.

"Don't worry, Frank. We've got the facts on our side."

As expected they're steaming mad when we stroll in five minutes before show time. A harried young male assistant makes a pretense of welcoming us but is swept aside by the volcanic Shelly Rakoff, a raging butterball of frizzed hair, who blows in dragging a clipboard and sweating mightily.

"Well, well, Elliot McGuire. Thanks for being so prompt and making my life worth living. Do you realize we go on the air in about ninety seconds?"

No matter. "This is Mr. DeForrest."

"I'm sure." She rushes us directly into the chattering confusion of the studio, where a male stand-up comic with headphones is jumping around enticing the crowd to riot.

"Come on, get rowdy, folks! Make some noise or we'll turn the rats loose! Hey, Yugo's rating's down this week, we wanna keep the poor guy on the air, don't we? Don't we? Yeah! Come on, one more time . . . !"

Frank seems confused, disoriented, a haggard old survivor of the Lost Generation, dropped into the jibbering dreamworld of contemporary talk TV.

"Sit here," says Shelly Rakoff, indicating two front-row seats.

"Wait a minute," I say. "Frank and I are panelists. Why are we down here in the audience?"

My deal with Yugo was to share the stage with Pappy. Now

here we are out among the busloads of real people from Queens, tourists, passersby hawked in from the streets. Here we have the co-author/co-conspirator in the matter of *I Killed Hemingway*, plus the one true witness to Pappy's self-fabrication, and where do they put us? In Siberia.

Up on the stage, radiating pink under the intense lighting, are the rest of them, gabbing like monkeys, kidding around, floating in their temporary renown as if it were a bubble bath. I'm about to raise a protest when Frank collapses thankfully into his chair. There is no more time. I settle into my own seat, in a fury of resignation.

And here he comes, bounding down the aisle, face spraying light, teeth bared in a frantic grin. The show is on: it's YUGO!

Applause. Wild applause. Half of it is real, the rest piped in electronically. Yugo begs and pleads for silence, gives up a few times, simpering with gratitude, then, sternly, waves the crowd off and talks into the camera.

"Folks, what would you say if I told you America's greatest novelist, a Nobel Prize winner, was the victim of a brutal murder, made to look like suicide, and that the confessed murderer—a free man, mind you—is right here today, on our stage? Shocked? Well, come with me—" He leaps on stage and settles next to Pappy. "And meet this man, Eric 'Pappy' Markham—how're you doing, Pappy?"

"Just fine, Yugo!" Grinning, beaming, Yugo's arm draped around his shoulder.

"Pappy has a story to tell, and he's told it in this spellbinding book, *I Killed Hemingway*." Yugo waves the book high in the air. "It's a story that may astound you, may disgust you, may stir you to anger, but when it's all over, can't help but leave you with profound doubts about the death—and life— of the great writer. That's our subject on today's *Yugo*— Ernest Hemingway, death—who did it?"

Yugo leaps back to regard his gang of experts.

"Okay—let's jump right in and introduce our panel. From Florida Southern University, Professor Howard Ritz, Hemingway scholar, writing an article for—is it *Esquire*, Howie?"

"Right, Yugo."

"It's called 'Pappy Meets Papa . . . When Legends Collide.' Howard Ritz says it was Pappy, not Papa, who pulled the trigger."

Howie squirms and shrugs, opening his mouth to lodge a qualification, but Yugo rolls on.

"On his left, Bernard Lyttle, writer, traveler, columnist, close friend of Hemingway. Bernie has written nineteen books of personal reminiscence dealing with his friendship with Hemingway."

(Maybe his next one should be *How to Write the Same Book Nineteen Times.*)

"And next to Bernie, Pappy's editor from Warren and Dudge, Craig Vandermeer. Welcome, Craig."

A curt nod from a heavily bespectacled, very dignified, very literary Craig.

And in the audience? In the audience——?

"Pappy, let's begin with you. It's 1922, you're living in Paris, an expatriate poet. Get us started here, how did you meet Hemingway?"

"In a café. He started talking to me in bad French, so I switched us to English and we went on from there. But Yugo, I've got to correct you on a couple of things: one, I wasn't a poet, just a writer. I wrote a page a day, just as a hobby. I had no interest in publishing or calling myself an artist. I was a boxer and an ex-soldier, that's all. The fact that Ezra Pound and Hemingway and Amy Lowell and God knows who else figured out how to write after seeing my stuff—well, you can make what you like out of that——"

Frank turns to me with a grave look and shakes his head.

"Great, Pappy, great," says Yugo, nimbly cutting off the flow. "Howard Ritz, fill us in. What's the essential story here?"

"Yugo, it's a story of youthful friendship spoiled by envy and betrayal."

"And who betrayed whom?"

"Yugo, from my reading of this text, I'm afraid Ernest Hemingway is guilty as charged. That is, he appropriated both his famous persona and much of his early work from Pappy here——"

"Wait a minute! You're saying that Ernest Hemingway was a copycat and a plagiarist? What do you say about that, Bernard Lyttle?"

"That's bullbleep, Yugo. I think what we've got here is a

criminal type, Eric Markham, who's trying to pump up his early years. I don't buy it for a second—"

"Go shit in your hat—"

"Pappy, Pappy—"

"—but I will say this: Ernest Hemingway did *not* take his own life. Nor was there any way that what was done to him could have been an accident—he knew guns too well. No, he had to have been murdered and that part of Markham's story is right on. I believe we really are sitting here with the homicidal maniac who ended Ernest Hemingway's days on this earth."

Pappy smooths his feathers and nods with satisfaction. Yugo spins, pirouettes and paces meditatively into the audience.

"You say he didn't take his own life. Why are you so sure? And why have we been so unanimous till now that his death was self-inflicted?"

"Yugo, Ernest Hemingway held suicide in contempt. His own father had gone out that way and he branded him a coward. I knew Papa well in those days. He was a strong, tough man who could beat anything and anybody. He loved to eat. He loved to drink. He had a few health problems, but suicide? Well, until now we've had no other explanation, no suspects, no possibility of a murder scenario."

"Until now. Until now." Yugo twirls and advances on Pappy like an avenging angel. "Are they right, Pappy? Are you the missing link between the long-standing hypothesis of suicide and a new version of the great Ernest Hemingway's death?" He aims a prosecutorial finger at Pappy's reddening face. "Did you or did you not—in cold blood, without pity or remorse—murder the century's leading American author?"

Before Pappy can huff his reply, Yugo swings to face a camera. "We'll give Pappy his day in court when we return. But first, these messages . . ."

Yugo freezes, then on a signal from the floor manager, relaxes and ambles toward the stage.

"Great, fellas, keep it up."

Pappy is irritated. "What're ya pointing a finger at me for? This ain't the People's Court, you know."

"Just some theatrics, Pappy, for the folks at home. You're fabulous. You're a star, baby. Keep it up, keep it up."

So far Yugo hasn't even glanced at me or Frank. Does he know we're here?

"Yugo?" I call out. He's not responding. I stand up. "Yugo! Yugo!"

A young flunky approaches. "Sir, can I help you with something?"

"Yes, you can get Yugo's attention."

"Sir, Yugo has a lot to think about right now. He'll be taking questions from the audience in a little while—"

"Damn it, I'm not the audience! I'm a guest. I ought to be up there on the stage with the rest of those bozos."

"Sir—"

"Yugo, get your ass over here!"

Yugo's head snaps around. "Elliot, Elliot, hey hey, how ya doing, my man!" Vanishing into a grin, he bounds over and grabs me with both hands. "We're cooking, okay? Don't worry, I'm gonna pull you right in, right in here—two minutes, okay? You and Frank here, how ya doing, Frank?"

"Why aren't we on the stage?" I persist in a loud monotone.

"Don't worry about that. We're going to spotlight you, right here. This way you don't get lost in the pack."

I pull him close and whisper in his ear. "Don't fuck me over this time, do you understand?"

Yugo pulls away, smile faded, his eyes cautious. Then he's gone, sprinting to his marks in front of the camera, and *we're back!*

"I want to introduce someone very special in the audience—Valerie Markham, Pappy's wife."

Valerie stands and you can cut the prurient interest with a cleaver. She looks good, hair permed, wearing a thin little nothing that looks designed to drop to the floor at a moment's notice. Some low whistles. Yugo moves in and takes the mike from one of the stick girls. His eyes drink her in.

"Valerie. Pappy's some man, isn't he? I mean for a ninety-three-year old."

"Sure is."

"How old are you?"

"Twenty-five."

"Mm." The audience buzzes with delight. "Now tell me something: who is Roscoe?"

Valerie blushes and breaks up. "Yugo! You said you wouldn't."

"Friend of the family?"

"Yeah, I'd say one of our best friends, huh Pappy?"

Pappy glows, a radiant lump of pride.

"Just a little in-joke, folks," says Yugo, spinning away but continuing to ogle Valerie. "There's a little age gap, but I want to tell you, this is a fun couple. No problems in bed, Valerie?"

"Nope. Too few hours in the day is all."

Pappy chuckles. The audience hoots and breaks into applause.

"Some girl, huh folks? Pappy, you're a lucky man."

This is too much. I can't stand it. I jump to my feet. "Yugo! Yugo!"

A camera swings in my direction. A stick girl arrives at my side with a mike. She stands so close I can feel her breasts boring into my side.

Yugo starts to yammer. "Okay, okay, let me introduce, in our audience, Elliot McGuire, also a Hemingway expert, who is going to paint another picture for us altogether. Right, Elliot?"

"He's a complete phony."

A murmur of disbelief goes through the audience as Pappy throws up his hands, trying to laugh it off.

"You shut your face," Valerie yips from her seat, but she's off mike. A producer shushes her, but not before her outburst has provoked a ripple of cheers from the crowd.

"A phony!" Yugo is running with the ball. "A complete phony, he says! Elliot McGuire, tell us more!"

"He's a pathological liar, a publicity seeker, a psychotic. And I ought to know, I spent enough time in Key West listening to his crazy fantasies—"

I watch Craig go white with panic.

"Listening to his fantasies," Yugo booms. "And what else, Elliot?"

"Ghostwriting his book."

Another murmur, this time with a distinct edge of hostility.

"You're saying that you, Elliot McGuire, not Eric Markham, are the true author of *I Killed Hemingway?*"

"Yes."

"Not so!" Pappy blats. His fingers flail in my direction. "This man is a certifiable nut, he's just out of a private mental hospital, I can substantiate that. He's been following me for months, calling my house, frightening my wife—*get offa my back*, you psycho!"

"What about it, Craig Vandermeer? You're Pappy's editor. Is what Elliot says true or false?"

Craig clears his throat several times. "It's . . . he's—"

"Or is Pappy right? Is Elliot McGuire really a nut, into harassing the legitimate author of this book?" Yugo swings toward a camera. "Hold your answer—we'll be back in a moment. Ernest Hemingway! Who killed him? Who's telling the truth? Who's a liar? It's happening now, on today's *Yugo*—stay with us!"

During the break, Yugo disappears. I notice Valerie is gone, too. Craig keeps signaling at me. I ignore him. Pappy seethes and snarls. I ignore him, too. I turn my attention to Frank, who is getting paler as the show goes on. This is not good. He is my link to the truth; I need his credibility.

"How are you doing, Frank?"

"Just fine, just fine . . ." He trails off, his lips moving. His eyes seem to be looking through the studio walls, to some other universe of time beyond.

"Just relax, be natural."

The stand-up comic, who turns out to be Si Bardo, Yugo's executive producer, stops by and bends over to talk to us.

"Gentlemen, we're going to spend a few minutes on who wrote the book, then Frank, we'll go to your story, who's the real Eric Markham et cetera et cetera, okay?"

Frank smiles gamely and settles back into his thousand-yard stare.

As the seemingly interminable break draws to a close, Valerie slips back in, flushed and disheveled, followed by Yugo, who is smoothing his shirt. Pappy is oblivious to this little subplot—

"We're back! Craig Vandermeer, editor-in-chief, Warren and Dudge, help us—who's telling the truth? Elliot, when he says *I Killed Hemingway* is a fake, a literary forgery? Or Pappy, when he says Elliot McGuire is insane, a creep, a pervert, a certifiable nut, as he puts it, on a mission to spread lies and harassment?"

Craig has pulled himself together and is ready with an official statement: "Yugo, we stand by Pappy's version. To whatever extent there is error in the book, it is the error of memory. This is an exciting potential breakthrough in Hemingway scholarship, it shouldn't be besmirched—"

I can't stand it. "Yugo, Craig Vandermeer and I sat down months ago and planned the perpetration of this hoax on the American reading public. And what's more, Craig's boss, Sir Harry Taymore, was the prime mover behind Warren and Dudge's decision to create this book, even after we discovered that no such manuscript existed."

"That's a lie!" Craig erupts.

"Craig, you know it isn't a lie."

"Yes it is." Craig's eyes are bulging. "It is, it is!"

Yugo steps in. "Well, let's leave it hanging for a moment. Folks, I want to introduce a very special guest. Next to Elliot McGuire is the real McCoy, a man who was on the spot— Paris, the 1920s—knew Hemingway, knew Eric Markham. Tell us, Frank DeForrest, who's telling the truth? Who and what was the Eric Markham you knew in those days?"

Two stick girls descend on Frank, one to hold the mike, one to help him to his feet. Jaw flapping, eyes flicking from side to side, Frank attempts to answer.

"He was, well, a sort of *boulevardier*—"

"Did he know Hemingway?"

"Well, yes."

"See there?" Pappy crows. "Case dismissed."

I leap to my feet. "Not so fast—of course he knew him. But tell them the rest."

Frank has developed a pronounced palsy. "Of course. The rest . . ." He wags his head back and forth in prolonged silence.

"Frank"—Yugo steps in, laying a hand on his shoulder— "we'll come back to you in a few minutes, okay?"

Frank smiles in relief and crumples back into his seat. Something is wrong.

"What Frank was about to say—" I begin, but Pappy drowns me out.

"Yaa, he said all he had to say. You're a phony, Mr. McGuire, and everyone here knows it, right, folks?"

Here and there cheers break out like noxious weeds. Craig seems to relax—actually flashes a grin at the crowd. I may be flying into rough weather here.

"Hold it, everyone," says Yugo, raising both hands. "On the phone is Sir Harry Taymore, owner and publisher of Warren and Dudge, as well as syndicates of newspapers, magazines, and TV all over the world. He's in the midst of negotiations now to acquire Paramount Pictures, but he must keep his set tuned to Yugo. Sir Harry, you've got the floor."

"Well, Yugo, I couldn't help responding to the attack on our honesty and credibility. We think I Killed Hemingway absolutely deserves its place on the best-seller lists of several countries. It's a book that comes from the heart, it's deeply felt, it's compelling, and it pulls no punches. We think that its refusal to back down from a difficult subject will make it a classic of American confessional literature."

"Sir Harry, the question of authenticity—what about it? Have you checked the facts that are alleged here?"

"Of course we have, of course! As fully as possible, Yugo. You must remember, we are dealing with history in the making, and with history there are always conflicting views, you could even say conflicting truths. You must let one hundred flowers grow, to quote whoever that was—"

"Mao Tse-tung."

"Dear me, well let's just say you must give every dog his day, let them fight it out, so to speak. This is the sifting process that all history must go through."

"I'm sorry," I shout. "I can't sit here and listen to this puke. This is pure sophistry, I don't care how much money the man has—"

Pappy aims his finger at my head. "Oh yeah, Mr. Smarty-pants? If you're so smart, if you're so all-fired damn smart—then why ain't *you* rich!"

A cheer goes up, shockingly lusty. In all honesty, I have no answer for that question. I never have. I sit back in disarray.

"Let's let our audience get in on this. You sir—"

A tall, sober midwesterner: "Yes, I don't see how this man [me] has the right to criticize, if it's true, as he says, that he wrote the book." Applause. "Well, he's in with 'em it seems to me. How come he's complaining?" More applause. In with 'em . . . I fear my message isn't coming across.

A question for me: "I just wanna know why you're going to all this trouble. I mean, to like trash the book, when you wrote it, if that's true, or—like—even if you didn't write it, like why come in here and trash everybody and stuff?"

I stand. This is going to be my summation. If this doesn't go down, I will button my lip like the hated Iago and answer only with dignified silence.

"I came here because I had a change of heart. Yes, I participated in this sick joke on history, but now I'm not laughing. I'd give anything now to go back in time—to tell Craig Vandermeer to keep his money, that I'm not interested in helping some maniac turn his private delusion into a bestseller."

Pappy rises. But I anticipate him.

"Let me finish!" I shout him back into his seat, nearly blowing out my voice, "LET ME FINISH—!"

"Elliot, I think we get your point. But I want to go back to Frank DeForrest, because—"

"Wait, damn it!"

"All right, all right—finish."

"This . . . psychotic old man has waged a lifelong vendetta against Ernest Hemingway, who once caught him in an act of plagiarism. Everything he says about Hemingway is a lie. Even his claim to be a writer is a lie, he can't write a grocery list. I know because, unknown to Craig, unknown to Warren and Dudge, I made an under-the-table deal with this creep to write his book for him and the result is the book that now sits on the best-seller list poisoning Hemingway's reputation. Well, I'm here to tell you that half of the noxious crap that oozes out of the pages of this book is *mine*, my own craziness, mine alone. I'm as guilty as he is, but today I'm confessing to the world. I started as a biographer. Now I'm a tramp ghostwriter. I've been working on a way to make biography serve mankind. It's called LifeForms. But after today, that's all over. LifeForms is finished, I'm going to be untouchable because I've poisoned the well, I know all this—but guess what? I don't care. Doing what I'm doing right now feels so good that it's worth it. So right here and now I call upon Warren and Dudge to withdraw this book. Get it out of the stores. Do the right thing, gentlemen—just say *no*. I call on you, Craig—one of my oldest friends—I call on Sir Harry Taymore—one of the richest or most powerful or whatever the hell he is—to stand up and swear off this insult to literature and history and the living memory of a truly great man, Ernest Hemingway!"

Absolute silence. Si Bardo waves his arms wildly, begging for reaction—applause, boos, something, anything, because the studio has become as quiet as the inside of a snowball. Even Yugo seems to be skulking irresolutely, waiting for Si to make the next beat happen. Have I hit a home run? Was I inspired? Has my harangue struck the mark?

Then I realize, as a groundswell of restlessness grumbles out of the crowd, that no, I haven't made a fucking dent—I've only embarrassed everyone. Now they're regarding me as a simple pain in the ass; I'm nothing more than an obnoxious fender bender in the middle of the road; all they want is to drive around me. No, it's worse than that: they want to drive *over* me. I'm the old Scrooge who's arrived to kill Christmas. They want to put a stake through my heart.

"Okay, time's up, blabbermouth!" Pappy rises to a solid wall of cheers. "Awright, Mr. Purity, now it's my turn—and don't anybody tell me we're breaking for a commercial!"

Ecstasy! They love it; they love him. They hate me. He mugs like Mussolini as the cameras close in.

"This twerp, here, Elliot McGuire, this messenger boy, turned up at my house one day, and you know why? My publisher, Warren and Dudge, had sent him down to type my manuscript for me and bring it back up to New York, secretarial stuff, right Craig?"

Craig, dear Brutus, nods assent to this ridiculous notion.

"Now you see him here, denouncing everything and everybody, the world's biggest poor sport. He's come to rain on our parade, folks. A boy unable to do a man's job, a Mr. Softy that can't even stand up and—"

"I'm sorry, this is outrageous—"

"Let him finish!" yells a voice.

"He says he wrote my book. I say he should only live so long. He says the book ain't true. I say he lies like a dog and he ought to have his nose rubbed in it, whaddya think?"

"Yaaah!"

266

"But the truth, folks, the truth of the matter is he had a boner on for one of my girlfriends—"

"Watch your language, Pappy," says Yugo.

"Val knows all this—he wanted little Lynnie in the worst way, right, Val?"

"Right, honey."

"But when it came to blast-off, he had a little trouble getting his worm to turn—"

He shambles to the lip of the stage and points down at me.

"Yeah, you, you limp rag—"

Where the hell is Yugo? Isn't there a commercial? They're always cutting people off in this business, why aren't they shutting this maniac up?

"—you wimp, you know what your LifeThingy is? A noodle, a sliver of linguini!"

Yugo suddenly takes control. "Whoa, big fella, whoa," he says, striding forward, a shit-eating grin disfiguring his face. "Pappy, I want you back in your seat now, because there's a man here, a very important voice who still hasn't had a chance to be heard. Frank—"

Frank, who seems to have been dozing through the brouhaha, cringes protectively in his chair as the stick girls descend on him.

"Stand up, Frank. Atta boy." Yugo moves in and rests a hand gently on Frank's shoulder. "Now you've sat through this craziness . . . I'm confused. Who's coming, who's going? What's the story? You were there, Paris, the nineteen-twenties—help us out. Is Pappy the man he says he is—Hemingway's friend and mentor, the man Hemingway stole his image and his early work from? Or is he making it up, as Elliot says, for reasons that only a psychiatrist could fathom? But I want you to hold your answer, we'll be back in just two minutes with Frank—and then . . . it's up to you folks here in the audience and you folks at home. We're going to take a vote: is it truth or fiction? Suicide or murder? Who's been the most convincing this morning? Who do you believe? We're going to tie up all the loose ends on today's *Yugo*. Stay with us!"

But Frank isn't waiting.

"He is a sham."

"Frank, can you hold on to it? We're into a break—"

"He is a sham and an insult to civilized humanity." Frank ignores Yugo and struggles to his feet, swelling like a Big Bird from the Macy's Thanksgiving parade. "I was, as you say, an eyewitness to these events, perhaps the only one still alive."

"Frank, Frank—"

But nothing can stop him now. He trembles with indignation and his voice takes on a resonance I had no idea it possessed. Yugo signals the control booth to keep taping.

"He arrived in Paris, a nobody, no talent, but desperately ambitious. A sham from beginning to end—a pathetic poet, a liar, a social disaster wherever he went. All he had was good looks and a bit of trashy charm, which he used to win Hemingway over. Then he turned in some counterfeit work. I knew it was a fraud. Too good to be true, this sheaf of poems. But Hem . . . Hem just beamed when he read it. 'Look at this, look at Ricky's work!' "

Pappy is up, white-faced. "Is somebody gonna shut him up or do I have to do it?"

Yugo raises one hand. "Pappy, Pappy . . ."

Frank swivels sharply toward Pappy, teeth showing like an angry terrier's, and points a finger.

"I accuse you!" he shouts. "If we lived under Islam, both your hands would be gone by now, lopped off at the wrist. You are a hyena that has somehow gained entry to a hundred million minds. Who could live in a world that supports and encourages such as you? If this book is allowed to stand, I shall gladly retire to my grave."

"Then go ahead, Bozo, fall in!"

Frank drops back into his seat, stunned. I squeeze his hand with eternal gratitude.

Yugo bustles up. "Great, great! That's in the can. But I've gotta have it again, okay? We're almost out of this break—can you give it to me live, Frank?"

Frank's eyes are like big wet pools of confusion.

"He doesn't look too good," says one of the stick girls, smoothing Frank's hair.

"Frank. Are you okay?"

He pipes up gamely: "Fit as a fiddle. Couldn't be better."

"Thirty seconds, Frank."

"Can we wrap it up, Yugo?" Craig says in a whine, as a

makeup man powders his brow. The strain is getting to him.

"Ten seconds, everybody," shouts Si Bardo.

"Ready, Frank?" Yugo gives him a confident wink and looks directly into the camera. "We're back. Frank, you've been waiting a long time. The floor is yours, baby."

Frank struggles to his feet again, gathering his thoughts. That's what it looks like, anyway. His lips move fitfully. His eyes roll back and forth. Only this time he isn't saying anything. The look on his face is that of a man waking from a bad dream to discover that they've bound him hand and foot and are burning him at the stake.

"Frank? Frank?"

Then, like an ancient apple tree toppling in a sigh of wind, he lurches to one side.

"Catch him!" shouts Yugo.

I divert his fall and wrestle his frail body into the chair. His eyes stare dimly forward. His tongue lolls out the side of his mouth.

"Get a doctor."

"Don't let him swallow his tongue."

Like an underwater swimmer I go through the motions of laying him down, loosening his collar. Things move so slowly I begin to think all motion might cease, down to the molecular level and below. We will congeal into a plasma of sorts. Time will reify and condense, a kind of mute clear Jell-O. None of us will ever leave this studio, this space, this moment. We are talking eternities here; it takes me a millennium to slump hopelessly into my seat. The paramedics spend several centuries charging down the aisle with a stretcher to bear Frank away. Maybe they'll take me. Please God, take me, too . . .

FIFTY-SEVEN

THEY'VE GOT ONE hell of a nerve, not letting me into Frank's room. So what, I'm a little loud, so I smell a little strong, so I can't quite stand up right—still he needs me: he's my only friend. (Did I get that right?) Listen to me: he's eighty-seven years old, he has no family in the area, don't you understand—I'm as close to next of kin as you're going to find. Don't you get it? Let me in, you jackasses! People are dying in this place, this is serious! What is this, a hospital run by shoe clerks? *Frank! Frank, I'm in the hall and they won't let me in*—

All the same there's something likeable about the two security guards who escort me to the street. Izzy and Pepe, both of them as big as you can get without spilling over into slobbiness. I don't know how the subject comes up but Izzy tells me he's a Puerto Rican Jew.

"Me too," I say. "Me too! Isn't it confusing? Are you circumcised?"

"Last time I looked."

"Now be a good boy and don't come back," says Pepe gently as they push me into the fluvium of Eighth Avenue.

"Izzy, did you ever think you might be special? I mean really special?"

"Negatory."

I'd love to continue this conversation but Roosevelt Hospital has declared me persona non grata and Izzy would have to join me in the street and he's not about to do that.

Goodness it's dark out here—must be close to eight o'clock! Time flies, doesn't it, now that I'm drinking again? It seems like only five minutes ago that I emerged from the bloodletting at Yugo's. Yes, they took my blood in there, Pappy opened a vein and drew it right off, leaving me bereft of fluid, a dry husk. If we hadn't been on national TV, he would have sucked it right from my neck.

I drift over into the theater district. It's all lights and gaiety here, with the occasional purse-snatching or throat-cutting off to the side. I drop into Sardi's and toss off a couple of Scotches with a young doctor and his wife, up from North Carolina. Turns out they saw *Yugo* this morning in their hotel.

"I never miss him," says the wife. "He's so cute."

The husband is peering at me with his doctor's eyes. He has nice southern manners. "I'm sorry, but . . . aren't you—didn't we see you—?"

"You sure did, Doc, why do you think I'm clinging to the bar, here, recovering alcoholic and all."

"I want you to know I was on your side." (Whatever that was. I can't recall.) We shake hands. He takes a professional interest in Frank's stroke. I tell him what the doctors told me before they called Security to have me thrown out. Partial paralysis. Aphasia. Rehabilitation. He nods with clinical weariness. He knows it all by heart. Oh, Frank, Frank, you were the best of us all—what did I do to you . . . ?

Hey, drinking isn't so bad, what was I scared of all those months? There's nothing to it. I could have been happily drunk the whole time. Oops, here comes the floor! I just have to learn to keep my legs under me—the doctor is helping me back up, holding one arm while his wife holds the other. Halfway to the door, the bouncer bows in fastidiously. "I'll get you a cab, sir." Oh yeah, what does he take me for, a fool? He's going to get me out of sight and then jackboot me into the gutter.

"Don't touch me, I'm having a heart attack!" I shout.

He hesitates.

"I'm a doctor," says my buddy from the South.

"Well, get him out of here, okay?"

We hit the street like an impression of the Martha Graham Dancers and while the doc's wife holds me up he waves for a cab. I start to tell him he'll never score one here, when all of a sudden he's opening a yellow checkered door for me and shoving me in and as they recede into the happy splash of theater fronts, it's good-bye y'all, good-bye, have a nice life. . . .

"Where to?"

"Anywhere."

The cabbie sets his meter. "It's your dime, sir."

Why do I always get these cabbies from hell? This one (his license reads "Salvatore Ricci") is bucking for the Demolition Derby Hall of Fame. He burns rubber instantly, scattering traumatized pedestrians, and makes three lane changes in half a block. Then he runs a red light and swerves in front of a bakery truck. Continuing the physics experiment, he bounces off the curb on the other side of Seventh Avenue and we're headed downtown on what feels like three wheels and a cinder block.

"Smooth ride."

"Thank you."

And he's an old guy, too! A great grizzled elderly demon. Another one of these wild ancients, like Pappy, with scary mind powers and seventeen-inch dicks, out to pound the rest of the world into specks of submission.

"Right? Right, Salvatore?"

"Whatever you say, sir."

"So what do we do, huh?"

"You tell me."

"I mean, what do we do about these guys, these geriatric psychopaths. They're out there. There's no protection from them. They're like killer dogs that wag their poor old tails one day and chew your child's face off the next. They shouldn't be allowed to mix with ordinary human beings. I know one. He's a LifeForm suck, a spirit vampire. Somehow I let him get fangs into my soul and now—I walk and I talk but, hey, there's nobody home anymore. I mean, Salvatore, tell me, man—what would you do about a guy like that?"

"You wanta know the truth, sir?"

"Sure."

He holds up a fat black handgun. "I'd take this and decompress his head."

Flashing a horrible smile, he swings around to wink at me just as a parked car slithers into our path, a giant battered fleeing roach of a Buick. There is no time for a horn or even a screech of brakes. All I hear is a loud bash of sheet metal and we are careening across several lanes, as about twenty vehicles whistle past, twisting and pirouetting, a miraculous dream ballet of avoidance. Salvatore whams a lightpost, destroys a newsstand, and comes to rest inside an adult video arcade.

I grab for the door but Salvatore has locked them all with the master lock control.

"Let me out."

"Stay put, I need a witness."

"Let me out, damn it, I'm going to throw up!"

He relents; the lock pops up. I struggle out. All around us are porno buffs in shock. I push my way out to the sidewalk and fade into the street scene. As I lumber down Seventh Avenue I can hear Salvatore cursing in the distance, horns blowing, a police siren whooping. I stumble on, veering from side to side—three blocks, four, five—Fourteenth Street is coming up and at last it's all just something that happened once upon a time, far, far away, somewhere else in the Naked City. I want to go home. I want to sleep. . . .

FIFTY-EIGHT

I PARAPHRASE *The New York Times:* cutting-edge research has shown that sleep releases rare nocturnal hormones whose purpose is to bathe your cells, massage them, manicure them, tone them up, oil your nerves, mend your synapses, anoint you with an inner fragrance, a suffusion of peace, the secret chemicals of maternal love. So sleep, my baby, sleep. Round and round and round the clock. Close the blinds, turn on Fox, run the air conditioner, rip out the phone. Don't be afraid to dive deep into blackness. You won't disappear in it. Don't worry if the grogginess is heavier and more paralytic than anything you've ever felt. You will walk again, my baby, you will breathe and stand tall, that's a promise.

But in sleep what dreams may come . . . ?

O, and yet again O, what whoppers they are!

In the spiral of time since the Yugo show (don't ask me how long it's been) a demonic homunculus of Pappy has camped out in the murk of my unconscious. When I close my eyes he is there, wounding me with his sulfurous presence. He'll take any role in the repertoire of my dream theater—laughable clown in the absurdist farces, scary nemesis in the nightmares—anything to keep himself center stage. Sometimes his sidekick Roscoe bursts from the roiling old crotch like a playful boa, slithering forth to crush the helpless lamb. Sometimes there is simply the awful promise of Pappy's teeth, row upon row of them, lurking among the shadows. I awake whimpering, frothing with sweat, knowing he is out to drink me dry, over and over again. *What dreams, what dreams . . .*

Yes, it's ridiculous. But wise old Sven always said that above all, you *must* respect your reality, no matter how ignominious, degraded, laughable, deplorable, or mortifying it is. Spurn it at your peril; it will go underground and return, a marauding monster seething with the power of the rejected.

Magdalena from upstairs brings me food from time to time— thank God she's moved on from chicken (now it's Chapter Ten: Soups and Aspics). She claims I'm depressed.
    She doesn't know the half of it.

This is the kind of hate mail they've been forwarding me from Yugo's office:

> *Dear Asshole:*
> *Its* [sic] *asshole's* [sic] *like yourself who rub America's face in shit. This letter should have been a pipe bomb. If I ever see you on TV again I'm going to put TNT in your high heels.*
>
> > *Sincerely,*
> > *I spit on your grave*

They did actually rerun Frank's denunciation several times, but, judging by the mail, to little or no effect. I keep asking them to throw away anything that comes for me. But they send them on anyway, in noxious little clumps. Of course, I can't resist reading them:

> *Shame, Mr. Elliot McGuire; shame, shame ...*

—this one in a tiny cramped slant, ten pages of it.
    Oh, well, it's the closest I get to entertainment these days. At least these nut cases keep my box full of cheap thrills.

This morning I ventured out for my first walk, a bit shaky from all this notoriety. Would I be recognized? Hounded? Photographed? Stoned? Lynched?

No such luck. Not even a dog to pee on my leg. Then I rounded a corner and there, in a splendid vision of SoHo royalty, were Astrid and Sophie Luxembourg, arm-in-arm, lesbionic lovers for a new decade. Seeing me, they fell into a forward-and-reverse state of discombobulation, Astrid wanting to stop, Sophie pulling forward, her nose in the air. I actually laughed at the sight of it, this new beast with two backs.

"Jerk," Sophie muttered under her breath. Her skin was clear. Love suits her, I thought. Nobody had to say anything else. We all knew instantly how things stood. This, I realized, was just another judgment, just another message from the world to me. Do you ever get that feeling? That the world is sending you personal messages? On the street, in world events, through the radio . . . ?

Well. Then they were gone. I walked around the block several times, then several times again . . .

And damned if I'm not still walking around this same old block (it's endlessly fascinating, crack for crack) although it is now dark. I've no idea what time it is, does anybody know? I suppose I should go back to the apartment . . . but not yet. My reality meter (hey, respect it!) is telling me that if I do, some potent animal distillation of Pappy will be waiting in the dark, curled like a cobra.

Why do you think I'm sticking to this one stupid block? Otherwise I pass a newsstand—and his face is leering at me from the cover of the *Voice*. Yugo was just a start. The controversy there (for which I take bitter credit) has succeeded in whipping up Pappymania everywhere. He's like a new yuppie fruitcake that everyone suddenly has to serve. PR campaigns don't last forever, but this one seems to be going on and on and on—or else I've lost my sense of time (a distinct possibility: call it Biographer's Disease)—

Wait a minute. Isn't that Brantly Swann, the UFO guy? Sure, he lives around here—

"Brantly!"

"Excuse me?"

"Brantly Swann?"

"I'm sorry . . . I can't understand you."

"Are you Brantly Swann?"

He tries to walk away.

"Oh come on, don't pull that crap with me. I'm your neighbor, I'm an author myself—"

I'm following him down Greenwich Avenue, past the movie theater, where there's a long line of people waiting to get into the eight-o'clock showing of *Star Trek V*.

"Brantly, I'm talking to you."

"Go away."

"Now wait just a minute, I resent being brushed off like I was some kind of wacko. I'm Elliot McGuire, I live around the corner, I've written thirteen books and I simply want to talk to you, as one author to another. What's so awful about that?"

He swings to face me and whips off his gold-rimmed spectacles. "I'm not an author, I'm a doctor. I help sick people. I'm late for work. Now leave me the hell alone."

"Brantly—"

"My name isn't Brantly."

This is infuriating. I appeal to the people on line. "This is Brantly Swann, isn't it? Doesn't anybody recognize him?"

Everyone zips up tight and won't look at me.

"You imbeciles, you're standing on line for *Star Trek* and right here is a man who's been there—!"

Brantly jogs off toward the corner. I get a brief look at myself reflected in the marquee glass. I'm bent, disheveled, ratty-looking. Next to the marquee, a man I used to know—he once did my taxes—is standing with his wife, gaping at me. I instantly read the emotions on his face: horror, sympathy, disgust, caution. He wishes he could help me. He wishes the line would move so he could forget he ever saw me.

All right, I'm going home. . . .

All I wanted to ask Brantly was this: If the apocalypse Lynn fears is true, why should I shed a single tear over the demise of *LifeForms*? How could a time-based theory make any sense at all in a context of Götterdämmerung? And why (my lips are moving) should I be concerned over my own silly LifeForm if the Biggest Bang of all might just be on its way?

This is all I wanted to talk about.

On the floor of my foyer, as I pass through, I spot a piece of junk mail that never made it into my box. Kneeling for it

I almost don't make it back up. Spasms. Bad knee. You'd think I'd been playing rugby all weekend—

"*Dear Elliot...*" How nice. After all these years I'm still on a first-name basis with HA, the Hemingway Association. There is something *awfully* civilized about this: no matter what you've done—raped, pillaged, committed genocide, betrayed your country, dismembered your spouse—you still get the Christmas card, the newsletter, the appeal for funds, still personalized after all these years: "*Dear Elliot...*" This mailing plugs the annual meeting in Key West next week. Hm. Yvonne Scudder Vinson to receive the "Ernie" Lifetime Award. Crap like that. Nothing much of interest . . .

Hold on—one item jumps out at me like a punch in the face:

Dinner, Saturday Night. Memoirist Eric "Pappy" Markham will speak on "The Job of Hemingway Studies." Author of I Killed Hemingway, *Pappy will be introduced by Yvonne Scudder Vinson.*

No. Dear God, no. I can't permit this.

A flower opens in my mind. How easy it is for fear and rage to progress in invisible increments, step by rickety step, climbing to heights so rarefied that even breathing is not possible. And at the top, unfurled in lonely malignancy, the flower, the horrible flower. No, I can't permit this.

Part Four

FIFTY-NINE

IT'S BEEN RAINING for three days.

It rained solid all the way from Myrtle Beach to Miami, then a break, then just as I rolled into Key West in my big shiny rented Plymouth or Olds or Mercury or whatever it is, more rain right down to the present moment. (It's Saturday, cocktail hour, I'm sitting in the Raw Bar at the Mallory Square end of Duval Street, listening to a bunch of Hemingway scholars complain about the weather. None of them recognizes me. They will in a few hours.)

"Anybody seen Wesley's new book?" says Chuck Stam. I "gored" him in Pamplona in a drunken bullfight pantomime sixteen years ago. He's talking to Ray Strekker, who once tried to lure me into taking a job at Princeton.

"Yeah, I saw it in manuscript. He trots out his sex-trauma theory again. Nothing new except he claims little Ernie walked in on his mom who was in bed humping the housekeeper."

"Ruth Arnold?"

"No, some Irish temp."

"Oh, that's bullshit."

"He's trying. Makes a tough case for it."

HA bar chat. *Plus ça change . . .*

This morning, in my room at the Windjammer Guest House (a come-down from the Blue Conch), I watched the ceiling fan spin around fifty thousand times (approximately—I lost count after thirty-two thousand.) That was clearly going nowhere, so I set off on a rain-soaked sentimental journey in my scraggle of new beard, top thatch of dripping seaweed, sloshy flip-flops, impervious shades. I shuffled over to Pappy's old shack on Gruntbone Alley, wondering who, if anyone, had moved in there since Pappy and Valerie went uptown. As I stood across the alley in the shelter of a banyan tree I spotted Roland's head passing by the window.

I extended a finger and whispered, "Bang."

His head went off like an exploding grapefruit.

Oh, not really, but that's the sort of movie that plays on the screen of my mind these days. Just as you are what you eat, you are what you think, there's no way around it. Didn't Jesus say this, or something like it, in the Sermon on the Mount? And wouldn't it work the other way, too: whosoever becometh an assassin, so too doth he think assassin's thoughts?

"Don't bother with handguns," I was told by Rod Brattigan, a suspense author I met at the bar in the Lion's Head. I had just told him I was working on an assassination yarn. "Have your character do it with a shotgun. They're so much easier to acquire. More firepower. Fewer legal problems."

My character took his advice. In fact it's standing on its end right beside me here at the Raw Bar, a sawed-off 12-gauge concealed in a trombone case. I got both of them at a Cuban pawnshop in Miami. I figure no one should have any trouble entering the banquet room of the Key Hilton with a trombone.

About the trip down, I'll say this: glad it's over. The decision to drive was only partly financial. I needed time to get here, time to think, to grow my beard, time to evolve, to catch up with myself. After all, I'd covered a lot of ground in a few months—from scoffing at Pappy's assassination fantasy to embarking on my own real-life adventure in asset removal. So I spent several nights in motels along the way trying to determine whether I had crossed a significant line—whether I ought in fact to be veering into the nearest roadside lunatic asylum and handing myself over.

I worked it out: No, I'm not a lunatic. I'm like someone who has taken a drug. By accident perhaps—a very unfortunate accident. But I *know what's going on*; I can still connect the dots. As soon as I read that Pappy would be addressing the Hemingway crowd down here, everything became so very, very simple. All the pulling and tugging over my spirit ceased. I was no longer a Rube Goldberg twittering machine, I was a guided missile. The silo covers were sliding back, I was already on my way to incise this wart from my life, from the playing field of Hemingway scholarship, from the face of the poor wounded literary earth.

So here I am, sitting in the Raw Bar, eavesdropping on the HA-HA's as they breathe the air that Hemingway breathed and oil themselves up for the big dinner. Interesting to note that if you dropped The Big One on Key West this weekend you'd reduce the entire edifice of Hemingway scholarship to a thin dusting of coral powder floating on the oblivious sea—

"You a musician?"

I jump as if stung by a bee. "Um, yes."

She slides onto the stool beside me. She's pretty, a little tipsy, thirtyish, obviously one of the Hemingway crowd, bored with the bar chat, saw me, I looked like an interesting sort of oddball, a side trip.

"What is that, a trombone? Or are you just glad to see me?"

"It's a trombone."

"You in a band or something?"

"Not exactly, I just . . . carry it with me wherever I go. It's extremely . . . rare. Only two or three of them made. I'd never be able to replace it."

"I see. My name's Susan Vector." She thrusts out her hand. "I'm one of these strange mythological academic beasts down here for the Hemingway Association riot."

"Oh?"

"Yah, I teach Papa studies at Methodist Union, Elyria, Ohio, groin of the galaxy?"

"Oh."

"Yepp." She blows smoke over my head. "M.U. the Big

Blue. The Germans have a word for it and it's not *fahrvergnü-gen*."

"I don't know much German."

"Just a little quip. I bet you know a lot more than you let on. Ever read Hemingway?"

"A little. Basic stuff. I had a course once, years ago. Kind of an interesting course. With a guy named Elliot McGuire?"

"Elliot McGuire, sure, *Hemingway on the Terraces!*"

"He was my professor."

"He's a wild man. He poured champagne down Yvonne Scudder Vinson's dress at a Hemingway dinner years before my time. Did you see him on *Yugo?*"

"Missed it."

"I've got a tape of it. Chris Abbott has been selling them. Want to come to my room and watch it?"

"Ah, no thanks, but you could tell me about it."

"It's outrageous—the guy stands up and claims he ghost-wrote *I Killed Hemingway*, claims Eric Markham is essentially a nobody looking for his fifteen minutes of fame, claims the book ought to be recalled, and so on. You look kind of like him, you know? But younger. You look more . . . mmm, coordinated or something, more of a rough ride, like a hungry wolf or something. Am I rambling? You really should come up and see this tape—"

No. Keep her talking. "Hey, what about this *I Killed Hemingway* thing, anyway? Is it true or not?"

"Who cares? You want to know what I think? Hemingway never told the truth about anything, ever! Fantasy, reality—who knows? It'll get sorted out eventually. Meanwhile I guess it's good for business. Ultimately, y'know, everyone assembles their own custom Hemingway doll. I have mine. You want to know who my Hemingway is? The poor sick old hulk who wrote that little letter to a dying kid, the most heartbreaking, selfless thing you ever read. Do you want to hear it? It's very short. I know it by heart."

"No, thanks."

I know it by heart, too. She's right. It's Hemingway the man on his best day—even as he was depressed, decomposing, facing the mother of all *nadas*.

"That's okay. I'd cry. I don't want to cry. We're here to have a good time, aren't we?"

"Absolutely."

"Hey, I'm a little shitfaced, but—I like you. D'you have a name?"

She puts her face about three inches away from mine and waits. Jesus, where are we going with this? There's only a half hour until the dinner begins. I can't get involved in a flirtation. I have to think.

Her face toughens. Have I tripped her shit detector? Does she recognize me?

"What's your hustle?" she says after a moment.

"Well, you were right the first time, actually. I'm a trombone player."

"No you're not. I can't put my finger on it, but something else is going on here. Are you gay?"

"I, ah . . . yes."

"I see, I see." She softens. "Well, hey, that's okay. I love it. Maybe we can be friends. I think gay men make the best friends of all."

"Absolutely." I offer my hand. "Friends!"

She grabs it and we shake. She tries to buy me another drink, but I've had enough. I've got to get over to the Hilton and prepare myself.

We say good-bye. Susan Vector hugs me. Can she smell the truth? Apparently not. I have to be sure to avoid human contact from here on out.

The rain is gone. The sun is out at last, low and red in the west. Tomorrow will be bright and dry—if tomorrow ever comes. I've had enough to drink. I'm decidedly loose. Any more and I'll start warping and woofing.

Well perhaps one more Scotch.

I think it over, watching the sun set off the wharf with several families of tourists. A man shaped like a water balloon approaches me with a camera.

" 'Scuse me, could you take our picture?"

He lines up his brood, a pudding of a wife and three little custards. I keep grinning and aim carefully. What a story they'll have when it's all over. *Click.*

I walk into the Hilton. The young doorman (who wears three earrings, probably plays air guitar and deals dope off the job) ogles my instrument case and grins in brotherly fashion. He'll have a story too: *Jesus, how did I know it wasn't a trombone . . . ?* Inside I follow the sound of cocktail piano. Yes, a Scotch. I'll nurse it. That'll give me an excuse to sit in the bar until the dinner is under way—

"Hee-hee-hee."

A Mohawk rises from the base of my neck to just above my third eye. It's his laugh. He's right here in the bar somewhere. Relax, relax. It's dark, he's preoccupied. Stay down, don't attract attention.

The waitress glides by to take my order.

"Scotch, rocks."

Now where did that giggle come from? I let my eyes adjust to the dim light. I swivel my head discreetly this way and that until I have him in my coordinates. He's in the corner, all scrunched up with a lady (not Valerie). He's whispering, holding her hand. Her face is averted in a genteel listening attitude. She isn't young. She seems almost as old as he is. The punch line comes: he snorfles explosively and she throws back her head in a silent mask of uproar. It is Yvonne Scudder Vinson, the Dragon Lady of Hemingway studies.

The pianist finishes "Stardust" with a flourish and stands up to take his break. In the silence I can hear their voices.

"You wouldn't dare."

"Want to bet?"

"Let me see . . . oh, my God!"

"Hee-hee-hee."

"Put it back right now."

"Hee-hee—"

"Put it back, the waitress is coming!"

Then the jukebox starts, drowning out any further chat from that moisty corner of the geriatric sandbox. "Let's take a boat to Bermuda," Sinatra groans. I signal the waitress for another Scotch. Oddly enough, it never comes. At least that's my initial impression. Then I look on the table in front of me and it's there, only the ice cubes have melted. I'm slumped in my seat. The pianist is at work again and someone is gently shaking my elbow. It's the waitress—

My God. I've been asleep. I jump to my feet, startling the waitress and spilling my drink. Craning into the darkness, back where their table was . . . nothing. They're gone.

"How long have I been asleep?"

"About two hours."

"Jesus Christ, why didn't you wake me up?"

She jumps back and looks at me as if I were a live flame-thrower. "But I just did."

"I slept for two hours at this table and you only just woke me?"

"You looked so peaceful. I'm sorry . . ." She is going to cry.

"Never mind," I mumble. "That's all right, that's all right. Here." I give her a huge tip. My last ten dollars.

She lights up. "Oh. Hey, thanks!"

Of course, it's just to pave my getaway, as I saw the bartender start to zoom in on the situation. I can't afford to get snarled up in some minor hassle. I've got to get to the banquet room—

"Sir, your trombone!"

Jesus! "Thank you very much." Slow down. Don't attract attention. "Oh, and have a nice day."

The South Wind banquet room is just down the hall and around a corner. The door is open and a couple of waiters are sitting outside having a smoke. I hear Ronald Vinson's quavering voice over a loudspeaker. He seems ancient—can it have been that long since he almost made me crown prince?

Inside, the lights have dimmed. On a small ballroom stage there is a dais. I can see Pappy, Yvonne, a few other HA functionaries. Ronald Vinson is at the lectern introducing his wife. He turns and totters back to his place, making way for Yvonne, who looks like an aerobics champ by comparison. She helps him into his seat and pats his hair, then hits the podium in full stride, introducing Pappy flirtatiously as "a possible figure from literary history . . . one of the most *impossible* possible figures we've seen in a long time." This calls forth a generous laugh. All eyes drink in Pappy. My God, these people act as though they're about to hear from Buckminster Fuller—!

"Sir, your trombone."

It's one of the waiters, coming at me with the damned thing. Jesus, what's going on? I'm going to have to tie it to my wrist!

". . . a man who has a lot to answer for in Hemingway circles [another ripple of warmth], Mr. Eric Markham."

Applause. *Applause!*

As he stands and shambles toward the podium, I begin my dread move forward, trombone in hand. I suppose my feet are in fact walking me along, but the effect is of a slow inexorable camera move forward. P.O.V. ASSASSIN: *closing in on prey.* Images swim past on my way— Susan Vector, blowing smoke and holding hands with Ray Strekker; Howie Ritz, glancing at me, then glancing again, stifling an uncertain wave.

I slide into a vacant chair at one of the front tables. Someone across the table is signaling to me. I have occupied someone's chair. "Don had to go pee. He's coming right back." I nod affably and lean over to open the trombone case.

"I want to talk to you tonight," Pappy is saying, "about the job you folks have got ahead of you. You've got to look hard into the ugly mess that was Ernest Hemingway and shine your lights on him, good and true."

I pop a shell into the breech.

"Y'ever shine a light under a rotten log? What happens? All hell breaks loose. Every creepy crawly in God's universe runs for cover."

I stand up.

"I'm just the opening act of this process, y'know. Just the harbinger. It's up to you folks to take up the standard, shine that light, that, that— *Holy shit!*"

He sees me, shotgun in hand. Oh, what a feeling. Almost orgasmic, this moment of recognition. He knows his future. He knows he's going to die.

Only, I don't raise the gun.

Something is keeping my muscles from raising the gun.

The gun weighs a thousand pounds—

Then I'm hit from the side with the force of a small moving truck. Someone has thrown a flying block and I'm on the floor, rolling and grappling with whomever it is.

Roland.

Several screams. I hear Valerie shout, "Get the gun! Get the gun!"

On the podium, there's a commotion of some kind. Pappy scrambles under the dais and emerges, front and center, glaring down at me in the spotlight. He has his pistol and is aiming in my direction, using a two-handed squat that he must have learned from TV.

"No, Pap! No, no!" Roland shrieks, loosening his grip on me, raising his hands and wriggling desperately out of the line of fire.

Then—a scuffle onstage as Yvonne Scudder Vinson, coming around the table like a racehorse, throws herself heroically on Pappy's shooting arm and claws at the pistol. Pappy can't quite hang on to it and for a moment they are locked in a gruesome tango for possession of the thing.

Bang!

The room erupts in panic as the pistol goes off. Yvonne lets out a long scream of pain and hops to the table on one foot. The gun clatters to the stage floor. "Get it, you idiots!" she blats. Several HA-HA's try to fall on the thing, but it squirts hither and thither, finally skittering to the floor almost at my feet.

There follows a strange moment, almost a tableau, as everyone stops moving at the same time. Why? Who knows, perhaps the Angel of Paralysis passed overhead. But I take advantage of the tiny opening to reach over and pick up the pistol—yipe! it's hot—and begin a strategic retreat (tell it like it is: a rout!), which reverses direction and turns into a broken-field run as I realize someone has bolted the exits, leaving the kitchen as the only way out. The rest is a blur of foodstuffs, stainless steel, tile, organic garbage, black faces in white puffy chef hats, eyes, eyes following me, faces frozen, gaping at me as I sprint full-tilt past the steaming tureens, the monumental freezers, the security check-in and punch clock, the loading dock, and into the moist Key West night.

"Stop him. He's a killer!" somebody yells.

SIXTY

NO, I AM not a killer. I am a LifeForm Terminator doing the business of history.

This is what I tell myself as I slow to a walk and regain my breath. For the moment I am a nonentity again; just a casual breeze among the tourists all around me in the sultry darkness. The gun is in my hip pocket. I sense it pressing against my butt. It makes me feel deadly. Can you believe this—I start to go erect! Could this be what the NRA is all about?

Repositioning my wang I realize I'm on a direct glide path to Lynn's house on Eton Street.

A light glows in her window. Her door is unlocked.

"Elliot!"

A candle burns beside her bed. She was asleep. Or, by the musky fragrance of the room, up to some private naughtiness. No need for that— Here I am, springing the very erotic surprise she longed for, just the way she pre-visioned it.

"Elliot—I can't believe it!"

But she doesn't know the half of it. How can I tell her what I just tried to do?

Don't. She's waiting for a wordless kiss. I know this by reading the imperceptible slant of her body, the slight glint of bare breasts as she lets her robe fall open.

Later for confessions, I owe her something.

I draw her to me and part the robe. She makes a little sigh as she feels my revivified status up hard against her. She opens her mouth and bites at me hungrily. I bite back. I'm lingering over the pungent wetness of her mouth, when I realize her hands are working their way steadily down my back. In a moment those hands will slide down to my hips.

She'll feel the gun!

I rush to drop my pants.

"Yes!" Her voice is husky with desire. She staggers a bit as we tandem-walk to the bed. Falling backward, she pulls me over with her and we hit the bed in a muddle of flesh and clothes.

The gun's muffled weight strikes the floor with a dull clunk. Her legs have parted, knees outspread, and by happenstance we are keystoned, belly to belly, in exact entry position. "Go," she whispers. I thrust once, twice—and it's over almost immediately. "Oh, shit, Elliot—!"

"Don't worry," I say. And truly, there is nothing to worry about. Machine confidence is possessing me. The transition to a new round is seamless; I don't even break rhythm. I have chanced upon a piece of magic: at the slightest hint of softening, I picture the gun. We ride on without stopping, through various comings, together and apart, until by mutual agreement we roll apart, exhausted. I am still hard. She looks at me, as if not sure who I am.

We move out onto her little balcony and drink beer in the musty twilight. Vines cover our nakedness. No one can see, so Lynn climbs aboard again. Later we sit back in breathy silence, staring into the frangipani jungle from separate galactic windows light-years apart. My boner is refusing to subside.

They are on the way, she tells me. She has sensed it for days, like an approaching storm. She can't shake this idea that arousal, like mosquito repellent, keeps them off. Before I walked in, she tells me, she'd been masturbating for days. As she talks, she kisses my chest—

A police siren wails.

"Lynn, we have to talk," I say. "I'm in a lot of trouble."

"I know."

"You know?"

"Pappy called from the hotel. He warned me you might show up."

A flicker of panic. But she's shaking her head. "Don't worry. I lied: I promised him I'd call the police the moment you rolled in. Have I touched the phone?"

"Nope."

"He can take care of himself. Don't worry, nobody's gonna spoil this." She rests a fingertip gently on my cheek. "Just don't do it again—shoot at Pappy, I mean."

"I never even got a shot off."

She looks at my dong. Oblivious to anxiety, it juts like a bald palm tree on a nuclear test atoll.

"Thank God you're a lover, not a fighter."

Through the night we sleep and wake and (crazy as it seems) continue to make love. In the morning we lounge in bed. Yes, still hard. Only now I'm not thinking about the gun. As she feeds me toast and honey, as she spoons passion fruit into my mouth, as she goes to the door to talk to somebody pushing "The Watchtower"—my erectile unit is monotonously perpendicular. Occasionally her desire recycles and she slides under me or climbs athwart. At this point I am mostly a dead tower of tumescence. I let her work her way to her orgasms. Through the day she has seven, eight . . . eleven, twelve. Who's counting?

I am. Although I'm no longer getting anything out of it, I must keep score.

Fourteen. *Take that, Pappy.* Fifteen, *and when we're through, bring me your child bride.*

Late afternoon. We have no idea what's been happening outside. Have they set up roadblocks? Have they called out the National Guard?

Lynn is starting to behave erratically. As night falls, she wants to go again and again. I don't think I ought to keep this up. Not that I'm unready. Au contraire, after a stray nap's worth of soft time, once again I'm stiff as a pole. But I worry about this thing: *nothing kills it off.*

As for space visitors, what if she's wrong about love as prophylaxis? What if they *do* come down? I mean, in full force, not one of these furtive guerrilla missions, but to stay, once and for all. Actually, the more I think about it, the more I lean wistfully toward the idea of some kind of metaphysical police taking control, setting things straight. Let them install Eternity Now so we can rest our tired sex organs, put minor temporal concerns (like my certain arrest, my failure as a human being) aside forever, and bury time where it ought to rest—in some hazardous waste dump where it can no longer harm us.

She is lapsing into sullen compulsiveness. More, more—as if successive orgasms conjure up bizarre new strains of hunger. She has begun to carry on running breathless monologues while rocking up and down like those prairie oil wells you see out west.

"Mmm, and who can predict? Shit just happens, doesn't it? Pappy has his sob story—you have yours. Shit just happens. Space goonies walk into my head. Pappy walks into your life. Howard Ritz walks into Pappy's—"

Howard Ritz?

"Did you say Howard Ritz?"

"Yeah."

"What about Howard Ritz? *He walked into Pappy's life?* Is that what you said?"

"Yeah."

"When? When did he walk into Pappy's life?"

"Well you know him, don't you? Isn't he your friend?"

"But when did Pappy first encounter him?"

"A couple of years ago? I don't know."

"A couple of years—?"

"I don't know exactly—I don't really know anything much—don't make me think. Oh, don't stop! Oh, Elliot, ohhh!"

Hey folks, is it just me? Does anyone else notice the night springing to life with interstellar fault lines, light-year time-tables, hints of visitations, warps, holes, Other Purposes? And what about this disturbing sensation that the raw nub end of my life is about to be atomized, sucked into a cosmic straw, sprayed across some endless black void of other spaces, other worlds?

Is it just me? Hello out there . . . !

SIXTY-ONE

WITH A LITTLE imagination it doesn't take much to change your appearance radically.

In a discount Walgreen's on Truman Avenue I find what I need: a Roto-Rooter baseball cap that I wear backwards, a stick-on mustache, a pair of reflecting shades, a "Zero Tolerance" T-shirt. I appropriate some scissors and snip my slacks into cut-offs. I pick up a coiled length of clothesline and a pocket knife.

As I predicted, they don't even recognize me in the lobby of the Hilton.

"Howard Ritz, please," I say into a house phone, desperately hoping that instead of skipping out on the rest of the conference, he has stayed around to schmooze.

"Howard Ritz? One moment, sir."

While the operator rings his room I rearrange my still-looming pecker, which feels like it's been Novocained and leased out as an industrial-strength dildo.

" 'Lo?"

"Mr. Ritz?"

"Yah?"

"Sir, this is the bar calling. In conjunction with room service, we're offering a complimentary beer and schnapps to each of our Hemingway Association guests. May I send one up to your room?"

"*Sure thing.*"

"Your room number, sir?"

"*Oh—it's 302.*"

"Thank you, Mr. Ritz."

The door opens a crack but I help it with a thunderous shove that sends Howie reeling across the room. I lock and bolt it behind me.

"Whoa now, take it easy! Elliot? Is that you?"

"Sit, Howie."

He sinks in a semisquat on the edge of the bed. "Whatever you say, guy."

He grins, reaching out for some sign of friendly intent. His eyes peek at me wildly over the ruddy redness of his cheeks. I could flash the pistol, but I'm not here to terrorize the poor scoundrel.

"So tell it, Howie: let's hear the rest of it."

"The rest?"

"Oh, I know my little part of the story, I don't need any help there. The part I'm vague on is your part—which I'm beginning to understand goes all the way back to the start."

Howie forces a laugh. "Elliot, I wish I could help you, but—"

The gun comes out. I slap it on the table in the manner of gamblers or drug dealers.

"Aw, you're not going to hurt me, are you?"

"I don't think so."

"Jeez, you're being so scary, Elliot. There's something different about you, your eyes are farther apart or something."

"Talk to me, Howie."

"No beer and schnapps, huh? No matter, I've got a bottle over here, let me pour you a Scotch."

"*No!*" My voice resounds, freezing him in place.

He stares up at the ceiling and, spewing a sigh, makes his decision. "Okay. Here's all I know, and it isn't a hell of a lot. I first ran across him a few years back, in Captain Willy's, where they have the cheap happy hour specials. We were regulars at the bar there. . . ."

And a pretty tale it is, too—how back then Howie was just an ordinary scholar cum tourist and Pappy an anonymous Hemingway-basher who cadged drinks on an unending flow of wiseguy tales from the Twilight Zone. Howie made it a point to drop in and buy for him so he could listen to the old coot's cockeyed Lost Generation garbage. He heard all the choice stuff: the mortician, the penis-stretcher, Gertrude Stein—

"Hadley's valise?"

"Yeah."

"The assassination?"

"Eventually. But that came a lot later. At first it was just a lot of sick jokes on Hemingway. I don't think he believed half of the crap himself, not in the early days."

"Then what?"

"Then he started believing it. That's when we parted company."

A little cloud of wistfulness drifts into my soul. "No truth to any of it? None at all?"

"Well, it's pretty much like Frank DeForrest said. Eric Markham was in Paris, did know Hemingway briefly, did screw up and drop out of sight, et cetera. But that's about all."

"What about the Hadley manuscripts? Isn't it possible he could have stolen them, as he says?"

Howie pauses awkwardly. "You're kidding, of course."

"Why kidding? I mean, if anything is true to form, wouldn't it be that? And don't forget the fragment he claims he snatched back from the sewer. A version of it, five pages, was the basis for his whole goddamned publishing contract. What do you think?"

"What do I *think*—? Elliot?" He can't seem to look at me. He's blushing.

Make way for the hammer of truth.

It takes a long time, but finally I force it out in a whisper: "You. It was you who wrote it."

He shrugs miserably. "Just a hobby, guy. Little Hemingway imitations. I used to do them and throw them away, like crosswords. One day Pappy and I were drinking and he said, hey, we could get ourselves on the map with this stuff."

"I see."

"Well, I just laughed. We never gave it a hell of a lot of thought till Pappy got the idea to send in that fragment. Then . . . along you came—"

"Heaven-sent. A schlemeil."

"No, Elliot, no." He reaches over to comfort me, then withdraws his hand, as if from a snake cage. "By the way, let me congratulate you on *I Killed Hemingway*. You did a terrific job. The stuff you threw in. Le Chat and all that—" He gives me a thumbs-up.

"Howie, I have to ask an obvious question."

"Shoot—I mean, ask."

"How the hell did *I* end up ghosting the memoir? Why didn't *you* do it?"

"Oh, I tried. I even wrote a few attempts. But I didn't have the touch: I couldn't get Pappy's voice right. Neither could he. Everything we did turned out sounding like warmed-over Hemingway. Like the fragment he sent up to New York."

" '*I stood on the train tracks and looked up into the darkness . . .*' "

"Yeah. Just doesn't sound like Pappy, does it?"

"I suppose not."

"The whole memoir thing wasn't my cup of tea anyway. I bailed out. I said, take the fragment, get a publisher in on it, get 'em hooked."

"Exactly . . . exactly. One last thing, Howie: that color snapshot, the bloody one. Hemingway lying dead . . . ?"

He breaks into a grin. "Me. Me and about a quart of ketchup. Lord, we got smashed that night!"

Silence opens like a gorge.

Howie rushes to fill it: "Well hey, you want my take on Pappy? Borderline schizo. Ever since Paris he was haunted—Hemingway yelling in his ear, paralyzing his hand, shutting his mind down. He really did want to pull the death-trigger—but Hemingway himself beat him to the punch. That drove him crazy: Roland remembers the day Papa blew his brains out—Roland was ten. Pappy heard about it on the radio in his house and went catatonic. He lay around for a week, couldn't even get out of bed."

I release my breath in an endless sigh.

"Howie, thank you for sharing this with me."

"Not at all, Elliot. Can I go now? There's a colloquium I really want to get to—"

"Negatory."

"How's that?"

I reach for the clothesline. "Face down, please. The night isn't over for me."

SIXTY-TWO

FROM THE VACANT lot across the street I see lights on in Pappy's place. I see the ridiculous crystal chandelier through the ridiculous bay window. I even see somebody—Pappy or Valerie—sitting in front of a TV screen. The fool, he hasn't even pulled his blinds. One shot from a high-powered rifle— But wait: the head is too still. Of course—it's a dummy! They've set up a decoy to trick me into overplaying my hand. And there—didn't I see something move in the shadows of the front yard? Someone's out there. A bodyguard.

I circle silently, commando-style, until I am in a strip of high weeds and scrubby trees behind the house. The bodyguard—Roland, with an automatic rifle—passes through the backyard and returns to the front of the house. I sneak forward and take a hiding place in some bushes beside what looks like a half-finished chicken shack.

I'm still packing a ramrod in my groin. This thing is past the curiosity stage; it's starting to resemble a medical problem—some crazy form of mock-priapism. But what can I do about it? Drop into a drugstore? "Got anything for mock-priapism?" I'll simply have to put up with it while I carry out my mission, then let some prison urologist (or shrink) have a crack at it.

Here comes Roland, on his rounds of the house. He stops a few yards from me and sniffs the air like a dog. A neighbor's screen door slaps shut and he jerks in place. "Jeez," he says to himself and pulls out a half-pint of something from his back pocket. He glugs it down and flips the bottle to one side. Some bodyguard.

"Roland!" It's Pappy at the back door. "Go for some beer."

"You sure about that?"

"Yeah, I'll take over the watch. Gimme Old Betsy."

Roland hands over the rifle and takes a wad of bills in return.

"Case of Bud?"

"Yeah."

He stumps off toward his truck. Pappy ventures farther into the yard. He sights the rifle at a star and then slips it over his shoulder, resting his hand on the strap. I hear Roland's truck fire up and take off. Then silence, a few snuffles, a raspy sound as Pappy scratches his chin.

"You out there, wimp?"

Me? Is he talking to me? Momentarily, I panic—but wait, wait, I'm well hidden here in the weeds, there is no moon, no significant light from the back of the house. There is no possible way he could know I am here. He chuckles, as if enjoying a private joke. Relax, it's okay, he thinks he's alone.

Well then, why not jump up and do it? Here, now, in the pitch black, no warning, no witnesses? In my back pocket the gun heats up, or seems to. My drowsing member rises mercilessly. Readiness, the readiness is all. But no. Something's incorrect about this moment. I want him to know what's happening and have time to think about it. I want to get an unmistakable message through, something morally expressive, not just a gunburst in the night.

What's this? He's shuffling toward me. Ten more feet and he'll be walking on my chest—!

He stops. What's he doing?

"C'mon out, big fella."

The voice is intimate, barely audible. What's he doing? His hands are messing with his pants. No. This can't be happening! Three feet from my head Pappy has hauled out Roscoe and pointed him directly at me. For God's sake, stand up! But once again paralysis has gripped me. I can't reach for the gun, I can't move. I can only stare back at the implacable one-eyed beast—

"Pappy!" Valerie's silhouette appears in the back doorway. "What're you doing out there?"

"Just stepped out for a pee."

"You can pee inside. Where's Roland?"

"I sent him for beer."

"Beer! There's a maniac out gunning for you and you send your protection out for beer?"

A chuckle. "I don't need protection against that fuzzball."

"Just get in here, okay?"

He flashes with testiness. "I'll stay in the yard as damn long as I want."

"Fine. Get your head blasted off then."

In the exchange, Pappy has moved a few feet to my left, thank God—he lets fly and it's as if a rogue pipeline has just been opened bringing stolen lake water from the Adirondacks. For some reason the very sound of it drowns my spirit. I could no more rise to confront this cascading demon than I could recite the Book of Job backwards.

Nada. This assassination business is not as cut-and-dried as some would have you believe.

Between the small-animal action around me (crabs? rats?) and this Louisville Slugger between my legs, I am miserably awake the rest of the night. There are comings and goings: a police cruiser stops by . . . Roland leaves, apparently sent packing after arguing with Pappy . . . Key West's fun couple can be heard sniping at each other and the TV plays loudly until late. Around three, with everything quiet, comes a downpour of rain. My joints stiffen. With first light I stand to urinate, but one leg has gone numb, making me yaw to one side, then drop to my knees. The urine issues forth in a timid festoon from my inert flagpole. Dogs bark. I topple back into the weeds. God, what I would give for a drink!

I close my eyes and open them with a start: it's full morning, hot and steamy. Nine-thirty. Jesus, have I missed my chance? Wait a minute, wait a minute, don't panic: Roland's truck is nowhere to be seen, and I hear no voices from the house. This may very well be it—the perfect moment. If I don't make my move now, I'll never make it.

I rise from the weeds like a swamp thing, dripping, hulking, gimping along, inflammation screaming in every joint as I nurse the pain of this relentless penile bloat—I'm a brilliant specimen of assassin for sure! As I approach the back door, I hear the TV running quietly. My hand turns the imitation Spanish doorknob and I let myself in.

He's up. Sitting in a recliner in front of the tube, his back to me, watching *Mr. Rogers*. Valerie is nowhere to be seen. I grip the pistol and slide it from my back pocket.

"Dinosaurs don't have names like mine and yours," says Mr. Rogers. *"Their names are very long and hard to say, like 'stegosaurus.' Can you say stegosaurus?"*

"Stegosaurus," says Pappy.

"Pappy! Turn around! *Now!*"

He swivels the recliner to face me, smirking, not afraid, not even startled.

"Hey, Bobby!" he shouts. "Look what the cat drug in!"

Bobby—? Have I walked into a trap? I drop to one knee and turn this way and that, aiming the pistol at phantoms.

"Hee-hee-hee!" Pappy cackles, vastly entertained. "Relax, there isn't a soul here but you and me. And Val, of course, but she's asleep. Want to go peek at her? She sleeps with her bare butt in the air—"

"Be quiet."

His hawk's gaze drops to my groin area and refocuses. "Well, well, what's that?" He addresses the TV screen. "Oh, Mr. Rogers, Elliot has brung a model rocket ship for show-and-tell, one of them little hot-doggy ones—*Hee-hee-hee!*"

I thrust the pistol toward Pappy's head and click off the safety. In spite of himself, he tenses. His voice drops to a snarl.

"Gonna shoot me? Go ahead. I made it easy for you—no bodyguard, no Uzi in my hand. I could've had an army out here. Don't it make you wonder?"

Defiance! Even as he stares directly into the muzzle of his own pistol—this is hardly what I had in mind.

He reads me and chuckles: "You think it matters whether I die in my sleep or you put a bullet through my head today? Go on, you might as well pull that trigger as sit there and make faces, because you won't see me whimper and cower and beg for my life. I'm not scared of you or death or nothing." Rays emanate from his eyes. He sees me all over, inside and out.

Neither of us moves for at least a full minute.

"Drop it!" Valerie's voice cuts through the soft yammer of the TV.

Somehow she has managed to sneak out of bed and find the assault rifle, which she now holds on me, sighting it as though it were a BB gun.

"Haw!" Pappy explodes. "I'll be damned, what a girl!"

"Drop it, Elliot!"

I continue to aim at Pappy's head. Let her shoot—only from the looks of it, she doesn't know how.

"Pappy, he won't drop it! What do I do now?"

"Well, don't pull the trigger, for Christ's sake, you'll blow us all to Kingdom Come."

"But he's about to, to, to—"

"No he ain't." Pappy spits to one side, keeping his eyes on me.

Valerie lowers the gun and narrows her gaze on her ancient devil of a husband.

"This is ridiculous! Here I am trying to save your stupid old life and you just laugh at me like I'm some kind of fool. Okay, Mr. Cool, you just take it from here."

Pappy spits again.

"Goddamnit, stop spitting!"

"Aw, dry up."

"I will not dry up. And you know what? I don't give a flying fuck who does the shooting. I'm only a step away from doing it myself. You're lucky I don't know how to work this thing. I've had it, you're on your own, both of you. Just don't leave any goddamned bullet holes in *my house!*"

Stiff with wounded righteousness, she rushes to the back door and throws the rifle into the yard.

And that's when I start to *hear it*—low at first, then louder, more articulate and organized, as if the house is surrounded by a fleet of Mack trucks all revving up at once. Is it a trick? Some hideous diversion? I look back and forth from Valerie to Pappy. My voice cracks: "What is it, what's that sound?"

"What sound?" Pappy looks shifty, uncertain. I'm out of my crouch now, and the gun is in his face. Moment by moment the noise grows louder, transmuting like a monstrous synthesizer, a chorus of church organs.

Confusion suddenly flows into Pappy's eyes. Something in my face is saying to him that I *might just shoot.*

"Wait a minute—" He raises his hands.

Surprise, surprise. He's not ready to go after all!

But this noise, *this noise*—it's not just outside, it's *over* the house. It's *hovering!*

"You want my heart on a stake, don't you—" Pappy is saying, licking his dry lips. "—just because I played a little hardball with you. You oughta be ashamed. A real man takes his lumps."

Doesn't he hear it? Could it be for me, for me and no one else?

Suddenly my eyes squeeze shut. With wraparound clarity I *see*, on the inner screen of my eyelids, complete and whole and out of time, *see* the source of this cosmic roar, all 360 degees of it. It is *up there*, hanging over us like the shadow of a whale . . . thick but atmospheric, lighter than smoke, denser than lead, like the bottom of a dark planet. Imbedded in the shadow is a forest of city lights. Through them and beyond, I can see things so unimaginable that it breaks my heart to look. In what must be mere seconds, I see the whole sad story of creation—the final sputtering of the world, the simple futility of LifeForms, the blasting of the Garden, the literal end. Then, past the farthest rim and on, a vision of something else, a hereafter so vast it makes the entire chronicle of earth seem like the merest blip.

My eyes pop open. Through a skylight in Pappy's ceiling, what I'm seeing now—what I'm *really* seeing—is just a wide-open Key West sky of crisp blue in which, like a dragonfly, a small police helicopter is hovering. It's going *yada, yada, yada.*

I realize I've fallen to my knees.

Slowly I'm coming back, back to the gentle vision of Mr. Rogers, back to an awareness that Pappy and Valerie are maneuvering frantically, comically, behind my back.

Outside, the copter lands and the roar is replaced by nothing more than the windy *whomp* of its blades slowing down.

The pistol still hangs limply from my hand.

Pappy has retrieved the assault rifle and has it leveled at my heart. I don't care—it doesn't really matter anymore—but to keep the game going I raise the pistol until it's pointed at the middle of his head.

Valerie shudders audibly.

Pappy studies me with infinite care. He is trembling. I'm a little shaky myself. In fact, as the minutes stretch on, I feel myself becoming decidedly feverish. My bowels start to churn so loudly that we can all hear them over the noise of the TV. With a blend of relief and shame, I feel my mock-priapic affliction subside and curl gratefully into wormlike repose. Sweat trickles down my forehead and burns into my eyes.

My arm gives way, the gun sags.

Pappy lowers the assault rifle and lays it gently on the floor.

"Lost the burn, McGuire?" Pappy says after a moment. "We've both lost it." Pulling a footstool beside the recliner he motions me to sit. "C'mon, let's forgive and forget. I'll forgive you if you forgive me."

Forgive him? Forgive this man? What an idea!

I sit—

—but what is that oddly peristaltic wave activity shaking the room? Is there more to endure? Has the Seventh Seal been torn asunder?

It takes a moment to grasp the fact that it's me: I am doing the shaking myself, in tumultuous spastic throbs. I'm sobbing, I'm hooting and hollering. I'm coming apart, melting like a Dairy Queen in the wind. My cells are liquefying. Apply more heat and I will turn to steam and be gone, no more than a wispy memory in the surrounding atmosphere.

"Now, now, now, son," Pappy croons. "It ain't worth all this."

Oh, Jesus, I'm weary. Could this finally be the end? Let's release these poor molecules that were Elliot McGuire, let them disperse mercifully, flesh to mist to cosmic dust, like the dying universe. Let's make space for other possibilities. . . .

And so when they arrive—Roland, two cops, a local TV news crew—we are sitting just like that. Pappy holding me in a kind of burlesque of a pietà. The two assassins. The two hopeless aspirants. The wanna-bes that never were. Twin gods. What a pair of *men*.

Part Five

SIXTY-THREE

I DIDN'T GET off scot-free, of course.

I was a perpetrator: they jostled me around, there were handcuffs and footcuffs, a ride in the police cruiser. I had to spend a few nights in jail while they figured out what to do with me.

I had visitors, the human kind.

There was an attorney, a big, rich-looking Cuban. Smily, gum-chewing. Optimistic. I assumed he was court-appointed. "This is no-problem stuff," he said. "No drugs involved here, nobody hurt, you're a white first offender. Shit, I could do this in my sleep."

A writer from *Vanity Fair*, real this time, found her way in, but I declined to talk. Her assignment: "Deceit, Violence, and the Postmodern Biography." She had a copy of the *Miami Herald* with a front-page picture of me being led from Pappy's house in chains. Glad Mom never saw that.

When Lynn finally got in to see me, she was smoking a cigarette and there were deep, grim circles under her eyes.

"I've been at the hospital," she said. Something grabbed at

my innards. I knew what was coming next. "Pappy's had a heart attack."

"Is he . . ."

"He's okay. For now. It was close."

Suddenly she broke into a ravaged grin and shook her head. "He's such a rotten patient!"

It had happened like this, she told me: the night of my arrest, Pappy and Valerie wound themselves down by watching an adult tape called *Backdoor Nurse*. This stirred up the irrepressible Roscoe, who lured Pappy atop Valerie for one last quick sprint, and triggered the massive coronary.

Lynn and I sat for a while, glum, full of unsayable things. *All, except this, will pass, please God*, said a small voice in my mind.

When her time was up, looking straight into my eyes, she put her fingertips against the glass partition and I met them with mine.

Compared with Pappy's ordeal, jail was nothing to complain of. They fed me, sheltered me, I even got some mail. This came from Frank, forwarded by my vigilant upstairs neighbor Magdalena, along with a tin of brownies.

> *Dear Elliot:*
>
> *I beg you to excuse this illegible scrawl. Although I'm hale and hearty once again I still have some trouble making my right hand do what I want it to.*
>
> *With all that has happened since the day you first came to visit me in Connecticut, I feel as though a new life altogether had been grafted onto my waning days.*
>
> *I must tell you that an astonishing number of female viewers of that Yugo program tracked me down at the hospital and kept the phone in my room busy for some time. One in particular, Estelle Halsey of Summit, New Jersey, made regular visits to my bedside, and—well, the gist of it is that, miracle of miracles! we shall be married next week! We would be absolutely thrilled if you could attend. After all, you are directly responsible for her apotheosis in my life—you and, funnily enough, Ricky Markham, and indeed Hemingway himself! Isn't it rich?*

Imagine if one day, back in 1924, I had remarked to Hem, "You know, sixty-odd years from today, I will land a new wife as a result of a best-selling memoir by Ricky, in which he will claim to have murdered you." Can you see his face! How could God be so whimsical?

I never tire of the passing show, Elliot. I do so hope you will come and meet my new love.

And thank you once again. Thank you so.

Sincerely,
Frank

Well. If that's not proof that attitude is everything, I'm a monkey's uncle.

When they turned me out, it came as something of a shock. There had been a lot of legal nattering that I didn't pay much attention to. As a bumbling first-time LifeForm Terminator (unsuccessful), I was deemed an unlikely repeat threat to humanity. The judge imposed a ninety-day jail term and immediately paroled me.

I walked out of the courtroom a (somewhat) free man.

Against doctors' orders, Pappy had broken out of the hospital to be there at the sentencing, small and pale, struggling in a walker. We stumped out together, arm in arm, into a firestorm of shouted questions and flash cameras. Pappy (not the state) had paid for Herrera, my lawyer, even filed an affidavit in my behalf. We had made peace, he told the cameras. He was right: peace through some mysterious riddle of forgiveness, peace through divine exhaustion.

"It's true, ain't it?" he said later, over a root beer in the hospital cafeteria. "We *are* at peace."

"Whatever that means."

"Well, I asked you to forgive me. I've forgiven you. This is important, y'know."

"Why? Why are we being so solicitous all of a sudden?"

"People can change, y'know. Look at me. Don't I look different?"

He did—and not just sicker. Something had gone out of him, some piece of his craziness.

"Forgive me while you can, Elliot. I could die with this thing."

"You, die?" I laughed.

"It's certainly possible."

Forgiveness. You grit your teeth and let your animus shrink to utter insignificance. Or a vision reorders your way of thinking from soup to nuts. *You could choose peace . . .*

It was easy: "I forgive you, Pappy."

Today, weeks later (sunning on Lynn's porch), I am finally getting around to answering Frank:

> *Dear Frank:*
>
> *You may have heard by now, I'll be staying on indefinitely in Key West. It's lovely this time of year—the soft smells, the fruit blossoms, the lazy bees. I too have a new lady out of all this, one who is keeping me together, body and soul. We live a clean life. No drinking, no compulsive behavior.*
>
> *She has taught me to tend bar and we share a shift at Sloppy Joe's. In our off-hours, I work away at my newest project, a novel. Odd, isn't it, how much storm and stress I had to endure in my twenty-odd-year struggle with reality, only to discover that the real reason for my being here—was to make it all up! As you said: "How could God be so whimsical?"*
>
> *But I'm hedging my bets: this novel is based on someone from history. A very big someone (more on this some other time).*
>
> *New York never enters my thoughts these days, Frank, but it's great to hear from you.*
>
> *How about a Key West honeymoon?*
>
> *Very truly yours,*
> *Elliot*

The day of my release, the day Lynn took me home, we were still a bit shaken by our scary sex marathon. We acted like just-ripened children, awkward, tentative, chaste by default. I slept on her couch until the middle of the night, when she shyly asked me into bed. We both lay on our backs, holding hands, looking up at the ceiling, through the ceiling.

"You know what you're taking on, Elliot," she said after a while. "With me, I mean."

"I do, I do."

"I still believe it could happen. They could come anytime."

"But remember your letter?" I said. "You asked, would they steer clear of someone who's happy?"

I could hear the smile in her voice. "Someone in love? Sure I remember."

A siren keened in the distance.

"Well. Want to try?"

She sat up and turned to me. She wiped her eyes, and then her hands, wet from tears, touched my face.

That very night, we later learned, Pappy defied the hospital's orders and bolted for home, clattering his walker up Duval Street, barhopping, gossiping, carousing, tying on one big final bender.

The next morning, Valerie found him, slumped in front of the TV, gone.

Yes, we had all made peace.

SIXTY-FOUR

WORKING IN SLOPPY Joe's is honest, sweaty labor. I get to make a lot of small talk. I've become a kind of cult figure here. People tell me they've driven all the way from Tampa, St. Louis, Atlanta "to meet an honest man."

The other day a local booster asked if I would enter the next Papa look-alike contest, representing Papa's middle period, "when he still had a brain and a crank."

A woman from Miami gave me a Crayola and some creamy white paper and asked me to draw her portrait. She wanted to know what she looked like "seen through the eyes of a saint."

These things really happen.

Lynn and I just keep smiling, get our shift done so we can

cross-fade into the real work. Little things mean a lot to me these days: a new writing table found at the dump. A smooth pen. A window with a breeze blowing through it.

Sven once told me that visions happen when the pot boils over: you clamp a tight lid on the unconscious, scenes from heaven or hell rise up and blow the lid away. Visions change you. They reset the course of your life.

Once I was Elliot McGuire, creator of LifeForms. But try as I might to change my own life for the better, it took a vision to succeed where my noisy clatter of an intellect had failed. A mere glimpse of *something else* and I was alchemized.

The present Elliot McGuire is no longer the same person who came down here to expunge Pappy. I've forgiven and forgotten that person. Not only that, but I've forgiven Pappy. I've forgiven Craig, too. And Howie. And Yugo. And Sir Harry Taymore. I've forgiven everyone, everything.

I am a goddamned forgiving machine.

On Fridays I often work an extra half shift by myself. The tips are good. I do pretty well. Usually it's still daylight when I meet Lynn. Sometimes we walk to the cemetery and visit Pappy's grave (an imposing black marble mausoleum, built with my money, of course—but let it go, let it go). Sometimes we're still there at nightfall. We sit among the graves, with the stars reeling over our heads, and hold hands. All over the universe, moorings are loosening.

"I'm ready if they come," Lynn insists.

I'm feeling okay about it myself, I tell her. I have become half crazy with love for this woman. I'll say anything to comfort her.

And who the hell knows? When you've left history behind, things look awfully different. Maybe they really are on their way. If so, I have a major message for them and it is this:

Wrap it up! Punt! Move on! You have nothing useful to learn from us!

Meanwhile I'm three-quarters through my novel and making stately progress. It's called *I, Jesus,* the story of a minor galactic prince who designs a cosmic experiment: comes to earth as a common Jew and ends up crucified and the figurehead of a vast new goyische religion. I'm having lots of fun with it. I'm even using first-person narrative (Jesus tells his own story). Renwick warns this will get me into all sorts of trouble in the Bible Belt, but I just can't make myself care.

If you want to know the truth, I really don't care what anybody anywhere thinks about *anything* anymore. I'm free. What a feeling! Where is Hemingway, for instance? Where is the derisive snort, the foul breath of contempt over my shoulder?

SIXTY-FIVE

THE OTHER NIGHT, Lynn tells me, I was whimpering inconsolably in my sleep. In the dark I wrote down this dream:

He and I are walking in the hills around his place in Idaho. But something doesn't make sense: everywhere I look there is ocean. In every direction we see rough gray seas. It dawns on me that he is about to embark in a rowboat. Once he's gone, he tells me, I'll never see him again. But we can write letters—and this time there won't be any foul-ups. This time we'll write good letters and not hurt each other. As I help him into the boat, the gray Idaho day suddenly turns sunny and hot and the sea is clear and green and calm. In the heat, he strips to the waist, revealing a pair of withered old tits. He is delicate and small, like a weatherbeaten baby. As he rows away, I know this is forever. There will be no letters. There will be no more big fish, he'll row till he falls off the earth. And for a moment I want to go with him, so much so I almost jump in, to die among the feeding sharks, the sea scorpions, the eels, the barracuda. But in the end, only my eyes follow him, until he's nothing but a speck on the horizon, until there is no more light to see. . . .

I forgive you, Papa. Forgive me while you can.